CARAVAN

Lady Eleanor Smith

CARAVAN

Doubleday, Doran and Company, Inc.

Garden City, New York

1943

PRINTED AT THE *Country Life Press*, GARDEN CITY, N. Y., U. S. A.

"To Oriana"

Contents

CARAVAN

PROLOGUE

It was on a bitter December morning when young Mr. Edward Scales set forth on the first important assignment of his journalistic career. He was a slender youth, of deliberately casual appearance, who looked very much indeed as though he had taken a vow never to be startled by anything. His clothes possessed just that touch of flamboyance so sedulously cultivated in the Fleet Street of his time, but beneath this confident exterior he was still a somewhat bashful young man, with qualms concerning the assignment to which he journeyed with so outwardly blasé an air.

He caught his train at Paddington in an inferno of blackish-yellow fog, with engines snorting, wagons and cabs clattering, people shouting, and porters jostling the crowds. It would soon be Christmas, and country visits in 1892 were never undertaken without mountainous and majestic luggage. Young Mr. Scales, however, was apart from such problems, since he would return from Oxfordshire that same night. Rather disdainfully he elbowed his way into a smoking carriage, lit a cheap cigar, and reflected once more on the extraordinary luck of being sent down to Steeple Courtney in Frensham's place. On the extraordinary luck, that is, of poor old Frensham having collapsed with a feverish cold the day before. There had been nobody else to send. Well, he only hoped he'd acquit himself well and return with a story that would be a credit not only to himself but to *The Morning Globe*.

The train started, after a prolonged series of jerks, and then he glanced down at the book on his knee.

Of course he'd lied when the editor asked him if he was familiar with the works of James Darrell. Who wouldn't, in his place? And he would have plenty of time to mug up one of the books before he arrived. He had never read one, because they were not in the least his style—of that he was sure—but it had been easy enough to buy a copy of *The Spanish Journey* on his way to the station. It was a long book, too, and he was dying to read the next Sherlock Holmes adventure, but he knew well enough that duty came before pleasure.

He wondered, as the train rolled on, what had made the "old cove," for so he irreverently described James Darrell, consent to an interview on his seventieth birthday, when for the last few years he had curtly refused similar requests from *The Morning Globe*. Perhaps, Mr. Scales thought, it was just the awful knowledge of being seventy. Seventy! No more girls, no more racing, no gay suppers with the other chaps, no more trips to Brighton, or even to Boulogne in the summer. There wouldn't be anything left for you to do, once you were as old as Mr. Darrell. Perhaps it was some consolation to be famous, and famous in rather a mysterious way, as the old cove undoubtedly was, because nobody knew much about him, and it was years since he had last written a book.

Edward Scales reflected for some moments and decided that nothing would induce *him*, should he achieve fame, to live buried away in some forgotten dead-alive Oxfordshire village. Not he; he'd stay in London and keep a carriage and pair! He thought, happily, and in a possessive way, of London; of the huge, dark city of lamplighters and sweeps and muffin men and cabbies; of barouches and flunkies and red carpets in Belgrave Square; of swarming Fleet Street with its taverns; of gaslit alleys at night; of Jack the Ripper and Neill Cream; of Madame Tussaud's Waxworks, and of the ballet girl that he was going to take out to supper.

Reluctantly, and with a sigh, he opened *The Spanish Journey*. Must have been a long journey, he thought; the book was heavy enough.

He read:

"I stood on plains that were burnt to the tawny hue of a tiger's flanks, and remembered how a friend of mine, a certain Spaniard, had told me long ago that in summer the whole country seems on fire . . ."

Well, why *go* to such a place, Mr. Scales wondered? It wasn't as though this chap hadn't warned him. He turned a page. At first he fidgeted and glanced frequently out of the window, but gradually he became absorbed in what he was reading.

Soon he was no longer in the smoky, ill-lit carriage; he was no longer even in England. He was walking along a straight, dusty road with a comrade at his side. He was in James Darrell's company, and together, beneath the sun that flamed from a purple sky, they were experiencing much that was strange and curious. The bullfight, with its grace and brutality, its blood and bright silks; the scented dusk of vast cathedrals, where, in the gloom, lamps winked, silver and gold, beneath the pale images of saints and Virgins; sometimes they were joined on the road by gypsies in gaudy rags, who led shaggy dancing bears, and then, when the sun went down, there was the sound of wild and wicked music to be heard beneath the evening star. Somehow James Darrell made him see all this so clearly that he could smell blood wafted from the bull ring, incense from the churches, and the piercing sweetness of the jasmine blossom with which at dusk the women decked their hair.

In fact, so deeply was Mr. Scales immersed, so profoundly was his imagination stirred by James Darrell's *The Spanish Journey,* that it was only by sheer good fortune that he remembered to get out at Oxford Station. Here, as he waited to hire a fly, he looked with hatred at the iron-grey, freezing sky, heavy with its burden of snow, and wrapped his muffler round his throat to protect himself from the arrow-sharp east wind.

A few minutes later, driving out to Steeple Courtney in a draughty old fly with straw bursting from its interior, his thoughts were as bemused as though he had been for a time enchanted, as indeed he had.

How *could* old Darrell live in a climate like this, after what he'd written about the sun? And he could write too! He made you *see* places—made you want to turn the next page! Vaguely he tried to remember the titles of Darrell's other books—*The English Journey,* of course, which he recollected having heard described as very rum stuff indeed, all about prize fighters and jockeys and such-like. Then there was *El Moro,* which he believed to be about North Africa; also a book on gypsy tribal customs, the name of which escaped him; *The History of Piracy, The History of Witch-craft,* and, of course, the fairy tales.

Not many books, yet enough to have made the man famous. And the fairy tales, it seemed, had made him rich into the bargain, for they were as much a part of every Victorian nursery as were the tales of Grimm. Well, Darrell hadn't much to complain of, Mr. Scales decided, apart from his venerable and fearful age, and if he chose to live in this appalling climate it was his own affair. Seventy. A bit old, perhaps, for wandering about foreign countries. And doubtless he had a wife, who wouldn't like that sort of thing at all. Wives didn't, as a rule, approve of roving husbands, and the old cove had certainly done more than his share of roving.

At this point the fly, which had been passing through a little hamlet, drew up near the village green before a small Queen Anne house with two yew trees on either side of the front door. Mr. Scales descended, advised the driver to wait at the local tavern, and rang the bell. It was answered, after a pause, by a dark, foreign-looking man in dingy black.

"Mr. Scales, sir?"

Mr. Scales signified languid assent.

"Will you please come this way? My master will not keep you waiting very long."

Mr. Scales found himself in the most unexpected of rooms—a panelled, eighteenth-century parlour containing everything condemned by dashing Victorian taste as old-fashioned—a damning indictment this. A grandfather clock ticked, as it must have ticked away the passing of time for more than a hundred years; there were samplers on the walls, together with some inferior portraits, and the chairs were Hepplewhite. The panelling was dark with age, and although a bright fire burned on the hearth, the general effect of the room was that of having somehow been left unaccountably behind from the mists of the past.

Disappointed by the lack of taste shown by the old cove, Mr. Scales walked over to the window. There, beyond the wintry garden, was a paddock where two milk-white Arab horses grazed. That, he supposed, was better. A bit better. And the manservant was certainly a foreigner. . . .

At this moment the door opened, and Mr. Darrell came into the room, followed by an enormous Saint Bernard dog.

The young man started, for here, at least, was no disappointment. James Darrell looked exactly right. He was an immensely tall, very erect old man, and although he walked with a stick, his back was straight, and he held his head high in what Mr. Scales thought of as a "stiff-necked" way. And this head of his was thickly covered with hair as silvery as snow. Beneath the white crown his aquiline face was oaken dark; he looked as though at least a century of fierce sun had burnt his skin a deeper bronze than that of his own gypsies. Amid so much darkness his eyes were surprising; they glittered, light granite-grey, beneath strong brows that were still jet black.

"Good morning, sir!" he said, in uncompromising tones. His voice was deep and musical. "Sit down!" He indicated a chair. He sat down himself and took a pinch of snuff. "Well?" he asked.

Mr. Scales, despite his bravado, was terrified. The old cove certainly looked just as he should have looked, but there was no benevolence about him, or any nonsense of that sort. He was frankly intimidating.

"It's very good of you to see me, sir," he began ingratiatingly.

"It is," Mr. Darrell retorted to this, "very good indeed. Glad you realise it."

A pause ensued. Mr. Scales felt beads of sweat dewing his forehead. Worse—he could think of nothing whatever to say. The silence was eventually broken by Mr. Darrell.

"Lost the use of your tongue, eh? Well, I suppose I'll have to help you. You want to know how I became a writer?"

"Yes, please, sir." Mr. Scales licked his dry lips.

II

It was half an hour later, and Mr. Scales, now brimming over with gratitude, insinuated himself in a curious serpentine fashion from his chair to announce that he had better return to Oxford.

"So you pick my brains, do you, and then decide to run off when I've nothing more to say to you?"

No, Mr. Scales was understood to mumble; such a supposition was very far indeed from being the case.

"You'll stay and eat birthday dinner with me, young man! I seldom receive visitors, and I dine in the middle of the day!"

He got up to ring the bell, and the great dog, Lion, got up, too, and thumped his tail.

Mr. Scales, James Darrell thought ironically, was not unlike a dog himself: almost, in his eagerness and gratitude, he wagged *his* tail. The journalist, after the foreign manservant had received various directions:

"Those are two splendid-looking horses out there in the field, sir."

"Yes. Thoroughbred Arabs. I've had some here ever since I was in Morocco. Bred 'em in the old days. Only these two left now."

Violently against Mr. Scales's private inclinations, they strolled out for a few minutes into the wind-swept garden towards the paddock. Mr. Darrell wore no hat and seemed impervious to the cold. After he had given the horses sugar, conversation languished, and Mr. Scales, casting desperately in his mind, at length perceived a thickly wooded hill about half a mile away. Above the trees rose lovely twisted chimneys, and he hazarded:

"Looks like a nice place over there, sir."

There was so long a pause that he began to think his host could not have heard him.

"We'll go back to the house," James Darrell decided. Then, as they retraced their steps: "You mean the old Hall. Been empty for years. I'm told it's gone to rack and ruin."

They dined in a shabby, rather draughty room, where the fire was inclined to sulk at them and smoke. The chops were tough and the treacle pudding stodgy, but they drank a bottle of excellent claret.

Mr. Scales, recovering slightly from his earlier cataleptic state of awe, began furtively to observe his surroundings. The old cove, of course, couldn't be married, for no wife would tolerate the discomfort, the neglect even, of the house. There hadn't been, either, now he came to think of it, any specific mention of women in *The Span-*

ish Journey, and somehow he seemed to recollect a similar criticism being made of *The English Journey.* Perhaps Mr. Darrell had been one of those monkish sort of chaps, more interested in poking about old buildings and among odd languages than in the good things of this world. In that case, Mr. Scales was sorry for him. Despite all his fame, he seemed lonely enough, and he was a fine-looking old fellow. Must have been handsome as a young man. Pity he'd wasted his time.

"My England's gone, vanished," Mr. Darrell was saying as they drank some Turkish coffee, which was better than the dinner had been.

"How is that, sir?" Mr. Scales enquired, humbly accepting a very tolerable-looking cigar.

"When I was your age," James Darrell answered, speaking perhaps more to himself than to the young man, "when I was your age, the English countryside was unspoilt. Anybody who wanted adventure on the road had only to walk out then to find it by the wayside. Now that the railways have ploughed their foul way through the fields, they've chased away the last ghosts from the road I remember so well."

(A good job, too, Mr. Scales privately decided; nice lookout if everybody had to go back to the days of the coaches!)

Aloud he asked deferentially:

"Do you ever see much of the gypsy people nowadays, sir?"

"Very seldom," replied the other indifferently. After a slight pause he added: "There's a woman, Rosaina Lovell—I knew her parents long ago—when she passes this way, she comes to see me with her family."

His tone was sombre, and it was obvious that he had not the slightest desire to discuss the gypsies. Mr. Scales, nervous once more, sought to turn the conversation, but succeeded only partially with:

"I've always thought it must be pleasant to stay in a caravan—just for the Epsom races, let's say!"

James Darrell smiled and answered:

"A caravan, you know, doesn't necessarily mean a gypsy wagon. In Morocco a procession is known as a caravan. But the word can be used, too, to mean a cavalcade of any kind. Don't, pray, start me musing on the curious significance of words! Your time is short;

tell me instead how do you like this old-fashioned house of mine? I was born here, you know. I spent my childhood in the village."

The wine had mellowed him, and he was now more genial in his manner, but Mr. Scales regarded this last question as what he termed a poser, not perceiving any charm whatever about the house in question. He blurted out something to the effect that Mr. Darrell must feel the cold after so many years abroad.

"Yes," was the brief answer. "I miss the sun."

(And then, as though a bell rang somewhere in his brain, came the perplexing thought: *"Someone else said that once, long ago, here . . ."*)

There was so long a pause that Mr. Scales at length struggled nervously to his feet and said there was no question about it, he positively must be getting on his way. This time he was not detained, and as he bade farewell to his host, he muttered something incoherent about the great honour of being received, and only hoped he should do justice, etc., etc.

"Good-bye," James Darrell said, and smiled again.

The young man's last view of the writer was that of a very tall, erect old man standing alone on the doorstep, his hand on the collar of his dog.

Then the fly drove off, bearing him towards the railway so much despised by his host, towards the lights of London, towards all the clash and clatter of the streets he loved so much. He was glad; he thought once again how terrible it must be to be old and forgotten, having once been famous. Poor old chap! Talk about loneliness! And there was no doubt that he'd missed a lot of fun, despite all that wandering about! Probably he never had been in love! Then Mr. Scales's active mind immediately became occupied with the composition of his interview, and he began furiously to scribble on the back of an envelope.

James Darrell, followed by Lion, returned to the parlour and put another log on the fire. Then he sat down, lit a cigar, and patted Lion's head, but his thoughts were far away.

He had at last granted an interview, because he knew, just as well as Mr. Scales, that people were beginning to forget him, and he was still vain enough to resent being forgotten. He knew something else as well: he knew that he would never write another book. He wondered what sort of rubbish that young man would print about him. Nothing, in any case, that would have the power to trouble him, for he had kept his secrets. No one knew those secrets that had been so rigorously suppressed from all the books.

There was nothing, now, to connect him with that grave just across the fields in the churchyard, nor with that other grave so far away across the seas. He had not been near the Hall for years, and in any case the place was said to be tumbling down. That reserve which had always, even in youth, been his, served him well in his old age, since he had supposedly become a recluse. People had been inquisitive enough once.

Reserve was a good thing, too, he mused. Look at that fellow Dickens. A nice mess he'd made of his private life. Well, James Darrell had never talked. Nobody suspected any mystery, except such as was cunningly and deliberately manufactured in the books, and that, of course, led nowhere. It was pure showmanship. Now it did not even matter, since they were all dead, all forgotten. He had just happened to outlive the others. It was a strange thought.

In a way he was sorry. It was a damnable business, growing old alone. He had always been as tough as a yew, but it could not be for very long now. He didn't think that he would much mind dying. He threw away the butt of his cigar and closed his eyes. His memory had never been good since all that trouble so many years ago, and the wind was high—howling about the house and down the chimneys—so that for a moment he thought he heard children calling outside, and he wondered why no one let them in.

Of course he could not really hear the voices of children. And that other sound—that faint, distant strumming of a guitar—was simply another distortion of the raging wind.

His head nodded then, and, as he slipped into a fitful, uneasy sleep, he dreamed that time rolled back, and he was young again.

PART I

The Cuckoo's Child

CHAPTER I

IT WAS DARK in the parlour, and the pale evening light was in no way aided by the struggling green creepers that clustered against the windowpanes. Inside, a fire burned fitfully, flinging black shadows against the faded walls. The shadows leaped and danced, casting fantastic shapes upon the furniture.

The children were supposedly playing on the hearthrug. Their mother, who sat knitting by the window, thought they were playing at Noah's Ark, and her daughter Emily was indeed happily engaged with a troop of tiny wooden animals. But the boy, James, sat on his heels and stared straight ahead of him into the fire. It seemed to her that he had been for a long time motionless.

She called sharply:

"James!"

"Yes, Mama?"

Outside in the street a coach or a carriage passed, hooves clattered, and a cockney voice swore at the horses. A burst of wind rattled the windowpanes. The March day was nearly over.

"James! Why do you not play with your sister?"

He turned his head slowly, thinking this a foolish question indeed. As he deliberated, a lock of dark hair fell over his eye. Why wasn't he playing with Emily? His mother was always asking him why he did, or did not do, something so obvious to him that it seemed ridiculous even to protest.

So he said coldly:

"I am looking in the fire."

He knew then, perhaps for the first time consciously, how much he hated his mother's French accent. He was eleven, and he realised his own ingratitude. He spoke French nearly as well as he spoke English. She had taught her own language to James and Emily since first they could remember: almost her sole contribution to the welfare of these children she had borne to an obscure Oxfordshire doctor.

Henriette Darrell was the granddaughter of *émigrés* escaped from France during the Revolution. She herself had never seen her own land, and her youth had been lived while a long war raged between her country and her adopted country. But the war had been over now for many years, and for a long time she had been married to Robert Darrell.

She had met him on one of his rare visits to London, and married him gladly, although he was old enough to be her father. Whatever rural English life might be, she was wise enough to know that it could not be worse than the precarious existence of a young lady who depended on fine sewing for her daily bread.

And so Henriette Duval came to Oxfordshire with her small green trunk, her workbasket, three books by Voltaire, some pretty bonnets, and a dark, sad-looking picture that had belonged to her Spanish grandmother.

All that, she recollected, was nearly thirteen years ago. All that time she had lived quietly, but as a stranger, in the remote hamlet that was nearly three miles from Oxford. She had been a slender creature with a certain attractiveness of ebony and ivory colouring so sharply defined as to make her resemble a black-and-white drawing. She was thin now, and her eyes were haggard, for the marriage soon failed, and she had been for many years intolerably bored.

To the villagers and peasants she would always be the French-woman: an alien, even an enemy, for the long wars were still remembered bitterly. To her elderly husband she was a bad house-keeper and a moody companion. To the children? Because she did not know the answer to that question she now said sharply to James:

"Staring at the fire isn't a game. It's doing nothing. It is just being lazy."

"I shall go and see Betty in the kitchen," James retorted to this, and slipped away.

She supposed, since he was her son and resembled her physically, that he should have been her favourite child, but he was not. If she had an affection for anything in the world, it was for the flaxen, fairy-like beauty of her daughter. James was a thin child, dark-skinned, with grey eyes still too big for his face. He was reserved, as she was. Secretive, his father called it. She would have used another word to describe herself and James. Remote.

Many years ago, living in London, she had expected more from life than the swift quenching of her youth, this imprisonment in a house that would always to her seem strange. She had dreamed then, as other girls dream, of a youthful lover, of gaiety as well as hardship shared; of colour, and noise, and all the glittering clamour of city streets.

She had married for safety, and safety brought her to a little Queen Anne house in a scattered village where the countryside was wild and where her husband acted as doctor to a handful of peasants more ignorant than animals.

Such neighbours as there were found her "odd," sarcastic, and unfriendly. Sometimes, still, for her husband's sake, they asked the pair to Sunday supper, or a game of whist, but Robert Darrell was seldom free, and for weeks, months, at a time she saw no one but her family. And the winters were long in Oxfordshire.

One of her few interests was that of making pretty dresses for her daughter Emily. The beautiful little girl was dressed always in fine muslins and delicate gauzes; her sashes were of the best silk and her slippers of coloured kid. In contrast, James was both shabby and untidy. But, as his mother said, what did that matter? He was a boy.

Now, in the dingy kitchen, with its huge old grate and glowing copper pans, the boy sat down by the fire and talked earnestly to his friend Betty, the overworked servant. This plump, middle-aged woman with cheeks like picotees and a rich Oxfordshire accent was at that time accustomed to see more of him than any other person. If anyone had questioned him, he would have said that she never "fussed" him.

"When will the pedlar come again, Betty?"

"Which pedlar?"

"The Jew. The one who said I would sail across the seas to foreign lands."

Betty smiled. It was dusk now, and she went to light the candles. Her pattens clicked on the stone floor.

"And find a crock of gold at the end of the rainbow? The old rascal's not been back. Give over teasing that cat, Master James!"

"Well," he sighed, releasing Tib, "I wish I were a pedlar—the one, I think, who sells toys and ribbons and gingerbread . . ."

"A nasty, low thing to want to be," Betty reproved.

They talked comfortably for hours together, these two, much as though they were contemporaries.

"It would be very fine," James persisted; "no more lessons with the parson—no staying always in one place! I'd like to walk in Ackland Wood as much as I please, Betty, and when I was tired of one village, I'd tramp on to the next!"

"When the primroses are out, in a week or so from now," Betty promised, "we'll take a picnic to Ackland Wood and spend the day there."

James sprang up with a shout of joy as the clatter of horse's feet in the yard heralded the doctor's return home.

He ran out into the yard, where John, the sulky manservant, waited with a lantern.

Robert Darrell climbed slowly from the back of his flea-bitten grey mare, for he was stiff and tired.

"Rub her down well, John; we've had a long day, the pair of us. Why, child, you're out late!"

"I came to meet you," James explained.

Robert Darrell was a big, rather stout man, in the middle fifties. He was sturdily built, with broad shoulders and a square, darkish face. His nose was beaked, his eyebrows bushy, and his thick hair steel-grey. As a physician he was old-fashioned, and his manners were offhand, but the village people liked him, for he was strong and tough, and resolute in the pursuit of his duties.

Floods and snowdrifts never daunted him, nor the fiercest gales, nor trees blown down across the country lanes. In hail and sleet and storm he rode doggedly forth to the loneliest, most remote of all the scattered farms and cottages. He swore robustly, and always insisted on a bran mash for Judy, the grey mare, before he would consent to glance at his patient, but he understood the Oxfordshire peasants, and they trusted him. Not that they ever said much. At the most they admitted that they might have fared worse.

"Well, come in now," he admonished his son. "I'm stiff and cold, and you can bring my grog to the study."

CHAPTER II

THE STUDY was a shabby room with book-lined walls, a large old-fashioned smoky fireplace, and a general air of dilapidation, of being somehow down at heels. Yet to James it was the most pleasant room in the house; more attractive even than the attics under the roof. Perhaps its chief attraction lay in the fact that his mother never came near it; she and Robert Darrell had little left to say to each other, and even their meals together would have been eaten in silence but for the children.

The doctor now sank into the worn armchair near the fire with a grunt of satisfaction, and while he lit his long clay pipe James hastened into the kitchen to fetch the grog that was an evening ritual.

Relaxed and warm for the first time since early that morning, Robert Darrell surveyed his son with a lazy curiosity. The thin little dark boy in the nankeen trousers returned his gaze earnestly, a lock of hair falling over his eyes.

"What have you been doing, eh?"

"I found a book here, Father, this morning, and I want to know if I may keep it."

"What is it?"

"Look. It's a Spanish grammar and phrase book. Can I take it upstairs?"

"What on earth do you want with such a book?"

"Why, to learn Spanish, of course!"

"Will that help you," Robert wanted to know, "to become a better doctor when you grow up?"

James evaded this question.

"I'll learn at night," he suggested artfully, "when my lessons are over."

"As you will. Not that the book is mine. It must be your mother's."

Not for the first time the doctor regarded his son with perplexity, for he was attached to the boy without in the least understanding him. The parson said he was intelligent but idle. When reproved for his reluctance to master Latin or Greek, he replied that he could not see the use of learning languages no one spoke. His mother complained that he liked low company, and he was certainly often to be found up at the blacksmith's forge, or gossiping in the cottage of a very dirty old woman reputed to be a witch.

When questioned, he merely answered that he told old Mrs. Hoskin stories.

"Stories?"

"Yes. Not lies. Made-up ones. She likes them."

The father thought, looking at him: "There is nothing of me in this boy of mine. He is all his mother, and yet they dislike each other. And he will never make a doctor. He is too dreamy."

Once again he wondered what to do with his son.

He himself had succeeded to his father's practice; he was Oxfordshire born and bred. With the exception of visits to London and professional sojourns in Edinburgh he had never travelled. The remote situation of the village and its extreme loneliness never troubled him, since he was accustomed to solitude. He saw nothing wrong in his son's bird's-nesting with the blacksmith's boys. There were no other children for him to talk to. In Robert's youth there had been the squire's sons from the Hall, a mile away; but the Hall had been shut for years now, and its present owner, Mr. George Camperdene, preferred to live abroad.

When Robert Darrell thought of his youth he thought always, and still with nostalgia, of the Elizabethan house on the hill behind the village; of rooks cawing in the elm trees near the lake; of black cedars casting their shade on grass as soft as down; of glowing flower beds, and greenly rolling parkland, and space, and graciousness, and comfort.

Well, there were no longer any Camperdenes living near by to associate with his own children, and the house was shuttered and desolate save for the peacocks on the terraces and the red deer in the park. Even the coverts were deserted, except for poachers who sometimes lurked there on moonlit nights. The end of an epoch, he thought, sighing; the end of those gaudy, glittering Regency days he had glimpsed only as a spectator, as a youthful visitor to the great half-forgotten house.

Aloud he said:

"You'll go to the grammar school in Oxford when you're thirteen, James."

He sighed, for the squire's sons had been educated at Eton.

James, having heard his destiny before, was not impressed. He promptly changed the subject.

"When the primroses are out next week, Betty is to take us picnicking in Ackland Wood."

Robert frowned.

"Take care not to lose yourself, or your sister. It's a wild place and used to shelter many a rogue when I was a boy of your age."

"Highwaymen?"

"I expect so."

James digested this information in fascinated silence. Vividly, half closing his eyes, he visualised the scene—a green ride sweeping mysteriously beneath darkly arching trees. Silence, ice-blue moonlight, and then, out of the silence, the frantic thunder of galloping feet, and a black, panting horse appeared, caked white with lather, and crouching on its back a cloaked, mysterious rider. The rider, of course, would be masked beneath his gold-laced tricorn hat. For a moment he visualised the phantom flight so clearly that the jingle of a bit rang in his ears and he smelt the sweating horseflesh. He——

"For the Lord's sake, stop staring!" his father was exclaiming in exasperated tones. "Or do you not want your supper tonight?"

James had not even heard the bell.

Later that evening, when the children had been sent upstairs, Robert Darrell paid one of his rare visits to the parlour. Here, as he had expected, his wife sat listlessly before the fire, her embroidery on her lap, her eyes veiled, her lips thin. She glanced at him briefly and began to sew.

For a moment he looked at her hopelessly. What an insane and futile marriage! His mind flickered back thirteen years, to an Adam room in London and the freshness and youth of Henriette in a dress sprigged with lilac. He had wanted to do it, and he had done it: he had brought back this alien woman to his home and fireside.

"With the result," he thought, "that my son is a changeling."

Aloud he grumbled:

"That boy—I can't understand him. Now he wants to learn Spanish!"

"His grandmother was a Spaniard."

"What has that to do with it? The boy is English!"

She said nothing. As usual, when the children were discussed, she consoled herself with the thought of Emily's flowerlike prettiness.

Robert continued:

"What's he to do, and how earn a living, if he continues so feckless?"

She made no reply, nor had he really expected one. She didn't care very much what happened to anyone but her daughter. He yawned and heaved himself from his chair.

"I've had a hard day. I shall go to bed."

"Good night," Henriette answered quietly.

When he had shut the door behind him she dropped her listless airs and listened for a moment with an expression of intense vigilance. She heard him take his candlestick from the hall and tramp heavily upstairs. In a moment his door shut, and there was silence. She folded her embroidery and rose from the chair. At the parlour door she listened for a moment. No sign of Betty.

She crossed over to the cupboard in the wall and took a key from her reticule. Then she returned to her seat by the fire, hiding beneath her shawl, as though even from herself, the bottle of gin.

Soon she would no longer be oppressed by the prim parlour with its ticking grandfather clock, its faded green covers, its framed samplers, its cabinet of Chinese "rubbish," as she called it, and the wooden, simpering portraits of Robert's parents, which she so much hated.

Soon, before she took off her shoes to stumble unsteadily upstairs, under the futile delusion that her household ignored her nocturnal consolations, she would find, a pitiful pilgrim, the only world she cared about.

It was a world where Henriette Duval was rich, powerful, fashionable, and young. There was nothing wild or savage in this world of hers; no desolate winters where the wind howled across the downs and the breath of snow was in the air; it was a land of spacious rooms and blazing wax lights, and flowers bloomed there at all seasons of the year.

More, she had her own carriage, to drive about St. James's.

Soon her head nodded, and she smiled to herself. She really didn't hear the wind battering at the windows.

Upstairs, in Emily's room, James sat on the end of her bed.

"Go on with the story about the mermaid with blue hair, James."

He hesitated, for while she was warm and comfortable, he shivered in his nightshirt, but since there were only two people who listened to his stories—Emily and Mrs. Hoskin—the temptation was too great to avoid.

"I won't tell about the mermaid tonight," he decided thoughtfully, "but I'll tell you something that happened to me in Ackland Wood the other day. Well, I was walking along, when, greatly to my amazement, I saw a great coach pass. A gold coach, it was, drawn by six chestnut horses, and all its panels were painted, like the lid of Mama's musical box. I said to myself as I watched, 'That coach will surely be robbed by highwaymen before it goes much further.' And, sure enough, as I watched——"

Here he glanced at Emily, and perceived that she had fallen asleep.

He was not surprised, but he felt slightly discouraged.

With a sigh he got up and went across the passage to his own bedroom.

His world was more real to him than Henriette's, and he lived in his nearly all the time.

CHAPTER III

ACKLAND WOOD had roamed for many years behind the hamlet of
Steeple Courtney. Originally an old hunting forest, the village itself
had at one time been encircled by those oaks and beeches that had
drawn back beyond the hill in the last hundred years, while men
dug roads, and built houses, and took timber for their ships. James
thought that the forest must have retreated reluctantly; must have
dwindled not without unwillingness to cede any of the splendid
woodlands haunted by the shades of Malory.

Even now the thick trees clustered for more than six miles, and
the dark, encroaching mass of the woods could be seen from far
away. Beneath grey Gothic arches, resembling aisles, formed by the
beech trees, the woods were densely overgrown with thickets of
briar and thorn and bramble. Here were fortresses of holly and
sloe, towers of yew, and citadels of gorse and broom. Bracken grew
knee-high, and in the spring the leaves of the young beeches were
the translucent green of sea water. Here, at this time of year, were
to be found amid the tangled brambles enchanting hidie-holes—
nests of primroses, golden yellow as the April sunshine, and, later,
glades mantled in azure bluebells, as though the skies had spilled.

Ackland Wood was common land, but the game found there had
always attracted the attention of poachers, tramps, and other vagabonds. There were fat coneys to be snared; there were pheasants
and deer, and even a hare or two, run in from the fields outside. Nor
were these the only attractions for the lawless.

Vagrants, rogues, and people of the road knew that it was easy
to disappear, as so many periodically wanted to do, among the dark
trees, there to live secretly, in glen or thicket, until the hue and cry
died down and they were free once more to take to the road. In the
bad old days footpads and other "flash coves" had sheltered in the
woods from thief takers and Runners; now, in rural England of the
early thirties, there were still queer customers whose desire to avoid
the constables occasionally led them to take refuge in so wild and
unfrequented a spot.

But no such thoughts troubled Betty's head on the fine spring morning when she started off, as she had promised, to take the children picnicking in Ackland Wood. She was a village woman, born and bred; as a child she had nutted in the woods, and gathered blackberries there, and picked her faggots in the winter; her own uncle had been a poacher. The times in which she lived were lean enough for country people, and the poorer among them would have suffered often enough from hunger had it not been for an occasional stolen rabbit finding its way into the cottage pot.

Now in heavy clogs and with her skirts kilted, Betty strode down the village street, a child on either side, a heavy basket slung about her shoulders. Emily, for once in a plain dress, moved with an odd, precocious sedateness, but her cheeks were pink with excitement, and she, too, carried a smaller basket—for the primroses she intended to gather. James was not interested in flowers. His desires were two: to search for birds' nests, and to invent a story based on the ghost of that highwayman whose possibly mythical adventures so much intrigued him.

Robert Darrell's small Queen Anne house stood near the village green. The hamlet itself consisted of one street, or road, where the two- and three-roomed cottages nodded beneath topheavy thatched roofs, like brown and drowsy toadstools. Before each door glowed a patch of garden, gay, now, with full-blown daffodils and budding tulips. The April wind rushed up the road to billow, like sails, rows of mended, shabby garments dancing on the lines, for this was wash-day, and Betty exchanged chaffing salutations with a dozen red-cheeked, red-armed women so like herself they might all have been her sisters.

Past the forge, where the blacksmith hammered away in his smoking crimson Cavern, while two elephantine horses waited meekly in the adjoining shed, and then, as they approached Mrs. Hoskin's tumbledown cottage, James rushed forward with a whoop of greeting, for the old woman stood at her doorway, blinking with red-rimmed eyes upon the radiant April sunshine.

Mrs. Hoskin might have been any age from seventy to a hundred. She was really rather a horrid-looking old woman, for she had not only a moustache, but a tuft of grey beard, and there was enough scanty grey hair on her head for these locks to be perpetually in a state of dishevellment. She had few teeth, with a resultant nut-cracker appearance which made it easy to understand why simple people not only called her a witch, but firmly believed that, on certain nights of the year, she flew round the church tower straddled upon a broomstick. She was by no means overclean, and her dress was ragged in the extreme. She much enjoyed being dirty, and took a sardonic pleasure in her own sinister reputation. She had once confided to James that, in her great-great-grandma's time, she would have been burned—"alive too. Don't you believe they strangled 'em first."

Added to these charms she was as thin as a gnawed bone, lived in one room that would have put a pigsty to shame, and possessed a furtive-looking ginger cat supposed by James to be her familiar spirit.

No one understood the friendship between himself and Mrs. Hoskin, nor did it occur to anybody that the old woman, being lonely and unpopular, thoroughly enjoyed the company of a high-spirited, vivacious boy. From James's point of view the problem presented an even simpler solution; she was, being a sorceress, the most interesting personality he had yet encountered. When his common sense told him that she was no more a witch than, say, his own mother, his imagination, already that of a creative artist, immediately convinced him that she was, and he believed himself.

While he talked to his disreputable friend, Emily shrank behind Betty's skirts, and Betty beckoned angrily.

"That dirty old body!" Betty protested when at last he had been extricated and they had resumed their way. James did not even bother to reply. He had long ago learned that it was of no avail to defend Mrs. Hoskin. Instead he repeated to himself:

"I know a witch. A *real* one."

He straightway forgot her as they turned down a lane leading towards the first grey stems of Ackland Wood. Outside, in the fair sunshine, green fields smelled sweet, the hedgerows were thick with budding pussy willow, and young lambs staggered in sunny hollows that were lined with violets. Silvery clouds raced across the sky, chasing their own light shadows that darted over the grass. A cuckoo mocked from an elm tree near the haystack, and the bright-ness of the day, the clear sky, the song of birds, the sharp contrast of sun and shadow, all combined to create some lovely pastoral of spring no more attuned to reality than the music of a faun's reed pipes.

Even stolid Betty remarked that it seemed a pity to "go in the woods when it's so nice here outside."

"But you promised!" James cried, disconsolate, and Emily insisted that her basket must be brimful of primroses before evening.

Betty laughed at their dismay and shooed them before her, like a pair of chickens, down the green ride that wound its way among the trees. At first, until they became accustomed to the shade, it seemed dark enough in the woods, particularly since this first path was bordered with tall firs and pines, and their foliage seemed more sombre even than usual against the delicate, feathery green of the young beech leaves.

They turned to the right and then to the left, where Betty remembered a favourite glade for picnics. Now they passed down a ride pillared silver and white with the trunks of beech and birch trees, and then, suddenly, the primroses were everywhere spread so thickly that there was no longer any sign of grass or moss—only a fragrant carpet the colour of the April sunshine.

It was there, beside a noisy little stream, that they ate their dinner couched on the primroses.

"Like *A Midsummer Night's Dream*," James said, but neither Betty nor his sister knew what he was talking about.

They ate cold chicken, and bread and jam, and drank milk from the bottle Betty produced. All three ate enormously, and even Emily showed a disinclination to pick primroses until she had rested for a few minutes. Betty, her back propped against a birch trunk, frankly bade them keep quiet until she had enjoyed her forty winks.

James immediately interpreted this demand by slipping away on his own among the trees.

Now, for some time, while the others gathered primroses, he would be free to pursue without restraint his own mysterious avocations. He asked nothing better of life. He slid down a steep bank, tearing his trousers, extricated one foot from a bog, and chased a rabbit across the path into a thicket of gorse. For the time being he had even forgotten the highwayman.

He was tremendously happy.

CHAPTER IV

MANY PAGES might be written to describe the activities of a boy running wild in the woods. This one differed not at all from his kind. He chased another rabbit, threw stones at a squirrel in a tree, wet both feet in a stream, and scratched his cheek pursuing through the brakes the first butterfly he had seen that year. He climbed a young fir that cradled a pigeon's nest, abstracted one egg, put it carefully in his mouth, and broke it, sliding down the knobbly trunk. Then, feeling a trifle sick, he sat down to rest in a primrose glade, and was enchanted by one swift glimpse of a fleeing dappled shape—a deer. Another chase, and then he found himself, panting, in a part of the wood strange to him—a coppice of huge oak trees beneath which thorns and brambles straggled in an impenetrable thicket.

Here, had he been wise, he would have confessed himself on unfamiliar ground and retreated whence he came, but he did no such thing. His head stuffed with tales of witches, and highwaymen, and knights who were all of them Lancelot, he became drunk on dreams, as boys will, and plunged straight away through the tangled undergrowth, greatly to the detriment of his already torn breeches.

James in moments of freedom was perhaps wilder than others. It was always to be the same with him. Then, as ever, the joys of liberty were like a heady wine. Betty and Emily were swiftly obliterated from his mind as he scrambled through the glen intent only on the exploration of what to him was a strange, fantastic land. Malory came true once more, and Robin Hood, and fiercely painted Indian braves stalked him mercilessly from behind the oak trees.

A hundred magical disguises were his. Sometimes he clanked down the green rides clad in shining armour; sometimes, Turpin-like, he spurred a goaded horse; sometimes, again, he sailed the ponds he saw, captain of a pirate crew, and then his ponds became the Spanish Main. His every wish came true, for this was his kingdom, and his word was law. In fact, for more than two hours he played every role that every boy has ever wanted to play.

And then he was lost.

He was hot, now, after so much scrambling, and tired, and thirsty. Looking about him, he found himself in a ride like all the other rides. Pausing first to drink from a stream near by, he wandered on past the grey flanks of the beech trees, only to find himself overlooking a ravine where boulders slanted down to a bog overgrown with reeds and rushes. These rocks were covered with a dark green moss, and stunted fir trees grew crookedly from among their crevices. It seemed to the boy a dismal spot, and silent too; as he paused, hesitant, something clattered noisily from one of the firs, and he watched, his heart beating fast, an enormous raven wheel into the sky and disappear. The dark silence of the ravine and the startling apparition of the great black bird combined to frighten him so much that he took to his heels and fled.

When at last he halted to look about him, he found himself surrounded by dense and briary thickets. But he was no longer afraid, only cross and weary and greatly in need of his tea. So he plodded on again, trying to believe that at any time now he would turn a corner to find the primrose glade, and Betty waiting with a cup of milk.

But nothing of the kind happened, for he had wandered more than three miles since his picnic, and he was walking directly in the opposite direction to the village. His spirits were high until suddenly he observed that the sun was setting. He had no watch, and only then did he realise how many hours he had been wandering. He called to the others, cupping his mouth with his hand, but his voice rang out desolate and thin in the quietness of the woods, and there was nobody to answer him.

Even the birds, he realised, had long since ceased to sing, and then the silence of his surroundings seemed to be filled with menace. He stopped, breathing hard, sweating, and knew that his feet were blistered. Frantically he tried to calculate his way back to the village, but his efforts were of no avail, for the trees and winding paths all looked the same, and he could not have been more hopelessly lost had he been one of his own legendary heroes benighted in the jungle.

Then, as he limped a few steps further, conscious that dusk was falling, he heard from behind some thickly growing trees the sound of voices. At once his spirits rose; he was no longer alone in the darkening woods, and he was ready to welcome anything living as a friend. He pressed on towards the trees, ready enough to meet a witch with a sugar-candy house, Robin Hood and his men, or a party of gnomes digging gold.

But he saw none of these as he came towards a clearing among the beeches. What he did see was sufficiently curious to make him forget his weariness and his aching feet, for this was an adventure.

Two curiously tilted carts, not unlike carriers' vans, were drawn together on the sward, surrounded by a cluster of low, arched tents. A huge fire burned, two or three nags and donkeys grazed near by, and some dark, strange-looking people, dressed in ragged, bright-coloured clothes, sat about the fire on their haunches and stared at him, but not with surprise. Rather, he thought confusedly, as though they had been expecting him.

Gypsies. He had seen such in the lanes near the village, and he knew that they bore another name—the peasants called them Egyptians. A very old shepherd once in James's presence had referred to them as the moon men. By any name they sounded curious and wild enough to satisfy the boy who loved adventure. Now, staring at them, he was assailed by a trio of wolfish-looking dogs.

"Call your dogs off!"

To his own astonishment his voice sounded authoritative, and he started when the dogs were whistled back.

James advanced slowly towards the fire. It was only later that he learned to differentiate between those dusky and impassive faces. He vaguely noticed that the men wore their hair long, so that their black and snaky locks flowed to their shoulders. Some of the women seemed comely in a savage way, and at least one, a young girl who lay on her stomach feeding a donkey with stolen hay, was possessed of a rich and vivid beauty. The almost ferocious wildness of their aspect, their raffishness, and bright-coloured rags did not dismay him, as such matters would have dismayed most children. On the contrary, he forgot his weariness and his blistered feet; he advanced almost gladly towards his destiny.

An old woman growled:

"Lost, my mannikin?"

She was a vast old woman wrapped in a cloak of poppy red. Her face was walnut brown and furrowed. She wore a straw hood, but her long, grizzled hair fell like a pony's tail below her waist. Her eyes blazed so brightly that it was easy to believe the devil himself peered out from these two dark windows.

James walked straight up to face her.

"Listen," he said, "will you give me supper if I tell you a story?"

He could not, had he studied this entrance for many weeks, have devised one that amused the gypsies more. The coolness and impudence of his address was a form of impertinence after their own hearts, and they all began to laugh. Their laughter was not so gay as the rags they wore; it was a dark chuckling that reminded him of the sound a spring makes when the water is deep.

"A story?" guffawed the old woman. "Do ye think then we're a parcel of *chavés,* of children like yourself?"

"It's a grown-up story," James assured her, unflinching.

He had certainly won the attention, for what it was worth, of the gypsies; he stepped forward, his eyes fixed seriously upon the old beldame, who appeared uncertain whether to box his ears or to treat him with the stupefaction she would have accorded to a pixie, had one sprung up from the ground at her feet. While she hesitated, his solemn gaze swept the gypsies seated about the fire, and, after a short, dramatic pause, he began his story, speaking without hurry, standing very straight and still before them. .

"I know a witch," James began, and his clear voice carried across the glade.

CHAPTER V

It is always gratifying to taste power for the first time. Long before James had finished a sinister tale based on the supposed supernatural activities of Mrs. Hoskin he perceived that the gypsies were not only attentive, but enthralled. Indeed for them—supposed sorcerers—this fire-and-brimstone tale was one that could not have delighted them more had he especially designed it with the object of weaving enchantment. They were younger than he as they listened; they sat motionless, their black eyes fixed unwinkingly upon him, while simply, seriously, and with immense conviction he related one fantastic incident after another.

When at last he stopped, they wanted more, but the showman was already dormant in the eleven-year-old boy, and he refused almost abruptly.

A few minutes later he was seated, cross-legged, on the right of the old beldame, eating stew from a wooden platter and drinking steaming coffee from a mug. The stew tasted of rabbit, pheasant, hare, and other delicacies, seldom encountered at home; while he ate, he peeped at the gypsies beneath his lashes and listened to the strange, outlandish tongue in which they chattered to one another.

The men, he thought, looked like Red Indians, with their long hair, their sheepskins, and their odd slouch hats. He thought that it must be very fine to be a gypsy and loll before the fire smoking a clay pipe and drinking out of a black bottle. Now that he was no longer hungry, his spirits rose; he was living in an adventure, and his quick wits told him how much his story had impressed his hosts.

And indeed he had impressed them, more profoundly than he knew Superstitious as savages, the gypsies were not at all sure that this *gajo* brat was not indeed the familiar imp of witches, and some, as they discussed him, were in favour of packing him off before dark, lest he mischief them as they lay in their tents. Others, braver or more mercenary, were in favour of keeping him for the night and returning him to his family the next morning, in exchange for a suitable reward.

This faction was led by none other than the formidable old woman herself, whose name was Hagar Brazil, and who was listened to with authority, as being the *daia,* or chieftainess, of the party. The other gypsies, a dozen or so, were mostly cousins, members of the Stanley, Buckland, and Boswell tribes.

James was asked his name, and where he lived, and if his father was a grand gentleman.

While he was engaged in answering these and other questions, a whistle sounded from the darkness of the trees, and a newcomer approached the encampment. This was a boy of about his own age, an alert ragamuffin, brown as a hazel nut, raffishly untidy, and the possessor of a moleskin waistcoat which seemed to James the most splendid thing that he had ever seen. The boy, who brought with him two rabbits still warm from the snare, looked at him roguishly, but without ill nature, sat down beside him, and began skilfully to skin the rabbits.

Despite the fascination of this new companion, James was by this time so sleepy that his eyelids pricked and everything swam before his gaze; as though in a dream he heard Mrs. Brazil inform him he should sleep that night with her grandson and be returned to his parents in the morning.

Then at once he seemed to be asleep, although he could not remember in the least how this phenomenon occurred; he was in a low tent, for he could see a patch of starry sky; he lay on a bed of bracken, although he did not know this until the morning; he was covered in a blanket that smelled, comfortably enough, of rabbits, and beside him, warm as a puppy, lay sprawled the gypsy boy who had said that his name was Sylvester.

Sylvester Brazil—a strange name. James slept as peacefully as though he were in his own bed.

In the morning he was aroused by Sylvester.

"What's your name?" the gypsy boy asked, resuming, as though without a break, the conversation that had been interrupted the night before by both of them falling asleep.

"James Darrell."

"James—Jamie. Well, Jamie, get dressed, and come out. It'll soon be breakfast time."

The encampment still slumbered. Already the morning was radiant with sunshine, but there was a tang in the air, and dew glittered silver on the cobwebs. In a coppice near by the cuckoo called, and the scent of wet primroses haunted the woods. Following Sylvester's example, James knelt down by the stream and plunged his head into the stinging freshness of the water. He felt suddenly, blissfully happy. He was at peace as he had never been at peace before.

He knew then, definitely, that he did not want to go home, and his head was stuffed with romantic dreams of living forever with these wild people, of becoming the king of the gypsies.

"Sylvester," he said, "what's the language your people talk together?"

"That's **Romany**," Sylvester returned in his rough young voice that was like no voice James had ever heard.

"Will you teach me to speak it?"

"Aye, if you were to stay, happen I might. But my dad's to take you back this morning."

"I don't want to go."

This Sylvester understood perfectly.

"No more would I. Not to a house. Steeple Courtney is your village called, Jamie?"

James nodded.

"Well," Sylvester reflected, "five weeks from now we'll be at Lyndon for the Mop Fair. A week we'll bide there."

"Lyndon's not far from us," James agreed eagerly.

"No. If you come to me then, I'll learn you Romany—on a condition you do summat for me."

"What?"

"Tell me the story of the chouahauni you told 'em last night."

"You mean about the witch?"

"That's it. Do you really know her, Jamie, or was you gammoning my granny?"

"I know her," James asserted obstinately.

"Granny's a bit of a witch too," Sylvester contributed.

James looked affectionately at his new friend. Already he liked everything about him—his rough raven hair, his dirty roguish face, the slim brown naked feet that were prehensile, like a monkey's. There was, too, the glory of the moleskin waistcoat with its buttons of real silver. Already, although disreputable, Sylvester was something of a dandy. To James he was perfection—he was everything a boy should be.

"Jamie," the paragon was asking, "can you box with your fists?"

James shook his head. His humiliation was great.

"Green, aren't you?" Sylvester taunted good-naturedly. "Well, I'll learn you that, too, or my dad will, or my uncle Saul."

"Thank you," James replied humbly. He added: "I can speak some Spanish. I taught myself."

This, incredibly, did not impress, and so he was forced to change the subject.

"Sylvester, where do the gypsy people go from here?"

Sylvester grinned.

"Over the hills and far away."

"Really?"

The gypsy boy relented. They sat down on a fallen tree near some gorse bushes, and Sylvester began to talk. James listened, as though bewitched, as indeed he was, for he heard then, for the first time, the lore of the Romany people, more fantastic than any of his own stories. Sylvester would not normally have confided in a strange gajo child, but this one, he knew from his grandmother, was different. This one, after his occult performance the night before, was even suspected of being a *beng's chavé*—a devil's brat, and therefore pleasurably different from others of his detested race. So Sylvester talked and James listened.

He heard that the gypsies were descended from the Kings of Egypt, and that Sylvester's own father was called the Duke. He heard for the first time that the lure of the *drom,* which meant the road, was inexplicably more fascinating to these people than any form of security the world could offer. The roistering life of the road was preferred, "because of wanting to see what happens round the next corner." It seemed to James as he listened that many vivid adventures could happen on this road of theirs that had no ending.

He heard of knuckle fights and brawls with knives; purses of gold passed mysteriously from one brown hand to another; there was talk of something called horse whispering, and there were stallions charmed from fields on moonlit nights. He listened to tales of fairground traffic; of crystal gazing, palmistry, and other magic. As Sylvester talked, it was as though the music of gypsy fiddles sang in green lanes, while all over England and Scotland, across the mountains into Wales, the painted caravans crept forever along winding roads, and the Egyptian people scarcely tarried anywhere long enough even to extinguish their own nomad fires.

It was a violent, lawless life, as described by Sylvester, and the other boy listened to many a tale of dark misdeed. But the freedom so fiercely prized by the gypsies dominated every legend; they called no man master; they were a people apart, wrapped in the secrecy of their own mysterious traditions; they wandered the world as they pleased, and were free as the air they breathed. They would have scorned to exchange their tents for palaces, and so long as they were at liberty to roam the face of the earth, they were content. Wherever they went, they trailed always with them the glamour of their vivid music and their dancing, their necromancy and magic, their potions and horse charming, and their love of everything wild and strange.

"Sylvester," James implored, "ask your grandmother to let me stay with you!"

Sylvester shook his head.

"She never will. She said your dad might pay a golden *balanser*— a guinea—to get you back. Hungry, Jamie? I can smell the bacon."

CHAPTER VI

AN HOUR AFTERWARDS, despite every form of entreaty on James's part, he found himself seated before Sylvester's father, the Duke of Egypt, upon a weedy young horse, riding firmly in the direction of his own village.

His consolations were two: his arrangement to meet Sylvester Brazil at Lyndon Fair and the majesty of his own return home seated thus before so spectacular a figure as that of Sylvester's father. The Duke as an escort was not lacking in attraction; tall, sun-scorched, and black-a-vised, his sheepskin, his peaked hat ornamented with a peacock's feather, his whip, its handle turquoise-studded, and the gold ring glinting in his ear, all combined to invest him with a fearsome grandeur flattering indeed to James.

As a companion, he lacked his son's charm, being in any case a taciturn fellow, but he somewhat grudgingly agreed to instruct his charge in fisticuffs at some future and unspecified date.

It was only as they approached the village that James's heart began to sink. For the first time since his adventures began he realised how dastardly had been his own behaviour. Not one thought for the anxiety his family must be enduring had obtruded itself upon his bewitched imagination. He had, on the contrary, most passionately besought the gypsies to let him stay with them forever. He did not care for Henriette, but he loved his father,

Betty, and his sister. The worst of it was that even this realisation of his own selfishness and affection for his family did not in the least prompt him to return to them of his own free will. He knew that he wanted, more than anything else, to stay with the gypsies.

"Not forever," he told himself; "only just till I get tired."

As he reflected thus, the Duke lit a short black pipe, and asked curtly if they were not approaching their destination.

As he spoke, the village children, emerging from the dame's school, perceived the horseman, and yelled to the skies their amazement and delight at the prodigal's return. Soon several mothers emerged at the doors of their cottages, only to join the procession, which was soon swelled by the blacksmith, the shepherd, two milk-maids, and the old weaver. Mrs. Hoskin, hearing the noise, prudently barred her door. She had no reason to like village junketings, which were usually celebrated by children pelting her with stones.

James was embarrassed and the Duke indifferent to the attention their arrival created in the village; later, when they arrived at the doctor's Queen Anne house, and John, the manservant, rushed indoors to break the news, James felt even more guilty. Betty wept over him, Emily embraced him, his mother had taken to her bed, and his father's joy could be seen gleaming behind his face of wrath.

"Happen the little squire lost hisself," the Duke contributed, pocketing a guinea with quiet satisfaction.

"Father, the gypsies were very good to me. This man's son, Sylvester, was so kind as you would never believe——"

"Be quiet, James. I'll speak to you later."

And when the Duke had ridden away down the street, darkly mysterious as ever, Robert did indeed speak vigorously to his son. He did not beat him, because, curiously progressive for one of his epoch, he did not believe in beating children. But he made it plain that James had behaved with monstrous selfishness, and the boy hung his head, once more uncomfortable at the memory of how little he had missed those who were so attached to him.

His mother did not attempt to conceal her contempt.

"As always, you prefer low company. Peasants and pedlars are bad enough. But these vagabonds—— Go out of my room—you may be covered with vermin!"

Even Betty, his warmest ally, refused for some time to forgive him.

"You done it on purpose, Master James! Just took to your heels and run the moment my back was turned!"

And Emily:

"Why, James, we might never have seen you again! Everyone knows the gypsies steal children——"

"That's nonsense. They didn't steal me, did they?"

His only sympathetic audience, in fact, was Mrs. Hoskin, who listened with passionate attention to the recital of his adventures, hearing with particular relish the impression produced upon the gypsies by his account of her own nefarious activities.

A week later James wrote his first story, an effort named "The King of the Gypsies." When he had finished it, he put it away in the chest in his room with other treasures—the strand of a rope supposed to have hanged a man, a hair ball from the stomach of an ox, his Spanish grammar, a book about Jack Sheppard, a conch shell, and a Roman coin.

There, of course, the matter should have rested, and that should have been the end of the adventure, for his parents had forbidden him to go near Ackland Wood, nor was he ever again to associate with the gypsies.

But in this matter he was incapable of obedience. He slipped away to Lyndon and met Sylvester clandestinely; he began to study the Romany language, and Sylvester taught him how to use his fists. Even when Lyndon Fair was over, he found the gypsies a few weeks later camping in a green lane the other side of the village. In the summer they wandered mainly about Oxfordshire; it was only in the winter, they told him, that they migrated down to Hampshire, to the New Forest.

It was easy to find them. Sylvester lured him away by means of a "patrin," a leafy track left for him at the nearest crossroads. Whenever he saw it, he knew that his friends were somewhere in the neighbourhood and traced them by the secret leaves to their camping grounds. Sylvester and he soon called each other "brother," and were as David and Jonathan. Old Hagar seemed fond of him, and listened to his tales; even the Duke and his moody brother Saul were not above teaching him the advantages of a straight left.

Soon, as these meetings became more frequent, the gypsies appeared less strange to him, and he took their company for granted, although they must never be mentioned at home. They, too, became accustomed to him, and learned in time that it was safe to discuss their Romany secrets in his hearing. He was no longer "the little squire," but "Jamie," and by the end of the summer they had almost accepted him as one of themselves.

That autumn, while he neglected his lessons to run wild with the Brazils, to write fairy tales, and to learn Spanish, he heard a piece of news which, while it meant little enough to him, gave the village cause for much gossip and excitement.

It seemed that Mr. Camperdene, the squire, was coming back to live at the Hall.

Robert Darrell was delighted. Although George Camperdene had never been his favourite of the brothers, he looked forward with joy to the prospect of renewing any friendship after so many lonely years.

"Why has Mr. Camperdene never come home before?" James asked his father.

"His wife was always delicate. This was no climate for her, and so they lived in Italy. It seems she died a year ago, the poor ailing body, and now he wants to come home. He has a daughter, too, about Emily's age, so let us hope they'll make friends together."

The doctor beamed as he sipped his grog.

"If Mrs. Camperdene died a year ago, why didn't the squire come home before?" James wanted to know.

"That's no business of ours. You're too fond of asking questions, boy. Get on with your studying!"

James shrugged his shoulders.

He had, after all, no interest in the Camperdene family, although he would have liked to visit Italy himself. But only that morning Sylvester had shown him how to doctor a broken-winded horse, and he had begun to write a story about the most bloodthirsty of all pirates. He had no time to spare for the squire or his daughter.

Pretending submissively to be working at his lessons, he lay very still on the hearthrug and began to write the third chapter of Captain Skull's adventures.

He was a hundred miles away.

CHAPTER VII

ONE AFTERNOON in November, a dusky day of lowering clouds and
gusty wind, a grand carriage sped down the village street and vanished before the watchers realised that at last Mr. Camperdene had
come home.

The next day, of course, there was much gossip. Betty talked
excitedly of the crest on the carriage doors, of the shining bay
horses. The Hall, it appeared, was full of servants—"stuck-up
London bodies"—who had been waiting for more than a week for
their master to return. And then he had arrived without so much as
a word to anyone.

"And the little girl?" Emily asked eagerly.

Miss Camperdene was with her father; Betty knew that from the
gardener's boy, who was her cousin. It appeared she had a strange,
outlandish name that no one could remember. And the squire, Betty
knew for a fact, had returned from foreign parts looking as yellow
as a guinea. He felt the cold too; fires burned all day in the big
house that had not been lived in for so long.

James for the first time pricked up his ears. He liked the sound
of the yellow Mr. Camperdene who had given his daughter an outlandish name, and who sounded so pleasantly unlike his own family
and the village people. He thought that he would like to meet someone who had lived in "foreign parts," and he wondered why on
earth the squire had ever troubled to return from them.

"To come here," he reflected, "where nothing ever happens. I'd
not do that in his place."

About a week afterwards Robert and Henriette went forth to
pay their respects at the Hall. Everyone was astonished that Henriette should even for one afternoon venture forth in the doctor's
gig. In any case, she caught cold returning home and took to her
bed for several days, so that, his father proving for once uncom-
municative, James was forced to rely upon Emily for a secondhand
account of the Hall and its inhabitants.

"Only fancy, James, the big drawing room is filled with statues, like a church, and there were flowers, although it's nearly Christmas time. And the squire's very grave, and laughs seldom. Oh! James, what do you think the little girl is called?"

"Well, what?"

"Oriana. Did you ever hear the equal?"

"Often. Gypsy women have names as strange. What's she like?"

"Mama said old for her age, and no wonder, being alone with her father, and some old governess, and an Italian maid. But she is to come here soon, so we shall see for ourselves, and perhaps she and I are to do lessons together."

The twelve-year-old James lost interest, and it was only some days later, when Miss Camperdene was to spend the afternoon with them, that he remembered how much her name reminded him of Romany names and allowed Betty to chivvy him into his best suit without registering more than a formal protest.

Mrs. Darrell was still ailing in her room, so that it was supposed the visitor would bring her governess with her.

But she did not; to Betty's shocked astonishment she arrived entirely alone, driving up in the grand carriage with two liveried servants seated upon the box.

To James and Emily, waiting stiffly in the parlour, this was the most sensational arrival ever known, eclipsing even James's return home from the gypsies; to the visitor it might have been the most commonplace in the world. She wore a red cloak and hood the colour of holly berries, and she exclaimed at once, without even waiting to greet her hosts:

"Why, Emily, how pretty you are! Your mama told me about you, but she didn't praise you enough; you're like the fairy doll I had last Christmas!"

James scowled, such flattery of Emily being considered by all save Henriette as prejudicial to her modesty; but she turned to him and said, holding out her hand:

"I wanted to meet you, because you're the only person I ever heard of who ran away with the gypsies!"

Betty, taking the visitor's red cloak, here made clucking sounds of disapproval, and James asked:

"Who told you that?"

"Why, my father's groom." And, looking at Emily's flower-sprigged gown, "I'm not fine enough, am I? But I thought we might run wilder if I didn't dress up."

This was Oriana at ten, and she was never to change greatly. She wore a dress of clear white muslin, with a red sash, and her shoes were scarlet to match. Her dark, silky hair hung loose upon her shoulders, and her skin was very white. She seemed strong enough, bubbling with vitality; she was slim, but tall for her age; her eyes were large, brown, and lustrous; even then James noticed that the tip of her nose turned up in the most engaging manner possible, making her quite unlike anyone he had ever seen before.

She was herself so free from shyness that all constraint immediately vanished, and when the three sat down to saffron cake in the parlour they might have known each other all their lives.

"We thought," Emily volunteered, "you were to bring your governess with you."

"Mrs. Bloomfield? Oh no—I didn't want her! Isn't it more agreeable by ourselves?"

It was, but since this explanation by no means satisfied her companions Emily persisted:

"Does she do as you wish, then?"

"Nearly always, so long as I don't plague her, and you see she hates the cold. She's lived a long time in Italy, and so she loves to stay indoors."

During this conversation James stared quite openly at his guest. Despite his vivid imagination, it had never once occurred to him that any girl could be like Oriana Camperdene; Emily, for instance, was often prim; she disliked rough games, and at nights Betty put her hair in curling rags. It seemed to her brother that she cared only to look pretty; to dress up in her best.

But this girl, who was as frank and impetuous as a boy, combined, with the freedom of her manner, a glowing charm that seemed to him far more attractive than his own sister's prettiness; when she talked, her whole face danced and sparkled, and her hands talked, too, he thought, but perhaps that was because she had lived so long abroad and was accustomed to speak Italian.

It was after the saffron cake that she suggested going out into the garden, and when Emily protested that it was damp underfoot, and would soon be twilight, she looked at James and said:

"You'll take me, won't you? *You* don't mind getting your feet wet?"

He asked slowly, his anger mounting:

"Do you think me such a milksop?"

"I know you are not a milksop," Oriana answered. She looked at him for a second, and dropped her eyes.

Emily watched them from the parlour window as they walked, sedately enough, across the sad-looking, wintry garden, and her eyes stung with angry tears. How like James, she thought, to lure away this fascinating new companion! Oddly enough, it never occurred to her that James had been lured. She went, crossly, to her dolls' cupboard and took out the favourite she had hoped to exhibit. It seemed to her that James was a bad, wicked boy, who only liked to plague people, and run away, and associate with the lowest, most disgraceful characters. She was sure that Oriana's papa would not approve of him. Choking back her tears, very meticulously she began to fold up her dolls' dresses.

Betty came in noisily, her arms as red as her face.

"He's never taken Miss out in the fields at this time of day?"

"He's a bad boy," Emily agreed sadly.

"That's what comes of sending her here alone! You'd think they'd know better up at the Hall!"

Emily said nothing. She was conscious of an intolerable sense of loneliness, and only pride prevented her from running upstairs to complain to her mother.

CHAPTER VIII

"Can we go across the fields into that farmyard?" Oriana asked at the end of the garden.

"I can, yes. But you—in those red shoes——"

"It doesn't matter about my shoes. They aren't new. Come on, James!"

For as long as he could remember James had been free to play in Hunter's yard, Hunter being the neighbouring farmer and a patient of the doctor's. Now he was conscious that the farm looked "mucky," with its piles of wet straw trampled into slimy mud, its dishevelled haystacks, its dejected-looking hens clustered broodily about the yard. He made a sudden discovery.

"Oriana, this is an awful place!"

"It's all right. Is that a barn?"

"Yes, it's the big barn. It's dry. Let's go inside."

It was better inside the barn. The walls were whitewashed, and the heaps of straw smelled sweet and clean. They sat down, and James perceived, not without horror, that the little red shoes were plastered with mud.

Oriana came straight to the point.

"I wanted to speak to you alone," she announced. "Why did you run away with the gypsies?"

James reflected.

"I didn't exactly run away with them. I was lost, and I stayed with them. That isn't running away."

"But you run away to them now whenever you have a chance, don't you?"

He was startled.

"Did your groom tell you that?"

"Yes. He told me a lot about you. Do you mind? I'll never tell anyone."

"You never must," he urged. "You see, they'd try to stop me— send me away, or something dreadful!"

She said imperiously:

"Grownups are fools!"

"*You* seem to do as you please!"

"With Mrs. Bloomfield? Yes, usually I can, but that's only because she's so lazy. I'm glad she is; I couldn't endure her otherwise."

"And your father?"

"Papa?" She considered, her head on one side. "Papa doesn't bother his head very much. He didn't want to come back here to live, you know, but in the end he thought it was his duty, and so we came. I miss the sun."

James was conscious of an ignoble envy. She was younger than

How frankly, the day before, would he have answered the question in the affirmative! He thought, for a moment, of Sylvester's cousins, of Darklis, Philomena, and Fézenta—all handsome girls, his own age or older—black-browed, sloe-eyed, jetty-maned, and insolent. Then he looked beneath his lashes at Oriana's ivory skin, at her mischievous nose, and observed her little precocious air—which vaguely annoyed him—of knowing so much more than he knew himself.

"Not so pretty," he at length achieved gruffly.

"Not so pretty as *what?*"

"You're a spoilt miss!"

"And you're a savage! But we are friends, aren't we, James, and I'd like you to ride my pony whenever you want!"

Long afterwards, when neither one was a child, he would still hear those words echoing in his ears. They were friends, she had decreed, and she wanted him to have everything that was hers. That was her way: she was high-handed, impetuous, and passionate. She was a child, and so was he, but for a moment there was nothing childish about the detachment with which he viewed this intrusion of his secret life; he knew, instinctively, that she would disrupt the freedom he enjoyed already with so much difficulty.

That she was possessive, he realised without even comprehending the word. At the age of ten she was dominant, ruthless, and utterly feminine.

He, aged twelve, was merely perplexed. He tried to laugh. He said:

"Thank you, Oriana. You're very kind to me."

"Oh no!" She dismissed that. "It's not being kind."

"Isn't it?"

"Indeed no! You see, we shall be friends."

And then came the abrupt intrusion of Betty into the barn. Never had James looked upon Betty with greater disfavour. No one, then, would have thought them allies. No one would have guessed how often they had gossiped comfortably in the kitchen!

"Master James! Are you daft, to take Miss out in the damp?"

Oriana got up then. She brushed straw from her muslin dress, and James forgot that the little red shoes were muddy.

She said haughtily:

"I'm afraid I'm to blame. It was I who made Master James come out. Is my carriage here?"

And she returned to the house before them, casually flinging on the red cloak as she went, as though forgetful of the friendship she had so recently pledged.

PART II

Road to London

CHAPTER IX

FOR THE NEXT FEW YEARS, as the children grew up, they continued to see much of each other.

James now attended the Oxford Grammar School, riding there on a cob purchased by the doctor. But most Saturdays and Sundays were spent up at the Hall, and Emily shared Oriana's lessons with Mrs. Bloomfield. Emily, however, was never admitted to the same intimacy as was James; even a nature as easy-going as hers was sometimes conscious of jealousy. Mrs. Darrell naturally hated Oriana, a sentiment vigorously returned by the young girl, who privately described her as a "soured-up, neurotic woman." Another grievance was Henriette's indifference to James.

Oriana's affection for James was sometimes curiously mature; where he was concerned she was possessive and often imperious; yet she and her father were the first persons to appreciate his half-developed gift for writing tales.

Mr. Camperdene, a tall, pale man with taciturn manners, at first intimidated James greatly; but on finding, to his surprise, that the boy had taught himself fluent Spanish, he began to question him, and learned with increasing interest of his absorption in languages and customs remote from his own secluded life.

Mr. Camperdene had travelled in his youth, and fascinated James by tales of Bavaria, Austria, and Italy. Sometimes he found himself talking to this solemn boy as though to a contemporary, and then Oriana, usually herself a chatterbox, kept still and quiet on the arm of her father's chair.

45

"So you're to be a doctor, James, when you leave school?"

"No sir. I haven't told my father yet, but I know I shan't."

When Oriana read a tale of his, she persuaded him to let her show it to her father, and when he agreed, only on condition Robert Darrell should not learn of his private activities, Mr. Camperdene found himself oddly impressed. A strange boy, he thought, but undoubtedly clever.

He said as much to the doctor, who only answered with some abruptness:

"I'm glad you think so. It's more than his schoolmasters say."

James was in disgrace. He had recently exchanged his quiet cob for a green colt obligingly supplied by Sylvester Brazil, and Robert's permission had not been asked.

James refused to feel guilty. At fourteen his grammar-school life was so distasteful to him that he only endured it by accepting it with complete detachment, as a bad dream from which he thankfully awoke when he returned from school. He hated the tyrannical, narrow-minded masters, and formed few intimacies among the boys, who thought him a singular creature, with his love of gypsies and their gibberish. But his skill with his fists earned him a wholesome respect among his schoolfellows, and a few hints from the Duke of Egypt had turned him into a fine horseman, so that, if not popular, he was at least an object of admiration to other boys.

His real life began only in his leisure time. Then, when he was not writing, he was with Oriana, and she, at twelve, was as wild, or wilder, than himself.

Together, on Sundays and holidays, they roamed the countryside. Soon they learned to know every path and glade of Ackland Wood. They fished in the river, and rode their ponies, and never minded how wet and muddy they returned home.

Once Mrs. Bloomfield felt compelled to protest that Oriana was growing up a sad tomboy, but the squire only shook his head.

"Let her be young while she can. Soon, all too soon, she'll grow up."

He had deeply loved his wife, and in his daughter he saw a replica of the dead woman's gaiety, vitality, and that independence so rare in a young lady of the period. So he checked her seldom, allowing her to do very much as she pleased.

When James was fifteen, and the two girls thirteen, the old King died, and Princess Victoria, who was not very much older than James, became Queen of England.

The last link with Regency days snapped at William's death; they were all gone now, those roistering Georgian princes with their mistresses and their bastards, their drinking and their debts; the rosy-faced young person who was soon to be crowned at Westminster would be symbolic of changes so vast that none, in the early years of that interminable reign, could have prophesied their magnitude.

Oriana went to stay with her godmother in London for the Coronation. She was away a month, and James knew then, beyond all doubt, that he loved her more than anyone else in the world. He was at first perplexed, even troubled by this knowledge that had come to him too soon; perhaps, had she not gone away, he would not have realised how deeply he cared for her, but he missed her so desperately that he knew immediately, and for the first time, how great was her power. That was growing up, he reflected, and he was by no means sure that he was going to enjoy the process. When he grew older, he would marry Oriana, and that was going to be difficult, since he was poor, and she was, he supposed, very rich. Perhaps, on the other hand, he might become a famous writer and make plenty of money. He sighed, and confided in his friend, Sylvester, for the gypsies were once more to be found in a green lane near Lyndon.

"When I'm eighteen, brother," Sylvester told him, "I shall marry my cousin, Darklis."

"That's easy for you. You can look after a wife."

"Aye, to be sure I can, Jamie. By then I shall be fighting in real mills, for real purses, and there's always the horse whispering, and Darklis makes her own way with fortunetelling."

Not for the first time James envied his friend passionately. Life was easy for Sylvester, and always would be; so long as he had his tent, his horses, and his fists, his pockets would never be empty. Now, it seemed, in two years' time Sylvester would have Darklis, in addition to these other lordly possessions. James knew her well— a golden-skinned young girl with a mane of raven hair. He sighed, and Sylvester said:

"Listen, brother, you talk Romany, and you know our ways. One day you come and bide along of us and marry one of our girls. You'd be better off!"

"Thank you, Sylvester," James answered, touched, but he added shyly: "Somehow it would never work."

Then Oriana came home, and he went up to the Hall to see her. He was very conscious of his new, perplexing feelings towards her, and determined at all costs to keep them to himself. Sometimes it was difficult to remember that Oriana was not yet fourteen.

He was shown into a small library which opened off the large drawing room so seldom used. This room was octagonal, and lined with books; it was formally decorated in bygone Regency taste, with drapes of dark green brocade, and the clawed feet of gilded chairs and narrow couches showed that they had been fashionable yesterday—when Napoleon menaced the English Channel. It was summer, but a fire burned in the basket grate, for the squire had lived long enough abroad to fear the cold.

James was warm enough in his riding clothes. He went over to the window and stood there looking out at the mossy lawn, upon which starlings gathered, twittering, and for the first time it struck him that the Hall, which to him, as to his father, represented all that they knew of luxury, seemed faintly neglected, perhaps even a little forgotten, despite its grandeur.

Surely there was too much clover on the lawn, and the grass needed cutting? And there were some weeds in the rose beds. He turned as Oriana came into the library.

She saw James, who was so familiar to her—an extremely tall boy with untidy black hair, granite-grey eyes, and a sensitive, obstinate mouth.

He, for his part, saw a stranger—a fashionable young lady straight from Belgrave Square.

CHAPTER X

She wore a plaid silk frock, smarter than any he had ever seen, with white frilly pantalettes, and her dark hair fell upon her shoulders in glossy curls. It was coquettishly bound with a red ribbon, and at the sight of him her face danced with glee.

"I've missed you, James!"

"Why, Oriana . . . "

He smiled, and his heart beat faster, and yet he was confused by the new maturity she wore with such apparent carelessness.

"Have you nothing to say? How's Emily, and the colt, and how are the woods, and have you fought anyone since I went away?"

He reassured himself; she was the same. And yet, instinctively, he knew that she was different.

They sat down on the sofa.

"Nothing's happened here," he said, "but I want to know all about you."

"Will you pull the bell, James, and we'll have tea? Mrs. Bloomfield has a headache, and Papa may be late."

"You never wrote to me," he remarked as he obeyed.

"I know, and it was very bad of me. But there seemed so much to do, and we were always busy. James, I love London!"

"Well, tell me about it!"

While she talked, swinging one foot, of processions and bazaars and tea gardens, he watched her covertly, scarcely listening. She was far more fascinating than he remembered. The impertinence of her face was surely more mischievously charming, the whiteness of her skin more startling, the beauty of her great brown eyes clearer and more limpid.

"James, I don't believe you're listening to one single word!"

"I am! You were talking about the music at a place called Ranelagh!"

She hesitated for a moment, smiled, patted his hand, and said:

"Then I met my cousin, Frank Castleton."

"I never heard of him," James said.

"He is really my second cousin. He's grown up—eighteen. He would have liked to go into the Guards, but he's delicate, has been ever since he was at Eton. His father died a year ago, and when Frank is twenty-one he will inherit a lot of money and a beautiful house in Hampshire."

"He's fortunate," James commented, as she seemed to expect some remark. The butler came in with a silver tray. He knew, then, why she was different. Before this visit her only interests had been identical with his, but now, in one brief month, she had stepped alone into another world, and he could no longer accompany the darting flight of her fancies.

She said:

"Later on this summer Papa will ask Frank Castleton to stay here. We'll all ride and picnic together, shall we?"

"If you like, Oriana."

They were silent for a moment as they ate gingerbread. Then she said:

"You've told me nothing about yourself. Have you been writing?"

"Yes, thanks to Mr. Camperdene, who lets me borrow books from the library here. Without his help, I could do little enough."

"And the old witchwoman? Have you seen her?"

"Mrs. Hoskin? Yes, once or twice. She's grown very feeble; she likes to hear children's fairy tales."

"And the gypsies?"

He put down his cup and saucer.

"Oriana, you need not talk to me as though I were a child—indulgently!"

She looked both surprised and hurt.

"Indulgently? What do you mean, James? What's the matter with you?"

"You needn't condescend, just because you've been in London! I am not the ploughboy!"

She got up abruptly, and her white skin was suddenly rose red. He noticed, even in his own unhappiness, how tall she had grown; her head would always top his heart. She raged at him then, her dark eyes flashing:

"Condescend? To you? What right have you to think me so hateful?"

He, too, was angry, partly because he knew himself to have been ungracious.

"I had better go. I—I'm in a bad humour—it's my fault!"

"If you go, you need not come back!"

"I'll remember that, and take you at your word!"

But as he rushed towards the door she stopped him. He would always remember, whenever he thought of that moment, the rustling of her silk frock. She reached the door before him, in one swift movement.

"You shan't go! I'll not have you spoil my first day home!"

He felt immeasurably relieved. He could scarcely push her away from the door, and since the initiative was no longer his, he could submit without loss of pride. Therefore, he returned to the sofa.

"You know," he reminded her with cold dignity, "that I can't push you about, since you're a girl. So I'll have to stay."

She was still angry.

"You are the most disagreeable person I ever knew! All the time I was in London I looked forward to coming home, and talking to you, and seeing you again! And then what do you do? You fly at me, and——"

The storm clouds rolled away, and the sun streamed down once more. He was wildly happy.

"Oriana, do you mean that? Did you miss me?"

"Who else," she wanted to know, "is there for me to talk to in all the world?"

"I thought—you were speaking of your cousin—this Castleton——"

Unerringly her femininity had from the first divined the exact truth.

"You are just simply jealous, James Darrell," she pronounced with detached severity.

And at this unfortunate moment Mr. Camperdene saw fit to come in for his tea.

James watched her beneath his lashes. She looked after her father delightfully, taking the greatest pains to see that he was comfortable. Once more she was enchanting, deliberately so, he thought, and all ill temper was smoothed from the April curves of her charming face.

But he was by no means happy.

By some uncanny means she had already guessed how much he loved her. The secret he had stumbled upon, swearing never to tell her until they were both older, had, for some incalculable time, been hers. How, or why, he was never to know. Her intuition, he supposed, was swifter, more subtle, than his, and she had always been the more precocious of the two.

Afterwards they resumed their careless and youthful companion-ship as though nothing intimate had ever been said between them.

But that same summer Sir Francis Castleton came to stay at the Hall, and James's dislike of the young man became a sick and fretting ache, tormenting him from the moment he woke until the hour he fell asleep.

Frank Castleton, threatened at fifteen with a consumption which had not yet materialised, was a slender, willowy youth, with a fair skin, clear-cut features, and bright, brilliant blue eyes. Educated privately, he was, when his health permitted, to go up to Cambridge until he attained his majority. Then, apparently, he would return to Hampshire, there to administer his considerable estates. He had charm, a certain intelligence, and considerable self-confidence.

James hated him.

Those summer evenings at the Hall, when moonlight blanched the flowering lilies, when stocks and tobacco plants wafted their sweetness into the bird-enchanted air! Those sad evenings of adolescence! How long would he remember his own unhappiness!

Once, when the three of them were riding on a late August morning fresh and cold as spring water, a morning of vivid blue skies, dew scattered like frost upon the meadows, and cobwebs draped gauzily upon the brambles, they passed an encampment of some gypsies named Stanley, who were cousins to the Brazils.

James, recognising them, laughed and waved his hand. Oriana would have reined up her black mare, but he pressed on, and they cantered down the green, elm-shaded lane.

At last, when they reached the road and stopped to rest their horses, she said:

"What was the hurry? Am I never to be permitted to meet these gypsy friends of yours?"

He shook his head, smiling. Her question had revived an old argument, for, easy-going as he knew the squire to be, he had never taken it upon himself to introduce his daughter to the Romany people.

"Why," Frank Castleton asked, in his pleasant voice, "should Oriana's fortune not be told, if that is what she wants?"

"It isn't only that," Oriana protested. "I don't particularly want my fortune told. I want to meet the gypsy people because they're James' friends, aren't they, James?"

"It's better not," was all he said.

"But why?" Oriana demanded.

"Oh, why, they're rough, and use low words. Sometimes they're dirty. Mr. Camperdene wouldn't like you to meet them."

From the corner of his eye he caught Frank's smiling glance at Oriana. It was as though Frank said:

"Never mind him—he's a savage! What do we care? We understand each other!"

Frank Castleton's summer visit to the Hall was renewed each year. Soon James came to accept his presence, as one accepts, in summer, the visitations of a gadfly, or a wasp. Yet that comparison was unfair; Frank was unfailingly courteous, invariably charming to his junior. But to James he became something detestable, to be feared and endured at the same time.

And every August found him at the Hall.

He brought with him gaiety and frivolous talk from London. Oriana enjoyed listening to him. He was to be at Cambridge soon, and then James, an outcast schoolboy, began to feel the other's power, for there would be no university education for him, and already he was known as an odd youth, who, in Oxford, frequented taverns where dubious characters, such as boxers and horse copers, mingled to talk their own cant, and it seemed that he was intimate with them.

Yet he still ran wild with Oriana.

To his chagrin, she treated him, when he was sixteen past, as a brother. But her treatment of Frank Castleton appeared to be the same.

Every year, when Frank came to the Hall, James, watching his bright hair, his girl's cheeks, and his slender body, thought himself safe. Then, when he remembered Castleton's worldly advantages, he trembled.

Since he had refused to study medicine, his father had insisted that he should be articled to a firm of solicitors in Oxford when he was eighteen. He meant to run away, but he said nothing.

CHAPTER XI

ONE AFTERNOON in late May James sat in a tavern with Sylvester Brazil, the Duke, and Saul Boswell. The taproom was clean and bright, with a sanded floor, and contained only a few customers— a couple of shepherds, a trio of postboys. The inn was near Lyndon, and the landlord was accustomed both to the gypsies and to James.

Now they sat apart from the others, talking little, tankards of ale on the table before them. The three gypsies sat very erect on their chairs, their impassive faces burnt to the hue of dark walnut, their black snakes' eyes, that so often appeared to be looking into space, in reality missing nothing that happened in the taproom.

Sometimes they spoke briefly in Romany. When they wanted more ale, the Duke tapped sharply on his tankard with a silver coin. Their attitude to the landlord was one of complete indifference.

Only to James, when they spoke, were their voices warm with friendliness.

James was nearly nineteen. For a year he had been articled to the solicitors in Oxford. He had accepted this destiny because, for some months, his father had been ailing, and he knew that he could not, in these circumstances, be base enough to run away. Now Robert Darrell had been for some weeks gravely ill.

So James looked serious enough as he sat among the gypsies and drank his ale. He had grown both stronger and taller the past year. He was just six feet in his stockings, with broad shoulders and narrow flanks. The gypsies were proud of his athletic build. Thanks to them, they said, he could use his fists and ride a horse as well as any Romany *chal*. And he knew how much he owed them.

Whenever he thought of his father's sickness, he felt deeply ashamed of his idleness during the past year. But it was useless for him to struggle with work so alien to his own nature. He felt as confined in the sleepy office as any gypsy would, and his friends in Oxford were precisely the type of person most disapproved of by his father. There was an ancient don whose spare time was devoted to studies of the occult, a Maltese priest, an old Jew from Fez, an Irish horse coper, and a retired sea captain with a wooden leg. These were the people who interested him and with whom he was most intimate.

Yet, save for his office work, he was not lazy. On the contrary, he was remarkably industrious. He had learned to speak fluent German and Italian, he had written two books, and translated a volume of Bavarian ghost stories. His ambition to be a writer had never for a moment wavered, and his longing to travel was stronger even than before. But now his father's illness had made any escape impossible. Sometimes, in gloomy moments, he thought that he would be condemned all his life to live in Oxfordshire, plodding at work he hated so much his heart was often sick within him.

At such moments he envied the gypsies, and he envied Sylvester more than any of them. A year ago Sylvester had kept his word and married Darklis. They were wedded gypsy fashion, by jumping over a branch of flowering broom, and later there had been a riotous feast, with a pig roasted whole, red wine, ale, and much robust merriment. Now Sylvester lived with Darklis in a gaily painted caravan, and they appeared to prosper.

Unlike James, Sylvester's problems seemed non-existent. He lived exactly as he pleased, roaming the countryside, horse coping, boxing, playing the fiddle. He returned to his campfire whenever he was hungry, and he was most certainly never lonely, for at night he held his tawny Darklis in his arms.

Was it any wonder, James brooded, that Sylvester should be a gay fellow, popular with travelling people all over England? Were he, James, in Sylvester's place—— Here he looked up, to observe that the gypsies were regarding with a guarded and peculiar expression someone who had just come into the taproom.

With a start he sprang to his feet.

Oriana must have known very well what she was about, for a young lady to enter the taproom of an inn was a solecism so utterly without parallel that indeed it could be measured by no standards of the unmentionable—there existed none.

She seemed, however, casual, and as though unconscious of her own appalling audacity. She wore a close-fitting riding habit of dark blue, with a feather of lighter blue curling from her brimmed hat. She addressed James cheerfully, ignoring his wrathful brow.

"I was riding by and saw your horse's white blaze looking at me from over the loose-box door. So I thought I would come in, to pass the time of day with you. Won't you present your friends?"

This, as she well knew, was aggravating her own wicked behaviour; for many years now James had kept her away from the gypsies, and this by order of Mr. Camperdene, who seldom thwarted her wishes. But in this matter the squire was adamant.

"I'll not have my daughter running wild with tinkers! Do you understand, James? I forbid it absolutely!"

Small wonder, then, that he glowered as she advanced calmly towards the table. The gypsies rose with a careless grace and greeted her imperturbably, but he could see that their eyes were hostile. They did not encourage their own women to accompany them to taverns. Now, in the presence of James's *rakli*, his girl of whom they had so often heard, they were constrained, although they seemed at ease. She was, after all, the squire's daughter, and squires are seldom regarded with affection by the Romany people.

"I've heard about you all, ever since I was a child," she told them, pulling off her gauntlet gloves. Her manner, he noticed angrily, was perfect. It was natural and friendly and free from the faintest hint of patronage. She seemed unconscious of the disapproval with which the other customers viewed her presence in the taproom, and James she ignored.

She put her hand on the table, and he saw the gypsies glancing at it out of the corners of their eyes. He was not surprised. He did not think they could ever before have seen a hand like hers. It was long and narrow and white as ivory. In any case, he observed that they no longer seemed hostile. They wore the somewhat insinuating look of men who are in the presence of a pretty woman, and who are enjoying themselves.

Roughly interrupting her, he jumped to his feet.

"Come, Oriana, I'm late already, and we must go."

To his amazement, she followed him quietly enough, smiling good-bye to the gypsies.

Outside, when they were both mounted, he began furiously:

"How dared you come into that tavern? What would your father say? Hasn't he forbidden you to go near the gypsies?"

She did not answer him impatiently, as he had expected. She looked at him innocently, with eyes as brown and clear as dark amber.

"There's no need to lose your temper, James. I was lonely and had nothing to do. And so I thought I'd see for myself these Egyptian friends of yours. You've kept them from me long enough."

He was slightly mollified by the gentleness of her tone. She had always been headstrong, and the earliest bond between them had been their mutual dislike of convention.

"Well, having seen them," he said, forgetting his anger, "what do you think?"

She looked at him again, over her shoulder, but without gentleness this time.

She said contemptuously:

"I think they're vile!" She spurred her horse, galloping away from him through an open gateway before he had had time even to grasp the import of her words, and slammed the gate behind her.

It took him half an hour to find her. At length he ran her to earth in Ackland Wood, where she was resting her blown horse at the end of a green ride. She glanced at him without surprise, without indeed any expression at all.

"Oriana, are you mad?"

CHAPTER XII

SHE ANSWERED SLOWLY, fidgeting with her horse's bridle:

"It's you who are mad."

"I?"

She met his eyes then, and in hers was a disdain he had never seen there before.

"James, how much longer are you going to go on wasting your life?"

"I don't know what you're talking about."

"Oh yes, you do! You know very well, I think. Have you really nothing better to do than to roam about with a pack of tinkers? Are those the only companions you care for?"

"Oriana," he said, *"you* know that's not true!"

"Do I? You had such wonderful plans once, when you were little. You were to do something great—you made me believe you. Well, I was only a child myself. But I'm not a child any more."

He retorted, stung beyond endurance:

"Have you forgotten my father is seriously ill?"

"No, I remember that. And I remember that before he was ill he worried about you. He said you would never settle down."

"If he was not a sick man, I'm damned if I'd be in a solicitor's office now!"

"I suppose you'd rather be tramping the countryside stealing chickens with your friends the gypsies?"

He had seldom been angrier. His face was pale and his grey eyes glittered.

"Oriana, you know, better than anyone, I'm going to become a writer!"

"I seem to have heard that ambition before! And what are you going to write about—the gypsies?"

The scorn in her voice made him want to strike her. He jumped from his horse and went up to her saddle.

"Yes!" he said, speaking quietly because he did not want his voice to shake. "Yes! If that is what I want to write about, I shall, and make people read my books, do you hear? I'll write about what I please, when I like, and suffer no dictation from anyone! Least of all from you!"

She laughed.

"I shall think of you, James, when you're starving in a garret."

"What would you have me be?"

"You've every chance of becoming a lawyer. You're studying law, aren't you?"

He said bitterly:

"Someone's tamed *you* these last months!" And with a sickening wave of suspicion: "Would you prefer me like Frank Castleton?"

There was an imperceptible pause before she answered calmly: "What's wrong with Frank Castleton?"

"*Wrong* with him! That sickly milksop! That helpless whelp! *Wrong* with him!"

Shadows were folding upon the woods around them. In the distance they could hear the drowsy bleating of sheep. A wood pigeon, seeking a place to roost that night, clattered noisily into the branches of a fir tree overhead. It would soon be twilight.

"I must go home," she said, as though suddenly exhausted by the violence of their argument, but he caught at her bridle.

"Oriana! You like Frank Castleton because he's rich, don't you?"

"Oh, I don't know, James! I shouldn't like to be poor, if that is what you mean."

"But Mr. Camperdene . . ."

"I believe," she said frankly, "that Papa has lost some money lately. Let go of my bridle, James, I am going home."

He said no more. Suddenly everything seemed to be hopeless. He stood watching her as she rode away up the long ride. She looked small and slight on the powerful black mare, but that was deceptive, for he knew that she was nothing of the sort. She was as strong, perhaps stronger, than he, and he knew her to be ruthless.

She vanished out of sight, and his mood became more hopeful.

Well, he would not let her go without fighting for her. Against her will he would force her to choose him because the idea of mating with anyone else was monstrous, against nature, and that certainty, he knew, was shared by both of them.

They were too much alike.

They were undisciplined and candid and at ease with each other. They laughed at the same jokes, fought each other frequently, and, until that last year, they had shared the same wild tastes and together flouted convention. Above all, they found comfort together, wherever they were, either in the most secret glade of Ackland Wood, or in one of the formal flower gardens of the Hall. In the gypsy language the words "divine" and "devilish" are the same. James and Oriana had always been divinely, or devilishly, together.

He got upon his horse and rode slowly towards home, thinking, in a daze, of the cruelty with which she had lashed at him. When he recollected her information regarding Mr. Camperdene's finances, he cursed himself for a blind fool. It was years since he had first noticed the shabbiness of the Hall. He thought then, as his horse picked its way along a ride heaped with fir cones, how thick, lately, had been the thistles in the rose beds, and the weeds, too, in that lake where water lilies bloomed. He remembered dust clinging like a film to faded brocades, chimneys that smoked, grass carpeting roads in the park, draughts everywhere in the house, and pictures, valuable ones, stained with damp now, in dark, forgotten corridors.

No, the Hall was certainly no longer the home of a rich man.

As he rode through the woods he remembered in colorful snatches his father's reminiscences of the Hall, when he was young, and the old squire's sons were young, and George IV was Regent.

He remembered tales of windows bright all night with the glitter of a hundred wax lights. There were cards in one room, dice in another, and powdered flunkeys to light and snuff the candles. There were ladies in diaphanous dresses, who played Mozart on the spinet, and who gambled, too, and the wine brimming in their glasses was no redder than their own vivid lips.

There had been laughter and music and gaiety.

All that was finished and done with, but for all Mr. Camperdene lived so quietly, James had never, in his ignorance, supposed him to be poor. Now, he was amazed by his own stupidity. Ever since he had first been privileged to visit the Hall, it had been slowly going to seed.

And then, thinking of Frank Castleton, his hopefulness vanished, and all the black misery returned, for Frank was rich, and he knew how suitable a match between himself and Oriana would be; how much it would please Mr. Camperdene.

And then some old jingle, heard in the village when he was very young, returned to tease his mind:

> *Change her name, and not her letter,*
> *Change for worse, and not for better* . . .

He rode up to the Queen Anne house near the green and was astonished to find the upstairs windows alight. He knew that he had missed supper, but he didn't care. He was exhausted, and stiff,

and weary. Oriana had hurt him so bitterly out there in the woods
that he thought he would never again be quite the same. Emo-
tionally, he felt lifeless and extinguished. Oriana would marry Frank
Castleton, because Frank Castleton was rich.

She had taunted him with being unable to write, and one day
he would show her that she was wrong. But one day would surely
be too late.

Meanwhile, his head ached, and his body ached. Desolation en-
compassed him as he rode into the stable yard. His horse's hoofs
clattered on the stones, and there, to his astonishment, his mother
waited by the back door. He saw at once that she was a little drunk.
She spoke to him in French.

"So you've returned! About time too! Do you realize your father's
worse and asking for you?"

He pushed past her, through the kitchen, and into the parlour,
where he found Emily huddled over the empty fireplace. He smiled
at her without speaking and tumbled up the stairs towards his
father's room.

There on the landing he found Dr. Richardson, from Lyndon.

"Why, James! He's been asking for you! Go in, and don't upset
him, mind! I give you five minutes."

He went impulsively into the room and across to the four-poster
bed, beside which Betty sat, her eyes swollen with tears. He did
not even remember until afterwards that Betty was there at all.

He looked at the odd, mottled, tragic face crushed on the pillows,
and whispered urgently:

"Father, I'm here! James!"

There was a long pause.

"Father, do you hear me?"

For a long time, it seemed to him, there was no response, and
then the raddled face began to twitch, the swollen lips to quiver.

James bent his head close to the pillow.

"James . . . back from Oxford . . ."

"Yes, Father."

"Bad boy—you go with gypsies—worse . . ."

James blurted out on a sudden impulse:

"Father, I'm going to be a writer."

There was a pause, while tears of weakness coursed down Robert

Darrell's hairy cheeks. He turned, heaving, as though twisted with pain, and James put a strong arm underneath his shoulders.

"Writer . . . You've got a good straight left for half a Frenchman. James, I'm slipping . . . Hold me up, James, there's a good boy . . ."

He died later that night, and seemed at peace. He died quietly, without struggle.

He died tranquilly perhaps because, as his soul departed, his eyes glimpsed all that he had found beautiful in life.

Simple things these, for he was a simple man.

Perhaps he thought vaguely, his eyes glazing, of rooks cawing and clustering darkly in the wind-swept tops of wintry trees; of an old horse plodding forth to drag a plough; of the wind and the rain beating on those familiar thatched roofs of an Oxfordshire village; of taverns, their windows glowing bright as marigolds; of mulled ale and crimson fires; and of roads, snow-blanched, leading to hovels where women lay in travail, and were helpless but for him. He thought, no doubt, of the wriggling infants he had brought into the world; of his wife, who had once been young and slim and gay; of old people dying, collapsing like tired dolls in their dark and tiny rooms, before fires that were dead because they were too feeble to put on fuel.

Doubtless he thought of storms and falling trees, and of many broken limbs clumsily mended. And of Judy, his grey mare, and the bran mash she had earned so bravely. He was too modest, perhaps, to remember that he had never, no matter how inclement the weather, refused to answer a sick call.

He had gone forth sturdily, for many years, in hail and sleet and gale and snow. Perhaps he forgot that, as he lay dying, and remembered only the sweet things that had softened an austere life: primroses and violets nestling in a sunny hollow; the skylark's song; harvesttime; cherry blossoms in the spring; the cuckoo's call; the babbling waters of the old millstream.

And so he died, a simple and a gallant Englishman.

CHAPTER XIII

A MONTH LATER James walked up to the Hall. He had asked Oriana to meet him in the garden, not having seen her alone since his father's death. There had been so much to do, so many wearisome details to be settled, and she had been exceedingly kind, taking Emily to stay with her until after the funeral.

He himself was leaving the solicitor's office, but it did not seem to him right that Emily should be left to live alone with anyone so eccentric, so abnormal, as Henriette, and this decision was one that had caused him much perplexity. In the end it had settled itself; as such matters sometimes comfortably do: the Queen Anne house had been sold to the new doctor, and Henriette and Emily were to lodge in Bath, with Robert Darrell's cousin and his wife. The Edward Darrells were poor, and their house in Royal Crescent was too large for them; Edward Darrell was a doctor, and would know how to deal with Henriette. Better still, they had a daughter of their own, so that Emily would meet young people and enjoy herself as much as any other pretty, sweet-tempered girl.

Yet James looked stern as he walked through the park, switching at the nettles with his stick, without even knowing what he was doing. When the will had been read, it was learned that such money as the doctor left went unconditionally to Henriette, in the event of her death to be divided between the son and daughter. James himself had fifty pounds in the world. Even to one so unsophisticated, it seemed little enough.

He walked on through the long grass, past the silken flanks of the cows that grazed there, returned from their milking.

Across the lake, beneath a clump of cedar trees, he could see the glimpse of a pale dress, and knew that she waited for him. His heart beat faster. They had met but once since the day of their quarrel in the woods, but so much had happened to him since then that he was conscious, not of that first sharp, intolerable pain, but rather of a dull and aching grief from which she, and she only, could give him the sweetness of relief.

She held out both her hands, behaving as though they had never quarrelled. She thought that he looked drawn and tired, and knew, despite many differences, how much he had loved his father.

They sat down on a seat that was screened by the dark layers of the cedar branches, and he told her about Emily and his mother.

"That will be good for her," Oriana said. "She should meet more people of her own age."

Exactly, he thought, as though Oriana herself were forty! It was typical of her. He laughed. She smiled back then, her own frank and charming smile, and put her warm hand over his.

He said, trying to make his voice sound casual:

"Oriana, I'm going away too."

"To live in Oxford?"

"No, of course not. I'm going to London, as I said."

"To try to be a writer?"

"To *be* a writer!"

She took her hand away from his and said:

"I shall go mad if I am to be left alone here."

"Alone? You need never be alone, I think. You have godmothers and aunts scattered all over England; you have—you have your cousin Frank Castleton, and a host of other people. You——"

"You are the one I love," she said, and turned her brown velvety eyes upon him.

It was then that he kissed her for the first time. He kissed her clumsily in his youthful diffidence. Her lips were full and soft and sweet.

He said:

"Then it will be all right! If only you'll wait for me, we can get married! Can't we? Oriana, say so!"

She was silent for a moment, staring at the grass by her feet.

Then she asked:

"How long would it mean waiting?"

"Until I establish some sort of position. Your father was so kind, the last time I spoke to him; he said he would give me a letter to a publisher he knew. And, you see, Oriana, there is all manner of work I can do—translations from several languages, and I could perhaps work for a newspaper, or review foreign books!"

"But, James"—she spoke, not chidingly, but patiently, as though to a child—"but, James, you will not be able to support yourself perhaps for many years. How could you expect to support me?"

"At first of course not. I said in the beginning we would have to wait! Does that matter so much? We're very young; so long as you love me would it matter if we waited five years, or even six?"

"I *do* love you," she repeated, after a slight pause.

"Then what's wrong? Is it that your father would never consent? Or do you not believe in me?"

"I wish," she said, "you would stay at the solicitor's in Oxford. If you did that, we might not have to wait so long. And, later, when you were established, you might begin to travel and to write. We'd be together then."

"But, Oriana, I want to write *now*. And I am not going to stay in Oxford. I hate it!"

They looked at each other.

No one, then, would have thought them lovers. The sweetness, the melting tenderness of her charming face was at once replaced by a dark and mutinous expression. And he, who had just with so much ecstasy held her in his arms, now looked at her almost with despair, for the barrier between them was up again, and he did not know how to pull it down.

"I can't wait forever," she declared, almost sullenly.

"You mean you have no faith in me? Well, that I can't help; I must do what I've waited to do for so long. I should have thought that you, of all people, would understand. *You* prize freedom, too, you've always had it!"

"Yes, but, James"—now she was coaxing, almost cozening, like a gypsy woman—"yes, but, James, you forget I'm no longer a child. I'm grown up now, and I like my own way of life. Can't you understand that? You see, dearest, I know I don't want to starve in a garret, and I don't think I should much like to sail before the mast in search of deserted islands, or buried Indian gold! I want pretty dresses, James, and a fine house to live in, and jewels for my ears, and, oh! many things that you could never give me! At least I'm frank in telling you so, aren't I?"

He got up from the seat. The sun had nearly gone, and it was cold in the shadow of the cedar trees.

He said, looking down at her:

"I never asked you to starve in a garret, as you call it. I never would do that. I asked you to wait, to give me a chance of being successful. If you're too cautious, I can do nothing about it. But there's only one part of you, Oriana, that plays for safety—the other part would like to come with me and see everyone else at the devil! That is *you*—your real self, which you're stifling now, with all your talk of money and fine houses."

"I suppose," she answered, sighing, "that everyone is divided. Everyone, that is, except you, or so it seems to me. You want something I would like you to have—but I can't believe you ever will have it. The truth, James, is that when we were children, we were alike. Now that we are no longer children, we have grown apart."

"We have *not* grown apart! Just now you said you loved me!"

"That's true, and always will be."

"Is it not enough?"

"Oh no!" She shook her head. "I wish with all my heart it were. But, you see, we're both so obstinate. You *will* run off to make your fortune. I suppose I must want a fortune made. We shall always love each other, but that doesn't mean we're made to marry."

He looked at her, still seated on the bench, her chin propped on her hand, her eyes a hundred miles away. It was dusk now, but he could still glimpse her cheek, pale as white lilac, her tilted nose, her dark, sweeping lashes. A moment ago, a century ago, he had kissed her mouth. Now, in the twilight, she was immeasurably remote. He did not know precisely what had happened, but he knew that he no longer dared even to touch her hand.

She got up, too, with a silken rustling of her skirts. Never, he thought, would they be alone again together. He was sick and strained with the misery of his last month.

He said, trying to keep his voice steady:

"At least promise me one thing: don't marry Frank Castleton too soon. Perhaps, you know, I shall be more successful than you think."

Her own self-control broke then, so that she wept.

"Oh, James! My poor James! You, who want to write about the gypsies!"

"Oriana, even so, will you not give me a chance?"

She put on her Indian shawl. She still wept, but now she was laughing at the same time.

"I'll wait for you, James, one year from now!"

"Two!"

"Two, then!"

The dusk grew deeper; the greyness was soon blue-black and stars pricked the sky. Quite suddenly he was no longer afraid; now he could not see her, but her presence was near and warm and sweet.

He took her in his arms and kissed her again, not diffidently this time, but with an increasing confidence. Soon he was kissing her passionately—her lips, her eyes, her throat, and her hair. So much sweetness had never come his way before. Her cheeks were still wet with tears, and his tongue tasted their saltness, delighting. The closeness of their contact exalted both of them.

"James!"

Suddenly he let her go, pushing her away from him.

"*Now* try kissing Frank Castleton!"

And then he was gone.

He tramped his way home, and the long grass was cold and wet with dew. Cows lowed, night birds called, and not far away from him a fox barked. All the sounds and scents of night were prematurely early; his senses, too, were sharpened; he sniffed peppermint from the millstream, and heard rabbits munching beyond the spinney hedge. A bat squeaked, blundering just above his head; the sweetness of young clover rose to his nostrils, and he knew that button mushrooms were thrusting through the grass beneath his feet.

Once again, with a bitter pang, he thought of Sylvester and his Darklis; of those two who had mated as simply as the birds flying above their heads.

Perhaps, had he never known Oriana Camperdene, he would have been happier with some gypsy girl from the tents; in any case, he would have been spared the chatter of dresses, riches, and jewels, that had distracted him so recently beneath the cedar trees.

But, knowing Oriana, other women, to him, were without meaning, and it was as though a spell had been cast about him. From that spell he could not escape. Even her kisses still lingered, glowing, on his mouth, and he was too confused to distinguish between their warmth and the coldness of her calculation.

That hay-scented summer night marked the end of James's boyhood.

PART III

The Spaniard

CHAPTER XIV

HE SAT IN A SMALL ROOM littered with manuscript, and wrote, painstakingly, but hunching a shoulder over his right arm, because he was weary and his wrist ached. His room was not the garret of Oriana's imagination, but a tiny, plain apartment with a small window overlooking the treetops of Russell Square.

Not that James inhabited so grand a neighbourhood; he did not. His nest was situated, along with similar rookeries, in a side street. It contained a bed, a washstand, a table, and a ramshackle bookcase. It was scrupulously clean and desperately untidy.

He wrote slowly, until the pain in his wrist, which had nagged at him for some hours, suddenly resolved itself into a jabbing anguish, forcing him to stop, to relax his stiff, cramped fingers. He looked impatiently at Robert Darrell's old-fashioned silver watch.

Always the same. His imagination was eager, and he could have worked on for hours had it not been for this damnable writer's cramp that gripped him every evening after so much work. Sometimes his right hand would be useless and swollen for two or three hours.

He got up then and lit the lamp on his table. The May evening was nearly over.

James was twenty-one. He had lived for two years in London, and he was no nearer to becoming a famous writer than on the night when he had said good-bye to Oriana. Now, in what he considered to be his maturity, he could have laughed at the picture of that shy, countrified boy travelling up to London on the coach, his box of precious manuscripts clutched upon his knees. How that boy had stared about him as he climbed down from his perch in the crowded yard of a hotel near Charing Cross! How dazed he had been by the roar of coaches and carriages and wagons, by the thousands of people jostling one another in the streets, by the vastness and indifference of the huge, unfriendly city!

His modest room had been engaged for him by an Oxford acquaintance, his only one in London, and his sole asset was a letter of introduction from Mr. Camperdene to a well-known publisher. The greenness of it all, as he looked back, amused him, but there was considerable bitterness mingled with the amusement.

Now, two years later, he got up slowly from his table, preparatory to attiring himself for an interview he dreaded. He washed, shaved, brushed his hair, and put on his best coat, a well-cut but worn affair of bottle-green cloth. He looked a presentable, even a good-looking young man; he was powerfully built, so that his height no longer appeared so remarkable, but he was well over six feet tall and carried himself proudly, in what Betty had been wont to call his "stiff-necked" way. His dark hair was still unruly; his face, very clear-cut about the jaw, looked fine-drawn, and there were faint hollows beneath his grey eyes. And these eyes stared out beneath black brows with a look of wary coolness in which there was nothing youthful. Mr. James Darrell has learned a number of lessons in the past two years, and now the only green thing about him is this best coat of his.

He let himself out of the house into a dark, narrow street, and wished, for the first time, that his publisher and employer, Sir Matthew Kent-Taylor, lived anywhere but in the neighbouring Russell Square.

He walked slowly, deliberately postponing the distasteful moment of their meeting. The early May evening was a silvery one of mother-of-pearl and peach-flushed skies; he felt like stifling in the city air, and once again he remembered, not without resentment, that he had not been in a position to leave London once during the two years of his servitude.

Nor had he seen Oriana. She had spent one summer in Scotland with her godmother, and he knew that she and her father were

..ravelling that spring in France and Italy. They had corresponded at first with much fervour on both sides, but he had had nothing of encouragement to tell her during the year just passed, and her last letter to him had remained unanswered. Perhaps, he reflected, that had annoyed her, but he was incapable of writing again until his situation showed some signs of improvement. Her last letter spoke frankly of Mr. Camperdene's financial embarrassments; the Hall had been let, and they were to travel abroad for some months. She never told him whether or not she saw Frank Castleton.

Musing thus, he arrived at Sir Matthew Kent-Taylor's prosperous-looking house and was admitted to the hall by the familiar spectacle of his employer's wall-eyed butler.

"Will you ask Sir Matthew if he would kindly see me for a few moments?"

"I'll *ask* him, sir." He was shown into the study he knew so well and disliked so heartily. He walked up and down, thinking how much he hated the dark, heavy furniture, the bust of Julius Caesar, the red, hot-looking draperies festooned about the walls and windows, and, most of all, the books crammed into the shelves behind the pompous desk.

"Dear God!" he thought, "that I could ever hate books as I hate these!"

Then he turned as the door opened and Sir Matthew Kent-Taylor came into the room. He was evidently dressed, save for his coat, his cravat was a waterfall of snowy starch, and his elegant lavender pantaloons strapped tightly beneath his shoes, but he wore a dressing gown of purple brocade, considerably increasing his resemblance to a turkey, for he was a large, florid man, pendulous of chins. At first sight his appearance was one of good-natured joviality, belied, upon a second glance, by his close-set eyes and by the mouth that turned down peevishly at the corners.

"Good evening, Darrell! Have you good news for me?"

"Good news, sir?"

"You have not called to tell me your compilation of *The Lives of the Saints* is finished?"

"Very far from finished, sir. I called to ask if you had read the manuscript I submitted to you the other day?"

The publisher sat down, shooting a sharp, mistrustful look at the young man.

"If you mean, my dear Darrell, that stuff about persons on the fairground, swindlers and vagrants, and I know not what else—I *have* glanced at it, and it is, believe me, useless."

"I see."

He should have become accustomed, he supposed grimly, to judgments of this nature. There was no longer any excuse for that sick thumping of his heart.

"Furthermore, young man, I have a bone to pick with you! You are paid—you are handsomely paid—you are, in short, *retained* by me to compile various works, the latest of which is *The Lives of the Saints*. You are *not* paid to waste your time and mine by scribbling of thieves and vagabonds!"

There was a pause, and then James said:

"There is another matter, sir. When you say I am paid, I must point out that I have not been paid for the last three months."

"Sir!" Sir Matthew's rubicund face darkened to an alarming violet. "Sir! Were you or were you not paid fifty pounds for your compilation of *Kings' Favourites?*"

"I was, sir. But that was ten months ago. I need some money now!"

"What for?"

"It is impossible," James answered dryly, "to live on air in London!"

He knew that he was safe. He was too valuable to Sir Matthew to be discharged. So he continued to stare him coolly out of face.

"Preposterous!" the publisher gasped, after a dramatic pause. "Preposterous! Like all young men, you're idle and extravagant! You——"

"If you wish to insult me, sir, then I'll leave your employment first!"

Damn the young puppy! He would too! And he had a certain facility for words . . .

"Now look here," Sir Matthew blustered. "I'll pay you five guineas on condition——"

"Ten."

"Ten, then! On condition that *The Lives of the Saints* is finished by the first week in June."

"Agreed," James answered, unsmiling.

When the guineas were counted out, Sir Matthew grumbled.

"Can you not perceive, young man, how hopeless it is to write of wild and vulgar subjects?"

"And the kings' favourites? Were they not vulgar?"

"Since they bedded with kings one hundred times, no!"

"Well"—he put the notes in his purse and smiled, since he had gained his point—"well, sir, I can only say I rejoice to think my compilations, as you call them, are published in *your* name, and not in mine!"

Without another word he turned on his heel and walked out into the street.

It depressed him to consider how great was Sir Matthew's power to infuriate him. This publisher, who could not write, but who enjoyed producing works supposedly by himself, had from the beginning employed James as a literary "ghost." Owing perhaps to the diverse subjects he chose, the books published under Sir Matthew's name were invariably failures, but he was so shrewd in other matters that he could well afford to indulge in this curious form of vanity.

Therein lay the rub. James knew Sir Matthew to be shrewd, and Sir Matthew invariably dismissed his own work as hopeless.

That the publisher was naturally reluctant to lose an efficient "ghost" did not occur to him.

He walked off, raging, in the direction of the Strand.

CHAPTER XV

HE HAD NO RIGHT, in his straitened circumstances, to dine at a coffeehouse, but for some days now he had existed mainly on bread and cheese, and his desire for a good dinner was a temptation too strong to resist. The ten guineas had to last him indefinitely, but he felt reckless, after an interview in many respects so discouraging, and he turned into a well-known coffeehouse situated near the Golden Cross.

He knew, in his hunger, exactly what he craved—oysters, two chops, and a bottle of claret. He could have eaten more but did not dare.

He had been to this particular coffeehouse three or four times before, and had once encountered there a party of gay young men, who had invited him to join them at their table. When they learned that he was a stranger in London they insisted upon escorting him to see the sights. They went to several oyster saloons, to the cockpit, to a dark and sinister nook where they drank gin called Blue Ruin, and finally, when they were all drunk, to a stew in Panton Street, where he awoke early the next morning to find a tousled blonde head upon his pillow.

He felt grimly ashamed whenever he recalled this episode. Somehow it seemed to separate him even further from Oriana. Not, he thought sardonically as he sat down in a box seat to give his order, not that there had been any need to make him feel more remote from her.

He ate and drank slowly, determined to prolong the enjoyment of every mouthful. He had not guessed the extent of his own hunger; he knew that it was some days since he had eaten a square meal, but that he was undernourished, and had been for some weeks, he did not realise. While he sipped his claret he looked round the room at the other guests. The place was empty, for he was dining late; apart from a sprinkling of grave gentlemen who looked, one and all, as though they followed the law, there was only one person who seemed different from these other diners.

This individual sat in a box alone; he smoked a cheroot and drank port. He was a man of about fifty. His features were straight and regular, his skin dark olive, his eyes, which stared downward, were heavy-lidded, and he wore a trim beard, blue-black, although his jetty hair was heavily flecked with grey. James decided that he looked distinguished, bilious, aloof, and lonely, all at the same time. Once, as he looked, the stranger glanced up, too, haughtily fixing him with a pair of dark, piercing eyes. He looked like a gypsy, but he was no gypsy; he was too richly dressed. While James paid his bill, this person threw a cape over his shoulder and walked out of the coffeehouse, leaving behind him, for a fugitive moment, an atmosphere of something exotic.

James was depressed by the extent of his bill. He waited a few moments for change, tipped the waiter, and went out into the cool sweetness of the May night. The darkness was lilac-scented, and suddenly he decided to avoid the gaslight of the Strand, the clatter of coaches and wagons, and to turn down a narrow side street leading past the Adelphi arches.

The silence of those early-Victorian nights was often broken by the sounds of violence, fighting, and blows. These were rough times, and the streets after dark were haunted by thugs who crept up from the river slime to prey upon their fellow creatures only when night fell, to facilitate their own chance of escape.

As James walked homewards, reasonably at peace, since his stomach was no longer empty, and he glowed with the warmth of food and wine, he heard, a few paces ahead of him, but mysteriously concealed from view, the sound of what seemed like a struggle, a thudding blow, and the noise of heavy breathing. He quickened his step, and perceived a slitlike alley illuminated by one dim gas jet. In this alley men were fighting, and although the murky light made it difficult for him to see distinctly, he thought that two of them were attacking a third.

He himself felt exactly in the mood for intervention. It seemed to him a long time since he had used his fists, and now he sprang forward with the lust of battle in his heart. He had been correct in his surmise: two burly ruffians, armed with cudgels, were in the process of cornering an unfortunate citizen whose face in the darkness it was impossible to see.

James could obtain but a most imperfect glimpse of the robbers, only enough to see that they were shabbily dressed and they both exuded a smell of beer; as he stepped in to swing a sideways blow at the nearest, something flashed for a second in the air, then tinkled down upon the cobbles beneath them, and he knew that one of the combatants was armed with a knife.

His blow missed in the darkness, and he felt the crash of a cudgel on his shoulder. Had he not slipped, his arm would have been broken; as it was the bruising pain enraged him, and, ducking in, he made short work of this assailant by delivering a short, jolting blow to the chin, which toppled the man over like a fallen tree.

He was still in danger, for the other thug, abandoning his prey, came rushing down upon him. For a moment his face was illumi-nated by the gas jet, and an ugly mug it was—unshaven, brutish, and distorted with fury at this unexpected interference. The vic-tim himself was of no assistance; he leaned against a wall in the darkness and made no move.

James rushed in to wrestle for the cudgel and received a kick on the shin which made him angrier than ever. He twisted swiftly, managing to imprison the heavy stick under his right arm, and then, with his long, jabbing left, he delivered three or four punishing blows to the villain's face. But this man had muscles of iron and soon wrenched his cudgel free. While he whirled round for a fresh attack James bethought him of a sly gypsy trick, and, shooting out his foot, tripped him heavily. The man fell sprawling on his face, and James flung himself upon the cudgel. Panting, brandishing it above his head, he prepared to crack it down upon the bristling skull, but the thief, a coward without his loaded stick, immediately took to his heels and fled.

James heard the sound of boots clatter away down the street and vanish into the distance. The other scoundrel was exhibiting signs of recovery, and James, without relaxing his grip of the cudgel, turned back towards the shadows to encourage the singularly un-helpful cause of the whole trouble.

"Sir! We had better be going before . . ."

A faint groan was his only reply, and as he went forward to discover how badly the man was hurt, he saw that he had crumpled onto the ground, where he lay apparently unconscious.

James did not particularly relish his own position. Quite apart from sounds indicating a return to consciousness on the part of the ruffian he had knocked out, it occurred to him that the fellow's companion was quite capable of returning to the scene with three or four other roughs.

Therefore he bent down over the senseless victim, slipped his arms about him, and began to drag him out towards the street. He was inert and heavy, but James was exceedingly strong. As they toiled past the gaslight he perceived, with surprise, that he was playing

Samaritan to the dark, foreign-looking gentleman he had seen that
night in the coffeehouse.

As they struggled along his foot struck against something that
tinkled. It was a knife, and he put it in his pocket. At this point
his companion spoke feebly, and in Spanish.

"I am recovering, señor. If you give me your arm, I think I can
manage to walk very slowly."

James answered in the same language.

"It will be best if you try. We must go towards the Strand and
find a hackney coach."

Their progress was horribly slow, and once or twice the Spaniard
groaned. He had been hit on the head and seemed dazed, but James
did not think he was seriously hurt. When they approached the
lighted street he saw that his companion was bleeding from the
scalp and his dark face had become olive-grey. He leaned more
heavily on James's arm, and soon they were accosted by the usual
inquisitive throng of gaping people. James swore beneath his breath
but managed to keep his temper, with the result that an urchin soon
returned in triumph with a hackney, into which the Spaniard was
assisted by a dozen willing hands. James climbed in beside him and
asked him where he lived.

He lay back in the coach, his eyes closed, and for a moment James
was afraid that he had fainted again. Then, without opening his
eyes, he gave an address in Berkeley Square. They drove off, and
James wiped the sweat from his face. From time to time he glanced
at his companion, but the man did not move. He no longer even
sighed.

"Perhaps he is dead," James thought, "and I shall have to face
his wife."

The hackney drove up to the door of a large, imposing house,
far grander than the residence of Sir Matthew Kent-Taylor, and
James got out, not without trepidation, to ring the bell. The Spaniard might, for all he knew, have been wandering in his mind when
he gave so fashionable an address, and his state of mind was by no
means improved by the driver, who announced cheerfully that the
party seemed in a bad way.

In a moment the door was opened by a grand-looking footman
in green plush.

"The Spanish gentleman," James began, "who lives here . . ."
The footman showed no surprise.

"Yes sir?"

"He has had an accident. He's in the coach. Will you help him?"

At this moment the majestic footman was joined by a colleague just as splendidly arrayed; even their impassive faces showed signs of agitation as they rushed down the steps to assist the man who was presumably their master. The Spaniard looked ghastly as they half led, half carried him up the steps.

James watched him until he disappeared inside the house, and then walked away before the driver began to pester for his fare. He had had, he decided, a wretched evening. His shoulder throbbed with a dull pain, and his leg felt badly bruised. He was no longer interested in the Spaniard's affairs, only immensely relieved that the stranger appeared to be wealthy and capable of paying the hackney coach.

"For I'm damned," James thought, "if it's anything to do with me."

It seemed a long walk to Bloomsbury.

CHAPTER XVI

He slept late, and it was only just before lunch that he discovered the knife. He had forgotten all about it. He looked at it in amazement, never having seen its iike before. Its long, wicked blade gleamed like silver, but it was the hilt that interested him most—a hilt encrusted in turquoises and plastered with glittering diamonds. Even if they were false, the workmanship was exquisite, and he realised, sighing, that he would have to return this weapon to the Spaniard.

He realised, too, that had the knife stabbed home before the robber's cudgel, a dead man would have been found in the alley and he himself would doubtless have been held as witness in a murder case of the most sensational description.

A weary disinclination to do anything else about the matter took possession of him, and he excused himself by arguing that the publisher had saddled him with so much work that he would be fortunate if he were able to stir from his room during the next two days.

When he found a letter addressed to himself his heart jumped, thinking that it must be from Oriana, but it was not; it was from his sister Emily, announcing her engagement to a young officer stationed down in Bath. He was pleased by the news, although Emily and his mother were no longer part of his life, but he was attached to his sister, and wrote warmly congratulating her.

He returned to his hack work haunted by melancholy thoughts, contrasting Emily's innocent happiness with his own lonely and embittered existence.

The next evening, unable any longer to postpone a tedious duty, he went off to Berkeley Square to return the jewelled knife. He consoled himself by reflecting that with any luck the Spaniard would be too ill to see him; he was in no mood for gratitude.

This hope vanished as the door was opened, not by one of the gorgeous footmen, but by a swarthy, grey-haired butler, who spoke English fluently but with a strong foreign accent.

"Sir, my master has been distracted because we had no means of finding your address!"

"I hope he is on the way to recovery," James answered curtly.

"Sir, will you please to follow me?"

"I thank you, but——"

"My master would never forgive me if you left without seeing him in person."

No hope, then. And perhaps it would be diverting to see the Spaniard's house.

"Very well."

He followed the butler across a large hall, paved in black and white, like an enormous chessboard, towards double doors which, when opened, revealed an amazing room. For a moment he stood confused upon the threshold, uncertain whether he had wandered into a museum or into a church.

Opposite the door hung a large Russian ikon of a Virgin and Child ablaze with precious stones, framed in gold and silver. There were four huge cabinets against the wall, and these contained, although he did not know it, an almost priceless collection of jade.

There were bowls and figures and carvings in all colours of the rainbow, and more beside—almond green, grass green, candy-pink,
and amber—gold, and luminous silver, and white jade, too, daz-
zling as Oriana's skin. The room also contained a Chinese temple,
exquisitely carved from ivory as delicately intangible as sea foam,
dripping with silver bells that tinkled faintly as he entered. There
was a sedan chair, hand-painted in the style of Watteau and lined
with oyster satin. There were two bridling Tang horses, and, in a
corner, the lifesize effigy of a Chinese warrior wearing armour over
gorgeous robes of vermilion and mustard-yellow brocade. By the
fireplace hung a Spanish crucifix, agonizingly realistic, carved in
wood that had turned walnut-dark with the passing of three
centuries.

As James paused, dazed, by the sight of so much colour, he was
addressed sharply in Spanish.

"Come here, young man! I have been expecting you for the last
two days!"

He then perceived the Spaniard, seated in an armchair near the
fire. It was a warm evening, but his host appeared to feel the cold,
and the blaze was fragrant with a scent of burning apple wood.
The mantelpiece, James noticed, was fantastically carved with fruit,
after the manner of Grinling Gibbons.

The Spaniard was dressed formally, in black, but his head was
bandaged and his olive skin looked pale and sickly.

"Come here!" he said again, and held out his hand. "What is
your name?"

"James Darrell, sir. I did not mean to disturb you. I came to
give you back your knife."

"Ignacio Fernando María de Zozaya, very much at your service!
You may call me Don Ignacio," the Spaniard announced graciously. "Sit down, young man, while I ring for refreshment! Ah,
the knife! Thank you. I should have been sorry to lose it."

James sat down, suddenly conquered. He was glad, now, that
he had come to this strange house.

"My sherry," explained Don Ignacio, "comes straight from Jerez
and is the best I know. When were you last in Spain, Don Jaime?"

James smiled at the unfamiliar mode of address.

"I have never, alas, been in Spain, Don Ignacio."

"May I ask, then, where you learned to speak my language with so much fluency?"

"I learned it when I was a child. I have a certain facility for languages. My grandmother was Spanish."

"That explains much that would otherwise be mystifying. The bone formation of your face, for instance, your high cheekbones . . . Well, Don Jaime, I owe you my life, such as it is, although I shall never forget the lack of skill with which I handled this the other night." He picked up the knife and looked at it reflectively. "It has served me well enough before in such brawls. I can only suppose I must be growing old."

"Sir, I hope you were not badly injured?"

"Oh, I received a scratch, nothing more. The loss of blood made me faint. Some more sherry, Don Jaime? Come—I insist!"

"I must be going. You have been more than kind."

The Spaniard smiled for the first time. His smile broke up the grimness of his face and made it seem suddenly whimsical and faunlike.

"You are dining, I suppose, with some charming young lady?"

James smiled too.

"Indeed I'm not, sir!"

"Then you will be kind enough to honour me with your company at dinner." He stretched out his hand to pull the bell again.

"But, sir . . ."

"Don Ignacio!"

"Don Ignacio! You are sick, and I've already stayed longer than I meant."

"But for you I should not be sick, but dead. Be so kind, then, as to humour me. Do you care for champagne?"

"I've never tasted it, Don Ignacio."

"No? Well, I have a particular brand of the wine here I would like you to try—a rose-coloured champagne considered by connoisseurs to be of some merit. I shall sip half a glass to keep you company. Now, before dinner, I will show you my collection of jade, and after dinner you shall tell me something about yourself."

James rose willingly enough to inspect the cabinets of jade.

He knew that he was going to enjoy the evening more than any he had yet spent in London.

The friends he had found so far in the city were scarcely of a type to impress Oriana—a Neapolitan pedlar who sold plaster images, some gypsies encamped near Battersea, another Italian who played the hurdy-gurdy and who owned a pet monkey, a Cornish ex-wrestler whose wife sang—out of tune—in the street, and a very old Jew who stuffed pet animals for a living.

He had written some sketches about these people and Sir Matthew Kent-Taylor had dismissed them as being more than usually vulgar.

Nor had he supposed, even in his more optimistic moments, that Oriana would have enjoyed reading about such oddities. But even Oriana might have been intrigued by the Spaniard; even Sir Matthew would perhaps have found that fantastic house impressive.

"I am only a collector," Don Ignacio was saying, "in my spare moments. Unfortunately they are rare enough. I am a busy man."

James, who had imagined his host to be some species of Castilian grandee, looked at him in surprise.

"I am a diamond merchant," Don Ignacio confided, sighing.

CHAPTER XVII

"It is usual," Don Ignacio observed, "for those ignorant of Spain to imagine my countrymen as a gay, volatile race, not unlike, shall we say, the Italians. Nothing, however, could be further from the truth. The Spaniard is reserved, austere, and sometimes dour. Occasionally he reminds me not a little of your Highlander."

It was after dinner, and they sat before the fire smoking cheroots. James felt happy and relaxed and well fed.

"That is not to say," Don Ignacio continued, "that the Spaniard and his way of life are not colourful. They are both intensely so. Possibly, my friend, it is difficult to be drab in a country drenched with sun, and Spain, in summer, is like a land on fire."

"Is it not burnt up?" James suggested.

"It is," Don Ignacio agreed; "but that does not necessarily mean it lacks colour. On the contrary, colour is everywhere. In our plains, that are tiger gold in the heat of August. In our snow-capped mountains at the glow of sunrise. In the bright flowers with which our dancers garland their hair; in the bullfighters' capes; in the brilliant shawls of our gypsies; in the gardens of the Generalife, where fountains play all night for the fireflies; in the blazing candles of our churches; in the gold and silver robes of our saints and Virgins. Above all, perhaps, in the wild music we call *flamenco,* which should always be heard beneath the stars or the sun, and never, never beneath a roof."

James said:

"It sounds like an enchanted land."

"To me it is," his host agreed with disarming simplicity. He added after a pause: "But I have talked too much, and now I would like to hear you speak. Tell me something of yourself—do. you work, and, if so, what is your profession?"

James found it easy to talk to Don Ignacio.

He described his life in London, his hack work for the publisher, his own interest in curiosities, and the discouragement with which his literary efforts had been received.

"I am pretty sure, Don Ignacio, that I can write, but the trouble is that other people don't appear to care for what I find interesting."

"How would you like to go to Spain?" Don Ignacio asked abruptly.

"To Spain?"

He felt his cheeks grow hot, and in his eagerness he stammered a little.

"I would like it, sir, above all things! But in what capacity?"

"I am reflecting," the Spaniard announced, blowing a cloud of azure smoke into the air. "I am saying to myself that you know, of course, nothing about precious stones, but that, I think, is not a matter of great importance. I have, you know, a business in Amsterdam, as well as a business here in London, and one in Madrid. Well, there must always be a beginning. You have, you say, no family ties of any kind, no other person to consider?"

"But I have, Don Ignacio," James protested firmly to this. "There is—— I hope one day to be married, although there are difficulties."

And somewhat to his own surprise he found himself describing Oriana to the Spaniard. He was completely truthful. He admitted that his situation was scarcely a hopeful one, but he said frankly that they loved each other, and that if only she could be persuaded to wait for him a little longer, he felt sure that they would in the end be happy together.

"Unfortunately," he said, "she has already waited two years, and there is someone else I suspect of being in love with her."

"And this young lady," Don Ignacio enquired after a pause, "if —I only say 'if,' mind you—if you were found suitable employment in Madrid, would she be willing to live there? For it might mean staying in Spain for some years, my friend, this post, or it might involve leaving Spain to live indefinitely in Amsterdam. Your *novia* appears to be a young lady of fashion; how do you imagine she would support the idea of exile in a strange land?"

James smiled.

"She's also a girl of spirit, Don Ignacio; I don't think that she would say no. But of course I would have to consult her first."

"Naturally. Well, Don Jaime, we can do nothing in haste, that is evident. In any case, but for my accursed accident I should have been by this time in Amsterdam, where my affairs await me. There is no hurry. Think the matter over, but write down your address for me before you go."

As James obeyed, the Spaniard mused aloud:

"And you like the gypsies."

"I have always been friendly with them."

"In that case, if you are what we call an *aficionado,* then Spain is most certainly the country for you, and you might write more successfully there than anywhere else. We shall see. You have saved my life, for what it is worth; you have shown yourself a brave and resolute young man, and one likes, does one not, to pay one's debts? I shall keep your address."

"I don't know how to thank you, Don Ignacio," James said, getting up.

"I have done nothing, so far, for which to be thanked. I like your company, Don Jaime, and the ease with which you speak my language; when you have talked to your novia, and when I have arranged my most pressing affairs, you will give me the pleasure of dining here with me again."

As James shook hands with him he felt a passionate curiosity to learn something of the Spaniard's life; there had been no talk,

for instance, of a wife, or mistress. It would appear as though Don
Ignacio lived alone, in solitary state, without so much as expecting
a guest. It would seem that he fed, regally, as a matter of course,
on buttered lobster, roast duckling, and ice pudding. He possessed
a cellar of precious wine, and the treasures in his house made it resemble nothing so much as the genie's cave in a fairy tale. His very
profession seemed fantastic to James: this traffic of diamonds, of
those white, glittering jewels, seemed to him something fabulous,
mysterious, apart from all ordinary standards of life.

As though Don Ignacio knew this, he observed, quite forgetting
to open the door:

"If I can read your thoughts, Don Jaime, I believe you are
thinking that my lot is to be envied?"

"Something like that." James smiled.

"Do not think so," the Spaniard urged him in tones of absolute
finality. "Do not think so, because it is not the truth! I have a splendid house, you think—two, three, splendid houses. That's true; I
have; but please remember I live in them alone. So much grandeur,
you know, can be very desolate. I have no son to defend me if I
am attacked, as you so valiantly defended me the other day. I have
no charming *novia*, as you have. Selling diamonds, you know, is
very much a commercial transaction, like any other of its kind.
The sparkle of the jewels is often hidden by the grime of the offices
where we work. Oh no, Don Jaime, don't envy me. I know this is
an irritating reflection, but I would relinquish all my treasures for
your youth, your ambition, your strong body, and the adventure
of your future. *Not* mine; I have little enough future left, but, thanks
to you, I am not yet dead!"

"Don Ignacio, you're a *brujo,* a magician, and you read my
thoughts!"

The Spaniard put his hand affectionately on the young man's
shoulder.

"Think over what I have told you tonight about Spain. If you
write about my country, you will be like Columbus, voyaging into
virgin territory, for no countryman of yours has written yet about
my own land. They are reluctant, perhaps, to venture somewhere
so primitive and savage. But you, as I have every reason to know,
are adventurous.

"Spain, Don Jaime, is both cruel and noble. Sometimes one side triumphs, sometimes the other. But nothing there is petty; everything happens on a grand scale. There is dirt, and there is glitter, and the sun pours down on both. For you, a writer, trained to observe, the little things may take your fancy too: a matador's fighting cape, fuchsia-colour lined with buttercup, will make your heart rejoice; you'll see the Virgin of Hope, crystal tears gemmed on her cheeks and a crown of diamonds—*my* diamonds—proudly set on her head; you'll see the grilled windows of an ancient convent where nuns—to enter on their novitiate—must once play fighting calves in the convent arena with that same matador's cape. Your heart, my dear Don Jaime, will rejoice even more when our horsemen, our riders from the ranches, gallop forth across the plains to test the guts of young bulls bred for the arena. Most of all, perhaps, your heart will rejoice when, for the first time, beneath the stars, you hear, in its fierce purity, the music called flamenco; when you see for the first time, again beneath the stars, some bitch of a gypsy dancer who will mesmerise you into thinking that she has jumped over the moon itself. Those are little things, my friend, but they are all a part of Spain, and one day, when you have known them all, you will write about them, and no one any longer will call your choice of subject vulgar."

James scarcely knew, that night, how he walked home to his lodgings.

His mind, considerably stimulated by pink champagne, revolved in some confusion between jade, ikons, Tang horses, flamenco music, jasmine blossoms, bright shawls, sun-scorched plains, and the waxen, jewel-framed faces of Spanish saints.

Since, for the first time, he had good news for Oriana, he walked on air—more, he soared above the stars. At last, soon, perhaps in a few weeks, they would be able to meet, and marry, and venture together across the seas to their destiny in that savage country which was drenched in sunshine.

He thought exultantly of his love: of her cheek, pale as the white jade he had seen that night; of her great, beautiful brown eyes; of her warm red lips.

For nearly a year he had been unable, in his own wretchedness, to visualise the loveliness that was Oriana; for a long time she had receded, a vivid ghost, somewhere into the background of his hateful life. Now, as though the Spaniard were really a magician and had flicked a wand, she was once more beside him, tangible, and glowing with all the zest for life, the mischief that was so much a part of her character.

Yet this ghost of her in the darkness was sweeter than he remembered, less mocking; the ghost crept close beside him and whispered charms into his ear, and told him how happy they would be together, the two of them, in Spain. . . .

It was late when he returned to his dingy room, and he was too tired, or too tipsy, to write to her.

The next day he received an imperious note from Sir Matthew Kent-Taylor, and for the following two days he was forced to concentrate on hack work until his strained right hand rebelled, finally to become useless. Until he rested, he could no longer have written his own name.

But he dreamed, those nights, of Spain, and of Oriana.

He had not dreamed of her for many months.

CHAPTER XVIII

ON THE FOURTH DAY after his meeting with the Spaniard he sat down to write to her.

He wrote at length, describing Don Ignacio's offer, trying to recapture on paper the longing he felt for them to see Spain together. He tried to describe to her what he had heard about the country, certain that so much warmth and colour would appeal particularly to one of her temperament. Although the Spaniard had not as yet discussed any salary, he felt certain, he said, that Don Ignacio was an honourable man—one who, conceiving himself to be under an obligation, would not offer him a post unless its emolument enabled him to support a wife in adequate comfort.

He described briefly Don Ignacio's amazing house, adding how much he hoped that she would soon see it for herself.

Then he wrote:

*My dearest one, for the first time I feel hopeful about our future.
Last night you seemed nearer to me than you have been for two
interminable years, and I dreamed of you, which I have been, I
suppose, too discouraged to do for a long time. I truly believe that
my fantastic Spaniard is destined to play godfather to us both; I
know that when he sees you he will find you as beautiful as I do.*

*My sweet love, I shall be in a fever of impatience until you answer
this letter by return of post. I kiss your hands and your lips, and I
worship you as always.*

JAMES.

When he had finished this letter he sealed it, directed it, and
decided to post it at once.

The day was cold and overcast, but he was indifferent. He ran
downstairs into the hall, where he found a letter addressed to himself. His heart leaped as he recognised Oriana's hand; he had not
heard from her for weeks, and the sight of her wild scrawl was all
that he needed to enhance his own mood of joyful confidence.

He opened the letter, noting to his surprise that it was written,
not from abroad, but from the Hall, and read:

DEAR JAMES,

*I am writing to tell you that I was married a week ago to Frank
Castleton.*

*This is the most difficult letter I have ever written, so please read
it carefully. My marriage does not mean that I love you any less,
although I love Frank, but not in the wild way we have always
cared for each other. That is what made me know it was wiser
for me to marry Frank.*

*You and I, James, love each other so passionately that we would
have been bound to wreck our lives together. That was the first
consideration. The other, of course, was money. You will despise
me for telling you how extravagant I am, but I must, because it is
the truth. I could never be the wife of a poor man. I love luxury,
I always have. Now you can hate me as much as you want, but
I have never lied to you.*

Perhaps one day you will be a great writer, as we have so often dreamed, but that would never give me the security I have found. I kept my word, and waited for you two years, and I have missed you so much that sometimes I have despaired. I knew that to see you once only would be fatal to my peace of mind, and so I have never tried to see you.

James, I know that this letter will make you hate me. In a way, I hope it will. You see, I love you. You will never know how many sleepless nights I spent before deciding to marry Frank. I had to uproot something so strong it was as though I tore up part of myself that is still bleeding. You won't believe me, I know, but it's true, and I've just said I never lied to you.

I knew when I gave you up I perhaps gave up much misery, but I know I gave up ecstasy as well. With Frank, I suppose that I shall be calmly happy. We could never have been that, even if we had been rich, and I would never have wanted it. There was nothing calm about our feeling for each other, and we were right, being so young, to love as madly as we did, for then it was perfect. But it would never have been perfect nowadays.

But if you think I shall cease to love you, you are mad. That is why we must never meet again, for I know I am too vulnerable.

Reading this letter over, I see that I have said Frank and I will be calmly happy. How smug that sounds! And how unlike me. You see, I realise my wildness, in my heart of hearts. I knew it when I first promised to marry him. That is why we were married in Paris, and there was no excuse then, when we stayed in London before coming home, for me to see you. As I have said, if I had still been unmarried then, and met you, all my ambition would have meant nothing, for we would just have been drawn into each other's arms, and lived to regret it, no doubt. But nothing else would have mattered, and I am glad, for both our sakes, that I was determined.

James, I am going to say good-bye to you, and since it is really good-bye, even Frank could not mind my saying that we were born to be lovers, and to be in love.

We always will be, so far as I am concerned. But I am too mercenary for your integrity, and so I can only finish this letter by asking you to forgive me for not being strong enough for both of us.

ORIANA.

He read this letter over and over again, standing there rigid in the shabby hall. Then, for he heard someone emerging from a room on the ground floor, he bolted out into the street, forgetting even to shut the door behind him.

He walked past Russell Square without in the least knowing what he was about. Suddenly, putting his hand in his pocket, he found the letter he had taken such pains to write her only that morning, but it seemed to him a hundred years ago. He tore it fiercely into shreds and watched the wind snatch its fragments, like snowflakes, down the street.

He thought he had come to the end of everything. The end of all joy, and dreams, and of ambition, too, he was sure. For many years now she had brightened all his life, so that his whole existence had been fiercely concentrated on her. Without her, nothing had any meaning, and the emptiness of life became something he could not endure to contemplate. He had thought her capable of nobility; impulsive and self-willed as she had always been, he could have sworn her love for him was steadfast as his own. Even in boyhood, when he had so frequently been jealous of Castleton, he had still secretly hoped in the end to conquer. And he had never thought her capable of treachery.

He walked on, dazed, unseeing, unconscious of everything but his own agony of mind.

The protestations of love she expressed so incoherently seemed senseless to him. She herself confessed to being "mercenary"; she had contracted a worldly marriage for the sake of security; she had, in his view, proved herself both coldhearted and rapacious; now he forced himself to think that she did not love him, that she had never loved him. In his bitterness he was convinced that she had only amused herself with him; she had coquetted, let him love her because there had been no one else for her to flirt with. All the time she had been coolly planning this rich marriage.

Yet, stunned and miserable as he was, he could not help remembering their last interview together, her tears, and the passion with which she had returned his kisses. He had had nothing to offer her then; even now his future depended entirely on the whim of an eccentric, and as a writer he had failed completely.

So, desperately, he tried for a while to defend her to himself, and then the memory of her beauty came rushing back to make him sick with longing for the sight of her, the touch of her hand, the sound of her voice. Once again he read her blotted letter, and once again his heart hardened. She intended to be "calmly happy"! That, he knew, knowing her so well, she would never be. She was a flame that Castleton could never quench. Now her wild protestations of love for himself—so unconventionally expressed for a girl of her period and class—seemed to him melodramatic and exaggerated, and he thought she was trying to combine two roles, that of the romantic she would like to have been with that of the realist she in fact was.

But no amount of confused thinking could in any way assuage his grief. He knew that he could not bear to sit still, or return to his room, and so he continued to walk, without the slightest sense of direction.

That afternoon he found himself in Cheapside, and it was there that he saw a notice in a bookseller's window—"Volume of tales wanted." He perceived another irony: how eagerly, on any day but this, would he have rushed home to collect his manuscripts! Now he looked at the notice with a lacklustre eye and turned indifferently into a pastry shop for a pie and a cup of coffee.

At last, after so much aimless wandering, he knew what he was going to do. He could not endure to stay any longer in London; that evening he would seek out the Spaniard, confide his troubles, and beg to be sent to Madrid, or to Amsterdam. It no longer mattered where.

All that mattered was escape.

CHAPTER XIX

THAT EVENING, having first returned to change his coat, he rang Don Ignacio's bell in Berkeley Square. After a pause the door was opened by one of the green-liveried footmen, slightly less immaculate, James fancied, than on the occasion of their last meeting.

"Will you ask Señor de Zozaya if he will receive Mr. James Darrell?"

The footman stared at him in a friendly manner and said:

"Sir, the señor's from home."

"What time do you expect him?"

"He's abroad, sir—in Holland!"

For a moment James could scarcely grasp this simple fact and only gazed stupidly at the footman, until he recollected, as though in a dream, that the Spaniard had talked of urgent business awaiting him in Amsterdam.

Then his heart sank.

"I see," he said. "I see. When do you expect him back?"

The footman thought that the young man looked as green as an oyster, or as his own livery; he seemed bewildered, too, and passed his hand over his brow, that looked wet, although the night was cold.

"Well, sir," the footman temporized, remembering that the enquirer was a favourite of his master's, "well, sir, we don't think he'll be away many weeks, but of course we can never tell. Sometimes it's as many months, although he *does* usually write to the housekeeper."

"I see," James said again, and turned away dejectedly. The footman watched him disappear, not without concern. James was, in the parlance of the servants' hall, a proper gent, a fine chap with his fists, and one who had saved their master from being murdered. There was a supper that night, below stairs, and the footman wished with all his heart that he dared invite the young gent.

James tramped on, cursing his bad luck, in the direction of Leicester Square. There he turned into a gin palace which advertised outside its blazing windows: "Drunk for a penny! Dead drunk for twopence!" He moved on, after a penny's worth of Hollands, towards the brothel where he had been once before.

There, in a salon glittering with mirrors, swollen with padded crimson sofas, he sat aloof, drinking a glass of wine with a voluptuous young woman whose hair was dyed a flaming red. Later that night they went to bed, in a room cluttered with sham French eighteenth-century furniture. He was not very drunk, as he had been on his previous adventure in this stew; he pretended to love the girl, but loathed her. He deceived her, and she clung to him all through the interminable night. He left at dawn and went downstairs in the grey light of morning to the florid, smoky room where the Madam waited to take his last five guineas and to detain him with salacious stories.

He tramped home, to fling himself exhausted upon his bed. He slept until the afternoon. It was then that he remembered his need for leaving London, the Spaniard's disappearance, his lack of money, and finally, as though in a haze, the notice he had seen outside a bookseller's shop, that notice demanding a volume of tales.

He got up to finish without a meal *The Lives of the Saints* he was "ghosting" for Sir Matthew Kent-Taylor. Stuffing another more precious manuscript into his case, he paused at Russell Square to leave a bulky heap of papers, and then strode on towards Cheapside.

He tried all that day, and tried most desperately, to put Oriana out of his mind. He did not think he would have felt so distraught had the Spaniard been in Berkeley Square. But he knew that he could no longer stay in London. He had to escape, or go mad. And so he went straight into the bookseller's shop in Cheapside, his manuscript clutched under his arm.

"Sir, I understand you wish to buy a volume of tales?"

Long afterwards the bookseller remembered him, and described him as a very tall young man, with grey eyes under black brows, a lock of hair falling over his forehead, and an abrupt manner.

He had presented, for reading, a volume of original fairy tales.

"I am only offering ten guineas," the bookseller told him, whereat the young man shook his head and seemed inclined to leave the shop.

"Ten guineas are no good to me, sir! I *have* to leave London. I must ask twenty!"

"Come back in an hour," the bookseller advised, "and drink a dish of tea with my wife and myself."

"Very well, sir."

He jerked his head and was gone.

When he came back, the bookseller's wife gave him tea and buttered toast in a comfortable room overflowing with books at the back of the shop. They were a pleasant, chubby pair of cockneys, and no doubt their company was excellent for him. In any case, as they remembered afterwards, he relaxed, stretched out his long legs, and smoked a pipe.

He persisted in his determination to leave London, and in the end, after a friendly interview, he consented to sell his fairy tales for fifteen guineas.

These transactions completed, they asked him where he intended to go.

He didn't care, he informed them. All places were the same to him. He just didn't want to stay on in London. Perhaps he would join the gypsies. In any case, he meant to tramp the roads and gain material for another book.

"And one day," he told them, with a charming smile, "one day I shall assuredly go to Spain and write a book about the Spaniards."

They liked his fairy tales, and told him so, but he only laughed and shook his head.

"They're nothing," he said; "only stories to amuse children, and I don't care for them myself."

When this book of fairy tales, *The Crystal Dragon* was published, they would often recall him, but that was to be no good, for when an eminent publisher rang their bell, they had no idea where he was to be found, and so, to this honest pair, he himself remained a mystery.

They believed, they said, that he vanished the night he left them, after receiving his fifteen guineas. They had no idea where he had gone. Much later, years later, when pressed, they were to remember long-forgotten details. He had seemed exhausted, odd, nervous in his manner. He had talked excitedly of the gypsies. He had confided that, if he found the gypsies again, he didn't suppose he would ever leave them. But he had qualified his statement by announcing that he wished to travel in Spain, to study the gypsies there.

They thought him charming but extraordinary. They had never met a young gentleman before, and this one, so interested in vagrancy, made a profound impression upon their mind.

They confessed later that they found him "a bit queer."

Yet theirs was to be the triumph of publishing *The Crystal*

Dragon and a dozen other fairy tales that will be remembered forever.

Not that they had any idea, then, that they were trafficking with future greatness—they only saw, being a solid, sensible pair, that here was an unhappy boy with a facility for telling tales.

Long afterwards the bookseller's wife confided:

"He'd put his hand on your arm and say, 'I'll tell you a story.' You had to listen, then . . . "

In his private hell he was unconscious of the effect he made that night in Cheapside. All he cared about was escape, and, with fifteen guineas in his pocket, escape, at last, was easy.

PART IV

On the Tober

CHAPTER XX

HIS PREPARATIONS were swiftly concluded.

He paid his landlady, left his manuscripts with his Oxford friend, and put on his shabbiest clothes. Such necessities as he took with him were bundled, Whittington-like, into an enormous handkerchief, and then he simply walked out of London. All roads were the same to him, and so long as he avoided going in the direction of Oxfordshire, it did not in the least matter where he went.

He had always been accustomed to tramp long distances, but the sedentary life of the last two years had scarcely prepared him for an indefinite journey such as he intended his to be, and he wisely took the coach at Chelsea, determined to ride as far as Kingston.

When he got down from his outside seat he ate some bread and cheese at an inn near the river. The weather had improved, and great clouds billowed like white sails in the sky. He was amazed to see masses of purple lilac in the cottage gardens and showers of laburnum, guinea-gold—he had forgotten all about spring in London. He breathed freely, he thought, for the first time since his self-imposed exile, and with pure air filling his lungs and the breeze on his bare head, some of the bitterness left his heart. But not for long. Such wounds as the one Oriana had dealt are never swiftly healed, and it was due to her that he felt no gratification in the thought that his fairy tales were to be published. His sole satisfaction lay in the fact that he had acquired, with fifteen guineas, the means of escape from London.

London had become to him, despite the colourful episode of the Spaniard, a place of grim and hateful memories. Quite apart from the emotional shock of Oriana's letter, he had been for nearly a year constantly discouraged and haunted by his own miserable failure to achieve anything. He had been overworked and vilely underpaid by Sir Matthew Kent-Taylor. Often, for days at a time, he had not had enough to eat.

Now he was free, and called no man master.

He walked out of Kingston and was enchanted, after so many months of city life, by the ordinary traffic he saw upon the road.

Once a coach tore by with foaming, lathered horses, the "yard of tin" pealing, and the coachman, heavy-handed, lashing his team round the next corner. After the bustle of their passing, some pack horses plodded by, and then a chaise, and then, bowling along scornfully, a nobleman's carriage with a crested door, and postillions bobbing like cherries on the shining horses.

In between such excitements a few gentlemen hacked quietly along the grass beside the road, and James thought, with a sigh, how long it was since he had last been on a horse.

He trudged on, observing, as one starved of beauty, the fresh, radiant green of the hedgerows, May trees that swam in a bloom of snow, bluebells surging like a patch of vivid tropic sea beneath the spreading branches of a huge oak tree, which made him think of Ackland Wood, so that he stopped then, and thought of Oriana. While he paused, wiping his face, for the day was warmer than he had supposed, a hoarse voice hailed him from behind.

"Cully! Wait a jiff, cully!"

He turned to perceive a short fat man who wheeled, panting, a small handbarrow. The man, who was followed by a scraggy white terrier, wore a full-skirted brown coat of incredible seediness, a shaggy beaver hat, and a scarf of scarlet spotted with white. His round chubby face was red, too, and he appeared not to have shaved that morning. He looked disreputable, heated, and, to James, somewhat endearing.

"Well?" James said, waiting for him.

"Why can't we tramp together, cully? I been trying to overtake you for the last mile. Vot's your hurry?"

"None," James said, with the simplicity that usually made him his friends; "we'll go on together."

They were silent for five minutes, and then the little man said: "So you're on the tober?"

"On the what?"

"God! You're green! The road, pal, the road, or a fairground pitch, if you like. Either one will do."

"I don't call the road the tober," James said, after a pause.

"You don't, eh?"

"Not I. I call it the *drom*."

"Romany, are you?"

"No, but I speak their language."

"I'm no Romany," his new friend said, not without hauteur, "and if I understand their lingo, vell, I don't adwertise it. I'm genteel; I'm a showman!"

"Really? What do you show?"

"I'm a Punch-man. Name of Jeremy Torch."

"Punch and Judy, you mean?"

"That's right, pal."

"My name is Darrell," James volunteered. "Shall I give you a hand with the barrow?"

"Thanks. I must say I'm sweating. The dolls veigh heavy. Sometimes I think old Punch does it to tease. Knowing, dolls are, specially when you've had 'em for twenty years, as I've had these. By the way, Toby, my *jukkal,* as your gypsies'd call him, my dog, seems to like you. Wery flattered you should be. Not but what she's not a bitch, and a randy one too. Three times she's 'eld up the show with litters. But she's a fine little artist, and I've not complained too much."

"Are you showing tonight?" James enquired, immediately fascinated by the personality and entourage of Mr. Torch.

"I am, cully. At the next village, half a mile from here. Listen: as we're both on the tober, how'd you like to busk—to take round the box and divide?"

"I'd like it," James assured him.

Later that evening they sat together in a barn while Mr. Torch, preparatory to producing his drama, most carefully unwrapped his puppets. James was enchanted by the seriousness with which he regarded them. He treated them exactly as though they were human beings.

"Now, cully, here's Punch, the chief artist, and a bastard he is, though I say it myself."

James picked up the doll and looked at it, smiling. Punch was an ugly, humped object clad in a tinsel dress, with a pointed cap and a waggish, red-nosed face.

"He looks a devil," James commented.

"And vy? Vimmen 'ave made him one, that's vy. Vimmen 'ave coddled him. Without vimmen, 'e might have been a good citizen."

"And Judy?" James enquired, picking up a ferocious female doll in a frilled mobcap.

"A nagger, cully, like all bitches in petticoats."

James burst out laughing—his first laugh for some time, and he did not even know it.

"And the beadle? And the hangman?" As he spoke, he put the limp dolls on the ground before him.

"Simple, isnt it?" Mr. Torch enquired. "Just laughing at authority. Nothing like it—nothing ever will be. We all vant to laugh at authority—makes us feel healthy."

Whereupon he thrust a piece of metal into his mouth and emitted a piercing squeak.

"That," he said to James, "is what we call the rozzer. No Punchman ever worked without one. Talking of work, you and me and Toby and the dolls had better start, since we're on the tober together!"

CHAPTER XXI

JAMES REMAINED with Jeremy Torch for about ten days. They wandered from village to village, pushing the barrow in turn, Toby trotting meekly at their heels. The show was an unfailing delight to James, and so was Jeremy, who took himself as seriously as any actor-manager. They gave their show wherever there were children, and then Jeremy, retiring behind his red-plush curtain, the "rozzer" in his mouth, ceased to be himself and became in turn many people

—Punch, Judy, the beadle, the hangman, and the ghost. James, "busking" outside the tiny theatre with his collecting-box, sometimes thought this drama of Punch the best play in the world, containing, as it did, the elements of all primitive tragedy.

When he told Jeremy this, the latter was disposed to regard his enthusiasm with suspicion.

"There's no call to poke fun at Punch just because you've had more eddication than him or me has. No call at all, there isn't."

"I wasn't poking fun at Punch," James protested indignantly.

"Punch was entertaining before Shakespeare. Never knew that, I suppose? And who knows but he may last as long, or longer !"

At night they slept in barns, luxuriously couched on piles of sweet-smelling hay or clean yellow straw. James slept better than he had ever slept during that last black year in London. He was becoming sunburnt, and the hollows in his cheeks were filling out. To say that he was recovering from the shock of Oriana's marriage would have been premature, but they walked so many miles, and worked so hard, that it soon became easy to sleep at night. In the evenings they ate at the nearest inn, drank ale, and listened to the local gossip. Their lunch consisted of bread and cheese, but it was some time since James had had even one square meal a day, and his health improved rapidly.

Their takings were good, Jeremy said. So long as they sufficed to pay for food and ale, James was satisfied. He astounded his companion by bathing—with soap—in every stream or pond.

"Terrible store of rheumatics you're saving up for, cully," Jeremy told him lugubriously; "vashing yourself all over isn't natural, and never will be. Look at me—old enough to be your dad, and never vashed myself all over, not once in all my life."

"No wonder that barmaid jilted you," James retorted.

He was referring to a romantic episode confided, late one night, by Jeremy.

"There was this girl, cully, behind the bar at the old White Horse in Shoreditch. A wery fine-looking doña she was, make no mistake. Vell, I was dossing near there all the winter, and I courted her. What occurred I don't know, but I can only tell you anything sentimental I had to tell the doña, I'm damned if I could tell her in me own voice. I had to put the rozzer in my mouth and make love to her in Punch's voice. She didn't like it, naturally, and even if she had, you can't very vell kiss a girl with a rozzer in your mouth. So it come to nothing, specially as it turned out Punch had always give her the creeps ever since she was first in short frocks."

"Didn't you mind?" James asked, moodily thinking of his own jilting.

"Oh, vell, I've always got the dolls to fall back on. They're companions, if you like, and never impident the way doñas are. Even Punch, who's a great artist, and knows it, can't answer me back unless I put the words in his mouth—vich I seldom do, knowing how he takes adwantage."

Life with Jeremy Torch and his puppets did much to restore James's fits of nerves and depression. Jeremy's prosaic common sense, his cheerful outlook upon a life that had never been anything but hard, the childish simplicity of his affection for "the dolls," were all effective antidotes to brooding and melancholy.

James would probably have continued his wanderings with the Punch-man had not Jeremy's partner eventually arrived to join him in Guildford. The tardiness of this individual was explained by illness, but James could not help thinking that Mr. Silas Dill's cadaverous face bore the authentic prison pallor. He did not like the man's little cunning eyes, nor his fawning manner; in any case, there was no longer any excuse for him to linger with the show.

He bade an affectionate farewell to Jeremy Torch, Toby, and the puppets, and then walked off, on his own once more, in the direction of Dorking. It was early June, and the countryside glowed in bright sunshine. The hedgerows were tangled with sweet-smelling honeysuckle and pink-and-white wild roses; the meadows glittered gold with buttercups, and cuckooflowers bloomed over the dried-up bogs and marshes. He passed near a noble forest, and, thinking of Ackland Wood, decided to wander down its shady paths.

He realised his mistake only when the quietness of the woods and the darkness of the ancient trees contrived to remind him of many a wild, runaway day spent with Oriana. His black mood returned, and, moreover, since he had no idea where he was going to sleep that night, these nomad adventures of his no longer seemed so enthralling, but began rather to assume the senseless windings and turnings of an animal at bay. He asked himself then, why, when it was no longer possible to continue with Jeremy Torch, he had not returned sensibly to London, there to await the return of the Spaniard. He forgot, in his fit of depression, the improvement in his own health, and only wondered why the devil he was tramping the roads like a rogue and a vagabond. Yet the mere thought of London caused him to shudder with distaste.

In such a mood everything is hideous; many things are haunted.

Therefore, when he heard a soft whistle, similar to the signals with which Oriana had so often summoned him, he started as though a ghost had whispered in his ear. But the whistle was repeated and his curiosity aroused; he turned in the direction of the sound, plunging through some bracken into a dell shaded with massive trees and carpeted in foxgloves. A fire burned here, and, thinking to have discovered some gypsies, he advanced impulsively.

But the woman who sprang to her feet, startled, by his approach, was most certainly not a gypsy.

She was an extremely tall girl of about his own age, eccentrically dressed in a man's coat—a soldier's coat of faded red and a striped petticoat. She wore rough shoes on her bare feet, and her hair, which fell to her shoulders, was palest silvery-gold, the colour of flax. Her features were strongly marked but handsome, and her deep-set eyes were vivid blue.

She said rudely:

"I was not whistling for you."

He glanced at the fire, over which she appeared to be cooking some species of meal.

"I did not suppose you were," he retorted, "but you must be more careful, you know, as to who you conjure up in forests!"

"Good evening!" she said curtly over her shoulder, dismissing him.

"Why? I've as much right as you have here; I propose to stay for a few minutes in front of your fire."

"You can't; I'm expecting someone."

"Is he such an ogre?"

She flashed one sharp glance at him, suspicious; he was shabby, but not quite shabby enough; most damning of all, to her, his voice was that of a gentleman.

She said:

"You come from *them!*"

"What on earth do you mean?"

Her voice sank to a whisper.

"Let us alone! For God's sake let us alone!"

James began to think that he had been unlucky enough to encounter a lunatic. Then, with a rapid look at her strange clothes and
her wild air, he gambled, addressing her in Romany:

"Your *nav? Pukker mande tute's nav, gajé rakli!*"

She looked at him fixedly, but to his relief she grew immediately
calmer.

"Oh, you're just a gypsy boy who's learned to speak like a swell.
I see. Well, I'll answer your question. My name's Silver, just Silver,
called so on account of my light hair. I was a workhouse *chavé,* a
parish child, that's all I know. Since then many things have happened. I was an army girl. Know what that means?"

He shook his head.

"I went off with a soldier," Silver explained, "and I sold barrels
of beer. I followed the camps all over England. There's a French
name for that. The redcoats told me, but I don't know what it is.
Low, I expect."

"I know," James said. *"Vivandière."*

"That's it. Then, in Hampshire, I met the person I expect here
at any moment. He's a gentleman—a real one, not like you. Not in
the army either. He's a squire. He wants to marry me. We met
again, but we had to run away. We are still running away. That's
why we're hiding in the forest. He has gone to find out if there's
an inn anywhere near here."

James stared at her in not unnatural astonishment, since his idea
of a squire was Mr. Camperdene, whom he could scarcely imagine
hiding in the woods with so eccentric a young woman.

"Where did you learn Romany?" he asked, after a somewhat
bewildered pause.

She threw him a scornful look.

"I've been on the road since I was thirteen."

And then, hearing a footfall too distant even for his quick ear to
catch, she whistled again, and someone came crashing towards
them through the bracken.

James rose, uncertain what type of person to expect.

CHAPTER XXII

HE SCARCELY KNEW for what fearsome spectacle he had prepared himself, but the parted undergrowth revealed nothing more terrifying than the sight of a slim and pale young man.

This youth, who was neatly dressed in dark clothes, appeared little more than eighteen years of age; he had highbred features, an imperious mouth, and dark-lashed eyes. On seeing James, he was obviously disconcerted, but appeared determined to be brazen.

"Sir?" he said haughtily, and James perceived that his hand trembled.

Silver said hastily:

"This is just a gypsy lad from the road."

"I'm not a gypsy," James protested, "although I'm tramping the roads! My name's James Darrell, at your service."

"I am Jeffrey Lucas, sir," the youth admitted after a pause.

"Another gentleman!" Silver commented scornfully, and for a moment there was an awkward pause.

"This young lady——" James began.

"We are eloping," Jeffrey Lucas admitted, "and we are in deadly fear. That is why——"

"It's his tutors," Silver said.

"Not entirely. My guardians!"

"Are they chasing you?" James wanted to know.

"I am much afraid they are, sir," Mr. Lucas confessed. "You see, I am under age, nineteen, in fact, and, well—they do not entirely approve of Silver, here."

No, James did not suppose that they would. Few tutors, few guardians, would feel benevolently inclined towards this road girl, this parish brat, who had since acted as a vivandière. He felt uncomfortable, and knew not what to say.

"We are eloping," Mr. Lucas repeated.

"But why elope into the middle of a forest?"

"Don't tell him!" Silver advised sharply.

"Surely," Mr. Lucas smiled to James, "we may regard you as a friend?"

"Of course you may," James assured him. "If the lady——"

"Oh! Silver, have done!" said the young man impatiently.

"So be it," she retorted. "If he's a traitor, in league with your fine tutors——"

"I'm no traitor," James protested crossly, finding her increasingly unsympathetic, "but I cannot see why hiding thus in the woods will further an elopement!"

He thought angrily how much better he would have managed such a business with Oriana, and even more he disliked the flaxen-haired road girl, with her handsome face and her surly manners.

"Mr. Darrell, sir," the young man urged, "we are being followed."

"Followed?"

"Yes. And our resources are limited. Our one desire is to reach Guildford. Once there, I have enough in my purse for a dash to Gretna. Meanwhile, we must hide until dark."

"Your supper's ready," the girl said sulkily.

There was a smell of toasted cheese, and Mr. Lucas commanded, with an authority James found extremely likable:

"Mr. Darrell is our guest!"

"By the bye," he continued a few minutes later, "there's a ditch tavern not a mile from here. We can bide there the night. Are you joining us, Mr. Darrell?"

"I am indeed," James assented, indifferent to an ice-blue stare from Silver.

So they ate toasted cheese among the foxgloves until dusk fell and Mr. Lucas announced that it was "safe" to make for the inn.

"Surely," James suggested, "no one is likely to follow you here to this forest?"

"We cannot be sure," the young man replied. "Since we left Hampshire we have been terrified of pursuit. You see, Silver is so remarkable-looking—— You follow my meaning?"

"I do," James agreed.

They walked along the narrow lane in silence, while James reflected on the attention this ill-assorted pair must have attracted ever since their flight from Hampshire. Had Lucas disguised himself as a vagabond, or dressed Silver as a genteel young female, they might possibly not have been remarked; as it was, they were bound to be stared at and, doubtless, discovered.

He did not think he would greatly mind if they were. The boy seemed to him as full of charm as the girl, despite her good looks, was charmless. Had Lucas been his younger brother, he would have fought with all his might to prevent so mad a marriage. But it was no business of his, and he was silent until they arrived at the inn, which proved to be a dilapidated thatched house encircled with huge and gloomy trees. But the windows glowed in the darkening twilight, and it was pleasant, after so many haystack nights, to think of sleeping in a bed.

They were received without enthusiasm by a surly-looking man and a crooked little rat-faced woman.

Lucas explained that he and James were brothers; the young lady was travelling with them, and they desired accommodation for the night. After a whispered consultation between the pair, they were informed that the two gentlemen could share a room; there was one small bedroom for "the woman." Obviously their appearance was considered suspicious.

They ordered ale and went to sit in the frowzy taproom. Here were one or two countrymen and a wizened little fellow with bent legs, who looked like a jockey. The peasants soon left, and the jockey, after various attempts to attach himself to their party, which were not encouraged by the young men, left too. They heard him going upstairs to bed.

Then Silver leaned forward and fixed James with the glacial blue gaze which had already made him feel hostile.

"You're no Romany," she pronounced. "What are you doing on the road?"

"Wandering to please myself," James answered shortly.

"How do you live?"

"I'm a writer. I have just made some money from a book of tales. This is my holiday."

She said ungraciously:

"It sounds suspicious."

"Why, Silver," Lucas chided, "Mr. Darrell's business is no affair of ours!"

"Perhaps not."

But once again her cold glance raked James, and a few minutes later, when Lucas left the room in search of flint and tinder for his pipe, she leaned forward and said:

"You think he's *dinnelo,* mad, to run away with me, don't you?"

"It's none of my business."

"Ah!" she laughed scornfully, "that doesn't stop you thinking, does it, Mr. Writer? Now, listen, there's something I want to tell you before he comes back—it's this: I love Jeffrey Lucas, and I shall make him a good wife if I marry him. If I don't, God help those who stop me. There's nothing I'll not do to them—*nothing,* do you hear?"

"Why tell me this?" James asked. "It isn't my affair, as I've just said. Keep such threats for Mr. Lucas' guardians—don't waste them on the likes of me!"

"Why do I tell you? I tell you because I'm not sure of you, that's why!"

He began to feel impatient.

"You might as well suspect the little jockey who was here not ten minutes past."

"I suspect everybody!" she declared fiercely.

He was glad when Lucas returned, gladder still when they went upstairs to a whitewashed room with two cotlike beds and one tiny window. Silver said good night briefly and left them.

"A wretched hovel," Lucas declared, taking off his coat and hanging it carefully upon the back of a chair.

"I've known worse," James confessed.

For some time they talked of his life in London, and of his adventures with Jeremy Torch, which greatly amused the young man. Later, when they were both in bed, James asked a question that had been burning upon his lips all the evening.

"You say, Lucas, your estate is in Hampshire?"

"It is. Not that it seems mine at the moment, what with mamas, and guardians, and tutors."

"Did you ever hear of a Sir Francis Castleton?"

"Frank Castleton? Of course. I know him well. Our lands march together. Why?"

James was silent for a moment.

"Why," he said at length, "I knew him slightly when he was a boy, and I hear he was married the other day."

"He married a Miss Camperdene, a connection of his. I visited them just before I ran away. They had only recently returned from their bridal trip."

James said nothing.

Young Lucas yawned.

"She's a lovely creature," he declared, "and reminded me of Byron's line, do you remember—'She walks in beauty, like the night'?"

"I remember."

"My lady is one of your dark, imperious beauties, and fashionably dressed, having come straight from Paris. But I love Silver, Darrell, and wouldn't change her for the Queen."

"They seemed happy?"

"Who? Oh, the Castletons. I think so. I am sure they were, but to tell you the truth, I wasn't paying much attention. You see, I was thinking of Silver."

Lucas fell asleep soon afterwards, but James lay wakeful and rigid. Sleep eluded him. It was not until the blue-black square of the open window turned to palest rose and roosters crowed that he fell into a fitful and uneasy slumber.

CHAPTER XXIII

HE WAS AWAKENED EARLY by his companion's enthusiasm for early rising.

"I shall have breakfast with Silver," Mr. Lucas remarked, "and discuss with her at what time we leave for Guildford. Will you join us?"

James shook his head.

"I had a bad night and shan't move yet."

"In any case"—and the young man smiled his charming smile—"we shan't leave without bidding you farewell. Later, when we're married, you must come and stay with us."

"You're very kind," James said.

When he was alone, he grimly reflected how unlikely he would be to visit one whose "lands marched" with those of Oriana. He did not think, either, that the proud Lady Castleton would be likely to befriend Silver, the road girl.

"The trouble with me," he mused bitterly, "is that I fell in love above my station. However successful I may become, either writing or selling jewels for Don Ignacio, I could never give her the life she wants. Yet she was wild enough, once; she loved adventure before they spoiled her."

After some moments of this profitless meditation he fell fast asleep, and slept for an hour or more.

He was awakened by the sound of wheels, shouting, and the clattering of horses' feet. A hay wagon, he thought confusedly, and then, as his senses became alert once more, he knew that this was no wagon, but a carriage—a carriage vanishing down the rutted lane even as he listened, for the sounds grew gradually fainter. He was uncomfortably aware that something must have happened. It seemed unlikely that any carriage should venture away from the highway to pause, however briefly, at this miserable ditch tavern.

Reluctantly, for he was still sleepy, James got out of bed. He was affectionately disposed towards Mr. Lucas, and it occurred to him that his young friend might possibly have been discovered. He might, indeed, have been apprehended. James disliked Silver, but if Lucas wanted her that was another matter, although he considered the boy a fool to marry her. In any case, he decided that he would investigate the matter.

He did not dress quickly, partly because he had been looking forward to the joy of washing himself all over in hot water. The water, he found, he had to get for himself. The inn appeared to be deserted.

He went downstairs half an hour later to find the little wizened jockey the only occupant of the taproom.

"What about it?" the jockey demanded excitedly.

"I don't know what you mean."

"The young swell! Didn't you know? A carriage arrived with a parson in it, and another chap, a valet, and a footman on the box! They nabbed the young swell, the valet and footman between them, shoved him in the carriage, and off they went at full gallop? The other chap knocked him out! I'll bet a guinea he doesn't come round for twenty minutes!"

James was silent.

Most unfairly, he thought that all this was Oriana's fault. Had he not been talking about her, and thinking about her, too, all night, he would no doubt have been there to protect young Lucas from his guardians. On the other hand, he could not help feeling extremely relieved that his young friend had been prevented, even by such drastic measures, from eloping with the fair-haired road girl. Yet, if they loved each other as he loved Oriana, the thought of their anguish moved him.

Unwillingly he asked:

"Where's the girl?"

"She! She was throwing stones like a wildcat! Made the footman's eye bleed!"

"But where is she?"

"She ran after the carriage, chasing it. Not that she'll catch it. They were a fine pair of horses, and travelling fast."

"Thank you," James said. He went out of the fusty room into the sunshine. His immediate and selfish design was at all costs to avoid Silver as a travelling companion. The mere thought of her recriminations appalled him. He wandered out into the untidy yard, where, in one of the sheds that did duty as stables, he saw a horse's head. James studied the head; it was that of a chestnut, with a white star gleaming from the middle of his forehead. Then, as he saw the race and breeding emphasised in the broad cheek, the flaring nostrils, the shape and delicacy of the head, his interest was aroused, and he walked inside the loose box, to find himself confronting a magnificent horse.

The animal was a showy-looking creature with mighty shoulders and front, a short back, and clean, strong legs. His coat gleamed like burnished gold in the summer sunshine. He had apparently just come in from exercise, and the only ominous sign about him was the manner in which his silken flanks were still heaving.

"Like a pair of bellows," James said to himself.

At this moment he was joined by the jockey.

"Great horse, that," observed the little jockey.

"I shouldn't wonder," James said, "if he wasn't a bit touched in the wind."

"What, him? He's not fit, that's all the trouble."

"I see."

"I'm selling him at the fair in the next town to Guildford—can't remember the name."

"I beg your pardon! I had no idea he was yours."

"Listen," the jockey said, swiftly closing the loose-box door. "You're right, young sir, this horse *is* slightly touched in the wind. That is how I bought him cheap. But I'll tell you, since you seem a knowing gentleman, that I intend to doctor him before the fair. He's not a young horse, mind you; he's ten if he's a day, but with those showy looks and my doctoring I wouldn't be surprised if he fetched fifty guineas."

"Nor would I," James agreed. "How shall you doctor him?"

"Easy enough. I shall give him a handful of shot done up in lard." James shook his head.

"That's not only wicked, but foolish as well, for if you didn't sell him at once, he might fall down dead as soon as he was tried out. There are better ways than that to doctor a whistling horse."

The jockey looked at him in some surprise and scratched his head.

"I *said* you looked knowing, young sir, but that's knowledge you never picked up in college! How, then, would you go about the business?"

"How many days have you," James asked, "before the fair?"

"Only four."

"That will do. Listen, you must pick a few sackfuls of ash leaves from the woods here, and feed him with nothing else for three days. Then, the night before the fair, give him a pint of sweet oil and a little clover. That's the best way I know of doctoring a whistler."

"I never heard of it before," the jockey said doubtfully.

"Well, it's no business of mine."

"I'll *try* it," the other said, after a pause, with the air of one conferring an enormous favour. He added: "Are you going on, now that your friend has been—taken away?"

"I have no plans," James said, "but I wish to avoid the girl who was travelling with him."

"Ah, she's a Tartar, isn't she? Well, I was going to suggest, if you have nothing better to do, that you stay here, and help me gather the ash leaves. Then, if you care to travel to the fair, and I sell the horse well, I'll be pleased"—he glanced rather nervously at James's shabby clothes—"I'll be pleased to pay you three guineas for your pains. That is, if you don't think it a liberty?"

James smiled.

"I'll be pleased to stay." He added, "And I don't think it a liberty!"

"What would you do with a whistler," the jockey asked a few minutes later as they walked out into the forest with a borrowed sack, "if it was winter, and there were no ash leaves?"

James did not hesitate.

"Give him a pound or two of black sugar and three pounds of bran mixed. If I wanted to sell a persistent kicker I'd feed him with a quart of ale with an ounce of snuff in it. I'd never give a horse laudanum; first, because I disapprove of drugging them; second, because opiates turn the whites of their eyes yellow, and any dealer can notice that they've been doctored. If I wanted to sell a horse that shied, I'd put a handful of lard down his throat just before they tried him."

The jockey's surprise was now mingled with considerable admiration.

"May I ask, young sir, where you learned all these tricks?"

"My name's Darrell. I learned them from the gypsies. Look—here's an ash tree!"

CHAPTER XXIV

THE JOCKEY'S NAME was Tom Hinkson. He was, it appeared, no longer a jockey, owing to the dark view taken by authority of certain escapades in which he had figured; he accepted his disgrace philosophically and bore no malice. He had started life as a sweep's boy, and made his companion's flesh creep by tales of his many grisly escapes from being lost in chimneys, beaten by his master, and given "less to eat than in the Foundlings' Home."

Until recently he had been a postillion, in the service of a noble lord of eccentric habits, and he amused James by describing how this employer, who never drove abroad without wearing his nightcap, insisted always that his carriages should be drawn by piebald horses. When he could not obtain any, he bought white ones and made Hinkson paint black patches on their coats. His lordship never travelled without a small monkey which he dressed as a ballerina, because it reminded him of an Italian mistress to whom he had been attached in his youth. When at home, he invariably ordered his bed put in one of his own loose boxes, so that he might be on the spot should a thief steal one of his beloved horses, and it was only after he had shot an inoffensive groom, painted himself piebald, adorned his body in harness, and neighed persistently for the black-smith, that his family succeeded in thrusting him into a lunatic asylum, whereupon Hinkson found himself without a place.

On his way to look for work, he bought the good-looking chestnut for a small sum and decided to sell him at the fair.

The ash leaves in two days produced such an improvement in the animal's condition that Hinkson declared James to be a miracle worker.

"In fact," he said, "if you care to stay with me, and set up a partnership, we might make a good business out of horse dealing."

James shook his head.

"I'm sorry. I've got other plans. I'm only on a holiday."

They were on their way to the fair, taking turns to ride the chest-nut. The last night they stayed at another humble tavern, and to James's delight there was no sign of Silver on the road. Every day the country grew richer and more verdant: the corn was ripening; the pasture lands were sweet with clover.

When they arrived at the market town where the fair was to be held their first precaution was to stable the chestnut. They then went forth to inspect the ground, which so early in the morning was almost deserted, except for the first arrivals, who were erecting their booths and tents.

Hinkson fell into conversation with some horsy-looking men, while James, after listening for a while to the usual boasts and ex-travagant claims, returned to the inn and ordered breakfast. The day was going to be a hot one; already the sun blazed through the windows, whipping the scarlet of the boxed geraniums to fire. He ate bacon and eggs alone in the parlour, wondering how much longer he would stay on the tober. He felt so much better after a fortnight's country air that the thought of returning to London was still distasteful, but, on the other hand, he did not quite see how he would ever, if he continued his wanderings, obtain any employment from Don Ignacio, and he was determined to travel abroad.

He thought that he would always be diverted by the people he had met on the English road, but already he was stretching his wings, longing to venture further. The Punch-man, Silver, Jeffrey Lucas, and the jockey, Hinkson, all had served their turn, as had a number of others—drovers, hostlers, postillions, and pedlars. One day, years later, although he did not know it, their prototypes would serve him once again—when he sat down to write their story. But the road then would have wound away around many turnings, and he would have passed many more milestones before evoking from the past the shades of that half-forgotten summer.

Later that morning he went out once again to the fairground.

Now everything was changed. The field was already crowded and ablare with the din of music and shouting. The bright stalls were pitched and thriving; dobbin horses revolved around a painted swan; people were hurling balls at coconuts; the medicine man yelled on his platform; in the boxing tent half-naked boys were fighting; and everywhere showmen bawled outside their booths. There was a stall for gingerbread men and another for sugar candy; there were giants, and dwarfs, and a fat lady, and a fortuneteller in a velvet dress trimmed with jet sequins. Everywhere there was a concentrated roar of sound, of hurdy-gurdies, accordions, fiddles, shouting, trampling feet, the thunder of hoofs, dogs barking, babies wailing, and horses neighing.

There was a smell, too, of freshly trodden grass, sweat, wine, beer, leather, coconut milk, toasted cheese, oranges, gunpowder, and rabbit stew from the caravans.

The red, honest faces of the country people were easily distinguishable from the wary eyes and traplike mouths of those who worked the tober; the dark, sidelong glance of an occasional gypsy was, as usual, apart from either, like no other glance in the world.

Here, unobtrusively, as on every fairground in the world, the gypsies were plying their trade. James, who knew none of them, watched the crowds for some time, absorbed. They were easy to discover, the Romany people. The girl with the yellow scarf, taking money on the swings, and the rogue who worked the pea-and-thimble trick. That black-eyed fiddler outside the dancing tent and the elderly fourtuneteller in her jet-trimmed dress. That tigerish, brown-skinned lightweight from the boxing booth; the little ragged boy fetching water for the horses, and the group of swarthy men in riding boots, clutching hunting crops, who stood in the lower meadow, where the horses were being tried. A dark, quiet group were these, and sinister in their very silence; James was astonished not to find Sylvester in their company.

For a time he watched them, studying their secretive faces. Once or twice, as a horse cantered past, he caught the flick of a swiftly dropped eyelid. That was their signal; otherwise they were impassive as stone images, save when a young black colt was shown, and then one of them sprang, without a word, straight into the saddle.

How he rode, that unknown gypsy! He only cantered round the meadow, an insignificant, sallow little fellow, with stirrups too long for him, and a green young colt between his knees, but the sculptured beauty of those two, the horse and the man, achieved for a few moments such co-ordinated loveliness of movement that a crowd stopped to watch, and it was as though a centaur passed through some glade of long ago, so that for one brief moment time wheeled back, and there was nothing strange in horse and man being one.

After three turns round the meadow, the gypsy slipped from the saddle and said briefly to his friends: *"Kek kushti* [No good]!" and sauntered away towards the beer tent.

He would never see the colt again.

That, James mused, was the way of the gypsies, and he wondered why. Because they occasionally played sentimental music, people were mistaken enough to think that they themselves were sentimental. They were, of course, determined to wrest their living from the gajo they so much despised; if the gajo desired sentiment from fiddler or fortuneteller he should have it; to that, with a shrug, the gypsy agreed, although his tongue was in his cheek, and all he cared about was the silver that would inevitably cross his palm.

That afternoon the showy chestnut was sold for fifty guineas. He made a brave show, never whistling once, and, had he been a younger horse, Hinkson would doubtless have sold him for double t⁻e price. As it was, his joy knew no bounds, and he invited to supper that night not only James, but two other men encountered on the tober. One described himself as a postillion, the other was a seafaring man with a wooden leg.

When it was time to eat, Hinkson scornfully refused to patronise the tavern where they were staying and directed his guests towards the principal coaching inn of the town.

Dusk was falling, and with twilight the fairground noise increased in violence. There was no longer any rustic charm about the picture, as there had been earlier in the day, when the meadows were freshly green and elm trees framed the gaily painted swings. There were no more glossy colts to canter proudly in the sunshine, and the innocent enjoyment of the day would degenerate, as night fell, into brutal horseplay, for there were crowds outside the beer tent, and a number of people were already drunk.

In silence the four men walked away towards the coaching inn.

CHAPTER XXV

THE LANDLORD of this superior establishment betrayed no particular willingness to serve such rough-looking customers, and it was only after James had assumed his most lordly manner that they were given a table.

Hinkson immediately demonstrated his familiarity with the ways of noblemen by ordering champagne.

"Pink," he added firmly.

"What do you mean—pink?" the landlord demanded.

"What do I mean?" the aggrieved host replied. "I mean pink champagne, of course. What do you think I mean? That is, of course, if this establishment of yours can take a gentleman's order."

So for the second time in his life James found himself drinking rose-coloured champagne, and his thoughts not unnaturally turned towards Don Ignacio and the problem of his own future.

"Come, Darrell"—Hinkson poked him in the ribs—"this is a celebration—not a funeral!" And, turning to his companions, "This young swell, who's just out of college, is the deepest one with horses I ever met! Better than Whispering Shamus! *You* remember Whispering Shamus, don't you?" to the postillion.

Listening to their conversation, which naturally turned upon the road, James felt restless and bored, and found himself thinking:

"I must be damned ungrateful not to be enjoying myself, or is it that I'm shabby enough to feel superior to these men and slightly ashamed of being seen with them in a respectable inn? If so, what sort of prig am I, since I myself chose the tober and chose to associate with them?"

But the feeling of restlessness increased, and he thought that perhaps he needed a woman. In that case, he had only to return to the fairground after supper. There were plenty of girls there, and he knew that he could take his pick. Yet the mere thought of the effort such a quest would entail increased his sensation of discontent, of loneliness perhaps, and even as he roared with laughter at one of the postillion's ribald stories, he saw himself at the same time, quite objectively, as a failure, as a gentleman tramp who roamed the countryside thinking, in the ignorance of his heart, that one day people would condescend to read the tale of his vagabond adventures.

It was dark now, and outside the inn he heard vaguely the rattle and clash of a fast carriage that stopped outside the door.

The sailor was talking, telling tales of haunted slave ships; of gold buried on coral islands in the bad old days; of seas James imagined as hyacinth-blue, curdled with creamy foam; of steamy jungles, where bright birds called; and of coloured women, in faraway ports the names of which were exotic as the Negro music he described with so much awe.

"Voodoo, they call it," the sailor declared, "and they make spells with it. They beat their bloody drums till you think you're in bedlam. So you are, too, if you listen too long. Nobody believes you here; nobody would. But when you're out there in the islands you know it's true all right. The heat blisters you, everything smells of flowers and mud, and these same bloody drums never stop. And when you know they're making voodoo, it gets to scare you in the end. It's said they can call people to each other——"

As though someone had picked up his eyelids, James looked across the room to see Oriana. He was tipsy enough to feel only a violent rage. He had tried to escape, he *had* escaped, and it was no good. Fate would not allow him even so feeble a victory.

She came sailing into the room preceded by the landlord, who guided her deferentially towards a table by the window. She was fashionably dressed in dark bottle-green, and a long plume curled from underneath her black hat. He thought there was a glitter of jewels at her throat, but he could not be sure. He could see clearly only that which was familiar about her—the lithe grace of her body, a flick of candlelight that caught the tip of her nose, making it seem particularly mocking, and her skin, pale as white hyacinths in the darkness of the ill-lit room. In a moment she would speak, and he would hear once more the warmth of her voice, that would remind him only that he was forever separated from her, yet still unable to escape her spell.

"Spells?" the sailor continued, as though nothing had happened since he first began to talk. "Why, there's nothing they can't do, these niggers with their voodoo. Not only spells calling people to each other, but ill-wishing too. Yes, you may laugh, but there's witches out there that can hold men against their will."

No. It was no good. He had tramped the roads to get away from her, and yet the moment he saw her again she was more vivid than ever before. He perceived, from the corner of his eye, that she was followed by a quiet-looking female who was obviously her maid; they sat together, and Oriana ordered supper.

He should have known better. The market town was on the highway between Hampshire and London; this coaching inn was the obvious place for persons of quality to lie the night.

It seemed to him that, from all England, he had been deliberately drawn onto this road; it was as though she had beckoned and he had followed, despite himself. It was as though their paths were always meant to cross. He cursed her then to himself and called her a bitch.

The sailor continued:

"They say around the islands that once a man loves a witch—a *sorcière,* they call her—he can never get free from her."

"We burnt witches once," the postillion remarked, burying his nose in his glass.

"We're wiser now," Hinkson shrugged.

"I believe in witches," the sailor asserted. He added darkly: "I've cause too!"

Once more James looked across the room, and this time her eyes met his. He stared at her blankly, without the slightest sign of recognition.

At first she seemed inclined to smile, then, meeting his cold stare, she shrugged her shoulders, lifting one ironical eyebrow, and returned to her supper. She moved slightly, so that she turned her back, that straight, elegant back of hers, upon the party. Oriana's back was expressive. To James, it expressed disdain.

Meanwhile, the others clamoured to return to the fairground.

They were in uproarious mood, and all were determined to seek women. They walked out of the room together, and James never once glanced in her direction, nor she in his.

Outside, on the pavement, he said good-bye to Hinkson. He had no possessions to worry about: all his worldly goods were bundled in a handkerchief.

"But you're not leaving me!" Hinkson protested tipsily.

"Yes, I am. I'm very sorry, but I've just remembered some urgent business."

This was lame enough, and he knew it, but fortunately his companions were too drunk to consider it anything but a highly reasonable excuse, and so they left him, slapping his back and wringing his hand warmly. Once more Hinkson told him that he was a better horse coper than Whispering Shamus.

He went back to the inn and bespoke a room. At first the landlord seemed reluctant to accommodate him, but when he perceived that the others had departed, he admitted to a small bedroom on the second floor.

"Now would you mind signing your name in my register?"

James obeyed, noting as he did so that Lady Castleton's room was number 18.

He glanced into the dining parlour and saw that she had gone upstairs, whereupon he returned to the landlord.

"Will you please tell someone to send me up hot water for a bath?"

"A bath now?" the landlord echoed stupidly.

"Yes. I have been on a walking holiday and am tired of cold water."

"Very good, sir."

He climbed upstairs to his bedroom, noticing, as he did so, that there was a ribbon of light beneath the door of number 18.

CHAPTER XXVI

HE HAD, naturally, only the one shabby suit, but he carried a change of linen, and when he had bathed, shaved, and combed his hair, he hoped that he did not look too much of a vagrant.

He had no idea of what he was going to say to her. He did not really stop to think. All he knew was that he had to see her, even if it meant breaking down her door. Then, perhaps, he would kill her. When he thought of this dispassionately afterwards, he was alarmed, but at the time he felt such hatred in his heart that he did not care. He thought of her as a bitch, a witch, a voodoo sorcière, and he thought that she would be better dead. He thought that he would be the cleaner for killing her.

He slipped downstairs and across the passage. He noticed there was still a thread of light beneath her door.

He opened it softly, without knocking, and walked into the room.

He remembered it vaguely afterwards. The room was spacious and oak panelled, and her bed was hung with crimson draperies. The latticed windows were open, and the curtains parted, so that the clover-scented night flowed in and made her candles tremble in the breeze. She was in bed, reading. When she saw him, she put down her book and looked at him steadily, saying nothing.

He shut the door.

She wore a pale garment that left her ivory shoulders bare. She returned his gaze without modesty, without coquetry. She looked him directly in the face, very much as one man would look at another. There was nothing feminine in her gaze, which was hard and straight, so that her eyes were more black than brown.

He came straight towards the bed.

She saw someone she had known nearly all her life—a tall young man whose face was burnt by the sun, whose grey eyes blazed pale in a frame of so much darkness. He was stern, his eyes were unsmiling, but that did not surprise her. His shabby clothes meant nothing to her, and secretly she was indifferent to the low company he had kept so short a time before down in the parlour.

She was happy, in a perverse way, to see him in her room. Had he stayed away, she would have known that his strength was the greater. Now she only knew, despite the astonishment of seeing him in the inn, that he was hers, that he had come straight to her. Nor would she ever have believed that he had found her only by accident. She thought that he had followed her deliberately, unable any longer to live without her. She knew how the gypsies whistled stallions out of fields. "Casting the glamour," they called it.

She held out her arms.

Without a word he got into bed beside her. And then they made love with a fury, a violence, that left him exhausted. All the gaiety of the attachment they had known in childhood vanished swiftly, as though it had never existed. What was between them became utterly physical, entirely removed from the romanticism of their youthful love. He knew her then, at last, for what she was—a sensual woman who had always wanted him. And, as he embraced her, he remembered the sailor's talk of witch women, of sorcières, from whom no man could escape.

Yet he could not stop loving her. She had been in his life for so many years, and now, when he lay there, indulging her wanton ways, he knew that she was strange, always had been, even from that very first day, when she had come to tea with the Darrell children, wearing her hood of holly red.

When the tempest of their love-making was at last over, he said to her: "Will this happen again?"

"I don't know." she answered, and turned away her face. Dawn crept through the windows, and the dark room was soon rose-lit. Only her cheeks, James thought, were pale as white moths.

"What do you mean, you don't know?"

"I want you to go."

"Do you mean tonight will never be repeated?"

"How can I say what will happen? I tell you I don't know."

"I see," he said.

He looked at her once more and felt suddenly ashamed.

He felt ashamed of himself, and of his manhood, for he knew then that he had never possessed her—she had possessed him all through the night. He knew, too, that he had failed, loving her, despite the pleasure she had had from him. Her masterful mind had controlled their bodies, and she had taken him to please herself, as though she had been the male.

He said:

"This is good-bye."

"Good-bye, James."

He went out of the room.

Downstairs he found a sleepy porter and paid for the room he had not used.

He walked away then, not caring where he went, or what he did. He was conscious of a paralysing exhaustion. He walked for about a mile, leaving the town behind him, and when at last he saw a haystack behind a hedge, he climbed the gate, and flopped, exhausted, into the hay. He curled himself into a warm nest, noticing only that it was brilliant daylight and that skylarks pierced the air with their song. He was so tired that his mind reeled.

He remembered, as though in a daze, that Oriana had been his mistress—or his lover—for a night, and that she had shamed everything virile about him by the passion with which she had possessed him, the insistence which had made her take him, sweeping his senses, so that she would remain in his mind as something a little sinister since her rich marriage, but something that, apart from his need of her, would forever make other women seem pale shades.

She was a she-devil, but never, now, would he be able to free himself from her spell. He thought of the sailor's talk—of voodoos, and witches, and sorcières. She was all three; she had emanated what the sailor described as the smell of flowers and mud; she was perverse, and he knew that to escape her he must travel very far. Then, as he fell asleep, her perverseness became entangled with the sailor's talk, so that she assumed the form of a witch woman, pale and dark, waiting for him against the bright tapestry of the jungle, holding out her arms towards him.

He fell asleep, and was only awakened by the sound of a sharp voice addressing him.

The voice said:

"I've found you at last!"

He opened his eyes, to see Silver, the road girl, standing over him in a menacing fashion.

He struggled vainly, in an effort to clear his brain. The girl's face, framed in straw-coloured hair, was white with rage, and her blue eyes were harder than flint stones. She still wore the faded military coat and striped petticoat. One hand was concealed behind her back.

"What do you want?" he asked, in no very gracious tone. The sun was high, and he thought that the morning must be nearly over. He felt at a disadvantage, lying there half buried in the hay, with this strange, angry girl towering over him.

"I want to tell you what I think of you!"

"I don't know what you mean."

"You'll know soon enough. So you were a writer, were you, Mister Spy? A fine sort of writer, you prying bastard!"

"Get away from here!"

"Do you think I didn't know all the time you were paid to follow Jeffrey? Do you think I didn't know you'd tell them where he was? Well, they took him from me, thanks to you, and now you'll pay for it!"

"You're mad!" James declared, preparing to get up. "I had no more to do with it than you."

"Don't move!" she screamed, and then he saw that a knife flashed in her right hand. "You stay there, or I'll use this!"

"Don't be a melodramatic fool!"

"A fool, am I? We'll see about that! And don't think I don't know how to use this *churi*, because I do! I worked the fairground with a knife-*engro*, and I tell you you'll pay for this, you stool pigeon! You'll——"

By this time James, having decided that the girl was mad, scrambled to his feet with the intention of snatching the knife away from her.

But she was too quick. With one flick of her trained wrist she flung the blâde straight at his breast. Instinctively he wheeled sideways, probably saving his life, but a stab of violent pain rushed through his left arm, and he felt his blood flow warm and sticky onto his right hand.

His fury was enough to shake even her iron nerve; as he stumbled towards her, she turned and fled through the gateway. He heard her running away down the road.

He pulled out his handkerchief and tried to tie it around his arm. But the blood continued to flow, and he began to feel a little sick. He walked round the haystack, looking for a stream in which to bathe the wound.

He found himself in a huge field, patched with heather, looking like common land. A rutty track led towards a dense clump of trees, and there he divined that there would be water.

If he could only walk so far! His clothes were daubed with blood by now, and his head felt oddly light. It seemed to him that he could hear the sound of voices from behind the trees, and he even thought that somewhere a child was crying. The feel of his own blood oozing from the wound turned him faint, and suddenly he fell onto his knees. The sky reeled round his head, and there was a singing noise in his ears. Desperately, determined to find the stream, he struggled to his feet.

Then the ground rose up to hit him, and he lost consciousness.

CHAPTER XXVII

WHEN HE OPENED HIS EYES he could remember nothing of what had happened. He felt languid and tired, and his head ached. He saw a patch of blue sky, and knew that he lay flat; there was a low roof over his head, but none of this meant anything to his feverish mind. He closed his eyes again and fell asleep.

When next he woke, he saw a strange-looking head, that was in reality bent over his, but which appeared, grotesquely, to be suspended in the air. Singular-looking as was this head, it seemed vaguely familiar; for a moment he thought that he was back with Jeremy Torch, watching a performance of his puppets.

The head was an old woman's; her dishevelled grey locks bristled wildly, like the spines of a resolute porcupine; the face was hirsute, leather-brown, and seamed with the network of a hundred wrinkles. But the eyes, which were fixed upon his, were still large and black and lustrous. There were gold drops in the old crone's ears, and a straw hood was perched upon the grey quills.

James attempted to smile, and, being still somewhat confused in his mind, especially as regards witches, murmured:

"Mrs. Hoskin . . . ?"

"He'll do," said a decided voice; "he'll be *misto* now."

He knew then that he had fallen into the hands of the gypsies. He was in the tent of his old friend, Hagar Brazil.

When next he woke he was ravenously hungry and eager to talk. Hagar fed him with bread and milk, and presently Darklis came peeping round the tent. She had grown very pretty, he thought; her white teeth flashed in the dusky oval of her face, and she wore her hair, glossy as blackberries in the sun, braided in a great plait across her head.

"Where's Sylvester?" James wanted to know.

"Over at the *gav*, the nearest town, on a little affair about a horse. But he'll be back by sundown. You shall see him then." She knelt down, leaning forward, and he saw that she wore a pink bodice, with a yellow *diklo*, or scarf, about her throat. "Jamie," she said, "we've got a little 'un, me and Sylvester. What do you think of us having a *chavé*, eh? A little girl, she is, six months, and we called her Rosaina."

"I'm glad," he said.

"Go away, child," old Hagar grumbled, "and tend to the chavé 'stead of hampering me *rokkering* your head off about it. His arm needs a new bandage."

Darklis vanished, and James asked:

"How did you come to find me? I fainted, didn't I?"

Old Hagar was skilfully dressing his wound, and he winced.

"Wasn't you lookin' for us?"

"No. I didn't know you were here. How should I?"

"You mean you didn't know we was campin' by the Nile?"

He thought he must still be lightheaded.

"The Nile?"

"We calls this field Little Egypt, and the stream that runs through it we calls the Nile."

"I've heard of it," he recollected.

"We couldn't get to the fair yesterday, owin' to one of the mares foalin' before her time. So we bided here in Little Egypt."

The wound, she told him, was fortunately a clean one, and had he not lost so much blood, he would have been in no serious straits.

"But," she said solemnly, dropping the "broken tongue" for pure Romany, "but whoever knifed you, Jamie, was aiming not at your arm, but at your heart."

"It was a madwoman," he answered, colouring, for the thought of being knifed by a girl was galling to his pride.

Later that afternoon Sylvester's dark, grinning face appeared in the tent.

"Why, brother, whatever was you adoing with that blackhearted little *grasni*, that trashy little mumping tramp of a gajo tinker's *brat?*"

James felt even more indignant at this assumption of any intimacy with Silver than at the recollection of being knifed by her; in a few well-chosen words he described his adventure with Jeffrey Lucas and his intense dislike of the fair-haired girl.

"The poor young *rye*," was Sylvester's comment on Lucas, and then, "Lucky young rye, too, since he ain't got to marry her after all!"

James slept well that night in the tent; he was able the next morning to walk about with his arm in a sling, and to admire Darklis' baby, a brown imp with hair like black silk. The Brazils intended to stay on for three or four days in Little Egypt, by which time their mare would be able to travel, and James agreed to stay with them until they left, when he himself decided to go to London.

"If you could only get that *gajé* woman out o' your head," Sylvester said, "you could marry Darklis' young sister, Mirella, and bide with us for good."

"No, Sylvester, thank you all the same, and Mirella is charming, but I've decided to leave England."

Once again, during the three days of his convalescence, he was forced to watch the happiness of Sylvester and Darklis, and once again moodily to contrast Sylvester's lot with his. The gypsy boy and girl loved each other with the frank, warmhearted naturalness of young animals; they were not demonstrative in public, but they liked to be near each other, and he could not help noticing how ready they were to go together at night into their gaily-painted caravan, the brasswork of which was so dutifully polished by Sylvester. The baby, Rosaina, they worshipped, and both hoped for many more children.

"A son next time," Darklis promised, and James saw Sylvester put his hand for a moment on her knee.

Sometimes wild thoughts came to him during those three days as he lay wakeful in his tent, staring at the sky; why not finish forever with civilisation and stay with the gypsies, as they had suggested? Why not forget these foolish dreams of becoming a writer and learn instead how to shoe horses and solder kettles? Would he not in the end be happier if he took one of these dark-skinned young girls as a wife, perhaps forever to forget, if he were fortunate, the torment of Oriana?

Naturally these fantasies in the end came to nothing, for the desire to write was still dominant, despite his many rebuffs. And there were other considerations—he knew that he could not for very long be happy without books to read, clean linen whenever he wanted it, plenty of hot water, and friends who could read and write.

The day before he left the camp he came upon old Hagar squatting outside her tent, staring into the globe of glass she prized above all her possessions.

"*Dukkering?*" he asked, well knowing her to be the most adroit fortuneteller of the tribe.

"Yes, I'm jest looking in the crystal, my Jamie."

"Do you see anything for me, Aunt Hagar?"

"Perhaps."

"Tell me," he urged.

"You'll not like it, my Jamie."

"It doesn't matter. When we first met, and I was a child, you thought me a wizard. Now I know that you're a witch! Please tell me what you see!"

Once more she began to speak what she called the old, dark language—the purest form of Romany.

She said:

"What you want, my dear, you must wait for, but it will come, all the same. It's just that you have to have more patience than most, and I doubt if you've got it. Listen, Jamie—something queer will happen to you when you sail across the seas. Something to do with bright beads, and Romany people, and there's blood spilt under the sun."

Her voice became deeper and hoarser; suddenly she raised her dark, piercing eyes and looked straight at him.

"You stay here," she urged.

"What do you mean—something queer is going to happen to me?"

"I don't know," she told him; "and that, my dear, is God's truth, but you stay here! Yes, even although that woman of yours haunts you worse than any ghost, as I see she does!"

When she spoke of Oriana, her grey locks bristled and her eyes flashed forth fire and brimstone. She seemed desperately in earnest; her aged body trembled, as did her clawlike hands; despite himself he was impressed by her talent as an actress.

"I'm sorry," he said, "but I shall still go abroad."

"Yes, headstrong. Well, you always were. But don't you forget, my Jamie, where the sun is, there's blood. And there are queer things I can't make out—a mist clouds the crystal just when I want to see deepest."

He laughed, sprawling beside her on the grass.

"One day," he told her, "I'll come back and prove you wrong!"

"Not me, my Jamie. We'll never meet again." And then, in broken Anglo-Romany, "You don't believe I'm dukkering proper, do you, love?"

He hesitated. The day was glorious; marigolds varnished the meadow where the camp was pitched; the stream they called the Nile babbled happily as the horses watered there, knee-deep, and dragonflies darted among the willow trees. Everything was peaceful in Little Egypt, and there was no reason for him to feel cold, for one moment, as though the sun had gone down.

She repeated, as he said nothing:

"You don't think I'm dukkering proper, do you?"

"As a matter of fact, I do," James assented unwillingly.

The next day, amid many protestations of affection, he left the gypsies. His arm was nearly healed.

He had spent surprisingly little money during his time on the tober. He walked to Guildford and took the coach to London.

PART V

The Diamond Necklace

CHAPTER XXVIII

AND SO HE FOUND HIMSELF, after an interval of three weeks, back in the same little room near Russell Square. Everything seemed the same, but he himself, and his circumstances that were so much changed. He no longer slaved for Sir Matthew Kent-Taylor. He had, in fact, no employment of any kind, and only about ten guineas left in the world. That in itself was alarming.

But just as alarming was his own state of mind. For one night he had been Oriana's lover, and now, although he imagined that he loved her less, he only knew that he wanted her more. Not for the first time he wondered of what strange stuff Castleton was made, so quickly to have changed an impetuous, warmhearted girl into the perverse and curious creature who had crossed his path on the night that he would never forget, no matter how long he lived.

Meanwhile, two idle days in London began to detract from the benefit of his holiday, and he was overjoyed, on the third day, to receive a note from the Spaniard, requesting his company that night at dinner. Superstitious, where Don Ignacio was concerned, he had been certain from the first that the diamond merchant would not forget him. In an odd way he had always been convinced that the Spaniard was somehow involved in his own destiny.

So he presented himself at Berkeley Square, where he was informed that he looked in better health; which compliment he was able in all sincerity to return.

The dinner that night was even better than on the occasion of his first visit. Truffles, breasts of guinea fowl, pineapple ice, huge Muscat grapes, and plenty of the rose-coloured champagne that for a moment made him sigh as he thought of the jockey's celebration and the night that had followed it.

During dinner he amused Don Ignacio vastly by an account of his adventures on the road; the Spaniard being particularly diverted by the thought of his own valiant defender suffering defeat at the hands of a girl.

"An Amazon she must be, that young woman!" he commented sardonically, but his voice showed genuine affection when he asked whether the knife wound was entirely healed.

That wound, James assured him, not without grimness, no longer troubled him, thanks to the care of the gypsies.

Afterwards, as they sat over coffee and brandy in the Spaniard's fantastic room, the guest plucked up his courage and began:

"When I saw you last, Don Ignacio, I think I mentioned that I considered myself engaged to be married?"

"I believe you referred to something of the kind," Don Ignacio agreed.

"Well, I want you to know I am no longer engaged."

Don Ignacio poured out some more coffee.

"No?"

"No. The—the lady in question decided my future was without hope. Before I had time to tell her of my meeting with you, I received a letter from her in which—well, in fact—she has married someone else."

"And I suppose," the Spaniard suggested, showing an understanding for which James could have blessed him, "I suppose that, in consequence of this lady's decision, you are more anxious than ever to leave the country?"

"I am, sir," James agreed firmly.

With a brief glance at the young, unhappy, and defeated face, Don Ignacio remarked:

"In any case, my friend, I have need of you. I was about to ask you if you would execute a commission for me in Seville?"

"Indeed I will!"

"Wait a moment! This commission is of a private nature—I will explain it later. But if you decide to undertake it I will then send you on to my business in Madrid, where a post is awaiting you. Since you have never been in Spain, and know nothing of the currency, I would greatly prefer not to discuss with you the question of your salary. I will merely give you my word that it should suffice you to live on comfortably, and that, as you improve, as I have no doubt you will, the salary will improve at the same time. I have given directions to this effect, and I sincerely believe that you will never have anything with which to reproach me."

James began warmly to thank his friend, but was cut short, for once, with scant courtesy.

"Regarding this private errand, Don Jaime, I would like first of all to explain that, for business reasons, I cannot in the near future travel very far myself either from London or Amsterdam."

James murmured words to the effect that he quite understood.

The Spaniard smiled.

"You don't understand yet, but you will, in a minute. I don't think I mentioned to you that I am a widower?"

"No, Don Ignacio."

"I am a widower with a daughter who is seventeen years of age. Since my wife's death, my daughter, Adriana, has been brought up by her aunts in Seville. It was better so; I travel too much, and my life is too unsettled, to involve in it a young daughter. But I have naturally visited her whenever it was possible, and it is no exaggeration to say that we are devoted to one another."

"Yes sir," said James, as the Spaniard paused. "I quite understand what you mean."

"Not at all," insisted Don Ignacio irritably; "as yet you understand nothing! Listen! A year ago my daughter became engaged to a Sevillano, to a gentleman of whom I approve entirely. Now the relatives of this young man are anxious for the marriage, and, with my consent, it is to take place in October. We are now at the beginning of July, are we not?"

"We are, Don Ignacio."

"Exactly! Well, there is no prospect of my being able to visit Spain for at least a year, therefore my daughter's marriage will have to take place without me. Naturally, Don Jaime, I wish to give her a fitting wedding present."

Yes, James now understood perfectly.

"If you undertake my commission, Don Jaime, you will sail direct to Cadiz, from where you will proceed to Seville, no very great distance. Your expenses will naturally be met, and once you have handed over the gift, and a letter to my daughter, you will be free to leave for Madrid as soon as you please."

"I will be delighted to act for you in the matter," James assured him.

"Wait a minute, my friend."

Don Ignacio got up, went over to a gold-encrusted Chinese cabinet, and unlocked its door. From a secret drawer he extracted a flat, shabby leather case, with which he returned to the table.

"Before you definitely accept my offer, Don Jaime, I would like you to know that this is the gift I am sending to my daughter."

He opened the case, and James gave a cry of admiration as he gazed upon a necklace of glittering gems. He knew nothing about diamonds, but even he could see that these brilliant stones were something out of the common. He said, his eyes dazzled by their blaze:

"I see that this will be a great responsibility, Don Ignacio."

"It will indeed," the Spaniard answered grimly. "I must explain to you that these stones are unique. Some of them are supposed to have been a part of the famous necklace that ruined Marie Antoinette—all of them are famous. And that, my dear Don Jaime, is precisely why I do not wish to send them over by one of my own couriers, or by anyone in my employment—anyone remotely connected with me. Do you understand?"

"I understand," James answered slowly. "The temptation such a necklace must be to robbers all the world over . . ."

"Exactly! But you, my friend, are so far in no way connected with my business. You are, as I have reason to know, a man of high courage. You are honest, as I knew first when you returned my valuable dagger. In fact, Don Jaime, I can think of no one more suitable for the purpose I have in mind, but, at the same time, I must warn you that the bearer of this necklace might easily find his life in danger should unscrupulous persons discover his errand. What do you say?"

"Of course I say yes," James answered promptly. "And I'm

honoured, Don Ignacio, that you should trust me in so secret a matter!"

"Well spoken!" the Spaniard returned delightedly, and then swiftly, in a low voice, he began to explain to James the precautions necessary for his journey. He was to travel as a gentleman of means, one desirous of visiting Spain with a view to writing about the country. He was to wear the diamonds, night and day, secured by a strap about his waist. He was never, until the necklace was delivered, to mention Don Ignacio's name, or the name of the Señorita de Zozaya, his daughter. When the necklace had been safely delivered, and not before, he was to write informing Don Ignacio.

Despite the responsibility, even the risk, of the enterprise, it appealed so strongly to everything adventurous in James's nature that his spirits rose wildly, and he was happier, then, than he had been for a long time.

"Do not forget," the Spaniard warned him, as he departed to await further instructions as to the date of his sailing, "do not forget, Don Jaime, what I told you once before—my country is savage and uncivilised. Coaches are to be found only on the roads between big cities, and Andalusia, in particular, is much as it was a hundred years ago. It is more than probable that you will have to ride from Cadiz to Seville. You will, of course, take a guide with you."

"I would prefer to ride," James answered, his eyes sparkling.

"In that case you will probably have a more comfortable journey should you decide to ride part of the way from Seville to Madrid, after you have delivered the necklace. For the coaches in my country"—here Don Ignacio shuddered slightly and closed his eyes—"are barbarous, my friend! Barbarous!"

James went home that night with instructions to wait in readiness until he heard from Don Ignacio. He was the richer for twenty guineas, which sum the Spaniard insisted upon presenting him "to purchase a wardrobe for the journey."

He felt pleasurably excited, and although he could not help thinking more than once how splendid the diamond necklace would have looked upon Oriana's white throat, he nevertheless slept soundly, without once dreaming of her.

CHAPTER XXIX

HE WAS IN PLYMOUTH, waiting for the *Southern Star* to sail. He did not think from what Captain Judd told him that the shipping of the cargo would delay them for more than another two days, and meanwhile he was content enough to stay at the most comfortable tavern and to spend his days wandering about the town. Never, he thought, had he seen so many masts in all his life before: they formed a veritable forest beside which those of the Thames dock-yard were, in comparison, negligible.

He liked the old-fashioned, bustling town, so noisy with the traffic of the sea. The weather was wild for the time of year, and the wind had a tang of spume and seaweed. So he spent four days pleasantly enough becoming accustomed to the feel of the heavy little leather pouch he wore strapped round his waist next to his skin. At this, the outset of his journey, the thought of the diamonds weighed lightly upon his mind, and he was inclined to consider Don Ignacio's fears as due to the exaggeration of a nervous temperament. The thought of bandits and robbers seemed too remote from this busy Devon town to exist anywhere but in the imagination of his friend.

On the day before he was due to sail he wrote to Emily and to his mother, explaining that he had obtained a post in Madrid, and that he would probably remain abroad for several months. He said that as soon as he knew his address, he would write again. Then, carefully replacing in his wallet Don Ignacio's sealed letter to his daughter, he wandered over to the window and beheld a crowd mustering down by the quay.

"What is that?" he enquired of the waiter who brought him a glass of port.

"Convicts, sir."

"What do you mean?"

"Prisoners from every jail for transportation to Botany Bay. There's a fleet of ships sailing as soon as the wind changes. Not the first lot we've had here, sir, and each time we hope it will be the last."

When he had finished his port James strolled out towards the quay, curious to see something of which he had often heard. A cousin of Sylvester's had been transported for horse-stealing some years ago, and nobody had ever heard of him again.

James looked distinguished as he sauntered down towards the crowds of people. Don Ignacio had insisted on his wardrobe being that of the gentleman of means he was supposed to impersonate, and he wore a plum-coloured coat with silver buttons, a shirt of finest lawn, and a silver-brocade waistcoat. His grey trousers fitted his calves sheathlike and were strapped beneath his varnished shoes. These new clothes set off his great height and his broad shoulders; sycophantically, the throngs parted to let him pass, and he found himself staring lordlike upon a herd of wretches so miserable that his cheeks paled, and he would have given much never to have left the inn.

The convicts, male and female, were chained together, and apparently lined up to await the arrival of boats to take them on board the transportation ships. The majority were the sweepings of Newgate and the hulks; only Hogarth, perhaps, could have immortalized so many brutal or vacant faces, so much ragged, tattered filth, so many starving skeleton frames. Some of the men, with hard mouths and evil faces greenish with prison pallor, were unmistakably criminal, as were their gin-sodden women, half naked, dishevelled, and verminous, some of them clutching tipsy babies that clung to their pendulous breasts. But bad as these were, and they kept up a ceaseless din of vilely obscene back slang, what sickened James was the sight, here and there, of a youthful or bewildered and *honest* face: a ploughboy, with ruddy cheeks and dazed eyes; a decent little clerkly man in a snuff-coloured coat; a white-faced young girl, who might have been a seamstress; a bronze-faced Jack Tar with a wooden leg; a pair of street urchins, about fourteen years of age. As he watched them, chained like animals, mute, these few, with all the dumb resignation of animals, he felt sick.

Then, suddenly, he saw Silver.

She wore the same faded red jacket and striped petticoat. She was chained to an aged woman as thin as a broomstick, and her chin was as defiant, her blue eyes as fierce, as when he had seen her last, only a month ago, free, upon the road that was her home.

As he watched her fair, shining head, he forgot all about her murderous attempt upon himself and thought only of young Jeffrey Lucas, who loved her, perhaps, as deeply as he himself loved Oriana.

"Silver!" he shouted.

She turned her head sharply, and her blue eyes met his without a sign of recognition.

Already warders were pushing the convicts down towards the waiting boats; he had a few guineas in his purse, and he called to her again.

"Silver! Catch!"

He flung the purse towards her, and it fell at her feet. Swiftly as a cat she grabbed it, then, fixing him with those steely eyes, she screamed a filthy insult in Romany. Unerringly, flicking her wrist as lightly as when she had flung the knife, she hurled the purse back at his head. It struck him sharply on the cheek.

As he caught it, pandemonium broke out among the convicts. There were those who yelled abuse at her for refusing the money and those who wailed, imploring alms of him. Warders sprang forward, swearing and cursing, and James turned his back, violently pushing his way through the heaving, shouting crowd.

When he regained the inn, he found that he was trembling. He still felt sick. It was more than half an hour before he could compose himself, and then he sat down to write another letter.

He wrote to Jeffrey Lucas and described Silver's plight. He did not know, he said, the name of the ship on which she sailed, nor the offence for which she was being transported, but he had always understood that the lot of convicts could, to some degree, be ameliorated by money and by influence.

When he had posted this letter to Mr. Lucas' house, Ardley Manor, in Hampshire, he felt a slight relief, but he was taciturn that night at dinner and thankful to go aboard the *Southern Star* early the next morning.

He had no love, only dislike, for the savage road girl; at the same time, the change in her fortunes was so frightful and the thought of Lucas' grief so haunting that he felt he would have done anything in his power to save Silver from transportation. The herding together of the shackled convicts, reminding him as it did of eighteenth-century brutality, inspired him to write, while waiting for the last consignment of cargo, a moving and poignant account of the scene which he sent off to Don Ignacio in a farewell note by the last boat to leave for shore.

He would have been exceedingly happy had he known that this account, published in a leading London paper, was to create a tremendous stir, and that people for the first time were to read the name of James Darrell in print. Oriana Castleton was among those, but he was destined to know nothing of all this for a long time.

Meanwhile, he was shown a tiny but clean cabin and informed that one other passenger, a Mr. Galbraith, was travelling as far as Madeira. Captain Judd would be pleased for both gentlemen to take their meals with him. The *Southern Star* was a steamship, a fact which had at first disappointed James, who had hoped to make his first sea trip in a windjammer. But Don Ignacio, arguing that his arrival might be delayed for days if he travelled by sailing ship, had insisted upon booking a passage on the *Southern Star*.

In any case, the novelty and excitement of the journey diverted him so much that he soon forgot his regrets.

He stood on deck as they slid away to sea, watching the misty outline of the shore recede, waver, and finally disappear. The sea was choppy and the waves foam-capped. A trail of gulls stalked the ship, and the sound of their harsh, eerie cries would forever remind him of his first voyage.

He wondered whether anyone had ever before left his native land with feelings of so much rejoicing.

CHAPTER XXX

JAMES LIKED CAPTAIN JUDD, a reserved, rather dour man with grizzled whiskers and bright blue eyes. They dined alone on their first evening out, and the captain, thawing over port, fascinated him with tales of sailing ships he had known in what he referred to as the old days. James listened to stories of wrecks, and storms, and white sails billowing over blue water. He heard legends of mutiny, of piracy, and of ghost ships, while Judd agreed with him that the manner in which convicts were transported was a disgrace to civilisation.

On the second night Mr. Galbraith, his fellow passenger, joined them for supper. He was, he said, travelling to Madeira for his health. He was tall and thin, and seemed to feel the cold, muffling himself in his greatcoat, although the night was pleasantly warm. His face was white as cheese, and he wore thick spectacles of dark green glass.

"So you're travelling to Spain, Mr. Darrell?"

"I am, sir."

"May I enquire with what object?"

"I wish to study the country with a view, one day, to writing about it."

Mr. Galbraith seemed to think this a devilish odd thing to do. He shook his head and asked:

"Surely you know, sir, it's a barbarous and primitive land? No comforts, vile inns, unspeakable roads, and, I believe, no systematic organisation of coaches or diligences?"

"I have heard all that," James returned; "and such wildness is what most attracts me towards the country."

"You don't fear the heat, or the mosquitoes, breeding fever?"

"I don't think I fear the heat, sir, and as for the mosquitoes, I must take my chance."

Galbraith hazarded after a pause:

"I was about to suggest, Mr. Darrell, that since your journey is one of leisure, you change your mind regarding Spain and stay aboard until Madeira."

"I fear, sir——"

"This will be a tedious voyage for me, with the captain occupied as he is. And Madeira, which I have visited before, is the most pleasant island in the world! A temperate climate, sir, with plenty of sunshine! Sea bathing and magnificent scenery! Why, sir, there's no comparison!"

"Thank you," said James firmly; "but my intention is to travel to Spain!"

Later that night, as he stood on deck, he wondered for the first time whether Don Ignacio's warnings were so exaggerated as he had at first supposed. He leaned over the rail, listening to the rush and tumble of the spray. The ship rose and fell, swaying so easily that the deck beneath his feet leaped like a living thing. A young moon rode the sky, and filmy clouds raced across her face. Mr. Galbraith, James reflected, wanted to know matters which concerned him not at all. And those dark green glasses looked uncommonly like a disguise.

That night he locked his cabin door, but in the morning he could have laughed at his own fears, for Galbraith, as they journeyed on, became more and more the peevish invalid and never once again pestered him to travel to Madeira.

It grew warmer every day.

At night the increasing moon floated, honey-gold, in the sky, and a silver road rippled straight across the ocean.

By day, an azure sky melted to meet a sea more vividly blue than cornflowers, and in the shimmering line of the horizon it was difficult to tell, amid so much misty golden haze, where one began and the other ended.

James, despite his eagerness to land in Spain, knew that he would be sorry to leave the *Southern Star*. He had not felt so well for years, and he loved the sea as much as he had thought to when he was a small boy writing the bloodthirsty adventures of Captain Skull, a pirate.

And that, he reflected, belonged to the remote past. He was reminded then of his father, and of the study in that Oxfordshire house of long ago. Perhaps thinking of his boyhood after so many months made him dream, the last night before arriving at Cadiz, of the gypsies.

Or rather of his friend, old Hagar.

He dreamed that she stood over him, her grey locks wildly dishevelled, and once again he heard her voice, hoarse and deep as he remembered it, repeat the dukkering, the fortunetelling, that he had heard one summer night in the field called Little Egypt.

Something queer was going to happen to him across the seas, something connected with what she called beads, and there would be blood spilt beneath the sun.

He woke then with a start, to find moonlight pouring through his porthole. He pulled out the leather bag he wore next to his skin and held the diamond necklace for a moment in his hand. The stones winked and glittered in the moonlight. They felt cold, and when he had looked at them for a moment, as though to reassure himself that all was well, he slipped them back into the leather bag, but their bright beauty remained in his imagination, and his moonlit cabin seemed sombre without their dazzle.

The next morning early he was up on deck as the first peach-coloured flush of dawn stole across the darkness of the sky. Soon the coast of Spain was a faint, sandy line, and then, as the ship stole closer in, he could distinguish, in the distance, a town, so far away that it looked like a heap of overturned dice. The sun rose gloriously, and he knew that the day would be intensely hot.

When he thought that soon he would be landing in Spain, his heart leaped with joy.

While he was leaning over the rail, listening once more to the harsh cry of the gulls that swarmed flashing silver in the sun, Captain Judd came up to speak to him.

"I need hardly say, Mr. Darrell, how sorry we shall be to lose you."

"Thank you," James said, smiling.

"I'd like to ask you, before you land—the Spanish inns are wretched—have you any idea where you will stay tonight?"

"None at all," James admitted; "but I shan't stay long in Cadiz. I want to be on my way to Seville."

"That might be as well," Captain Judd remarked, "owing to a superstition current in these parts. Not," he hastened to add, "that I myself pay any attention to their superstitions."

"All the same, Captain, what is it?"

"Well," said the captain, "it's only rubbish, and proceeds, of course, from the mouths of sailormen. They just say Cadiz is an unlucky city. That's all there is to it."

"In London," James observed, "actors will tell you *Macbeth's* an unlucky play."

"All rubbish! I told you so!"

"Probably. Can you recommend me a decent inn in Cadiz? I shall have to stay there a night or two."

"The Golden Bull is the best I know, and that's not saying much. Really, Mr. Darrell, I wish you'd listen to Mr. Galbraith and travel with us as far as Madeira!"

"I'm sorry, but that's impossible."

It was strange, he reflected, how everybody conspired together, trying to make him dislike the very idea of Spain. Never, for a long time, had he encountered such a pack of wet blankets, and old Hagar, with her dukkering, was the worst of these croakers.

"Great heavens!" he thought, "do they expect me to be murdered in my bed?"

And then he wished with all his heart that Oriana was with him, breasting this new adventure by his side. Oriana as she had been, gallant, impetuous, not Frank Castleton's spoiled, luxurious wife. Once upon a time she would have thrilled to this adventure as he thrilled to it now; he thought how eager would have been her tilted nose at sighting Cadiz; almost he could imagine her dark, silky hair, whipped by the wind across the whiteness of her brow; her gleeful smile; and her hand, pressing his, as they stood there together in the sunshine, a new life unfolding for them both.

CHAPTER XXXI

LONG AFTERWARDS he would always remember that his first impression, landing on Spanish soil, was one of intense heat. It was eleven o'clock in the morning; it was August, and the sun smote down in a white glare fiercer than that of an oven. He paused for a moment, confused by the heat and by a strange smell compounded of spices, rotten vegetables, some heady, exotic flower, coffee, tobacco, and unwashed human flesh. Then, following the porter who carried his two valises, he walked through the crowd of loafers on the quay, to find himself in a strange and narrow street.

It was so narrow, his first Spanish street, and the houses toppled together so closely, that those persons living opposite each other could easily have shaken each other's hands. He noticed the barred windows and the balconies of graceful wrought iron; once or twice he passed a doorway behind which green plants bloomed. It was blessedly cool in the street, but when they emerged into a plaza, or square, the sun flamed down again. He watched mules stamping impatiently, to shake off the teasing flies; busy little boys selling water from earthen pitchers; flocks of beggars; and a procession of donkeys gaily caparisoned in rainbow harness. All was new and vivid to his eyes and sharply outlined in the brilliant sunlight.

He gave an unconscious sigh of pure satisfaction.

"Señor," the porter said, "here is the inn."

The Golden Bull was a pleasant surprise after the gruesome accounts he had heard of Spanish taverns. He was shown a clean, bare bedroom facing the square, and was courteously received by the landlord, a stout man with a pockmarked face. As he sat sipping sherry in the patio, a courtyard open to the sky and shaded by a grove of orange trees, he briefly explained his needs.

"I want a reliable guide, with good references, and he must provide me with a couple of fast horses. I'm on my way to Seville, and I want to arrive there as soon as possible."

"I know of several suitable guides, señor, although I do not know whether they are to be found in Cadiz at the moment. However, I will make enquiries after the siesta, and at dinnertime I shall tell you whether or not I have been successful."

James, who had been inclined to scoff at the idea of the siesta, found himself only too thankful, after lunch, to draw his shutters and to fling himself upon his bed. The heat was intense, breathless; out in the square the sound of voices and the noise of stamping mules and jingling carriages were suddenly stilled, just as though the fairy story of the "Sleeping Beauty" had come true and all the city slept.

James slept, dreamlessly, sprawled half naked on his bed beneath a white mosquito net. If he had been competent to analyse his own confused feelings he would have agreed that he felt, although obscurely, that for the first time since his childhood he had come home. The blood of the unknown Spanish grandmother ran strongly through his veins that first night in Cadiz.

Far away, in his London office, Señor Don Ignacio de Zozaya sat at his desk talking quietly—and privately—to his manager from Amsterdam, Herr Vandervelde.

He said:

"You should have informed me when Da Silva first left Amsterdam. Two months lost! Do you realise that he could have reached Spain by this time?"

"Señor," the Dutchman said, "may I say I think you are exaggerating? You have no proof that Da Silva is so unscrupulous as you suppose—no proof even that he has not left you simply to work in Paris. May I say, señor, since I have been with you for twenty years, that when I think of the commissions you have executed in the past—successfully—I find your fears for your daughter's necklace almost unreasonable. That is, of course, if you trust your agent?"

"I trust him absolutely," Don Ignacio asserted.

"Then, my dear sir, because a rogue like Da Silva is missing . . ."

"A rogue I kept on when I should have dismissed him, solely because he was a clever workman!"

"He *is* a clever workman," the Dutchman repeated stolidly.

"No doubt! Vandervelde, would you call me superstitious?"

"I know nothing of your private life, sir. In business, you are the reverse."

"Exactly! Yet some of the stones in my daughter's necklace are so ill-omened, and Spain is so savage, I cannot help feeling anxiety."

"When the necklace arrives in your daughter's keeping, may I ask if you will still feel anxiety as to its safety?"

"Of course not," Don Ignacio retorted angrily. "My future son-in-law has a well-guarded house in Seville and estates in the country. He is surrounded by faithful servants. That he should be robbed is unlikely in the extreme!"

"Then, sir, I think you should cease to worry. Had I known your apprehensions concerning Da Silva, I should, of course, have let you know the moment he left us. But I think you have no cause for alarm; no one in Spain knows of your connection with the person who is acting as your agent in this matter?"

"No one! I am not a fool! But I would remind you, Vandervelde, that such necklaces are history; spies aren't wanting with stones like those; it wouldn't be the first time murder's been committed for some of the diamonds in that same necklace."

"May I ask, sir, who knows, *outside Spain,* of your daughter's wedding?"

"Outside Spain? Very few people, I should think, outside Seville, know anything about it. Da Silva probably thinks I am sending the necklace to Madrid. That's not the point; the point is that every rogue in the business knows that it is on its way to Spain!"

"Your agent, I believe, leaves Seville to take up a post in your Madrid business?"

Don Ignacio frowned.

"He does. Why?"

"I was only thinking that once he has safely delivered the necklace to Doña Adriana, it would matter very little what befell him on the road from Seville to Madrid."

"You're wrong," Don Ignacio informed him icily; "it would matter to me greatly! I would have you know, Vandervelde, that the young man is dear to me. You have behaved with a monstrous negligence, telling me only now of Da Silva's disappearance! You may go."

Alone, he sat for some minutes thinking of James. He had learned, in three or four meetings, to love James as his own son, and now he was afraid that the boy might be in peril.

"Great God!" he said to himself, "and I thought to help him! I should have financed some book of tales, or despatched him straight to Madrid. I was selfish, thinking of Adriana, but I'd never have sent the lad across Spain had I known that Da Silva was missing!"

"This is the only guide left in Cadiz," the landlord informed James that same day.

"Well, can he get horses? He's of no use to me if he can't."

"He says he can. Fine horses, he says. Would you like to see him?"

"Yes."

A tall, thin man came sauntering into the patio. His face was a pale dusty brown, and so was his hair. He wore a red sash about his emaciated waist, and his black, hooded eyes evaded any direct glance.

"I must be mad to consider him," James thought, looking at this unprepossessing figure, and remembering the diamonds. Aloud he said:

"What is your name?"

"I am Pablo, señor. A splendid guide."

His nose, James observed, was tremendous—an eagle's beak.

"You know the road to Seville?"

"Every inch of it, señor."

"What about the horses?"

"I have a five-year-old black gelding for you, señor, and for myself a fast chestnut mare. Is it necessary to find a pack horse?"

"No. I'm travelling light!"

"Excellent. When would the señor wish me to be ready?"

"Tomorrow at seven?"

"I shall be waiting, señor, outside in the plaza, with my horses."

James dined that night in his tavern and went early to bed despite the noise in the square outside his window. He thought he would wait until delivering the necklace before he began to enjoy Spain.

And so his only memory of Cadiz, the "unlucky city," as he rode out in the morning, was that of narrow, slitlike streets, shut-away patios, heat, smells, secrecy, and, in the distance, the pale turquoise wash of the sea.

He asked:

"Where shall we lie tonight, Pablo?"

"Don't disturb yourself, señor, I know all the *posadas* on the road. Tonight, if you can ride fifteen miles, I know of an excellent inn."

"I can certainly ride fifteen miles!"

"The señor is already an Andalusian!"

CHAPTER XXXII

THEY TRAVELLED all the morning. At first their road took them by the sea, and a light breeze blew in towards the shore. Later, they turned inland, and then, as it grew hotter, the horses were soon covered in dust and sweat. The country, James noticed, was bare and arid; so far it was ugly and unprepossessing. Occasionally they passed villages that were little better than collections of wretched huts. The loneliness of the road astonished James. They rode for miles without encountering a human being, and the sight of a boy herding goats became a novelty.

"Pablo," James asked, "surely this is not the main road to Seville?"

"Not any longer, señor. We left the main road about two hours ago."

"What the devil are you doing? Why did you not ask me first?"

"I beg your pardon, señor, but I understood you were anxious to reach Seville without delay. Therefore, naturally, I took you by the quickest path, which is a short cut. However, if you prefer it, we can always return to the main road."

"No. We'd better stay where we are."

At midday they found a *venta*, little better than a wineshop, where Pablo proposed they stay during the hottest hours of the day. There was stabling for the horses, and they ate a meal of rice and cheese. Afterwards they went into the barn and lay down on some straw piled within, since there was nowhere else to go. James's clothes felt stiff with sweat, and neither harsh red wine nor tepid water had done much to relieve his thirst. He thought he was beginning to know something of the discomforts of Spain, but he dozed for about ten minutes on his heap of straw, and when he opened his eyes again Pablo had disappeared.

James got up and went outside to put his head under the pump. Afterwards he drank some more wine and smoked a cheroot. In about twenty minutes Pablo reappeared.

"Where have you been?" James wanted to know.

"Saddling the horses, señor. It is time for us to be on our way."

It did not seem cooler to James, but they thrust their way down a rough bridle path, and to distract his mind from heat, flies, and dust, he decided to study Pablo, who was, after all, only the second Spaniard he had known in his life. Pablo, however, proved a difficult subject. He was courteous, but taciturn to the point of moodiness, and for the life of him James could find nothing likable about the man's sallow face and hooked nose. Yet Pablo's hooded gaze reminded him of something, or someone; he teased his mind, but his memory continued to be evasive. He was, in fact, tired, but determined not to admit as much to the sullen guide; he was just beginning to learn that it is one thing to ride fifteen miles in Oxfordshire and quite another to ride half that distance in sweltering Andalusian heat.

Soon they found themselves upon an immense plain. For as far as his weary eye could see, savage and barren land roamed on every side. Here and there were great rocks, and in the distance he could perceive scattered hamlets, but such an occasional oasis was rare, and the plains, naked beneath a burning blue sky, sweltered, swarthy brown, in the bright glare of the summer afternoon.

"Where did you say we lie tonight?" he asked Pablo.

"Not much farther on now. A good posada, not like this afternoon. Look, señor!"

James glanced over his shoulder, and saw, in the distance, cattle grazing behind a fence.

"What?"

"Fighting bulls!"

James rested on his saddle, easing his legs, and shaded his eyes with his hand. Bulls? They seemed more like black panthers, so swift and lithe were their movements. He was intensely interested.

"But what can they eat? Everything's burnt up!"

"They want for nothing," Pablo assured him. "Hay, oats, barley —several times a day they are fed. They are young, now, not four, but next year, when they are five, they will fight."

"Are there bullfights in Seville now?"

"Yes, señor. Every Sunday."

They rode on, and he forgot his weariness.

Suddenly it was as though Spain caught him by the heart. The dust and heat and flies no longer counted. He looked upon the tawny plains, golden yellow as a lion's flanks, and saw that they were beautiful. Those rocks and gorges farther down the road; the white jumble of distant, scattered hamlets; those lithe, quick-stepping fighting bulls; the pride and grace of carriage of the elderly peasant woman they had passed a moment before—all these were beautiful, but subtly so, and their beauty struck him as being as uncompromising as the sun itself.

He knew then that he had begun to love Spain.

That evening they approached the posada where they were to lie the night. It was a two-storied white building, with one big raftered living room, where James was received by the landlord and his wife. They seemed a dark, secretive pair, and he remembered, as he ate his supper, Don Ignacio's description of his fellow countrymen as being reserved, even austere. Don Ignacio, James reflected, had been correct in this statement. He was slightly piqued also that all these people should take for granted his excellent knowledge of their own language.

Later that evening the local priest came in for a glass of wine, and was ready enough to accept his eagerly proffered invitation. He was a thin, sallow man of about forty-five, who spoke with a more precise and formal accent than anyone James had yet encountered.

"I, of course, come from Valencia," he replied, in answer to James's question, "and although I have been in Andalusia for more than ten years, I still find it difficult to understand not only the people, but their language into the bargain."

"Why is that, Father?" James enquired cautiously, anxious not to involve himself in some complicated affair of politics.

"The people, do you mean, or their language?"

"Both!"

"Well, the people are unlike those of other provinces. More primitive, perhaps, certainly more colourful. It is said, you know, that many have a strain of gypsy blood, although I must confess I am scarcely an authority on such matters. As for their habit of clipping their words, you must remember that in this climate the least effort is something of an exertion, and the Andalusian has become an expert in the art of saving himself trouble!"

After a few minutes of general conversation the priest courteously asked if James was travelling far.

"To Seville."

"Unwise, my dear señor, in such heat! The time to see that lovely city is in the spring!"

"Unfortunately this is my only opportunity of doing so."

"But surely, señor, you are not visiting Seville in August for pleasure?"

James hesitated a moment. Already, during the brief time he had spent on Spanish soil, Don Ignacio's mysterious warnings had ceased to sound as melodramatic as they had appeared in London. Probably the priest was genuine enough, but that was no reason for relaxing his caution.

"I am indeed, Father. Later on my time will not be my own."

The priest shook his head, refused another glass of wine, and after warning the young man against fever, soon afterwards took his departure.

James began to yawn, and, having decided to start early the next morning, went up to bed in a fairly clean room with an old-fashioned tester bed.

But he could not sleep.

Some time in the night he was awakened by the sound of music. At first he thought that he must have been dreaming, but after listening for a few moments he got up and went across to the window.

A sweet freshness, herald of dawn, cooled his hot cheeks, and then, as he leaned out, he heard the music more clearly. He thought it proceeded from a large barn down the road.

As he listened to the distant strumming of a guitar, someone began to sing. This song was strange and passionate and wilder than the call of any birds. The voice was that of a woman, but it sounded unearthly in the distance, and his blood stirred.

Wakeful and restless, he returned to bed, but he could not sleep until dawn came, and then the music was stilled.

The next morning, riding down a narrow, rutty lane, he said to Pablo:

"What was that music I heard last night from the posada?"

Pablo was silent for a moment. Then he said:

"That, señor, was the song of the gypsies."

"I saw none. What gypsies?"

"The innkeeper, his wife, two cousins, and myself."

James suddenly knew where he had encountered that hooded glance before.

"You, Pablo? Are you then of gypsy blood?"

Pablo nodded, his profile more than ever resembling that of a starving eagle.

"Yes, señor. I am from the Caló quarter in Cadiz."

"I want," James said, "to learn the Spanish gypsy tongue."

CHAPTER XXXIII

HE RODE INTO SEVILLE just before sunset. After the wildness and desolation of the plains it was almost startling, at first, to hear the clatter of carts and wagons, to see crowded streets once again, and know that he had arrived, not, certainly, at his journey's end, but at his first destination.

Then he looked about him at the beauty of the city, and straightway fell in love with it. At first, until he became accustomed to the chalky whiteness of so many houses and walls, they dazzled his eyes; later that night he was to see them blanched in the pallor of moonlight, when they would seem mysteriously beautiful. As the sun sank in a red glow, the churches and convents he passed sparkled in the light, like the loveliest of jewels, and their spires seemed to float, delicate as lace, against the flaming sky. He caught glimpses of slit-like streets, mysteriously barred windows, patios, lush green where fountains tumbled, and it seemed as though all the church bells were chiming, in a sweet, deep-throated chorus.

The streets, he noticed, were crowded with people who had come out after their siesta to seek a breath of air. He observed the pride with which these Sevillanos moved; the men wore broad-brimmed hats and short jackets; many were booted and spurred, and all wore vivid sashes bound about their waists. They walked with arrogance, puffing smoke from their cheroots, eyeing the women who passed, their heads held high.

The women were black-clad and wore flowing mantillas draped over high combs. Despite so much darkness they were, as Don Ignacio had told him, intensely colourful; some sported blazing shawls, and nearly all wore flowers—bunches of jasmine, or bright carnations, or clusters of roses, crimson and white and pink. They snapped their fans as they talked, with a swift, rhythmic clicking which was soon to weave itself into his Andalusian pattern of summer sounds and to become as much a part of Seville as the strumming of guitars, the cry of boys' voices selling water, church bells, rattling castanets, and the jingling of donkeys' harness. He noticed that the women walked gracefully erect; they moved as though they were dancing.

He turned to Pablo, his eyes sparkling.

"Well, where are the lodgings?"

Pablo, in the intervals of teaching him the elements of the Spanish gypsy language, had assured him that he knew of clean, comfortable rooms, "fit for any milor."

"This way, Don Jaime—follow me!"

He had become Don Jaime to Pablo only during the last twenty-four hours, consummate proof of his powers to ingratiate himself with the Egyptian race. Pablo had promised to escort him to a bull-fight; better still, to take him somewhere "unknown to foreigners," where he would hear the best flamenco music in Seville.

"That, to me," Pablo assured him scornfully, "is by no means everything. Naturally the best flamenco music is to be heard in Cadiz."

"And Madrid?" James asked, amused.

"Madrid? A city of the north? No, Don Jaime, our music belongs to the sun."

The lodgings proved to be all that Pablo had said, and James was particularly delighted with the charming patio. Here, where roses bloomed, their scent mingling with the sound of falling water, he prepared, despite the guide's protests, to spend his first evening in Seville.

"Tonight, Pablo, I am staying in. Tomorrow I'll go anywhere you please. Did you see that the horses had a good feed?"

"But, Don Jaime——"

"It's no use, Pablo. I have a business appointment tomorrow, and I shall not be free until afterwards. Will you please deliver this letter for me?"

Pablo nodded, sullen once more.

But James had no intention of wandering about the thieves' dens of Seville until he had presented the diamonds to Doña Adriana. He wrote her a formal letter in his best Spanish, explaining that he was the bearer of a message from her father, Don Ignacio, and that he would be grateful if she would consent to receive him the next day at any time convenient to herself.

This done, he sat reading in the patio until he felt sleepy. He walked into the street for a few minutes before going upstairs, and thought that he had never seen more brilliant moonlight. Sharp as the stab of Silver's knife came the realisation that Oriana, had she wished, could have been beside him in the rose-scented loveliness of this dreamy night.

He turned his back on the moon and went slowly upstairs to bed.

Señorita de Zozaya lived with her aunts in a long white house standing in a garden thick with the dark pencils of cypress trees. Already James thought that one of Seville's greatest charms was the sudden discovery, in the midst of the town, of so many hidden gardens and patios. Each one seemed like another ferny oasis in a desert of sun-drenched streets and houses and squares. He was received by an elderly manservant and conducted immediately to the patio. Here, where fountains played in the shade of green orange trees, he was received by Doña Adriana and—inevitably—by the aunts, who would not for all the diamonds in the world have left their niece alone for five minutes with so dangerous an animal as a young man.

Don Ignacio's daughter was a slender creature dressed in filmy white. Her satin-dark hair was smoothly dressed, her features delicate, her skin ivory-pale. She was pretty, James thought, in a shadowy, rather remote fashion. The black-clad aunts were stout and heavily powdered, but they all received him graciously, and when sherry had been ordered, and Don Ignacio's letter produced, he sighed with relief at having successfully accomplished his mission.

"Now, señorita!"

He had replaced the diamonds in their original case, which he now slipped open, so that the three women exclaimed aloud in delight as the diamonds lay glittering in their nest of dark blue velvet.

James smiled, well pleased.

Once again Don Ignacio's mysterious hints of danger receded far away into the background of his mind. Out on those lonely, haunted plains the thought of thieves and brigands had been vivid enough to disturb him more than once, but here, in this pleasant patio, with its orange trees and fountains, in the company of this pretty girl and of her matter-of-fact aunts, even the cold light of the diamonds, flashing in his eyes could not make him believe that so many precautions were not the nervous fancies of an elderly man.

He was sorry, then, that he had stayed indoors the night before.

When it was discovered upon reading Don Ignacio's letter that the young man had saved the diamond merchant's life in London, the family could not make enough of James, and he was forced to stay to lunch with them. Doña Adriana's fiancé arrived, and proved to be a handsome, agreeable fellow of about thirty. The engaged pair seemed much attached to each other, and Don Luis cordially invited James to be his guest that night at dinner.

"If you have never been to Seville before, I could show you much that is *tipico* of the town."

But James thanked him and declined. He knew that he must proceed to Madrid before very long, and he was anxious to familiarise himself with the gypsy quarter of which Pablo had told him so much.

He parted reluctantly with Don Ignacio's family, having found them even more courteous in their hospitality than those who knew the Spanish people had led him to suppose.

"When we are married, and visit Madrid, you must lunch with us there!" Doña Adriana insisted.

He promised, lightheartedly; little did he think that he would never see them again.

CHAPTER XXXIV

JAMES sat in the Baile Flamenco with Pablo and Antonio, a picador. The Baile Flamenco was over the bridge, in Triana, the gypsy quarter of the town. It was a simple affair of whitewashed walls, and that was all. It had no roof, but was open to the stars. The trampled mud floor was hard as stone, and there was a low stage at the far end. Tallow candles lit the rickety tables, and the walls were hung with ragged, lurid posters of bullfights. The place was crowded with wild-looking people, many of them gypsies. Here was colour, and dirt, and music. Here were bullfighters, horse copers, mule dealers, acrobats, guitarists, dancers, street singers, and bootblacks. Never had James beheld so many dark, sardonic faces, so many flashing gypsy eyes, so much noise, laughter, and drinking. There were men whose jackets had once been rich with silver spangles that were tarnished now, but still worn with an air of inimitable bravado. There were peones from the ranches, in leather trousers and high boots with immense jingling spurs. There were male dancers from over the bridge, in tight-fitting suits of maroon colour and purple and plum and cinnamon.

As for the women, the majority of whom were dancers and singers, they were as bright as flowers in their flounced dresses of scarlet and orange and pink and yellow. Their lacquer-black heads were laden with bunches of gay carnations, and the poorest among them flaunted the brilliant three-cornered shawls known as *mantonés de Manila*. Some of the women were drunk, and all appeared to be drinking freely, but when the Cuadro Flamenco, the band of gypsy musicians, appeared upon the stage, there was a hush of absolute silence.

And so, as Don Ignacio had prophesied, James first heard Spanish gypsy music as it is meant to be heard, beneath the stars, and knew that a spell was woven about him as he listened. The enchantment thus created was a dark one, for the frenzied wildness of the singers, the wicked rippling of the guitars, the rhythmic stamping of the troupe, all combined to produce music of such fierceness that for a moment he felt sweat bead his forehead, and he thought of the tales he had heard of witches' sabbaths. Then the tempo changed, becoming wilder still, but melancholy, passionate, and haunted, so that it was as though the history of the gypsies unveiled itself in music; the endless road trailed on forever, and the caravans were already lost behind the next turning as a girl ran on to the stage and began to dance.

She looked young in comparison with the other women, for she was slim and angular in her flame-coloured dress that jingled with showers of gold sequins. Unlike the other dancers, she wore her hair loose, in a jetty curling mop that half concealed her face. She sprang into the air like a creature possessed, snapping her fingers until they clicked sharp as castanets. Lithely, rolling her hips, she crossed the stage, wreathing her arms behind her head, until they seemed like the flickering of tawny serpents.

Then, with another bound, as the music quickened, she began to contort her supple body as though it were boneless; now she flung herself into a series of lascivious and enticing poses, all with a little secret smile that could not have been more provocatively gypsy. She flashed and whirled across the stage, so that her feet seemed winged and her hair flew out in wild elf locks. Then, as the music swelled to a climax, she sprang once more into the air, to sink motionless upon the floor. In a second she was bowing to the sound of vociferous and noisy applause.

"That girl," Pablo said, in the grudging tones of one who hails from Cadiz, "is good. Who is she, Antonio?"

"She is a stranger," the picador replied; "that is, she belongs to those good-for-nothing nomad gypsies. Sometimes she comes to work here for an odd night or so."

James was so enthralled by the picador's elaborate explanation of the bullfight that only one part of his mind had consciously watched the dancer; he did not even notice that she was running around the tables collecting money in a tambourine.

As she approached their table, Pablo asked loudly:

"Are you staying for the Sunday bullfight, Don Jaime?"

"Well, today's Friday. Yes, I can stay if I leave early Monday morning."

The gypsy girl came up behind them and said impudently, in a husky, rather deep voice:

"Don Jaime, have you any silver for my tambourine?"

"Be off, little guttersnipe!" Pablo rebuked impatiently.

But James smiled vaguely and gave her a silver coin.

She was very young, with a wild little vivid face that was burned a clear, sunny brown; flashing teeth, and the usual devastating gypsy eyes.

"Be off!" Pablo repeated.

She went, then, with a muttered curse in his direction.

"You were saying?" James continued impatiently to the picador.

They went on talking about the bullfight.

The next Sunday found all three at the *corrida,* James in the middle, Antonio, who had lamed himself in a recent accident, on his right, and Pablo on his left.

James's eyes were at first dazed by the violence of so much colour: the fighting capes, of which Don Ignacio had told him, magenta, lined with buttercup yellow; the bright flowered shawls draped by women in front of their boxes; the sun glare on the sandy arena; and, best of all, the *toreros.* Skin-tight suits, their *traje de luces* of sky blue, rose, emerald, and cerise; suits richly encrusted with gold and silver spangles glittering in the sun against the vermilion of the cloaks loosely worn upon their shoulders.

He watched the corrida, absorbed.

Despite the admonitions of Antonio, he closed his eyes during the picadors' interlude, sickened, in the love he bore for horses, by what he saw. But afterwards, when the matador and the bull stood down there alone in the sun to start their mighty duel, he felt his heart beat faster. So much swiftness on both sides; such ferocity on the part of the great, lithe bull; such grace, skill, and dexterity on the part of the taut man who stood there in his bright silks, sword poised, waiting for that tremendous moment when, according to tradition, he must kill only by risking his own body in the thrust that would expose him, for one interminable moment, defenceless to the murderous horns.

After the second bull had been killed, Antonio went down to talk to some of his friends, and a gentleman behind James asked in excellent English if he might take the seat next to his.

"Certainly, until my friend returns."

The newcomer was a short, stocky man, quietly dressed, with a cigar-brown face, a cast in his eye, and a wide, smiling mouth.

"You speak Spanish so well, sir, that I hesitated for some time before addressing you in another language!"

"I might say the same about your English!"

"Oh, I speak many languages—none of them, alas, faultlessly!"

"And you're Spanish?" James asked, accepting a cheroot from this new acquaintance.

"I was born in Gibraltar, educated at Coimbra, in Portugal, afterwards spending some years in Mexico. Since then I have lived in London, Paris, Brussels, and Madrid!"

"I envy you."

"My name is Tomás da Silva. My profession is that of librarian. I am, in fact, on my way to Madrid, where I have some work waiting for me."

"I too," James informed him, "am on my way to Madrid. I leave tomorrow morning."

"Really? I suppose in that case you wouldn't do me the pleasure of dining with me tonight?"

"I should be delighted," said James, and then the picador limped back to his seat, primed with arena gossip, and the spectacle of the bullfight continued, brutal and vivid, beautiful and savage and brave, as the sun poured down upon sand that by now was dabbled with patches of dark blood.

CHAPTER XXXV

"IF I CAN BE OF ANY USE to you in Madrid, Mr. Darrell," Da Silva said, "you have only to make your wishes known."

"Thank you!"

James was moody for a moment. He was exasperated with the monk's life he had been leading, and determined to find a mistress in Madrid. Somebody, he thought, to share his home, someone to find waiting for him when he came back from work. He had little enough to give this as yet unknown woman, but he imagined that such a liaison as he had in mind would not be difficult to arrange.

He thought:

"I'm sick of living alone. I won't let her ruin all my life for me—that's what she'd like to do. She's got her rich husband; she doesn't care. But I am starting again, and I shall live, now, as though she had never existed."

They were brave words, and he meant them, after drinking a bottle of Valdepeñas wine. He decided that he would prefer a quiet woman, one without temperament, and, so long as she was not ugly, he would not even desire her to be attractive. What could anything of that kind mean to him, who was haunted, even now, by the memory of a pale scented cheek, a mischievous nose, and lips the warm sweetness of which he could never forget?

He started; Da Silva was speaking.

"Have you seen anything tipico here in Seville? Music and dancing?"

"Yes, last night I went over to Triana, to the Baile Flamenco."

"The gypsy dancing place?" Da Silva looked at him oddly. "My dear Mr. Darrell, aren't you afraid of such cutthroat dens?"

"Not in the least. Who would want to rob *me?*"

"Who indeed?" Da Silva agreed. He added: "I understand the flamenco artists there are the best in Seville."

"I well believe it. All the ones I saw were remarkable."

He thought then of the young gypsy girl in the flame-coloured dress. But he thought of her quite dispassionately, recollecting, for the first time, that the picador had scornfully described her as being a nomad. That contempt, he thought, really envy, which the sedentary gypsy must always feel for his wilder brethren!

Suddenly he smiled and said:

"I bought a horse yesterday. A four-year-old black stallion!"

"I do hope," Da Silva said, "that they didn't swindle you too much?"

"I don't think they swindled me at all," James admitted candidly.

"I was going to ask you," Da Silva hazarded; "you mean, don't you, to ride all the way to Madrid?"

"Indeed I do!"

"If I started tomorrow, would you have any objection to my travelling with you?"

"I should be delighted," James said warmly.

"It's dull travelling alone."

"Don't even think about it! Listen, my guide, Pablo, rides as far as Cadiz. He has now, naturally, an extra horse upon his hands! When we get to Cadiz, we will find you another!"

"Agreed. Do you think to engage another guide in Cadiz?"

"I suppose so. Why?"

"Because, my dear sir, I believe I can save you some money! I know every inch of the road from here to Madrid!"

"But that's splendid!"

After a few minutes' discussion as to the route they were to take, James suggested that they should visit the Baile Flamenco.

Da Silva shook his head.

"Mr. Darrell, I wouldn't consider it, and I beg you won't either!"

"I promise there's no reason to suppose you'll be robbed!"

"I assure you," Da Silva told him gravely, "that I am not exaggerating. Many people have been robbed there. Two, at least, have been murdered. The body of one was found in the Quadalquivir River. However"—perceiving by James's expression that these sinister tales were not deterring him—"I had hopes, tonight, of taking you to hear a famous flamenca singer who is to be found in the Macárena quarter. She herself is not young, but there are many pretty girls in the establishment, which is one of the most tipico I know in Seville."

"Good," James agreed. "We'll go there instead. It makes no difference to me."

The next morning they were on the road, and Pablo sulked all the way to Cadiz.

It was there, in the "unlucky town," that James took a final farewell of his guide, in the stables where he was bedding down the two horses he tended with so much care.

"Why should I take a guide?" James demanded for the hundredth time. "Have I not told you Señor da Silva knows every inch of the road to Madrid?"

"And what, Don Jaime, do you know of Señor da Silva?"

"I am not a child of five, Pablo," James explained impatiently.

"Look at the sore back this Da Silva has given to Brillante, to my little favourite horse! That in itself is against him!"

"Pablo, a man can be a bad horseman and still know the road from Cadiz to Madrid!"

"You think so, Don Jaime? Well, you are young. And, Don Jaime, do you know that to strangers Cadiz is supposed to be *la ciudad de mala suerte*—the city of evil fortune?"

"I should know by now. None of you get tired of saying so! And, Pablo, what are nomad gypsies in Spain? I should be interested to meet some on the road."

Pablo grunted.

"You mean the Ursari? They are no good. Of all the thieves——"

"The Ursari?"

"The Bear Foki. Those who travel the roads with their dancing bears, their music that is sometimes not even flamenco, who catch chickens like you catch fish, with hooks, and who would steal the gold from their own grandmother's teeth!"

James grinned.

"Where can I find them, Pablo?"

"I will never tell you how to find the Bear People. There are limits, Don Jaime, even to an aficionado of the gypsies!"

"I shall find them," James asserted.

"Not through me," Pablo insisted with finality.

The next day James and Da Silva set forth early in the morning on the first stage of their long journey. James was delighted with his black stallion and hoped to sell it for a profit in Madrid. Da Silva, a bad horseman, ambled along by his side on a sedate and elderly cob. James was in wild spirits. At last, he thought, he was starting his new life. He had delivered the diamond necklace, he had enjoyed himself for four days in Seville, and ahead of him lay the long, adventurous ride. Free to speak at last, he informed Da Silva that he was proceeding to the offices of De Zozaya, the diamond merchant.

"Did you ever hear of him?"

"No. But then in my own profession it's scarcely likely that I would have done."

James was becoming slightly mystified as to this profession of Da Silva's. For a librarian, he knew incredibly little about books. Apart from this peculiarity, he began to wonder whether he had not, after all, been impetuous in agreeing to travel so far in the stranger's company. The man rode badly and held him back when he was longing to test the swiftness of his new horse. On the other hand, the road appeared as familiar to him as his own pocket handkerchief.

The day was intensely hot; as usual, they paused for the afternoon siesta, and when they resumed their journey Da Silva suggested that they should press on until the evening, when they would reach a first-class inn. James assented eagerly, and so it came about that the sun was setting as they approached a gloomy, savage gorge.

Here rocks jutted sharply on either side to form a natural tunnel;

the dying sun was shut out, and the road became dark; the horses' hoofs drummed with a hollow, muffled sound.

"A strange, haunted sort of place," James commented, turning round to Da Silva, who was riding some paces behind.

At this moment his horse shied, and he saw that an ugly boy had run forward to beg for alms. James cursed the boy, but was searching in his pocket for some coppers when three men bestriding mules came abreast through the gorge to face him. They looked wild and uncouth enough in the dusk; there was something menacing in the silence with which they awaited the next move.

Politely James asked:

"Will you be so good as to let us pass, señores? You are barring the way."

There was no answer. The three men might have been carved from the dark rock surrounding them.

On James's repeating his request, less courteously this time, and on being ignored as before, he shouted to his companion:

"Come on, Da Silva! We'll charge these fellows!"

He remembered the tales he had heard of Spanish bandits and wished with all his heart that he had brought a pistol with him. He felt thankful that the diamonds were safe.

"Come on!" he shouted again, and, spurring his horse, rode straight at the three men. He was never to know quite what happened, although he saw that the bandits were flourishing great clubs, and one of these struck him violently on the back of the head. His horse plunged, and there was a clattering of hoofs.

He knew nothing more.

Ten minutes later, when Da Silva had searched his body and the saddlebags all in vain, his fury was ungovernable.

The diamonds were gone, and since he had no idea that they had ever been destined as a wedding present, he almost felt inclined to believe that they had been spirited away by black magic.

A heated altercation broke out between the hired bandits and himself; he tried to evade paying them what he had promised, and only his fear of their recriminations induced him to agree to their threatening demands.

"You've the body to strip, and there's the black stallion! There's a fine suit, isn't there, and a purse of money, and doubtless a watch! Such plunder as you seldom find! Now, out of my way—I've no wish to be caught anywhere near here!"

So saying, Da Silva rode away at breakneck speed through the gorge on his way towards the north.

When he had gone, and the sound of his horse's feet had died away, the bandits set about their work. When they had finished, they left James's naked body lying just outside the ravine, by the side of the road. Then they, too, rode away. The gorge was silent once more.

PART VI

Gitano

CHAPTER XXXVI

So LONG a period of darkness and oblivion as was to be James Darrell's lot can never, afterwards, be measured by known standards of time, since time has ceased to count; it is as though a sponge erases some portion of life forever from the mind of one who is thus struck down; those endless days and nights belong nowhere, mean nothing. Everything is black and blank and will always remain so.

That he was desperately ill, he of course knew afterwards. But how long afterwards he could never exactly determine. He asked at what time of the year they had found him, and was told the summer. So he thought, as he grew well enough to think at all, that he must have been near to death for three or four months.

During all that time there was a veil of darkness dragged across his mind, and, even later, his brief intervals of something like normality were shot with pain and clouded with a sense of utter bewilderment. Sometimes he noticed someone looking at him, and then when he asked questions, or complained that his head hurt, this person answered him clearly, and applied cold bandages where the pain was unendurable.

It seemed as though he had never known what it was to be without a headache. This, in his present state of weakness, was not only coherent thought, which was sensational in itself—it was more than that—it was a stupendous and advanced piece of reasoning. It lasted him for what seemed like a hundred years more of hovering on the fringes of blackness, then it was succeeded by another astounding reflection. The person who looked after him, and talked to him, and changed the bandages on his head, was a woman. Whether or not it was always the same woman he was of course unable to state. He couldn't, in any case, keep his eyes open for more than a few minutes. Sometimes he thought he heard people talking, and then he was even more confused, for their language, with the exception of a few stray words, was unintelligible to him.

Once he thought he heard someone say:

"I do as I please!"

Of course he was not entirely certain, and all might have been part of his interminable nightmare, but on another occasion he believed he caught the words:

"Better throw him back where you found him."

After many more periods of darkness and oblivion it was frightening, one day, to open his eyes and know for certain that the face looking down at him was a youthful one.

"Some girl . . . " he thought.

Some days afterwards, despite his headache, he was able to look at the girl quite sensibly. He had, of course, no recollection of ever having seen her before. She was smiling, her sparkling face was nut brown beneath a mop of black hair, but there was something wild and singular about her eyes. He was able, after that, to recognise her during these lucid intervals, and this, to both, was a step of major importance.

One day he asked, in a voice so weak he scarcely knew that he was speaking:

"Who are you?"

"I am Rosal."

He closed his eyes again, but during the next week the waves of pain were not so frequent, and he progressed enough to grasp the fact that sometimes an old woman looked after him in place of the girl.

"Where is she?" he asked the old woman in English, who replied that she did not understand him.

Mechanically he repeated his question in Spanish, without any idea that he was doing so.

"Out making money to keep you," was the curt answer.

A few days afterwards he saw the girl Rosal again. This time he was able to concentrate. He looked at her, recollected her name, and asked:

"Where are we?"

"Nowhere in particular. We're camping in some ruins, and staying until you are well enough to leave."

"I am in a tent, aren't I?"

"Yes."

"This all happened before," he said, bewildered, and then a band of pain closed round his head and forced him to shut his eyes.

Soon he was able to look about him, and then he perceived that he was in a roomy tent fashioned of skins. He lay on a divan of comfortable mattresses, and he saw that the girl Rosal sat cross-legged by his pillow, fanning him. When he heard the rapid clicking sound that was the snapping of her fan, he thought vaguely of some pattern he had once arranged in his mind, but it eluded him.

"You're good to me," he said suddenly.

"Maybe."

"Why?"

"I love you," she said frankly, in her young, husky voice.

"We love each other? Is that what you mean? I'm sorry, but I can't remember anything. . . ."

"I love you, yes. Don't talk any more."

"I can't even remember my name."

"You're Jaime. Don Jaime!"

"I'm not Spanish, am I?"

"No. Don't talk—your head will hurt!"

"I *must* talk! I feel better, and I want to know things. How long have I been ill?"

"Many weeks. Now you will soon be well."

"When will I remember what happened?"

"Ah! Don Jaime! Don't try to run before you can walk! You are getting well. Leave the rest until later!"

He slept then, but a few days later he resumed the conversation.

"Rosal, did you say we loved each other?"

"Yes," she answered, frowning.

"But I? My memory is a blank about that. You see—— Oh no, I'm sure—— It *wasn't* you. I loved someone else. I know I did!"

She said stubbornly:

"You loved *me*, Don Jaime."

"But when? How? I want to know!"

"I'll tell you when you feel better," Rosal said.

Later she explained:

"Don't you remember seeing me dance in Seville?"

"No," he answered. "I don't even remember having been in Seville. I just begin to know, now, that I'm somewhere in Spain, living with gypsy people, but that is all. I can't remember anything else. Why?"

There was a pause, then she said, looking straight at him with black, flashing eyes:

"You saw me dance, and you fell in love with me. But I went away. Then you had an accident on the road, and you were robbed. I found you at night, when I was driving home with the cart. I thought at first that you were dead, but your heart was beating, so I brought you here to the camp. Now you are nearly well."

"Who am I?" he asked.

"An Inglés. A traveller."

"I mean, what's my other name? You see, it worries me, not knowing . . . "

"I can't tell you," she answered, "but soon, as you get better every day, you will remember. Don Jaime, you love me, don't you?"

"Did I tell you I loved you in Seville?"

"You loved me when first we met. It was our destiny, our *baji*."

"But you married some rich man, whoever he was. Didn't you?"

"Don Jaime, I never married anyone! I'm a *mozita*—a virgin!"

He muttered, "I still don't understand."

She slid down beside him on the mattress and pressed her fruit-like cheek close to his.

"Don't you?" she whispered.

"Yes," he lied, for he was tired.

He didn't understand at all, and he could not help wondering why he had fallen in love with her, as she insisted that he had.

"Don Jaime?"

"For God's sake call me Jaime and have done!"

"Jaime! When you see me dance, you will love me all over again!"

"Rosal, what am I doing here in Spain?"

"You are a gentleman! You were travelling about the country and they robbed you!"

"Have I any money left?"

"No. But, *mi querido,* you mustn't worry—I make enough for both of us!"

"Wait until I get well!"

"Jaime, you love me, don't you?"

"Yes. It's only—I've been so ill—I've forgotten everything! I *must* have friends somewhere!"

"You have me, my Jaime."

"I know. You saved my life, Rosal, but I mean other friends—someone who told me to come here. Rosal, who was with me in Seville?"

She got up, stretching herself like a lithe young cat. She wore a rose-coloured skirt and a cream shawl. There were lumps of gold in her ears, and gold and silver bracelets tinkled on her tawny arms. She said:

"In Seville? When you told me you loved me? You were alone, Jaime; there was nobody else there. We were alone together."

CHAPTER XXXVII

ROSAL WAS SIXTEEN. Her parents were dead. Until a year ago she had lived with her grandfather, an astute old ruffian who was chief of the tribe with which they travelled. After his death she fended for herself. She was a remarkably independent girl and one of the best money-makers among the gypsies. She was an admirable dancer and an expert fortuneteller. She owned her own tent, cart, and pony. Since she was also exceedingly pretty, she of course had many suitors, but these she treated with a fierce contempt. She did, in fact, exactly as she pleased. When she grew tired of living with the Bear People, she disappeared for weeks at a time, visiting Jerez and Granada and Cadiz.

It was easy for her to find employment as a dancer. In Seville a rich gentleman was so impressed by her talent that he paid for her to enter the famous Académia as a pupil. But it was useless; she was too wild a bird to endure the discipline of the lessons; she ran away before she had been there a week.

When she saw James at the Baile Flamenco she fell in love for the first time in her life, and the love of such a nature as hers was of a passionate intensity. For her there were no halfway measures; she loved the young stranger, although he was a gajo; she wanted him more than she had ever wanted anything, and she was determined, if possible, to possess him and be possessed by him. But dauntless as she was, she did not quite know how to set about his capture.

He never returned to the Baile Flamenco, and she knew, of course, that he was a foreigner. She was a primitive creature, and she sat up at night preparing gypsy love charms, in the potency of which she firmly believed. One day, she assured herself, she would meet the stranger, and he would become her lover—her first and only lover. She was not quite sure how any of this was to be arranged, but she was prepared, if necessary, to follow him across the seas. She was very serious indeed about her magic, and it consoled her that she had overheard his name—Jaime. It made it easier for her to weave the spells that she had first gleaned from her grandmother, a noted witch.

And then she heard, by the mysterious grapevine system of communication current among the Egyptians, that the young man was to be robbed and murdered for the sake of some valuable jewels he was carrying to Madrid. She knew then, beyond all doubt, that the spells were as magical as her grandmother had always insisted.

She had not much time in which to work, but she made the most of it. She found the three disreputable gypsies who had been hired by Da Silva to act as assassins, and she bribed them to spare James's life. She would have preferred him unhurt, but when she was told that this was impossible, she wasted no time in arguing. She told them exactly where she would be waiting, and, in order to prevent any possible misunderstanding, she explained that she would be waiting with a loaded pistol. If the bandits killed James by mistake, she would kill them. That was her bargain.

And so she crouched near the ravine on the night of the robbery and overheard everything that passed. She was not in the least in terested to learn that there were no diamonds; she was possessed only by one idea—James.

When they delivered him into her hands, naked and unconscious, she put her ear against his breast, and satisfied herself that his heart was beating. Then, threatening the bandits with her pistol, she made them lift him into her cart, threw them the purse of money that she had promised, and drove away headlong across the mountains with her captive.

It was not until he was in her tent that she perceived the frightful extent of his head injury. In a panic, then, and terrified lest he should die, she saddled a fast horse and galloped off to the house of the nearest doctor. When the doctor refused to trust himself among the Egyptians, she swore that unless he followed her she would shoot him dead. She seemed demented, and he did not at all like the look of her pistol. So he consented to follow her, on the wildest ride of his life, and at the end of it he believed James to be dying.

Rosal possessed to a marked extent the art common to most gypsy women—that of knowing exactly how to charm and attract the gajos they so much despise. She now proceeded to charm the doctor, with the result that he promised to return the next day. He returned, and James was still alive, although the doctor, Don Matéo, thought that he might die before the evening. Rosal, fixing Don Matéo with her gypsy eyes, came closer, brushing against him, as she pretended to be weeping. Somehow, he never knew how, he found himself touching her young breast.

She said:

"If you save my brother, I will do anything you want. Anything in the world."

He asked her whether she would become his mistress.

"Yes, if you save my brother. But if you don't save him, I shall curse you, and then you will have ill luck for all your life!"

"My little gypsy, you must realise that your brother, as you call him, is gravely ill!"

"You heard what I said. It must be one way or the other!"

When James began slowly to recover, the doctor told her that his memory might be permanently affected.

"All the better!" She shrugged.

"And our bargain? When are you coming to my house?"

"When I know for certain that Jaime will live!"

"I am going to Madrid for three months. If you are not here when I come home, I shall report the whole matter of this 'accident' to the *gobierno,* and you will probably be put in jail. Do you understand? I'll put up with no gypsy tricks from you, my girl!"

She answered sullenly:

"I shall be here when you come back from Madrid. If Jaime is living, I will come to you."

This conversation took place while James was unconscious, so that he never even saw the gajo doctor. When Rosal first realised that he remembered nothing, she at once informed him how much he had loved her in Seville. She had no scruples where he was concerned. She wanted him, she was determined to have him, and that was the end of the matter. She had not the slightest intention of letting him know that they were strangers, or of telling him that he had had companions with him that night at the Baile Flamenco.

Rosal was, in fact, a wild and sensuous little animal. The strange life she led, sometimes dancing in dubious houses, sometimes wandering about the country with the Bear People, as the fancy took her, seemed in no way singular to her. She had been used, since babyhood, to scenes of violence—she had witnessed many fights with knives, seen many travellers attacked, as James had been, in lonely gorges, and had frequently watched desperate battles between gypsy smugglers and representatives of the law. She herself knew how to handle knives and pistols and guns. She could ride like a peón, lie like a trooper, and move more quietly in the woods than an Indian. Although her way of living was in many respects typical of the gypsy women of her age, she herself was more intelligent and more resourceful than her comrades. She was afraid of nobody.

She greatly enjoyed the adventure of her own life. She liked dancing, when she was in the mood; she enjoyed the bullfight, wine fiestas, horse fairs, and flamenco music. She liked to bake herself, lizardlike, in the sun, with a wineskin near at hand and a handful of tobacco with which to roll herself cigarettes. Because she had all the freshness and charm of youth, combined with a supple gypsy body; because her skin was tinted with a bloom like apricots; because she had red, ripe lips, and brilliant teeth, she naturally appealed to men, and this power, too, she much enjoyed, although it meant nothing more to her than the means of wheedling any number of small gifts from her admirers—bouquets of flowers, sweetmeats, tobacco, an occasional bracelet, and a prized collection of bright shawls, which she had sold in order to bribe the robbers who attacked James.

She was, until the night she danced at the Baile Flamenco in Seville, as lighthearted, thoughtless, and pagan as only one of her race can succeed in being. No one had ever touched her heart, and, apart from enjoying sunshine, music, wine, flowers for her hair, and the coaxing of money from gajos, she had probably never in all her life had an idea in her charming head.

Then, after one glance at the dark, grave young Englishman, her existence immediately suffered an upheaval as violent as any earthquake. Why it should have been James, no one knew, least of all herself, for she had not hitherto lacked a choice of attractive admirers. But she had always, until that fated evening, been as much boy—and street boy, at that—as girl. She had matured late for a gypsy. And perhaps she had forgotten, or ignored, during the birdlike freedom of her life, the fact that she was at heart utterly and ruthlessly feminine. She had nothing but this one quality in common with Oriana, the civilised lady from across the seas, yet both knew immediately what they wanted, both were equally determined to gain their objective.

Rosal's problems, compared to those produced by Oriana's complications, were simple. Whereas Miss Camperdene had wanted money and James, Rosal wanted only James.

Now, due, she was firmly convinced, to her gypsy spells, he lay in her tent, helpless, and she was convinced that he would never want to escape.

Soon, when he was better, he would know how much she loved him.

CHAPTER XXXVIII

When James was well enough to lie outside the tent on a mattress, he found that he was protected from the sun by the ruins of an old convent or chapel, inside which the tent was pitched. There was little left of the original building—three grey walls, with gaping eyes that had once been windows, overhung with clusters and tangles of creepers and vines. Where the garden had been there were a few old tombstones, half buried in moss, and here the roses had run riot, so that in summer they bloomed extravagantly, but already they had reverted to a wild, coral-flushed luxuriance.

"I was born here," Rosal told him one day, "that is why they called me after a rose tree." She added: "No Busnos—no Gentiles come here. It is haunted."

Sometimes they were alone in the ruined convent save for another tent, the home of the old woman, Joséfa. Sometimes, again, other carts and wagons came creaking up to join them, and although the shapes that crouched at night about the fire never came near to him, he did not need the sight of the enormous dancing bears to tell him that he was in a camp of the Ursari.

There was a forest surrounding the ruin, so that the overhanging branches of cork and chestnut trees formed a natural shady roof above the tents and carts. As soon as James became even vaguely aware of the passing of time, he perceived that Rosal frequently absented herself for periods of several days.

He disliked old Joséfa, to whom he scarcely ever talked, but once when the girl came back from one of these expeditions he asked her where she had been.

"Dancing, Jaime, in a town near here. I earned some gold *parné*."

"Of course! I'd forgotten you were a dancer. You will stay for a bit now, won't you?"

She knelt down by him, then, and put her cheek close to his.

"You are glad I came back?"

"Yes. You know I am. Are you staying?"

"I must go away tonight," she answered, after a slight pause, "but I'll come back tomorrow."

"Are you dancing again tonight?"

"Yes!" Her voice sounded abrupt, and he said no more.

A few minutes later she told him, stroking his hair and smoking one of her eternal cigarettes:

"You know, Jaime, before I was born, my parents, who were of the Ursari, had a dancing bear called Mara, who had cubs. My mother had been working too hard, dancing, and travelling, and when I was born, she died. So they gave me to Mara, the she-bear, and she suckled me with her cubs. Jaime, I loved Mara, and when she died, I think my heart was broken. I was eight. Since then I have loved nobody but you. I never will."

He smiled at her, touched. He did not think that he returned her love, but he supposed his indifference to be due to this serious illness. Soon, when he was well, everything would be all right between them, for he was sure that he was attached to her.

"That's why," she continued, "they call me the Daughter of the Bear." She added, after a pause: "Sometime, when you are better, I will tell you why I said this to you today—that except for Mara I have never loved anyone but you."

He thought that this story of her upbringing explained much that had intrigued him. Those fierce fits of rage he remembered overhearing as she railed at Joséfa for some imaginary forgetfulness regarding himself; the purring notes of her deep voice, when she told him that she loved him; those tawny flecks in the darkness of her eyes; her swift, soft movements; her passion for basking in the sun; her love of sweetmeats. Her moods of playfulness, even, had something of the animal: something wild and singular that, he felt convinced, was peculiar to herself.

Perhaps it was then that he felt sure he must have been mistaken to fall in love with her before his illness. But he was still too weak to ponder upon these problems, and he liked her company. She was, both as a nurse and as a companion, vastly preferable to old Joséfa.

So he said, pressing her hand:

"You will come back tomorrow, won't you?"

"I swear it, Jaime."

Later that evening, when he was fast asleep in the tent, she saddled her horse and rode away across the forest to the doctor's house on the other side of the pass. He had been pestering her since his return from Madrid, and she feared his threats. If the doctor reported the attack on James, James's friends might appear, and he would be taken away from her. To prevent this, she was willing

even to surrender the fierce chastity that is, despite their wild behaviour, proverbial among gypsy girls.

She tried to remember the doctor; she thought that he was a stout
man with a belly bulging above the *faja* swathed about his waist.
Not that it mattered. He could have been the best-looking, most
famous bullfighter in the kingdom, and still he would have sickened
her, because he was *not* James. She thought passionately, posses-
sively, of James: of the hollows left by illness beneath his grey eyes;
of his high cheekbones, too prominent now; of his generous, sensitive mouth. She loved him so much that her heart seemed to turn
with joy whenever she thought of him.

And then, recollecting the doctor, she stopped urging her horse
along the pass and rode slowly. Her charming face was no longer
pretty then; it was distorted with a fury of hatred.

Shadows began to fall from the gorges near the road, and the
sun was ebbing from the flushed sky. It would soon be twilight. She
rode on towards the doctor's house.

The next day James said to her:
"Rosal, you have been crying. What's the matter?"
She flashed back at him:
"Crying? What do you mean? Do you think me such a weakling?
I have *never* cried!"

Her cheeks were bright with a scarlet flush; she tossed the jetty
mop of her hair and moved swiftly out of view, to the other side of
the tent, but not before he had noticed, for the second time, her
reddened eyelids.

He lay quite still, thinking, as he had spent so much time in doing
for so many long and pain-darkened weeks.

Once again he was quite certain that whatever he might have
said to Rosal in Seville, he did not love her. For a moment, while
his tired brain tried to cope with so much that was still confusing,
he found that he was regarding her as a stranger—a half-savage
girl who was wild and hard and insolent. He forgot her devoted
care of him during his desperate illness, and said, with the petulant
ingratitude of a convalescent:

"Never cried? Well, perhaps if you had, my dear, you might be
a more sympathetic person. Did you never think of that?"

Rosal said nothing.

He tired then of his own fretfulness, and was silent too.

But he thought that her fantastic story of being suckled by the bear coarsened her in some strange way and made her appear curiously animal. Why, he could not say. She seemed fierce and cruel, except to him, but he did not think that that had anything to do with it. He had an idea that before his illness he had loved someone very different. Yet his mind was still so darkly clouded that he knew nothing more. All he knew was that Rosal, apart from being his nurse, was somehow vaguely distasteful to him. And he was growing stronger; he no longer needed a nurse.

A few days later she said:

"Jaime, do you mind moving to a village a few miles away through the forest? You're nearly well now; do you think you can bear the journey?"

"I can't go on staying with the Ursari," he replied to this. "If I'm well enough to travel, I'm well enough to find out who I am!"

She was prepared for this.

"I thought, Jaime, as you have no money, you would come with us and help us, perhaps, with the horses and mules. How can you trace your friends without a penny in your pocket?"

He pondered this.

"Will I soon be well enough to work?"

"Very soon!"

"If I learn to shoe horses, and to shear mules, will the Bear People give me my food free?"

"You know they will, Jaime. What do you think?"

"And of course my memory will soon get better. Yes, I'll stay. But I want my own tent—you must lend me the money for that! And I want to take off this beard—get one of the men to give me a razor!"

He said later, looking at a strip of mirror:

"Was my hair always so grey?"

"No," Rosal admitted, "only since you have been ill."

The night before they were due to leave she told him that she had an appointment.

"I shall take the fast horse and join you on the road tomorrow."

"Why? I don't understand."

"I have a debt to pay."

The next day he sat in the front of a wagon while the caravans of the Bear People wound their way through a country of rich woodland and frowning gorges. It was early in the morning, and still cool. He sat beside a dark, taciturn fellow named Lillo, and was unaware of the profound interest his appearance created among the gypsies. For months now he had lain hidden away in the ruined convent, tended only by Rosal and by old Joséfa. Now he emerged, Rosal's Busno, and was looked upon with veiled suspicion.

No other gypsy woman would have dared so openly to befriend a Busno. But Rosal was a law unto herself, and only stayed with the Bear People as long as it suited her. *Leis prala,* the gypsy laws, meant nothing whatever to her, and if she chose to defy them by marrying the Busno, then she would undoubtedly please herself. Threats of expulsion from the tribe would only make her laugh. The Ursari needed her more than she needed them.

While James looked about him, enjoying every moment of the journey, he heard behind them the thunder of horses' hoofs. Turning his head, he saw Rosal on her sorrel colt, galloping over the hill. She rode astride like a boy, easily, beautifully. He watched her leap the wide ditch leading onto the road. As she came up beside his wagon, he saw that her cheeks were vivid beneath the dusky tangle of her hair, and her black eyes flashed fire. She looked like a triumphant fury. The sorrel's flanks were heaving, and his neck was streaked white with lather.

"Where have you been?" James asked.

"I paid a debt."

CHAPTER XXXIX

SOME WEEKS LATER he said to her suddenly:

"This isn't the first time I've travelled with gypsies."

"You learned our language quickly."

"Yes. I may have spoken it before. Who knows?"

They had been to a horsefair near Cartagena and were returning together to the camp. She was in one of her melting and altogether charming moods. She had slipped her hand in his, and he retained it, finding it comforting. She wore a frilled dress of scarlet cotton with white spots—*"con lunares,"* as she said proudly, and a bunch of red carnations in her hair. He wore leather breeches, a blue shirt, and a scarf wound about his neck. It was she who had provided him with his gypsy wardrobe, and when he protested against any further obligations she silenced him with:

"You talk like a fool, my Jaime. How can you wear anything else when you have nothing? You can't walk about naked. Besides, you are working hard now, and the Bear People have accepted you as one of themselves."

This was true. He was strong enough, with the exception of an occasional bad headache, and it had been recognised by the gypsies that he was accustomed to the care of horses. So he fed them, rode them, groomed them, and learned to shoe them. He was happy, but his ambiguous relationship with Rosal troubled him profoundly. It was impossible not to know how much she loved him; her every glance and touch proved that, and the other gypsy girls were terrified of approaching him.

At first, in the weakness of convalescence, he had been irritated, even slightly disgusted, by her possessiveness. Now that he felt strong and well he regarded her somewhat differently. He was not, and never could be, in love with her, but he was beginning to need a woman, and she was the only one he knew. He was still dependent on her for everything. He was greatly in her debt, and every day, a dozen times a day, she did all she could to provoke him and to stir his blood.

As they were walking back from the horsefair, her hand in his, a heavy diligence came lumbering down the road, and they stepped aside to avoid it. She came close then, pressing against him. He could feel her heart beat; he could touch the swell of her young breasts. He kissed her. He had often wanted to do so before, idly, because she was pretty. Her lips were crimson, fresh, and sweet. He went on kissing her, half amused, half excited, by the passion with which she returned his caresses.

Then a frightful thought occurred to him. Remembering leis prala and that importance placed by the Caló people on the chastity of their daughters, he visualised with horror the trouble likely to be caused if he took Rosal as his mistress. He supposed that they would both be expelled from the tribe; he thought that he would be lucky indeed not to be found one fine night with a knife between his ribs, and he was sure of one thing—he had had enough violence to last him for the rest of his life.

To Rosal's consternation he at once stopped kissing her and remarked abruptly that they had better be on their way.

She followed him in resentful silence.

"Listen," he said after a pause. "When I was in Seville you are quite sure I had no friends?"

"You were alone, and a stranger," she answered sulkily. "When I had finished dancing you asked me to drink with you, and later that night you told me that you loved me. All this I've said before a thousand times! Jaime, why did you stop kissing me?"

"I never meant to kiss you!"

"That's a lie! My lips pleased you, didn't they? You wanted me, didn't you? You know I love you, and yet you torment me. You're a pig of a Busno, and I wish I'd left you to die upon the road!"

"Sometimes I wish you had!"

When they arrived, quarrelling thus, at the encampment, they both saw that something unusual had occurred during their absence, for although they were supposed to stay for the next two days in the glade chosen by the Bear People, the horses and mules were harnessed, the caravans and carts ready to take the road. The scene was wild and colourful, but already so familiar to James that he scarcely noticed the gypsies, with their bright rags, their streaming raven hair, the shaggy, mountainous shapes of the dancing bears, the painted carts, the string of young colts, the mules and asses and barking dogs. Already two boys were stamping out the fire, and as Rosal approached, the chief of the Ursari, a withered, pockmarked old man named Paco, beckoned to her, and they walked aside.

James's ears were sharp, and although they spoke in low tones he could not help catching the word "Busno," which at first he thought referred to himself, and then, more sinister, another word—"drao." He frowned, wondering what had happened, for the word drao means poison in the Caló language.

A few minutes later the gypsies were clattering away down the road, and James, who was responsible for three unbroken horses, had little time to think of anything but his own immediate problems.

The Bear People travelled all through the night, finally pitching their camp in a lonely ravine miles away from any village. Later, at supper, which they all ate together, just before the dawn, and were glad to huddle near the red glare of the fire, for the mountain air was cold, he caught Rosal's arm and asked:

"Why are we running away? What has happened?"

"Oh, just some trouble."

"What trouble?"

"Some dog of a Busno was sick, and the fool swore he had been poisoned by the gypsies. He had no proof, but Paco thought it best to come here for a few days."

"Is the Busno dead?"

"No. But he has been sick for some weeks. Now that he feels better, he finds nothing else to do than to accuse the Caló people!"

"How strange," James observed ironically.

She shot him a swift, mistrustful glance, but said nothing.

The next day he walked by himself for an hour or so, and tried, as he often did, to remember something about the past. But his efforts were useless, and he decided that to concentrate was fatal for his memory. It was only when he was thinking of something else that brief flashes of recollection returned to haunt his mind, and he stored them avariciously, a meagre hoard of treasure. At times he remembered some shadowy English village, with children, even more intangible, picking primroses in a wood. Then these phantoms merged into the panorama of a great city, and there were people whose faces were veiled to him, connected vaguely with writing upon many pages of paper. And there was someone else—someone who had made him very unhappy. His brain, struggling amid so much darkness, guessed that this person must have been a woman, but he could remember nothing whatever about her. He could not even remember his own surname, although it hovered tantalisingly near to him, and he knew that it began with D.

He returned tired and cross, as was his custom, from such expeditions, ready enough to forget Rosal, determined never again to kiss her. He was glad that she avoided him during supper, and soon afterwards he went to his tent, where he fell fast asleep.

He was awakened some time later by a rustling sound near him. Watchfully, without moving, he opened his eyes. The brilliance of a full moon flooded the tent, and by this argent light he perceived Rosal, wrapped in a dark shawl, kneeling beside his pillow. How many times she had knelt thus during his illness he did not remember, but he was well, now, and he sat up indignantly to confront her.

"Go away!" he told her, keeping his voice low, so that no one should hear them.

"Jaime, I *must* come to you! I can't stand it! Don't send me away!"

She slid nearer, with one of her supple movements, and dropped her shawl. She was naked, and the olive bronze of her body caught a silver sheen from the moonlight pouring into the tent. She was exquisite: the statue of a nymph straight from one of the formal Spanish gardens they sometimes passed on the road, and he knew that his heart was beginning to pound like a drum.

"You're mad!" he said. "You, a gypsy—a *mozita*—to come like this in the night——"

He stopped, for to his astonishment he saw that tears were streaming down her cheeks. Her tears glittered in the moonlight.

"What's the matter?"

She burst out sobbing and cast herself, despairing, at his feet, but he could not catch the sense of what she was muttering until he pulled her impatiently to her knees. Even then her voice was choked, and this was a Rosal he had never seen before. She clung to him, gasping:

"Jaime, I am not! That's what you don't know!"

"Not what? What do you mean?"

"I am not—a mozita—any more!"

"So you were lying?"

"I was *not* lying! I had to go with the Busno doctor! He wouldn't come to you otherwise!"

"What doctor? What are you talking about?"

"The one who looked after you! The pig—the filthy swine! I was a mozita until that night. I was waiting for you!"

He listened with horror as she sobbed out the rest of the story. No one knew better than he the proverbial chastity of gypsy girls, and for a moment the extent of her devotion almost suffocated him. Great heaven, he thought, what can I ever do for her in return?

"Rosal, stop crying——"

"And now you don't want me, Jaime! Oh, Mother of God, why was I born?"

"Listen to me! I *do* want you! Do you hear? I shall marry you! *Now* will you stop crying?"

A few minutes later her head was on his breast, and she was quiet.

"I might do worse," he argued to himself. "She'll be content to be married gypsy-fashion, and I'm no catch for anyone. I have no name, no money, no memory. I may as well stay with the gypsies. And she loves me. There are worse lives——"

These reflections were interrupted by Rosal herself, all trace of tears now magically vanished. She said with a sigh of pure bliss:

"And I paid my debt."

He was conscious of an awful suspicion.

"What do you mean by that?"

"I poisoned him," she said frankly. "I give the Busno doctor *drao*. That's why we had to run away."

He was silent, because he could think of nothing to say. Suddenly he shuddered, and she asked if he were cold.

"No."

"I am so glad I gave him drao," Rosal confided, snuggling against him like a sleepy kitten, "and I am very sorry indeed he is not dead."

CHAPTER XL

THE GYPSY WEDDING took place three days later in the ravine, suitable setting for a scene of so much wildness. Prompted by Rosal, James went the day before to the nearest town, taking with him two donkeys, which returned laden with boxes of sweetmeats—chocolates, sugared almonds, caramels, and *marrons glacés*. These were not for the feast itself but for use in a manner peculiar to Spanish gypsy weddings.

It was humiliating that he had no money with which to pay for the casks and skins of wine ordered by Rosal, for the suckling pigs and chickens and hams she considered necessary for the feast. Some of the gypsies, James noticed, were inclined to view the marriage with hostility, although they all knew, and defended fiercely, Rosal's attempt to poison the Busno doctor.

It was in the morning, while the gypsy women were roasting over spits, that he watched them idly, since there was no work to be done that day. He thought how long it was since he had accepted such curious scenes as a natural part of his life, and it occurred to him that when Rosal described him as a "gentleman," he must, before his travels in Spain, have been accustomed to a very different life.

"Whenever I can manage to get some money," he thought, "I shall go back to England and discover where I belong."

Then he remembered that he was just about to be married according to leis prala, and he sighed. He found Rosal's callousness unpleasant, despite her devoted and unselfish love for himself; she was ignorant, and bloodthirsty as a young leopard, and yet he knew, had he loved her, that there was much to reclaim, much that was fine about her nature. She was utterly courageous, and, where her own people were concerned, fearlessly truthful. She was recklessly generous, as he knew by experience, and he had found her a skilful, tireless nurse. He had watched with admiration her patient care of foals and bear cubs, and he could never remember hearing her complain of hardship. She was passionately fond of beauty—deeply moved by colour and music and flowers.

As against these qualities her hatred of his own race annoyed him. He disliked her savage, fiery temper, and her indifference to the sufferings of people other than her own frankly disgusted him. Thinking of these things, he picked up a piece of paper in which some chocolate had been wrapped, took a charcoal stick from near the fire, and began to scribble, in English, a description of her character. At first the words came awkwardly, and the language seemed strange, but soon he became absorbed in what he was doing and did not hear her when she called to him.

"Jaime!"

"Rosal," he said excitedly, "I remember something. I used to be a writer!"

"Jaime, it's time you shaved, and here's the clean handkerchief for your neck!"

"Look—do you see what I've been doing?"

She put her hand on his shoulder indulgently, as though encouraging a child.

"But of course you can write. You're a scholar, a grand gentleman! Come, mi querido, it's time to get ready!"

She herself wore the flame-coloured dancing dress that glittered with sequins; there was a bunch of white jasmine in her black hair, and her cheeks were carnation-flushed with happiness and excitement.

There would be no "white flag," no handkerchief flying from a wand to proclaim this bride's virginity, at the wedding, but she was past caring, although at first she had minded desperately. She only wanted Jaime, and soon, now, in a few minutes, he would be hers forever.

James himself never forgot his gypsy marriage.

There he stood, in the midst of the dark, frowning ravine, Rosal, brilliant as a rainbow, by his side, while old Paco, knife in hand, pronounced the words that would make them man and wife according to Egyptian law. On every side of them peered the dusky faces of the Bear People. Somewhere a child cried, a horse whinnied, and he could not help noticing that two large brown bears watched the ceremony with exactly the gravity of human beings.

He set his teeth as Paco's knife jabbed at his wrist, then, a moment later, when blood was flowing from Rosal's, Paco bound their two wrists together with a red silk cord, so that the blood mingled, and they were one.

At this moment the gypsies set up a deafening noise of yells, howls, and maniacal shouts. Guns and pistols were discharged into the air, the dogs barked madly, and one young horse stampeded away down the road.

The feasting began at once; he sat with Rosal by his side, eating hunks of savoury meat and drinking quantities of red wine. He thought that he might feel happier if he got drunk—very drunk. But the wine did not seem to affect him. Rosal was quiet. She put her arm through his, and sometimes glanced at him out of the corner of her eye.

Later that evening the guitars were produced, and flamenco music sang through the ravine. Strange and unearthly it sounded to James, as the eerie, wailing *coplas* echoed somewhere far behind the gorge. Rosal was called upon to dance, and she sprang forward like a young witch in the flame-coloured shimmer of her dress. In front of the fire, which cast a red glow upon her whirling figure, she danced, with every art and grace she knew, the seductive *farruca,* that dance of which the Spaniards say: "The devil taught it, and they dance it down in hell."

James was possibly less sober than he supposed. Half closing his eyes, it seemed to him that her body undulated like that of some jewelled snake, supple and lascivious, in the crimson firelight. And then, as though someone spoke in his ear, he recollected a voice from out of the mists of the past:

"Some bitch of a gypsy dancer will mesmerise you into thinking she has jumped over the moon itself."

"Diamonds," he thought vaguely, as he himself was pulled into the dance with the other gypsies, who were all flocking to take part.

The sweetmeats, without which no Spanish gypsy marriage festival can be complete, were strewn upon the ground in a great circle more than three inches deep. Upon this sugary crust the dancers ran forth with shouts and yells of delight. Then, as the guitars throbbed out the wildest of flamenco airs, the whole party began to dance the *romalis.* James, who could not dance, was whirled round once or twice, and then retired, to sit peacefully beside one of the bears, which, excited by so much noise and merriment, jigged frantically up and down, as though longing to join in the fun.

"*Meklis!*" said James solemnly to the bear.

He drank some more wine, flung himself on the ground, and watched the Bacchanalian scene with a dazed eye. In a few moments the sugar-candy floor was stamped into a pulp, and the dancers' legs were plastered with chocolate, turron, and sugar. Nearly all the gypsies were drunk by this time; they bounded wildly in the air, snapping their fingers in time to the music, screaming, singing, flinging themselves into indecent poses, dislocating their limbs acrobatically, as though determined to break every bone in their supple bodies. The spinning figures and the brightness of their gaudy dresses made him feel giddy; he shut his eyes, and was a thousand miles away.

"God!" he prayed, "for some peace!"

He hoped that he was not going to start one of his bad headaches.

In a second Rosal was beside him. Her black eyes glittered, her breast heaved, and her cheeks were as bright as her vivid lips. He noticed that her bare legs were spattered with a mess of sugar, and he said to himself:

"I've not married a woman. She's a wild animal!"

And he wished, in a sudden panic, that the bandits had killed him that night long ago when she had found him lying by the side of the road.

"You're silent, my heart," she said, putting her hand on his knee, and she hoped very much indeed that he was not as tired as he looked.

The fragrance of her jasmine flowers and of her warm young flesh was very close then, and he felt himself relaxing, thawing from the ice-bound fit of nerves in which she had found him.

"I wish we could go away now," he said. "How much longer is this hellish noise going on?"

"They will feast all night. But we shall soon be able to leave. In about half an hour. Don't you want to know where I am going to take you?"

"Yes, of course. Where?"

"I know a place in the forest, hidden away among the chestnut trees. There's a pool there, where the water is always snow-cold. Caló people call it the pond of the miracle. There's moss on the ground, thick and soft as the king's carpet, and you can make a pillow from the violets that grow there. There are birds singing in the grove of camellia trees by the pool, and the leaves are so thick that at night you can scarcely see the stars."

"Let's go now," he urged restlessly.

"Jaime, the Ursari would not forgive so easily if we left before the ramalis is finished. Remember I come of their blood!"

"The Daughter of the Bear! I shan't forget that."

Instantly sensitive to his moods, she knew that he was bored, perhaps disgusted, by the noise, the extreme licence, of the party. She herself was childishly delighted with the wedding feast and was prepared to enjoy every moment with gypsy exuberance, but Jaime was different: he was an Inglés, and a gentleman. She murmured as much respectfully, filling his glass. She said:

"I'll harness the pony now. The cart is ready."

"Good. Rosal, you'll wash all that sweet stuff off your legs before we go, won't you?"

"Of course," she answered, in surprise, "if you want me to."

"I do," James told her emphatically.

A few moments later he found himself making a speech. He supposed that he was very drunk. No one listened to his speech, for the noise was approaching a diabolical crescendo, and indeed, if they had listened to him, they would not have understood a word, since he addressed them sonorously in English.

"I, James Darrell, Englishman and scholar . . ."

It was not until the next day that he remembered his full name for the second time.

He fell asleep in the cart as they drove away to Rosal's forest glade, and later that night, as he lay in her arms, he called her by a name that was not hers, but which she immediately divined to be that of another woman—a woman from that secret past of his which so much tormented her.

He called her "Oriana" in his sleep, and smiled, resting his head on her breast. When dawn came, she was still awake.

CHAPTER XLI

IT WAS THREE YEARS LATER, and El Flamenco, the matador, was fitting his new fighting costume, his *traje de luces*. Twenty-two that day, the youth was of medium height, with the narrow flanks and square shoulders typical of his profession. He was a gypsy, darkly handsome, save for lips that were too thick, olive-skinned, with hair smooth as black satin. The *coléta*, that short pigtail emblematic of his trade, protruded jauntily from the back of his small, well-shaped head.

He pirouetted, well pleased, before a long mirror, puffing cigar smoke at his own brilliant reflection. The new suit was olive green, skin tight, encrusted with glittering silver embroidery.

"Not bad, eh, Jaime?"

"Not bad, Juan."

"Not flashy, you know, but in good taste, eh?"

"Excellent! What about these letters?"

James had exchanged his gypsy sheepskin for a maroon suit cut like that of any Andalusian peón. He wore riding boots with long spurs and a frilled lawn shirt. He towered above the young *torero,* but he was as darkly tanned as the other. Against so much sunburn, his hair, prematurely grey since his long illness, gleamed light as silver.

"What about those letters?" he repeated.

"Is there anything important?"

"Nothing that can't wait. Half a dozen from women."

"One from a girl called Clarita?"

"If you wait, I'll tell you."

El Flamenco hummed to himself as he stripped off the heavy embroidered jacket.

"Clarita—Calle Tetuan?" James enquired, after a pause.

"That's it. Take down this letter for me: 'Dear Clarita. Thank you for writing. Will you meet me after my fight on Sunday at the Café Antonio? You are beautiful, and—and——' How can I finish, Jaime?"

" 'And I will send you some roses red as your own lips'?"

"Excellent! Can you take that note—and the roses—on your way home tonight?"

"Very well."

El Flamenco flung himself, half naked as he was, onto the four-poster bed. The bronze of his splendid body was seamed white with the scars of his many *cornadas.*

"Where did you learn so much, Jaime? How to write, and read, and speak so many languages?"

"In England," James answered shortly.

"Will you ever go back to England?"

"I should think it extremely unlikely."

The matador watched him for a moment with a sly, cunning, street-boy expression.

"And Rosal? Where is she?"

"Making a new costume, I believe. She's dancing all this week."

"You know," El Flamenco declared, still watching James from the corner of his eye, "you know, I wonder, Jaime, that you let her travel about alone to fulfil so many contracts. And you—when you're away with me, as a member of my *cuadrilla?* Do you never feel uneasy?"

"Why should I feel uneasy, Juan?"

The young man burst into a fit of ribald laughter.

"She's so pretty, Jaime! All the men like Rosal! Have you never heard of San Marco's brotherhood? Of husbands with horns?"

"Juan," James said slowly, "last summer, here in Granada, I knocked you down for saying that. Do you remember?"

Juan's laughing urchin's face changed swiftly into a mask ugly with a furious anger.

"Do I remember? Did I not swear to shoot you if you so much as touched me again?"

"That threat doesn't frighten me. Threats from you don't. Is there anything else you want before I go?"

"No," the boy growled, turning away his face.

"I'll come to the café tonight."

"Don't forget Clarita's roses! Have you any money?"

"Enough," James answered. He walked downstairs and through the cool hall out into the shady patio. He stood for a moment beneath the orange trees there, and thought that if he owned the bullfighter's house he might be happy enough in Granada.

Once more, for the hundredth time, as he walked out into the glare of the street, he tried not to dislike the arrogant young man who was his master. Juan, in the arena, was a skilful and valiant killer of bulls. He faced death every Sunday with nonchalance and calm. When he was wounded, he suffered pain bravely and without complaint. It was part of his job. He was generous and gay.

As against these admirable qualities, he was common as only a spoiled gypsy can succeed in being, conceited, boastful, interested solely in himself. He was truculent in his cups and much enjoyed describing every detail of his amorous conquests. He was insolently rude to those he employed, and an arrant liar. In so far as he was capable of being in love, he was in love with Rosal and had been before she knew James.

Her indifference maddened him, and he was determined to possess her. Unlike other Caló men, the fact that she was James's wife according to gypsy law affected him not at all. He had lived too much among those who were not of his race, accepting their baser standards because they appealed instinctively to all that was ruffianly in his own character.

For several years now he had stalked Rosal, and he was quite sure that he would get her in the end.

It was Rosal who had obtained for James a post in El Flamenco's cuadrilla. With her usual shrewdness, she had divined from the first that his gifts as a scholar must be utilized to earn his living. She knew how deeply his pride had suffered during those months of horse coping for the Ursari. And so, using all her considerable powers of coquetry, she managed to insinuate him into Juan's cuadrilla.

A little later matters arranged themselves as she had always desired. James was soon promoted to the post of Juan's secretary, and this left him free to do what he apparently enjoyed doing more than anything—covering reams of paper with scribbled, incomprehensible writing. Why he should wish to do this was a mystery to Rosal, but it kept him quiet and happy, and was, incidentally, the most harmless of amusements.

James walked slowly back in the direction of the Sacro Monte, pausing only to leave some roses at the girl Clarita's house. For more than two years he and Rosal had made their permanent home up at the Albaicin, where hundreds of gypsies lived in caves burrowed like swallows' nests in the face of the mountain. Here again the decision was hers. She knew that he must have a permanent home, and this was the best she could devise.

He was acquiescent. He loved Granada, that lovely Moorish city of graceful, fantastic architecture, sunshine, and laden orange groves. They lived comfortably enough in their eyrie overlooking the blue, snow-topped mountains of the Sierra, and they were both earning money.

But, as Rosal well knew, his life was broken.

His memory had returned slowly, painfully, and with it full knowledge of the trick she had played upon him. If, during the first weeks of his illness, she had communicated with Pablo, the guide, Pablo could have been sent to Doña Adriana, in Seville. Then Don Ignacio would have known what had befallen him.

When at last his memory returned he wrote to Don Ignacio in London. Some time later a secretary wrote back formally, telling him that the diamond merchant had died that same winter after a heart attack. For a time, then, James thought of going to Madrid, to Don Ignacio's office, there to cast himself upon the mercy of those who controlled the business. But his letter of introduction had vanished with everything else on the night of the robbery, and with the news of Don Ignacio's death all desire to work in an office disappeared.

Still apathetic and moody after his illness, he shrank from communicating with Doña Adriana. He could not even remember her married name.

He decided that he had better make the best of a bad business. He had married, according to Caló laws, a gypsy; he was secretary to a bullfighter; and he could write as well in Spain as in England. When he had finished the book he had been compiling for the last year, he supposed that he could send it to some publisher in London.

When he discovered the extent of Rosal's deceit, there was a violent scene between them. He accused her of ruining his life with her lies and gypsy trickery, whereupon she raged back at him because so far there was no sign of a baby, and she wanted one with all her heart. James was thankful. He had not the slightest desire to have a child by her.

They quarrelled frequently, and sometimes, when he heard himself shouting at her, he thought he was no better than any other gypsy *rom* from the Sacro Monte.

At night, when she was out dancing, he sat down to write details of humble life in Spain, and had the consolation, at least, of knowing that he was attempting something no one else could do. What other Englishman, he wondered, could know what it was like to travel the country as a member of El Flamenco's cuadrilla? He himself was familiar with everything there was to know behind the scenes of a bullfight, and he thought that the most temperamental prima donna in the world would have been easy to manage, compared to coping with the arrogance, vanity, and jealousy of this young man who so bravely faced death in the arena every Sunday.

El Flamenco's pursuit of Rosal was another nuisance, he reflected, since it resulted in so many passionate complaints to him. He sighed, climbing the Camino of the Sacro Monte, and smiled at the acquaintances he met, but his thoughts were far away.

CHAPTER XLII

HE WOULD NEVER FORGET the day on which the memory of Oriana returned to trouble his mind.

They were still travelling with the Bear People, and one spring evening they were going after supper to the town of Jerez, where James was to look at a colt. Rosal, delighted as always by the idea of any outing, dressed herself in the red cotton dress with the white spots, and in her black mop of hair she tucked a spray of white hyacinths.

He came into the tent when she was ready and asked:

"What's that sweet smell?"

"These."

"What?"

"My white hyacinths."

He had at this time partially recovered his memory; he knew that Don Ignacio had sent him out to Spain with a diamond necklace. He knew that he was a doctor's son from Oxfordshire. But there was much that was still clouded, and the scent of Rosal's flowers seemed to open a door that led, through darkness, into a blinding light. He stood for a moment in silence.

"What is it?" she asked, as he did not speak.

The light flooding his mind still dazzled him, and he did not even hear her voice. Slowly his brain began to focus, and disconnected details became clear. A woman whose skin had reminded him of white hyacinths. A little girl who wore a hood of holly red. Someone whose silken petticoats had rustled in an English house hidden away in the trees of a spacious park. A witch woman, a sorcière, who had enchanted him, and yet, perplexingly, a child who had scrambled up trees in search of birds' nests. A child who had said, "Grownups are fools!" and a woman who had possessed him all one clover-scented summer night. And her name . . .

"Jaime, what is it? Why do you look like that?"

He did not hear.

He had no need to search any longer for her name, for it returned to him, there and then, together with a rush of memories so bitter sweet that for a moment he shut his eyes. She was very clear, then, to him, Oriana. Rosal receded somewhere far away. Oriana! She was so tall that she had always topped his heart; she was pale as lilies, her nose was tilted, and her eyes were deep and clear and brown as a trout stream. He remembered her wide white brow, and he could almost sniff the perfume of her dark silken hair. She was a baggage, a wilful woman, a mercenary creature who had driven him to despair. She had been what someone once called voodoo, and she still possessed his heart. Even the memory of her, after so many blank months, was enough to stir his blood, and he knew then, with a sad finality, that without her there could be no magic.

"Jaime!"

He turned then, having forgotten Rosal's existence, and the roughness of his voice surprised them both.

"Throw away those flowers!"

"What do you mean?"

"Throw away those damned flowers!"

"My white *jacintos?*"

"Yes!"

She obeyed him, as she always did. He was incomprehensible to her, but she loved him so much that she did not mind. Half the time he was somewhere far away from her, and then she was quiet, and did not bother him with questions. He would never forgive her for the trick she had played on him when he was ill. He had told her so frankly. She knew that he did not love her. He loved that other woman, to whom he had called in his sleep.

Yet he was dependent on her, and she, in her primitive way, was a philosopher. She hoped to make herself so indispensable to him that he would be unable to live without her. Let his fine lady try to keep him, living on his wits in Andalusia! Only Rosal could do that!

She thought that if they had been married in church it might have meant more to him. He probably would have been willing still to marry her, had she asked him, but her pride rebelled, and she refused to do so. She was simple enough to believe that a baby would hold him. She had no idea that he did not want a child by her.

Having on this fatal evening obediently discarded her white hyacinths, she remarked:

"It's time we went into Jerez."

"I'm not going," he replied in an absent tone of voice.

"Not going? But——"

"Take Lillo with you. He'd like it."

"Very well!"

She asked, after a pause:

"Don't you *mind* my going alone to Jerez with Lillo?"

"Mind? Why should I mind?"

"He's a very handsome man," Rosal informed him sadly.

"I can't help that. I don't feel like company tonight."

"Very well, Jaime."

She could think of nothing she disliked more than the idea of going into the town without him. As she was about to leave the tent, she suddenly exclaimed scornfully:

"Lillo! That pig—that brute! Mother of God—you don't care what happens to me!"

"I do! But sometimes I like to be alone! Can't you understand that?"

She could not, and, giving him her mouth to kiss, was repelled by his evasiveness. How could she know that he was haunted?

She ran out of the tent in a rage, took another Ursari girl with her in the cart, and boxed Lillo's ears for keeping them waiting in the *posada*.

"Your *rom*," Lillo said sourly as they drove back to the camp, "your husband should beat you."

She flashed him a wicked look, but said nothing.

Ever since that evening James was remote with her, and much of the physical pleasure they had enjoyed together was from then on lacking in their relationship.

He thought of these matters as he walked past the honeycomb of gypsy caves towards his own home, farther up the hill. Women sat on the low steps of their doorways and gossiped with one another. Children played in the dusty road, and here and there a mongrel dog sat happily scratching its fleas.

James passed a forge where two mules waited to be shod, and where an enormous gypsy smith, naked to the waist, hammered away at his anvil. He exchanged greetings with various friends, and one part of him mechanically noted that wild exuberance of colour without which the Romany race appears unable to live. He himself was now accepted by the gypsies as one of themselves—the greatest compliment they could pay. They trusted him, confided in him, and occasionally took his advice. They respected his prowess with his fists even more than they admired his skill as a scholar, and he, the Inglés, the Busno, was now one of the most popular inhabitants of the Sacro Monte rookery.

Not, he thought, smiling ironically, that that was much to boast of, yet, as a small boy, hanging about the Brazils' tents, it would have seemed a glorious destiny. Although he was young, his childhood, whenever he thought of it, seemed incredibly remote; due, perhaps, to so many months' loss of memory. Sometimes he thought that had he been alone in the world, he would have liked to return to England, and to the Oxfordshire village of his birth. It would have been pleasant to see Ackland Wood once more, and the Hall where he had so often played with Oriana. He wondered what had happened to Mr. Camperdene. But he himself had no ties now in England; he had written once to his mother in Bath, only to receive a letter from his uncle telling of her death, and he heard that his sister was still in India.

His only ties were those he had formed in this sun-scorched land across the seas, and any idea of taking Rosal to England he dismissed as fantastic. As for leaving her, even for a few months, that, too, was impossible, for once separated from her he doubted very much if he would ever have the will power to return. From what he knew of her he realised, without conceit, but rather with the increasing panic of being trapped in a gypsy snare, that she would be quite capable of killing herself.

He sighed as he left the glare of the road for the cool dusk of what he had learned to look upon as his home.

CHAPTER XLIII

The cave was large and airy. Like the other caverns honeycombed near by in the rocks, it possessed a rough fireplace and a small window scooped out of stone. It had no door, but at night they hung a faded bullfighter's cape across the arch, and this served them admirably as a curtain. Inside, the cave was whitewashed and bare. The huge mattress that served as a bed was covered with bright shawls, there was a plain wooden table, there were two or three chairs, and a brown bearskin rug spread before the fireplace. On a bench James's books were piled untidily, and by the bed Rosal had placed a small statuette of the Macaréna, the gypsies' Virgin of Hope, which stood on a three-legged stool, a burning taper before it.

Washbasins and cooking utensils were piled away behind a screen with which James had amused himself, more than a year ago, by pasting on it pictures of famous toreros. The cave was clean, and usually tidy, Rosal having mended most of her sluttish ways.

When he came in that evening she was no longer employed in sewing flounces upon her fuchsia-coloured dancing dress, which hung upon a chair in the corner. She was kneeling on the floor of hard, beaten mud, her back towards him, utterly absorbed in what she was doing.

He had no illusions as to her business.

"Rosal!"

She sprang to her feet, revealing on the floor a rough pentacle drawn in chalk, wherein lay a heap of white chickens' feathers, a bunch of withered herbs, a rabbit's foot, some ash twigs, and a small leather bag, doubtless containing some species of gypsy amulet.

She stammered:

"I didn't expect you back so soon!"

"I'm sure you didn't! Will you clear away that rubbish, there's a good girl?"

He threw off his hat, took a drink, by the simple expedient of tilting the spout of a wine jar into his mouth, and watched her out of the corner of his eye as she obeyed, her lower lip mutinous, her brow frowning. He knew better than to enquire into the nature of her spells; these were always either to excite his passion, or to enable her to conceive a child. Latterly, the former charm had not unnaturally become the more important of the two, the one usually practiced directly his back was turned.

"Rosal," he asked, sitting on the edge of the table, "do you really think all that mumbo-jumbo will help you to get whatever it is you want?"

She would have liked to remind him that her gypsy charms had succeeded originally in obtaining for her himself, but knowing only too well his opinion of her trickery in that matter, she evaded the question, and retorted:

"You believed in witches yourself when you were little! You told me so."

"When I was a child! You're not a child."

No, she certainly was not. She had developed into a beautiful girl, being, at nineteen, in the bloom of her brief, fiery prime. She was no longer so thin; she was gracefully but supplely made, and her sun-warmed skin had the flush of apricots. Her full lips were redder than the camellia tucked behind her ear, and she moved so lithely that she seemed always to be dancing. Even now, in her old rose-coloured skirt and yellow bodice, she was seductive, as she told him, tossing her head:

"I don't think I was even born a child, Jaime. There's an *arroz valenciana* for supper."

Later, as they ate together, he said:

"If I object to these spells, it's because they upset you and make you unhappy."

"There you're wrong. It's not my spells that do that."

Her black eyes met his directly, and, to change the subject, he said:

"Are you dancing here at the Albaicin tonight?"

She shook her head.

"No, mi querido. For the next three nights I'm dancing at the Baile in town."

He reflected. She was seldom free, the nights that she danced, until six o'clock in the morning.

He said:

"I'll go to bed early and come to fetch you about half-past five. You'd like that, wouldn't you?"

She hesitated.

"Wouldn't you?"

"Jaime, you look tired. I'd rather you slept late. I shall only be restless if I think of you waking up just to fetch me from the Baile!"

"Very well. As you like! We'll go down to the town together. What good coffee you make, Rosal!"

And he reproached himself for his own indifference, when he saw that this one word of praise sufficed to make her vivid face as radiant as a sunbeam.

When the dancing dress had been carefully packed, they walked together down the hill, and then, before the Sacro Monte colony, Rosal was, as usual, so proud of her rom that she forgot his strange, moody ways, and was able to imagine that he loved her as much as she loved him. She clung to his arm, gay as a hummingbird, and when he left her at the Baile—a famous haunt of gypsy artists—she kissed him warmly on the lips, and he thought once again that she had many pretty ways.

He walked to the fashionable café patronised by El Flamenco, and found, as usual, that the bullfighter had not appeared. He was not surprised, his patron usually being about an hour late for his appointments. He ordered a glass of wine and began to read the newspaper.

A few minutes later he heard behind him an English voice, speaking careful Spanish, call for some Valdepeñas, and impulsively, without thinking, he turned round to look at the first fellow country-man he had encountered for many months.

He saw a good-looking young man, obviously dressed by an English tailor, about whose face there was something so familiar that James, forgetting his usual caution, continued to stare, bewildered, since even now his treacherous memory occasionally played him false.

He should have known better, for suddenly the young man asked in English:

"Surely I'm not mistaken? It *is* James Darrell, isn't it?"

There was a pause.

"Yes," James admitted at length, "but I'm afraid—my memory is bad."

"I'm Jeffrey Lucas," the young man replied. "Don't you remember our evening at the inn, with—with Silver?"

"I remember," James said, speaking slowly, because his own tongue was unfamiliar to him. "Of course I remember. It was a long time ago."

"Near on four years."

"It seems longer to me."

"Won't you join me, Darrell?"

"For a few minutes, until my friends get here, there's nothing I'd like better."

Lucas was frankly mystified by the exotic appearance of this acquaintance from the past. James was burnt dark as oak brown, and his peón's dress, with the clinking spurs, frilled shirt, and high-crowned Andalusian hat, made him appear so foreign that he had at first hesitated before addressing this comrade of an English summer night.

When James removed the rakish hat, Lucas perceived with astonishment that his once-dark hair was blanched grey.

James grinned at his surprise.

"I was ill, here, for about a year. I wonder you recognised me."

"You wrote to me when Silver was transported," Lucas said, without any preliminaries, pouring out another glass of wine, "and since you gave me no address, I was never able to thank you as I wished. Now I can tell you how grateful I shall always be for your thoughtfulness. If I can ever serve you——"

"Silver!" James repeated, remembering the road girl and Little Egypt for the first time. "Why, tell me, were you able to help her?"

Lucas' boyish face looked suddenly drawn.

"She's dead," he said. "She died two years ago. But I was able to help her, and I owe you a debt I can never repay."

"It was nothing!" James answered impatiently. There was a pause, and then he enquired: "May I ask what you're doing in Spain?"

"I've been a year at the Embassy as honorary attaché," the young man replied, "and now I'm on my way home by Gibraltar. I know only Madrid, and so I took this opportunity of visiting Andalusia."

"How long are you staying in Granada?"

"I leave tomorrow morning, on my way to Seville. Are you staying here long?"

"I live here."

"I remember you were a writer! I suppose you find this part of the world an ideal place to work in?"

"I'm still trying to be a writer, if that's what you mean," James answered, not without bitterness, "but I've been wandering about Spain for some years. I'm acting as secretary to someone whose headquarters are here."

"I suppose," Jeffrey Lucas suggested, with his charming smile, "I suppose there's no hope of persuading you to travel with me as far as Seville?"

James thought of El Flamenco's Sunday fight and frowned.

"I'm afraid none. I'm so sorry, Lucas—there's nothing I'd have enjoyed more!"

"In that case," young Lucas insisted, "you must promise that when you're next in England you'll come and stay with me. Is it a bargain?"

James was silent for a moment.

It had taken this young man to remind him poignantly of all that he had for so long forgotten. Listening to Lucas talk, he thought of many things—of lush green meadows, far away in England; of rose gardens in June; of bright buttercups; cool, rainy skies; of rooks nesting in wind-swept trees; of crisp September mornings, with cobwebs spread like lace upon the brambles; and of winter frosts, with skating, and carols sung at Christmas in a snowstorm.

"Is that a bargain?" Lucas repeated, wondering why he looked so troubled.

"I'm afraid I'm unlikely to return to England. If ever I do, I promise I'll visit you. But—I have—commitments here. I can't leave. I'm sorry."

CHAPTER XLIV

LUCAS THOUGHT, "a woman," but naturally did not say so. James had attracted him during the very brief period of their friendship in England, and here, in Andalusia, he seemed a strange being—mysterious, haunted, secretive. The guarded reference to an unspecified illness, combined with blanched hair, an olive skin, and a peón's dress, all intrigued the young man immensely, but he saw that he had best keep silent.

At last he said:

"In any case, I have your promise, and you know my address, since you wrote to me from Plymouth."

"Better give it to me again," James said abruptly; "my memory's bad."

As Lucas scribbled on a piece of paper, a flashy-looking young man, accompanied by a pair of unshaven companions, arrived at a neighbouring table, where they sat down, noisily ordering some drinks.

"Surely," Lucas said, looking up, "that's El Flamenco, the torero? I once saw him fight in Madrid."

"It is," James replied.

"He seems to know you."

"He does," was the curt answer. James could tell that Juan was drunk and in a dangerous mood. He had no intention of introducing the young Englishman to the bullfighter and his ruffianly companions.

"Well," Jeffrey Lucas remarked, not without regret, "I suppose I must be on my way to my lodgings—I have an early start before me! Are you sure, Darrell, there's no service I can render before I go, to repay the good turn you did me?"

"There's one." James plunged suddenly, his reserve conquered by a passionate desire to learn something of Oriana. "You can tell me news of your neighbour, Lady Castleton. You see, she's an old friend of mine, and I'm so out of touch these days. I know nothing —nothing at all."

"Lady Castleton?" Lucas repeated, somewhat bewildered by this sudden change of topic.

"Yes. Is she well?"

"Why, she was a year ago, and I've heard nothing to the contrary since. Nothing! But it's common knowledge she and Castleton don't get along. You know that, I suppose?"

"I know nothing!"

"Well," Lucas continued awkwardly, "they don't. Never have done, come to that. He's a queer fellow, of course, and her ladyship likes her own way. There are no children, and for some time now they've agreed to disagree!"

James said nothing.

"They see little enough of each other," Lucas concluded. "When she's in Hampshire, he's in London, and vice versa. People say he drugs, but as to that I know nothing. Lady Castleton is a beauty. But that you know."

"Thank you," James said simply, and then, as the noise from the neighbouring table increased in clamour, "I'll walk to the corner with you!"

It was raining as they left the café.

As they parted Lucas suggested shyly:

"If you have any messages for Lady Castleton, I'd be delighted——"

"On no account," James protested with violence; "on the contrary, I want you to give me your word you'll never mention having seen me!"

"Of course, if that's what you want!"

"It is!"

He thought grimly of Oriana's mockery, should she ever learn of his life with the riffraff of Andalusia. If Lucas chose to make enquiries at his lodgings, he might hear of Rosal, of the Bear People, of the cave in the Albaicin, and of El Flamenco. Exactly, he thought, raging, the raggle-taggle future she had predicted for him once upon a time, long ago in Ackland Wood!

Lucas, disturbed by his stormy face, assured him:

"I won't mention your name!"

"Thank you! And—if I ever go back, I shall remember my promise too!"

And so they parted, Jeffrey Lucas to return, more intrigued than ever, to his lodgings, and James, reluctantly, to the café, where he was greeted by a remarkable variety of ribald jokes.

Juan appeared less truculent than when he had first sat down. Now, although no less drunk, he seemed in uproarious spirits, these appertaining to some private jest or witticism of his own. His companions were both known to James. The more villainous was One-Eye, an ex-picador, mutilated some years before in the arena, who was now a smuggler; the younger, Manoló, a rascal from Triana, who acted as El Flamenco's sword-holder. After many taunts as to the gentility, foppishness, affectation, pomposity, arrogance, and general vileness of James's English friend, Juan said, closing one eye as though in grotesque imitation of his friend, the picador:

"I have been to see Rosal dance."

James was unable to understand why so simple a statement should necessitate the complicated grimaces accompanying it; however, he replied, without paying much attention, that no doubt Rosal had been pleased and honoured; whereupon Juan collapsed into fits of uncontrolled and almost hysterical mirth.

"That's just it," he gasped, wiping his eyes, when at length he was able to speak; "that's just it—she wasn't pleased at all, little *gachi*—far from it, but, as I pointed out, and as old Madre Dora pointed out, a contract's a contract! Isn't it, Jaime? Don't you agree, Jaime?"

James was assailed by an unwilling suspicion.

"Have you and Rosal been fighting, Juan?"

Once again the torero burst into uproarious fits of laughter. James waited impatiently for this hilarity to subside, and then in a louder voice repeated his question.

"Shall I tell him, One-Eye?" Juan demanded, choking. "Manoló, shall I tell him?"

Something sinister in the way the two men shook their heads, while their evil faces remained impassive, made James comprehend that this was no idle prank of the bullfighter's, but something more serious.

"Juan, what have you done? Answer me!"

Because, despite his bravado, Juan was a little afraid of his secretary, his features suddenly assumed a forbidding scowl, and his mood of drunkenness, from being gay, became once more savage and sulky.

"Done?" he muttered, pouring out some more wine. "Done? Why, something I've always wanted to, that's what! And to hell with you, Inglés!"

"What have you done?" James persisted.

Juan began to chuckle.

"Seen Rosal naked, that's what!"

"Don't be a fool!"

"Don't you know it's Saturday night, Jaime?"

"What does that mean?"

Juan fixed him with dark, malicious eyes.

"You don't know some of the girls dance naked Saturdays at the Baile if the house gets enough *parné?*"

"Of course I know! And Rosal is one of those who don't!"

Juan looked at him mockingly.

"You believe that? Well, I've just seen her dance naked—I who am speaking to you! And very lovely she was! I congratulate you! Her body——"

James was in no sweet humour. Since talking to Lucas he was homesick, as he had never thought to be, for England, and the recent talk of Oriana had plunged him into a melancholy mood.

"Shut your damned mouth!" he advised curtly.

Juan grinned.

"I have two witnesses," he declared smoothly. "Come, One-Eye, and you, Manoló! Did I not pay gold parné to go upstairs with the señores from Madrid, to see Rosal dance, naked, with two other girls?"

"It's true," Manoló said, and spat.

One-Eye merely inclined his ugly head.

"You see?" Juan grinned. "And, once again, Jaime, I congratulate you! She has lovely breasts, while her——"

To his astonishment, he discovered that he was being dragged relentlessly to his feet. Some glasses crashed, tinkling, upon the floor, while James gripped the collar of his frilled shirt. He did not much like the grim look on James's face. But he was no coward, and so he taunted:

"Rosal keeps you, by these Saturdays, and you pretend to know nothing? Why, Jaime, you don't need to work! You——"

James's fist smashed straight upon the bone of his chin. There was the sound of a dull thud as the bullfighter slumped unconscious upon the floor. With a crash and a jangle of glasses the table collapsed on top of him, and James, accustomed by now to Andalusian gypsy fights, pulled out his knife, to face his patron's friends.

One-Eye made a swift gesture with his hand.

"No quarrel, Jaime!"

"No quarrel!" Manoló echoed, and spat again on the floor.

The waiters, distracted by this affront to El Flamenco, their god, ran forward to revive him, roughly ordering the others out of the café. They went together, the three of them. Huge, inky-black clouds masked the skies, and rain hissed savagely in the air, like the fury of a thousand snakes.

"Is it true?" James asked, before they separated, in the storm.

"Es verdad," One-Eye admitted.

"Manoló?"

"It's true he went upstairs. Are you going there to the Baile?"

"Good night," James said briefly, and left them.

Rain fell like prison bars of steel, and lightning flashed in a jagged flare across the sky. A low bourdon of thunder grumbled from somewhere across the lost and clouded mountaintops.

James, arriving at the Baile, softly let himself in by the kitchen door.

CHAPTER XLV

HE KNEW the place well.

The dance room led out of the kitchen and was much like other places of its kind, a whitewashed apartment crowded with little tables; it had a dais at one end for the orchestra of three guitarists.

The girls danced in the middle of the room, so close to the spectators that the latter were often brushed by the hems of their whirling skirts.

James, disregarding the waiters' astonishment at his sudden and bedraggled appearance in the kitchen, walked into the dance room, where he stood at the back, watching the artists. There was, he noticed, no sign of Rosal. He recognised the singer of flamenco, who was performing as he came in. Cautiously, so as to avoid being seen by the proprietress, a stout woman with a double-chinned, chalk-white face and sham flowers nodding in her hair, he skirted the crowded room, dodging behind the spectators, to find himself in an open patio.

He went through the rain towards a door which was, as he knew, the artists' dressing room, and, knocking, was admitted. Here, surrounded by piles of gaudy costumes, speckled mirrors, overflowing dress hampers, and posters of long-forgotten bullfights, he discovered two girls. One snored, her head on her arms, while the other, a sharp-looking young woman from Murcia, named Trinidad, was engaged in drinking from a black bottle tilted to her lips. There was no sign of Rosal.

It seemed to James that Trinidad looked somewhat startled by his abrupt appearance.

"Good evening, Trinidad. Where is Rosal?"

"In the dance room, I suppose," the girl replied, reluctantly taking the bottle from her mouth.

"She isn't; I've just looked."

"Perhaps she has gone out for a breath of air."

The bottle gurgled once more. James made no reference to the pouring rain; from the corner of his eye he observed Rosal's fuchsia-coloured dress hanging from a peg.

"Thank you," he said. "I'll go back and wait for her."

He thought vaguely, as he crossed the dripping patio and returned to the hall, which was in darkness save for one untrimmed lamp, of the many times he had seen Rosal dance, beginning with that night, long ago, in Seville, when he was new to Spain.

She was a fine artist, excelling in all that was typically gypsy, particularly in the farruca, that dance which is supposed to portray all passion in three acts—desire, seduction, and delight. Intensely critical where her work was concerned, he had come to the conclusion that no other dancer he had seen could rival the grace, the fury, the wild intensity with which she excelled herself during the ten minutes of this exhausting dance.

Now, as he walked softly up the dimly lighted stairs, his heart sank at the thought of the scene that lay before him. Before, her faults had been of a childish nature—a mania for love spells, an insane jealousy of other women, a quick and violent temper. But this behaviour, if Juan spoke the truth, was something so different that he thought he should despair of ever understanding gypsy women, although he knew that so long as they remained technically faithful they saw no harm in performing for the Busno songs and dances of the grossest indecency. He thought she must have known, well enough, that she was behaving badly, since she had not seen fit to ask his permission. He knew that the extra money received for such exhibitions would meticulously be spent, every penny of it, on obtaining various luxuries for himself, but he could not help reflecting that he had scarcely succeeded in taming her during the three years they had been together.

Despite her devotion, she was much as she had always been, a mischievous, careless, and reckless little savage. She was still the Daughter of the Bear, and of the Bear People, too, for the matter of that.

Having by now arrived on the first floor, he heard the strumming of a guitar, and, opening a french window, found himself upon a narrow balcony. Here another window blazed forth cheerfully into the night, and, pressing forward, he put his face against the rain-drenched glass.

He saw a smaller dance room brilliantly lit by candles. A guitar player, or *tocaor*, as the gypsies called him, sat in a chair at the end of the room. At the other end there reposed three elderly gentlemen in an awestruck row.

In the middle of the room Rosal and two other girls were dancing. They were naked, but they wore long black silk stockings and shoes with high red heels. They were performing, for the edification of the goggling spectators, a languid and somewhat disheartened *jota*. James watched for only one moment. Then, as he stared at that slender amber body posturing so ignobly in the midst of the abominable little garish salon, he knew that, far from taming the gypsies, they had made him as wild as one of themselves.

He smashed open the french window, crashed into the room, and advanced upon the dancers, who, not unnaturally, began to scream. He did not look at Rosal, but somewhere, on a chair, he saw an embroidered crimson shawl he knew to be hers.

Picking it up, he flung it over her, while she stood, petrified, as though rooted upon the floor, staring at him, her eyes dilated with horror. The other dancers fled from the room, and the tocaor stopped playing. The three elderly gentlemen rose agitatedly to their feet, not at all liking the desperate appearance of this wild man.

"Get out!" advised James, and they huddled towards the door like a trio of overexcited turkeys.

"Jaime——" Rosal began, whereupon he boxed her ears violently.

"Get downstairs and get dressed! We're going home!"

Rosal began to cry as he pushed her roughly down the staircase. In the hall he was forced to encounter Madre Dora, the proprietress, who assailed him like a tigress, screaming and swearing.

"Get dressed!" he shouted again to Rosal, who rushed away to obey him.

Madre Dora, shaking her fists in his face, began to threaten him with every indignity, whereupon he pushed her angrily aside.

"Don Jaime, I'll have the law on you!"

"You will? And what about you, whose Baile should be called by another name?"

"As God is my witness, I haven't one single bed in this house! You damned Inglés, I'll claw your eyes out!"

"If you touch me, I'll break your neck!"

A crowd had gathered in the hall, attracted by these heartening sounds of conflict; the majority, being acquainted with James and Rosal, were sympathetically inclined towards them, or rather towards James; but there were a number of travellers, strangers to Granada, who were only too delighted to witness a scene reputed to be typically Andalusian; as Madre Dora hesitated, not quite certain which side openly to favour, Rosal appeared from the dressing room draped in a black shawl, a bundle beneath her arm, pale and sad, her eyes downcast. There was a murmur from the crowd.

"Jaime . . ."

James could scarcely credit this rapid change of character. She now looked as demure as a young nun.

"Come on!" he said impatiently.

Accompanied by jeers, cheers, and catcalls, they disappeared together into the night.

It was still pouring rain as they left the Baile to climb the long Camino of the Sacro Monte. He clutched her arm in an iron grip, and she very soon began to cry again.

"How long have you been doing this?"

"Only since the Monday after Pentecost!"

"You know you deserve to be beaten?"

She brightened a little.

"You want to beat me?"

He shook her then until her teeth chattered, while the rain drenched them both.

He said:

"I'd like to kill you!"

She said nothing, but her expression became less nunlike, and if there had been more light, he might possibly have observed that the gleam of a smile flashed across her face.

"Kill me, Jaime, if you want!"

He said briefly:

"I've lost my post with Juan. I knocked him down tonight!"

She was serious then.

"Oh, Jaime, I never knew he would come to the Baile on a Saturday! He *can't* be angry. He'll take you back!"

"I am not *going* back! Have you got that into your head?"

They were buffeted by wind and soaked with rain as they climbed the steep mountain road of the Albaicin. Save for a few drunken gypsies staggering up the hill, the wet weather had driven most of the inhabitants inside their caves.

Suddenly, as they toiled along, James thought of Oriana. He remembered Ackland Wood and the future she had so scornfully prophesied for him. Well, he thought, even Oriana could scarcely have conceived a night so squalid as this one had proved to be. A night wind-swept and rain-beaten, on this wild hill tunnelled with Romany caves, with his gypsy wife discovered dancing naked, and himself dismissed by a drunken bullfighter! A night, he thought, worthy of François Villon!

"Get in!" he muttered, pushing Rosal, as they reached their own cave.

She obeyed and immediately lit the candles. She knelt before the fire, soon blowing it into a blaze, and poured out a glass of red wine, which she placed carefully upon the table. She then vanished behind the screen, from whence he heard sounds of the most furious ablutions, reminiscent of a stableboy rubbing down a horse. He was not impressed; whenever she had done wrong, she always hastened to wash herself, hoping thus to impress him, and to win his favour. Nor did a sniff or two, or a choked sob, in any way soften his heart. He had heard them too often.

He sat down to drink his wine and wondered what he should do, now that he was no longer El Flamenco's secretary. His book was not yet ready to send to England, and he had, in any case, little enough faith in such an enterprise.

Rosal sniffed again, close to him, and he perceived that she was on her way to bed, modestly and incongruously wrapped from chin to toe in a black shawl. He affected not to notice.

She curled up without another word, but sighed several times, peeping at him.

He thought:

"I'll take her to Morocco. I've always wanted to go there."

He had already forgotten his homesickness for England; his conversation with Jeffrey Lucas. He thought, in the bitterness of that lonely night, that England meant Oriana, and that without her he had no particular desire to return. Once again he sighed, and was glad that she would never know to what infamous depths he had sunk.

Rosal said faintly from the bed:

"You're wet, Jaime. You should take off your clothes."

He got up without a word. She watched him, peeping behind her hand, as he undressed. She was so excited by his behaviour that she no longer feared his anger. She was not even worried, in her exalted state, by his quarrel with Juan. Soon, very soon, she would put that right.

But she was happy. He must love her—love her very much indeed

—to have objected so passionately to her nudity at the Baile. She knew no other gypsy dancer whose rom would have made the scene that he had made. All her doubts, all her terrified misgivings left her then, as she thought affectionately of that wild scene. He was angry now, and queer, as he often was, but she did not care. He had taken the trouble to tramp out in the wind and the rain; he had climbed onto the balcony and smashed open the windows, and chased people from the room. He had carried her out of the place, and dragged her all the way up the hill to the Albaicin.

She lay in ecstasy, and did not at all mind if he wanted to beat her.

But nothing was further from his thoughts.

He got into bed with her. He was cold and wet; she was warm. He slid closer to her, and they embraced.

"François Villon!" he said once, in an odd tone of voice. She put her arms about him and rocked him upon her breast.

Later, much later, he called aloud a name he had once before pronounced, and that on the night of their gypsy wedding.

"Oriana!"

Rosal turned away from him. He slept then, but she was wakeful and suspicious, all her joy had gone.

CHAPTER XLVI

THE NEXT MORNING she got up early, while he was still asleep. When he awoke, she was busy combing her hair, neatly attired in a plain black dress.

"Where are you going?" he asked mistrustfully.

"To Mass, Jaime. It's Sunday."

She had not been to Mass for a long time, but he supposed that this new repentant mood prompted her desire. In any case, he felt disinclined to discuss the matter.

"I shall come back in time to make your coffee, Jaime."

"Very well."

She draped her head in a black lace mantilla.

"I am a very bad girl, I suppose," she suggested, with a deep sigh, looking at him beneath her lashes. James pretended to be asleep.

"But I washed myself all over again this morning. I also washed my hair—it's not yet dry. When I come back, I shall sweep out the cave. Then, if you want, I will try once more to learn the alphabet. Would that please you?"

"You'll be late."

"Is there anything you want that I can bring you?"

"I want to sleep!"

She went, walking down the Camino with mincing steps. For a moment she was absorbed, playing the role of a respectable young wife who had no connection whatever with the gypsies, and, although the morning was glorious and the storm had passed away, she wished very much indeed that she possessed a matronly umbrella. Some gypsy urchins taunted her, but she choked back the angry retort rising to her lips and ignored them, her head high. When she passed a flower seller at the foot of the hill, she could not resist buying a crimson rose, which she stuck coquettishly above her ear.

When she entered the sweet-smelling gloom of the nearest church, she knelt devoutly on a *prie-dieu* and followed the Mass, her eyes fixed intently upon the candlelit gold of the altar and upon the priest, so far away from her that he looked like some exotic beetle in the wings that were his silver vestments. When the Mass was over, she went instantly to do what she had from the first intended.

Beneath a huge stone pillar was set a waxen image of the Virgin, dressed stiffly in gold brocade, a crown of gold upon her head and a bouquet of bright carnations at her feet. She represented Our Lady of Hope, but, according to Spanish custom, her pink-and-white cheeks were gemmed with streaming crystal tears. Lamps of silver and gold winked on either side of her, and beneath the flowers a cluster of tapers, stuck on iron spikes, burned gustily in a blaze of weaving light.

Rosal bought a tall candle, stuck it carefully on a spike, and knelt down on the stone floor, her hands pressed to her eyes.

She prayed then, as she had never prayed before, aloud:

"Blessed Virgin, please make Jaime forgive me for dancing with no clothes on. Please let me never again hear him say the name of that other woman in his sleep, because I hate her. Please, Blessed Virgin, make Jaime know how much I love him. Mother of God, I am lazy about going to Mass, but if only Jaime loves me, I will come every Sunday, and I will light a candle afterwards, as fine a one as this."

She got up then and impulsively, pulled the red rose from her hair, to thrust it among the carnations at the Virgin's feet.

When she got back to the cave, James was dressed and had made his own coffee.

He said:

"Do you really want to go on learning to read this afternoon?"

"This afternoon? Aren't you going to Juan's fight?"

"I thought I'd made it plain to you last night that I've finished with Juan, and he with me."

"He'll never forgive you if you stay away this afternoon!"

"Do *you* never listen to what I say? We aren't staying here, either —we're going to Morocco!"

Rosal's face became radiant.

"Jaime, I'm so pleased! When are we going—tomorrow?"

"In a few days. I'm hungry. Aren't you going to cook dinner?"

"How shall we live in Morocco?" Rosal wanted to know.

"Much as we've lived in Spain. I can shoe horses and shear mules. You can dance—so long as you're dressed!"

"Yes. And all those books you're writing?"

"They can be finished as easily there as here."

Later that afternoon he said:

"I'm taking you to the Baile tonight."

"The Baile? But——"

"Nobody shall think we're afraid to show ourselves! I'll take you to supper there, and you must wear your prettiest frock."

"But, Jaime——"

"Oh, stop arguing, Rosal! If this is our last Sunday in Granada, we're going to show ourselves! Can't you understand?"

"Very well. I was only thinking that Juan might be drunk, and pick a fight——"

"Let him! I'd welcome the opportunity. And don't forget—your best dress!"

"My red with the *lunares,* or my white?"

"Your white!"

She took a long time to dress herself that evening. The frills of her best dress were crisp and white as foam; a scarlet triangle of fringed shawl draped upon her shoulders, there were her best shoes with high red heels and coral-coloured combs to stick in her jetty locks.

James was pleased with the result.

"You look pretty—very pretty indeed!"

She laughed, well pleased.

She had ironed and goffered his best lawn shirt, and he wore a suit of silver-grey. With his peón's boots and his long spurs jingling, she thought that he looked extremely distinguished. On their way down the hill he bought her a bunch of scarlet carnations, which she pinned, flamenco-fashion, in a topknot on her curly head.

He said:

"You're pleased at the idea of going to Morocco?"

"Pleased?" She laughed. "I'd be pleased to go anywhere with you, my Jaime!"

"Even to England? Where there's no sun, compared to this—only rain and grey skies?"

"England, France, Morocco—anywhere you say! It makes no difference!"

"I don't believe it would," he agreed, touched; "but God knows what you see in me! I'm bad-tempered and morose and impatient; I spend hours writing stuff you can't even read! Tell me, Rosal, why is it you love me?"

"You're my rom, aren't you?"

"But before? Before I was ill? That time in Seville?"

Her face fell.

"When I deceived you?"

"Never mind that! What does it matter any more? I just want to know why you liked me that night at the Baile Flamenco in Seville?"

She smiled, the secretive, provocative smile he knew so well.

"Why, Rosal?"

"I don't know—I swear I don't! I just saw you across the room, and I thought, Mother of God, that young man is my fate, my *baji!* Don't let's say any more about that—you might get angry, and if we're going to Morocco I don't ever want you to be angry again!"

"You think we'll be happy in Morocco?"

She flashed him an impish glance.

"On conditions, Jaime!"

"Well, what are they?"

"Many!" She began to tick them off on her fingers: "I never again dance with no clothes on. I never make love charms, because you don't like them. I wash myself all over every day. I learn to read and write. I can't say I will love you more, because that's impossible! But——"

She flung her arms about his neck and drew his mouth down to hers. It was dark, and they were only a few yards away from the Baile. Her lips were like sun-warmed fruit. She whispered:

"Jaime! I want me a little Inglés!"

He said unsteadily, moved by the passion in her voice:

"Those aren't things we can arrange. There's no reason why you shouldn't have a baby."

"If you loved me more, who can tell——"

"Rosal, we're not going to start all that again!"

"No."

"Well, here we are. Don't forget, if they ask you to dance, you won't, because you're not an artist tonight—you're a visitor!"

"She won't ask me to dance after yesterday. And, Jaime, if Juan is here, and wants to fight——"

"Come on, come on! We've been into all that before!"

They passed from the darkness of the street into the garish brightness of the Baile, while she still thought wistfully how much she wanted a "little Englishman."

CHAPTER XLVII

THE DANCE ROOM was much as it had been the night before; possibly more crowded. Their arrival created a stir and murmur of excitement, and as James ordered a bottle of wine, the bulk of

Madre Dora waddled swiftly towards their table. She said, addressing him:

"I thought you understood I dismissed Rosal last night?"

"She is not here to dance. She is here as a visitor!"

"I reserve the right to admit only those people I like!"

"Put us out, then," James said coolly. "If you care to try!"

"I want no more brawls," she answered sullenly; "so long as you behave yourselves . . ."

"Then be kind enough to leave us, señora!"

When she had gone he turned impatiently to Rosal, who had begun to say something.

"You'd have started a quarrel then! Can you never learn to keep quiet?"

"I'm sorry," she said submissively, drinking her wine.

He said no more. Once again he was moved by her passionate love for him, her fearless courage where he was concerned, her gay and gallant ways. He blamed himself then for the sorry exhibition of the night before; he had been too indifferent, too careless; he had let her run wild without ever enquiring how she earned her money. Now that they were going together to Morocco, he swore to himself that they would begin their life again; he would at least make her happy and keep her out of mischief. Easy enough he thought with a sigh; he had only to love her, or to pretend that he loved her.

"What are you thinking about?" Rosal wanted to know.

"I'm thinking we shall be very happy over there in Morocco."

"Yes. There will be Arab horses, faster than ours, and women with veils on, so that you won't be able to see if they are prettier than me, and there are snake charmers and fire-eaters in the market, and old gentlemen call from the minarets when it is time to pray."

"You talk," he said, "as though you had been there before?"

"But I have," she replied. "I was in Tangier, with the Bear People, when I was a child."

"Let's drink to Morocco," James suggested.

They did, and then she asked abruptly, staring into her glass:

"Do you know a tall, dark woman with a very white skin and jewels at her ears?"

"Possibly," he replied, looking at her. "Why?"

"I saw her in my glass just now, when we were drinking."

"You see too much," James said, disconcerted, "and in any case, this is no time or place to pen baji."

"I wasn't telling fortunes," she retorted. "I just saw her in my glass. For one second she was so close I could have touched her."

"To the devil with ghosts, anyhow!" he told her lightly.

"Yes."

She said no more, but she knew perfectly well that she must have seen a vision of the woman to whom James called in his sleep, and, intensely superstitious, she wondered why this omen had come to trouble her on one of the happiest nights they had ever spent together. She thought fiercely and with satisfaction:

"He's mine now! Nothing to do with her! Never again!"

"Stop brooding!" James advised, trying to forget what, to him, too, was an omen, and she looked up to smile at him.

The Baile was packed now, and the fun was wildly boisterous. There were very much the same shifting crowds of people here as were to be seen in similar haunts anywhere else in Andalusia. Bullfighters, peones, smugglers, dancers, singers, and street women. Violent, glowing colours of shawls and flowers and vivid capes. The wildness of flamenco music, a blue haze of smoke, a hoarse, noisy hum of voices, and a clash of glasses.

And then, suddenly, the entrance of a god, as El Flamenco strode into the room, followed by his cuadrilla. Following a custom of his time, he still wore fighting dress, although this costume was naturally not one he had worn that afternoon in the ring. But James remembered it well—that skin-tight suit of olive green bedizened with glittering silver spangles. Juan was drunk. His black eyes were brilliant, his tawny cheekbones flushed. He had fought valiantly that same day, and there were cheers as he came swaggering into the room.

"*Olé,* Juan! *Olé! Olé!*"

He flung himself down in a chair and ordered wine for himself and his comrades. Yes, he admitted, he had achieved miracles that same afternoon in the arena; had he not been awarded the bull's ear as a tribute to his skill and bravery? Whereupon he pulled this bloody trophy from his pocket and dangled it lovingly in his ringed hand.

"Drinks for everyone!" he shouted. "Drinks for all my friends!" Then, as his eyes raked the room and he repeated, "For all my friends, do you hear?" he saw James and Rosal, and the flush on his cheekbones became deeper.

"But only for my friends! Not for any cursed Inglés or for his mistress! Do you hear?"

"Be quiet, Rosal!" James insisted, then, as a bewildered waiter came towards their table, he said quietly:

"We are not drinking with El Flamenco."

Juan turned then, staring at him insolently, and roared, as the crowded room was suddenly quiet:

"No, Inglés, you are *not* drinking with me! I'll tell you why—I don't like kept men! Nor do I like the *putas* who keep 'em!"

James was ice-pale. He thought that he had never been so furiously angry before.

He got up and said slowly:

"The last time we met, I thrashed you for the impertinent puppy you are. Now I propose to thrash you again."

Juan laughed. He rose, too, and came sauntering across the room towards his enemy, in a silence so absolute that the two adversaries might have been alone together in the African desert.

"Yes," he agreed, his lips twisted in an ugly smile, "you hit me with your English box, didn't you, my fighting rooster? Did you think I'd forgotten that? No doubt you prayed I had! But you see I hadn't, and that's why I came here tonight—to call quits to your affair!"

Rosal, too, sprang to her feet.

"Your knife—quick!" she whispered to James. She glided close beside him, her own dagger hidden beneath her hand. He ripped open his knife swiftly, as he had learned from the Bear People.

"Since El Flamenco is afraid of my English boxing," he said, "then let it be knives—it's all the same to me!"

Juan's hand was in his pocket, and James waited tensely for the gleam of the bullfighter's weapon. He thought:

"This time it's him or me."

He felt stupid, dazed, when he suddenly perceived that Juan held a pistol in his hand. A pistol! Gypsy men fought always with knives, or with their fists.

"I warned you," El Flamenco was saying, the pistol levelled. "I told you if ever you laid a hand on me again I'd shoot you like a dog!"

James was never able to remember with any clarity what happened then. There was a violent explosion, and a flash of fire that was not so swift as the flash of fire that was Rosal springing across his breast, so that her warm young body shielded him, and the air reeked of gunpowder.

Then it seemed to him that everyone shouted at once; he had forgotten Juan, but he knelt on the floor beside Rosal, and, so far as he was concerned, they were alone together.

She was crumpled in a dishevelled heap of white, and a patch of scarlet seeping through the bodice of her dress did not look out of place, for her *manton* was red, and the heels of her shoes, and so were the gypsy combs stuck in her hair. What seemed strange was that the clear, sunny brown of her skin had faded in one moment to an ashen grey; her bright lips had paled, and her dark eyes, fixed on him, wavered, seeming unable to focus.

"Get a doctor!" he heard himself cry, holding her in his arms.

Someone, Madre Dora he thought, brought some water and tried to pour it down her throat. The water spilled over her face and breast, but she did not notice it, nor take her eyes away from him.

"Rosal!"

Her body quivered in his arms, and she gasped painfully for breath.

"Jaime . . ."

"Yes, mi querido—be quiet—don't worry!"

She looked up at him suddenly with those wild, beautiful eyes and seemed to see him distinctly, so that he perceived, with clarity, all the imperishable, hopeless, and passionate love she had lavished on him, and its intensity spoke to him then as she herself had never been able to speak. She smiled faintly and murmured:

"You make me happy."

"Rosal . . ."

"Happy, Jaime . . ."

She shuddered then, and sighed as though she were too tired to speak again.

One of Juan's men had gone for a doctor, and while they waited, and she lay in James's arms, it seemed as though she strained to keep her eyes open, to gaze at him, during the few moments that remained to her; it seemed as though she must look her last on him.

It was Madre Dora who said:

"Not a doctor—a priest!"

She made no sign of hearing.

Perhaps she thought, as her life ebbed away, so that even James's face was seen behind a mist, perhaps she thought only of him, her rom, her husband, and of how she had been determined from the first that he should belong to her. Perhaps she forgot everything that had happened in her brief, wild life before she came to know him—forgot even the Bear People, with their winding roads, their little fires flickering like stars on the wayside, their flamenco music, their fiestas, their sunshine, their witchcraft, and their dancing.

Perhaps she remembered only that she had found James in Seville, nursed him, loved him, and possessed him. He was hers, even though he had not been in love with her; she was never deceived about that.

But as her face blanched, and her eyes glazed, and her head fell limp upon his shoulder, the words she had just whispered to him were the truth.

He had made her "happy."

Nobody else had ever done that.

James could not believe for a long time that she was dead. It seemed impossible that so much gaiety, so much vitality, could be quenched utterly, forever, in a few moments. When he heard someone sobbing beside him, he did not know until afterwards that it was Juan, who had killed her, mourning.

For some days James could not believe that she was really dead.

She had been too passionately alive, too warmhearted, too impulsive and eager, easily to be forgotten. Her rages, her moods of jealousy and fits of tenderness, her selfless devotion to himself were all too near; sometimes he could not believe that he would never again hear the lightness of her step, or the husky tone of her voice; that he would never again see her dance the farruca with that leopardlike grace peculiar to herself.

She had been a little animal, but she had also been brave, truthful, loyal, and capable of great love; so that compared to other women, perhaps she had finer qualities than they.

When the drawn-out gloom of the trial was over and Juan had been committed to prison for ten years, James found that he had no desire whatever to return to England.

The shock of her death had been too great, and he felt an Ishmael. Perhaps later he would return, but not for some time. Not while he was still haunted by the memory of her hopeless love for him. She was too near, and her little ghost too impatient; it made him ashamed to know that he still thought of Oriana.

And so, perhaps to put temptation behind him, he sailed for Morocco.

PART VII

Oriana

CHAPTER XLVIII

MORE THAN TWO YEARS later, in England, *The Spanish Journey* was published.

Modestly, without much publicity, this book appeared.

It seemed that no publicity was required, for the book became an overnight sensation. There it was, to speak for itself, prominently displayed in every bookshop—wild, glowing with colour and adventure. To an epoch already drab with what was one day to be known as Victorianism *The Spanish Journey* came as a shock, a jolt. There, defiantly flung down before the taste of the time, was a gantlet electrifying to other writers of the period. Thackeray always regretted that he was not allowed, by convention, to describe the decline and fall of Becky Sharp. Dickens, writing of Bill Sykes's tawdry Nancy, wrote with one eye on his young ladies, suppressing many sordid details.

But James Darrell seemed indifferent to such delicacies. He wrote of Spain as he had seen it, and to his contemporaries the pages of his book were as though drenched with sun and blood. He wrote of gypsies, bullfighters, coppersmiths, and dancers. When he wrote of prostitutes, he wrote about them frankly. He seemed to understand a low and violent life.

Some people, of course, considered the book coarse.

It was at the same time vivid with his own observation of all the wild scenes he had, apparently, witnessed—his chalk-white towns were baked in a tigerish sun; his plains were scorched, copper gold;

brilliant, ragged gypsies tramped an endless road, gulping dust as though it were wine; his fighting bulls fed sullenly, flicking away flies with their lazy tails; and hordes of peones flocked across his pages, racing their swift ponies towards ranches over the mountains. His cafés and Bailes swarmed with wild and noisy people, flushed with wine, dark with the shadow of those jails that were never very far away from any of them.

James Darrell, suppressing only what was personal to himself, wrote with simplicity of all that he had seen, and awoke to find himself famous.

Victorian England, oblivious of slaving children, slums, and sweatshops, found his book peculiar, but was fascinated, since he had the gift of leading his readers, so to speak, from out of gloom into the brilliant sunlight of what they thought of as a savage and a primitive land.

His book was nearly suppressed by that element, ever contemptible, which is apt to consider anything advanced beyond its times as disgusting.

One night James was astounded to learn from his publisher, Mr. Grant, that his book had almost been banned on grounds of its frankness.

He was dining with William Grant, a quiet, silver-bearded gentleman, in that coffeehouse where once, long ago, he had seen for the first time Don Ignacio, the diamond merchant.

"Frank?" he said, astonished, looking very hard indeed at Mr. Grant, who answered:

"Well, my dear sir, you *do* write frankly, you know!"

"What would be the sense of writing otherwise? I wrote simply of what I saw!"

"You see such queer things, Darrell!"

James was silent for a moment.

Then he said:

"But you want me to write you another book, of my adventures in England?"

"Indeed I do!"

"But I shall have strange things to say about that time too. England can be as queer as Spain!"

"I'm not at all sure," Mr. Grant said, after a pause, "that people want to be told as much!"

"Then it isn't much use writing a book about it," James declared flatly.

"My dear Darrell, you, of course, belong to the Regency age! You're an anachronism in our present times!"

"Born too late, in fact." James smiled.

"Perhaps! But your book's jolted people out of their complacency! More than that—don't you understand you've given 'em a taste of colour, of wildness, of Bohemianism they'd never have had but for you?"

"Well," James said doggedly, "the next book—my English journey—will do much the same for them. There's just as much adventure here as in Spain. Only it's different!"

"And your book on Morocco?" Grant enquired.

"That must come afterwards. Long afterwards! I haven't got Morocco out of my skin yet—I'm too close to it!"

"You brought back two Arab horses and a Moorish groom, didn't you?"

"Yes. I keep them in Hampstead."

"And you didn't even know your fairy stories had made you famous when you brought this stable home with you?"

"No," James said shortly.

"Forgive my asking you, but how would you have paid their keep had not the fairy stories been so successful?"

"We should have worked in a circus," James said.

Mr. Grant laughed a little nervously.

"I'm not joking," James explained.

"My dear Darrell, I'm not so gullible as all that!"

"It's true," James said to this; "we *would* have worked in a circus. I trained my horses out near Tetuan, and very pretty they are too. I wasn't leaving anything to chance!"

"I never knew a writer like you," Mr. Grant confided.

James laughed.

"I don't ever wish," he said, "to depend on my pen! I did, once, and didn't like it!"

"I don't see," Mr. Grant observed, "what you have to complain about! After all, you're famous!"

"A bit late," James said to this, so bitterly that his friend remarked:

"I'll never understand how a cynical fellow like you could have written those delightful fairy tales!"

"I was very young!"

Grant thought:

"No matter how he writes—he's more a foreigner than an Eng-lishman when he's had some wine, when he tries to talk quickly!"

But James Darrell was a gypsy pheasant to Grant's firm, and so long as they put salt upon his tail, he would continue to hatch them golden eggs.

"Trouble is," Grant grumbled as he went home in a hackney coach, "trouble is, somebody will whistle him out of our coop! He's a wild fellow and won't be content to stay home long!"

Here he was wrong.

James went down the next day to Oxford, where, finding from the house agents that his home was to let, he drove over to view it, the keys in his pocket.

The house was silent, shuttered, and thick with dust, since the doctor succeeding his father had long since retreated nearer to Oxford.

James wandered about the dusty rooms, looking at the panelled parlour, the dark, twisted staircase, the hidden closets and cup-boards, the grave grandfather clock, and the kitchen where he once remembered having been so happy with Betty when he was a child. But Betty was dead.

He remembered his mother, with her strong French accent, and his father, who had so much liked to sit of a night in the shabby study, while he, James, fetched him grog. In the study a shutter was broken and clattered dismally against the wall, for the wind was high outside.

He went out then, towards the Hall, without thinking.

But the Hall, he learned in the village, was shut and desolate. Mr. Camperdene was dead, and there were no sons left to suc-ceed him.

He went into the churchyard, where so many farmers and plough-boys slept, enfolded in the wreaths of brambles and nettles that twined about their graves, and then into the church, where an old crusading Camperdene lay, his feet crossed, dripping tears of damp from the sepulchre where he had lain so long beside his lady.

The cold and chill of the little Norman church smote icily on James's bones, and he returned, with melancholy, to the neglected churchyard, where, he suddenly remembered, the later Camperdenes were buried, there being no room for any more of them in the mildewed church.

It seemed to him that the grave of his friend, Mr. George Camperdene, was neglected already, thick with briars and nettles. He thought then with anger of Oriana, who had never really been for long banished from his mind. She might have paid someone to tend her father's grave, he thought; and thinking of her, knew, somehow, as he knew by instinct so much about her, that she had done so, and been cheated.

He walked away from the churchyard as night was falling.

He had been brave; he had tried not to think of her. Now, as shadows crept close to darken the quiet mounds of that silent place, he thought of her with longing.

He had been away so long that everything in his own land seemed strange and unfamiliar.

The Hall was shut and dark against the blackness of the encroaching trees. There were no more candles or carriages; no more gaiety, no more parties, or music.

She, Oriana, had gone away somewhere else to live, to make another life.

She was no longer connected, and had not been for years, with his own troubled existence. But their past haunted him that night as he passed beneath the great yew tree shading the lych gate.

Then she seemed so near to him that he could almost hear her breathing at his side. Once, he remembered, on Christmas Day, they had walked in the churchyard together, when snow lay like icing on the dark roof of the yew tree, and she warmed her hands in a squirrel muff. How many times, in every season of the year, he seemed to have been her companion in the lanes and glades of Oxfordshire! He remembered walking with her in the park on starry summer nights, when her rustling skirts dragged in dew; he remembered riding with her on autumn mornings, when a feather curled about her ivory cheek, and she pressed her black mare homewards across the fields because she was hungry and there were muffins for breakfast at the Hall.

Musing as he did, thus reliving his youth, he almost forgot that she had been his mistress one breathless summer night more than five years ago.

Had that strange love affair between them really happened, or had he dreamed it, when he was sick to death in the wilds of Spain?

His passionate desire to see her again became, as he tramped back to the village, so acute that he could scarcely refrain from writing to her. Then it was that he remembered the truth: how casually, how cruelly she had parted from him on that dreamlike night of curious memories; how she had been interested only in possessing him; how he had been shamed, in his manhood, by her masterful ways.

"I'm damned if I'll write to her!" he thought on his way back to Oxford.

But he could not help hoping very much indeed that she, who once sneered at his gypsy friends, had read *The Spanish Journey*.

The next day he took a long lease of his old home.
Then he returned to London.

CHAPTER XLIX

"Mind you, he's a queer fish," Mr. William Grant remarked a few nights later to one of his old friends.

That evening he was giving a men's dinner for James Darrell, to which he had invited various representative writers and critics, and he was drinking a glass of sherry at the Kean Club before preparing to assume his responsibilities as host.

"Must have been, to have written that book," the friend rejoined.

"Wait until you see this *English Journey* he's planning! I don't think it'll catch on, like the Spanish stuff."

"Is Darrell married?"

"Not he! But I know nothing, absolutely nothing, of his private life—he shuts up like an oyster if it's so much as mentioned. All the same, one can't help thinking that in Spain and Morocco—— Well, he looks like a chap that knows his way around!"

"Is it true that he cares only for the.society of vagabonds?"

"God knows! As far as I can make out, he seems to have no friends. Not in England, anyhow. That's why I want him to meet some people. He strikes me as being the loneliest fellow I've ever known."

The friend grinned sarcastically.

"Just wait until the lion hunters get hold of him!"

Grant shook his head.

"They've tried; don't worry!"

"What happened?"

"Nothing happened! He went straight back to the wilds of Oxfordshire, where, it appears, he's taken some sort of ramshackle house!"

"Refused to be caught, in fact?"

"Refused in no uncertain manner!"

"Not by any chance the Byronic type?"

"Not in the least. Quiet, well-mannered, but the most damned reserved, independent young man I ever had to deal with in my life!"

The dinner that night was an ordeal for James. It was so long since he had met men of his own upbringing and education that he had almost forgotten how to talk to them. He was shy, but delighted, when they toasted him as "Don Jaime," and as long as they spoke to him of Morocco, it was easy enough to answer their questions, although, when they seemed curious as to the ladies of this country, he had not the slightest intention of referring to a casual intimacy he had enjoyed with a dancing girl of Moorish blood.

But later on, when they asked him about Spanish women, his replies became evasive, and he glanced about him at the blazing gaslights and the rose-brocade walls of the luxurious private room rather as though he had strayed there by mistake and would have given much to be anywhere else.

When he was asked if Spanish women were jealous, he replied briefly:

"Very." Then the conversation dropped, like a stone.

Grant, seeing that he looked ill at ease, began to talk of the bull-fight, and the other guests, remembering the young man's vivid descriptions of the arena, fired questions at him with a frank and lively interest.

At length an elderly and eminent dramatist enquired:

"You must have known these fellows pretty well, Darrell?"

"Very well, sir. In fact, I was secretary to one for about two years!"

Then he could have cursed his own unlucky tongue and the brandy that had loosened it.

"That's extraordinarily interesting," the dramatist declared; "tell me, what sort of man was this bullfighter of yours?"

James looked down at the great crystal bubble of his glass.

"In the ring, he was one of the bravest men I ever saw."

"But out of the ring? That's what *I* want to know!"

"I'd rather not discuss him out of it!" he said with unmistakable curtness.

"Ah! I suppose he's dead, since you speak of him in the past tense?"

"No. He's not dead, I believe."

Once again there was a little cold silence, and they thought him undoubtedly odd, this tall, abrupt young man with his grey hair and his dark, thin face.

Later they began to discuss a spectacular murder case, details of which were then absorbing London. Everyone had had plenty of brandy, and after dwelling upon some particularly gruesome details, someone asked James:

"What would your reaction be, Darrell, if you witnessed a murder?"

There was no doubt then that the author of *The Spanish Journey* looked odd. He hesitated, gripping his glass by the stem as though he would break it.

"Perhaps you have, in Spain?" the dramatist suggested, and there was a roar of laughter.

"Perhaps," James agreed facetiously, trying to laugh.

"Come, have you really?"

There was a moment's silence, and then the stem snapped suddenly with a tinkling sound.

"I've broken my glass," James apologised to Grant.

"Come, Darrell! Don't try to evade the question!" the dramatist bellowed.

James said quietly, as there was another pause:

"I *have* seen someone murdered, sir, so that I seem to have the advantage of you. But I'd give much to forget it, and I'd greatly prefer not to talk about it!"

"I believe the boy's serious!" declared a bearded critic, laughing across the table.

Grant, looking at the shadows darkening James's lean face, was sober enough to guess that he was serious, and once again he felt a passionate curiosity regarding those mysterious years in Spain.

Later, when James learned to trust Grant, he would confide in him, to discover the friend he so much needed, but that was not to be yet, and meanwhile he was as lonely and suspicious as a half-tamed wolf. Moody, too, for when he was reminded of Rosal, he blamed himself for his indifference; for having been unable to give her the love for which she had longed.

He was not a conspicuous success at the distinguished dinner party. While his merit as a writer was sincerely admired, he was thought—unjustly—to pose as a mystery man, to be lacking in social graces; and, although he seemed modest enough about his achievements, he was dismissed as an odd fellow, one who did not drink with gaiety, and one who seemed extraordinarily reluctant to answer the most simple questions relating to his own adventures.

"One wonders," the dramatist later hazarded to a friend, "whether he's really experienced what he's written about!"

James himself, walking home that night to his lodgings near the Aldwych, could not help wondering whether he was dreaming this part of his life, or whether he had dreamed the years in Spain; he came to the conclusion that London, with its richness, its sombre splendour, was more foreign to him, and always would be, than the wildest hamlet of any Andalusian plain.

He had been away too long to understand his own countrymen. All he knew was that their personal, impertinent questions would, even in humble Spain, be considered in the worst possible taste.

He felt such a stranger in London, especially since he had some money, that even his old, half-forgotten life of slaving as a hack writer for Sir Matthew Kent-Taylor seemed more familiar to him than this new existence of oyster bars, champagne, hackney coaches, and the company of men some of whom actually owned race horses.

He felt at ease only when he was working.

Then he was safe, shut up in his own secret world, happy, absorbed, as his pen raced across the paper. Later, when he revised, he knew the black misery of discontent with everything that he had done. But this, at least, was a familiar anguish; he was accustomed to a jumble of scratched-out sentences and barred, blotted pages.

It was only after he had worked and sought relaxation that he realised the extent of his own loneliness.

In Granada, at the Albaicin, he had only to wander out of the cave to encounter a dozen men with whom he could talk comfortably, as they sat together sipping sherry. It was never necessary to be alone for a moment.

But here, in London, in this vast, sunless city, it seemed impossible ever to find people to whom he could talk.

Perhaps, too, he missed Rosal, even after two years without her. He certainly thought of her often—always with a stab of misery. It was only since her death that he realised the full extent of her devotion, and then he felt very humble. Unobtrusively, she had struggled to make him comfortable. When he thought of the selflessness with which, when he was ill, she had nursed him, he felt a lump in his throat as he began to see her in perspective—gay, gallant, ready to sacrifice everything for him—even that life which she had appeared so much to enjoy.

No wonder, he thought, putting the key in his door, no wonder those sleek men had made him feel a stranger.

Probably they had no idea what life was like in Spain or in Morocco. Certainly they would never have believed in Rosal, or in the Bear People, or in smuggling. They would never have understood how the most chaste of gypsy wives could have danced, naked, in a Baile, nor could they ever understand why he no longer hated Juan, El Flamenco, but was only full of pity thinking of the bullfighter.

He returned to his comfortable lodgings, and once more was tempted by the idea of writing to Oriana. But here the reserve, the secretiveness, of his life again prevailed, and when he had written, he tore the letter up. He supposed that he was not yet prepared to meet her.

The next morning he was awakened by the tootling of a Punch-and-Judy show in the street, and when he looked down to recognise Jeremy Torch—despite his own faulty memory, it was impossible not to recognise Mr. Torch—he rushed downstairs, shortly afterwards to vanish for the best part of a week.

"You look a fair guy with that grey hair," Mr. Torch remarked subsequently, "and ven I say guy, I mean Fifth of November and no mistake."

"Well, I can't help it!" James replied impatiently.

"That's vhere you're wrong! Wery wrong, you are! Vell, I know a fellow sells wiolet-tinted hair improver at a bob a bottle! That's for the tober, mind you."

"I'll stay as I am," James retorted.

"What the doñas are going to say, I wouldn't presume to remark —not being a fortuneteller. Howsomever, to change an awkvard subject, you remember my Toby—that wery old bitch of mine as vas always holding up the show?"

"I remember!"

"On account of litters? You do? Vell, this Toby's her grandson— a dog at last! 'E's no trouble to me the vay *she* vas, but 'e 'as no idea of pathos—just vait till you see his performance! Drags the show down! 'E simply doesn't try!"

Here he shook his head ferociously at a somewhat rakish-looking white terrier busily engaged in irrigating a neighbouring tree trunk.

Mr. William Grant, anxiously awaiting the end of *The English Journey,* was scarcely mollified by a casual letter from Mr. Darrell informing him that he had gone away for a few days, with an old friend of his, proprietor of a Punch-and-Judy show.

CHAPTER L

JAMES RETURNED at the end of a week and sat down to finish *The English Journey*. As usual, he suffered crippling pains in his right wrist, and, as usual, apart from Mr. William Grant, he had few enough friends in London.

He visited a well-known gypsy camp at Battersea, and there learned that Sylvester Brazil, his wife, and three of their four children had emigrated to America. The eldest child, Rosaina, was being looked after by her Lovell cousins in Hampshire, and his old ally, Hagar, had been dead for more than three years.

It seemed to him that destiny was parting him from his gypsy friends, and, thinking of Rosal, he was glad.

He finished *The English Journey* and then, kicking his heels, could not decide whether to leave London for Oxfordshire. He dined once or twice with some of the men to whom he had been introduced by Grant, but he was so much a stranger that he never knew the names of those they were discussing, and although they seemed to like him, and although they most certainly admired him as a writer, they could not, unconsciously, have made him feel more of an alien than they did.

He wrote a dozen letters to Oriana—in fact, his wastepaper basket overflowed with bits of paper addressed to her, their fragments suggesting a paper chase on a grand scale.

But she had hurt him too much for the letters in the end to be posted, and his pride was always there to intervene.

He thought that she must by this time have forgotten him, and then, for the hundredth time, he determined to forget her.

Meanwhile, he wandered about a London where he was far more of a foreigner than he had ever been in Granada or in Seville. This huge, huddled city, of tumbledown medieval houses jostling the blackened cream of Regency façades and the red-brick monstrosities of the more modern era, seemed so strange that more often than not he lost his way as he roamed about winding alleys and dark little

lanes. Everywhere, it seemed to him, there were courtyards, and by-
ways, and grass-grown, deserted squares. There were labyrinths of
passages that led nowhere; there were haunted little churchyards
where the tombstones collapsed upon each other like a pack of
cards, and where weeds flourished; there were odd little fog-bound
taverns, and stables so hidden away that when the horses stamped
and rattled at their halters the sound was hollow, and sounded
ghostly enough in a silence that was broken only by the chime of
church bells and by a hum of wheels from the distant, busy streets.

Sometimes James thought that he could not endure to stay a moment longer in England, despite any pride he felt in possessing the
Oxfordshire house. It was late spring, but the cold chilled his bones;
it seemed to him that everywhere he sniffed dust and fog, and he
longed passionately for the vivid skies of sunnier lands.

Furthermore, to add to his depression, it seemed that Mr. Grant
thought *The English Journey* a peculiar book. He was not, he said,
inclined to prophesy a great success for it.

He explained:

"In the Spanish book you relied—very rightly—on colour and
sunshine and on adventures that could never happen here. Well, in
this second book of yours you. *make* the adventures happen here—
on this English road that's familiar to everyone. Don't you?"

"They happened," James said.

"But in this book there's no Spanish colour to gloss them over!"

"Do you still think they need glossing over?"

"Well," Grant said, "some of them are damned odd! Your account of a prize fight, for instance, is hardly likely to please the
ladies; your fairground chapter's somewhat coarse; and your gypsies, my dear Darrell—well, they're scarcely romanticised according
to custom, are they? They're pretty much in the raw, you know!"

"What about my Spanish gypsies?"

"My dear fellow, they were *Spanish*! They weren't depicted as
prowling about the lanes outside our readers' very windows!"

"All the same, they are!"

"Listen, Darrell," Grant coaxed, "your writing, in this book of
yours, is about as good as anything I've met yet. It is, on my word!
I don't think I'm exaggerating when I say that certain passages
will be remembered as long as you are. I'm sure they will! But

surely you see that while you can afford to be fanciful about Spain, you can hardly——"

"Fanciful!" James interrupted, thinking of all that he had omitted from *The Spanish Journey*. "Fanciful! Do you mean to say you think I invented anything in that book?"

"Well, I know how easily writers are carried away by their imaginations! The way, for instance, the other night, after dinner, you made everyone believe you'd seen a murder and didn't want to talk about it! Do you remember? You——"

"Damn you, Grant, I did see a murder!"

"Now, listen, you are not trying to tell me——"

With an effort he kept his temper.

"Grant, I'm *not* an inventive writer! I can't write fiction now, although I used to, as a child. Everything in that book was true. How much I omitted, I suppose you'll never know!"

"Then your life in Spain must have been like something they give us in the theatres over the river!"

"You mean melodrama?" James considered. "Well, that's about what it was! From start to finish it was just that! Jewel thieves, murders, jealous bullfighters—you've no idea what, for personal reasons, I omitted!"

"That may be true——"

"It *is* true!"

"—but still doesn't explain the extraordinary happenings you've put into this new book!"

"You don't believe in those, either?"

"My dear Darrell, here in England——"

James got up. He was pale.

"If you don't believe me, go out yourself on what's called the tober—go out on the road, speaking Romany, with no money in your pocket, and see what happens to you—just one week! Go to prize fights, and fairgrounds, and race meetings, and try to make a living! Just try! And you might see if your adventures are as pretty and as smug as you'd like to make 'em!"

"Now, Darrell, listen——"

"And," concluded James, glaring, "try living in Spain too—on your wits, or rather on someone else's! Then come back and talk to me of melodrama!"

This quarrel, needless to say, was soon settled. James was too lonely, Grant too sensible, for either to disagree very long.

It was then that Grant began to believe in James's strange adventures—to realise that the young man really had lived a life that might well have been described as melodramatic. He wasn't, as he said, an inventive writer. Shortly after their discussion he confided the whole story of the diamond necklace, Rosal, and El Flamenco. Grant said:

"You must write about that one day!"

"I never will," James answered curtly.

"But that, if you like, is melodrama! It's——"

"It's my private life!"

Occasionally, when he felt restless and disinclined to eat in his lodgings, he went out to dine at the old-fashioned chophouse where he had first met Don Ignacio.

There, in an ecstasy of creative imagination, he sat and pondered half an evening over a chapter, or even a sentence; sometimes he thought that he came alive only when he was writing; that he was happy only when his wrist throbbed, and his mind burned, so that he could scarcely wait to finish dinner and hasten back to his desk, there, often enough, to work until the dawn.

One night he sat alone trying to decide whether or not to invite one of the *coryphées* from the neighbouring ballet, to whom he had been introduced the night before, to supper. A humble *figurante* in the great Varsovina's company, she had appeared desirous of being entertained, and he remembered how delicate and intangible she had seemed as she floated across the stage in all the moonlit mystery of pale muslin skirts . . .

She was an Italian girl, and he thought her attractive.

He fished in his pocket for her card, and read:

"Signorina Maria Salvini, Ballet Varsovina."

Most suitable, he thought, as he asked for his bill. He remembered her as a slender creature, with satin-smooth dark hair and the brown eyes of a spaniel. She had confided how unhappy she was under Lina Varsovina's rigid direction. She had pressed his hand as he left the dressing room. Well——

"Darrell!"

He started, to find Jeffrey Lucas standing beside him.

CHAPTER LI

"Of all the unpredictable fellows!" Lucas declared, laughing.

"Mightn't I say the same of you?"

"I suppose you've got an engagement? You wouldn't keep me company while I eat a chop?"

Signorina Salvini was forgotten forever as her card dropped unnoticed on the floor.

"There's nothing I'd like better!" James laughed. "Let's have some wine!"

"Darrell, you've become famous since I last saw you in Granada!"

"A long time ago!"

"I never read a more vivid book in all my life," Lucas declared, "and I should know something of Spain, after a year in Madrid!"

"You should!" James's grey eyes twinkled.

"Suggesting that I know nothing, apart from the Embassy? Well, perhaps you're right! *You* certainly know a lot! I remember seeing you in peón's dress, in Granada, waving haughtily to famous bullfighters!"

James smiled but said nothing.

"Listen, James—can I call you that?—and you call me Jeffrey? Listen—I'm going to be marrried in October!"

"I congratulate you with all my heart!"

A shadow crossed young Lucas' clear-cut, charming face.

"That episode with Silver—don't think I've forgotten. When I was very young she meant so much to me—magic, and springtime, and romance. Did you ever feel like that, James?"

"Everyone does, I expect."

"She was youth itself. You've seen primroses in a hedgerow?"

"Many times."

"Well, that was the sort of business it was. We were—or I was—about as young and green as those primroses. I've grown up now, but I'll always feel the same about her. She had something I can never give to anyone else."

"And now you're going to be married?" James prodded, as his friend betrayed some tendency to brood upon the past.

"Oh, rather! Her name's Georgiana Chilton, and she's very pretty! I like her immensely—only, you know, she's not Silver!"

"No, I don't suppose she is," James felt impelled to agree, thinking of his knife wound, the scar of which he still bore.

"Nobody," young Lucas insisted, "will ever be like Silver!"

"No, I shouldn't think so."

"Let's have some more wine! And, I say, James, when are you coming to stay with me?"

James was silent for a moment. He realised then, not for the first time, that it was useless to fight against fate.

He said:

"Whenever you ask me, Jeffrey."

Lucas said nothing for a few seconds.

Like most people, he had been enchanted by *The Spanish Journey*. Perhaps more than most English people he understood the book. He had, at least, lived in Madrid. Now, in this London chophouse, he vividly remembered their last meeting, in a café at Granada. He remembered James's picturesque dress, his refusal to join the drunken bullfighter, his strange air, Englishman that he was, of somehow belonging, fitting perfectly into the savage scene of which he was so unobtrusively a part.

He remembered that his landlord, helping him pack that same night, before he left for Seville, had said:

"Don Jaime, señor? Why, yes, everyone knows Don Jaime, the Inglés. He turned gypsy and lives up at the Albaicin. In fact, he has a gypsy wife, a dancer. Everyone knows him here, but he only mixes with flamencos."

Then he remembered James's eager enquiries concerning Lady Castleton. He hadn't seemed to care much that night about a gypsy wife. And later, when Lucas was in Gibraltar, waiting for his ship, he'd heard some vague scandal—a murder, he recollected, somehow connected with an Englishmen in Granada, and he'd wondered then . . . A strange bird, James Darrell. . . .

"What's the matter?" James was asking irritably. "Why are you staring at me?"

"I am still waiting for an answer," Lucas said.

"An answer?"

"Yes! Will you come and stay in June, towards the end of the month?"

"I'd be very glad to," James responded.

"Come for as long as you like! You'll meet an old friend—Lady Castleton will be in Hampshire, I believe!"

"Is she well?" James asked, with a desperately overdone carelessness.

"Oh, I think so," Lucas replied.

"And their marriage?"

"Even worse than when we talked of it that time in Spain!"

"How is that, worse?"

"I believe Frank Castleton has to have nurses to check him taking drugs."

There was a pause.

Then James said:

"Someone said that over on the Surrey side of the river the theatres exaggerate when they give melodramas."

"Well, don't they?"

"I don't think they do!"

"My dear fellow, have you ever seen these melodramas?"

"I don't think I need to," James decided, frowning.

"In any case," Lucas repeated, dismissing the Surrey theatres, "you'll come and stay at Ardley for as long as you wish—a fortnight, say, or a month, if you like?"

"You're very kind," James said, "but we'd better say a week. I shall have the proofs of my next book waiting to be revised, and I'm going to take them down to Oxfordshire in July."

"Well, there's plenty to amuse you at home," Lucas said. "We even had some gypsies camping in the park a few weeks ago. Remembering you, I told my keeper to let 'em alone. Unfortunately, they've gone now. I'd like to have listened to you talking to them!"

A good thing, James thought moodily, that they had gone. He was no longer inclined to fraternise with the gypsies. Rosal's ghost seemed to lurk somewhere in the smoke of every nomad fire, and the memory of her death still had the power to pain him.

He reflected:

"If I had never been in Seville that night, she would probably

have married Juan, and they would have been happy enough together." Instead of which, entirely due to the intervention into
their lives of himself, Rosal was dead and Juan rotting in a Spanish
jail. . . .

His face looked so sombre, he seemed so remote, that Lucas once
again was puzzled.

He said at last:

"What are you thinking about?"

"Oh, I don't know! About the past, about Spain, about a thousand things best forgotten!"

"You must have known Andalusia wonderfully well to have written that book!"

"Yes," James admitted; "I knew it well."

"And loved it?"

"Well, I loved it and hated it too. Everything was mixed up. All
the same, I made my home there for a long time, and I am still at
a loss here in England. I feel a stranger here; I no longer understand the life and customs of this country; I get cold, I dread the
damp. . . ."

Jeffrey Lucas said:

"Why, then, did you return here? When I saw you, you seemed
happy enough. You must have had friends there. Why the devil *did*
you come back?"

"I *had* friends," James said; "but all that was finished before I
went to Morocco. There was a girl—— But I don't want to talk
about her—she's dead. She died violently. Looking back, everything
about Spain seems violent to me. Life is too vivid. There's so much
sun; blood's spilt too easily. Now that I'm here in England the
whole thing seems like a dream."

"But I remember how you appeared to fit in there!" Jeffrey
Lucas protested.

"Fit in! I know I did! But that doesn't make for happiness!"

"I suppose not."

"Just because you get involved with people, don't think either
that that necessarily means happiness—it doesn't!"

"The trouble with you is you've been overworking—it will do you
good to come down to Hampshire!"

But Lucas thought at the same time of Lady Castleton, and

wondered very much whether she would make his friend any happier. Somehow, he did not believe that she would, and when he thought of Miss Chilton, his own well-bred, youthful fiancée, he was glad that he had found contentment, although their relationship did not excite him.

Meanwhile, James knew well enough that his sole reason for visiting Hampshire was his burning desire to see Oriana once again. No matter how long he stayed away from her, it was impossible to dismiss her from his mind. There she was, eternally looming in the background of his life, always dominating that other ghost whose wraith floated in the smoke of gypsy fires.

Rosal's death had made him dislike meeting gypsies, but more haunting to him even than that was the scorn with which Oriana once had mocked him, long, long ago, in Oxfordshire, in the glades of Ackland Wood.

"And what are you going to write about—the gypsies?"

"Yes, madam," he thought sardonically, when he remembered her taunts; "yes, madam, I wrote about the gypsies and made my name! And you? Well, you married your rich, feeble cousin, and he's an invalid, because he drugs! I can scarcely wait to congratulate you, madam! Our fortunes have changed indeed!"

Jeffrey Lucas was talking.

"You can come by railroad, now, James, within ten miles of our village."

"I hate the railroad," James objected.

"You'd rather take the coach?"

"Good God, yes!"

"But these swift trains are astounding!"

"They've broken up all we liked when we were young," James observed to this.

"What do you mean?"

"Can you imagine eloping with Silver in a train?"

"Frankly, no!"

"That's what I mean. We owned the road, the tober, in our youth. We couldn't walk a mile without adventures then. Well, our sons, if we have sons, won't know what we're talking about when we tell them that. They'll fall in love with railways, with shouting, screeching, filthy engines."

"Progress," young Lucas remarked.

"Progress! I only wish I'd been born a hundred years ago!"

"As you haven't, and won't be, can I ask if you are definitely coming to stay with me next week?"

"I am indeed," James answered him; "by coach!"

"Good! A carriage will meet you if you let me know!"

"Thank you!" A little later he walked back to his rooms to sketch the outline of a book that would one day be called *El Moro*.

CHAPTER LII

JEFFREY LUCAS LIVED in a gabled, mellow Tudor manor house nestling among park and woodland. Ardley Manor had belonged to his family for more than three hundred years, and, in comparison, Sir Francis Castleton's graceful Palladian house across the fields still seemed, to those associated with Ardley, something that had grown up, mushroomlike, in the night.

Jeffrey was alone at Ardley now that his mother was travelling in France, and James had not been half an hour in the house before he succumbed to its charm.

His attention wandered from the silver teapot and softly hissing urn to the bowls of potpourri in the drawing room, to the sporting prints and foxes' masks in the hall; to the flowered chintz curtains on his four-poster bed; to the crystal and silver glittering at night on the dinner table. He had not been inside an English country house since his last visit to Oriana's old home, and now, experiencing once more the same familiar atmosphere of unobtrusive comfort, of a life that seemed changeless, of a past that was rich and interwoven with history itself, the years in Spain seemed more than ever like a dream.

How could he believe, as he played billiards with Jeffrey in a dark-panelled room heavy with the sweetness of stocks growing outside, that he had ever roamed Andalusia with the Bear People and taken his orders from a bullfighter who could not read or write?

Before going to bed they escorted the spaniels out onto a lawn grey with dew and moonlight, and while they stood talking beneath cedar trees that rustled in the breeze, a fox barked sharply from the woods near by, and then Rosal's phantom vanished somewhere far away, and he said to Jeffrey in puzzled tones:

"I can't believe I've really been away so long! I can't believe it!"

When he woke next morning there was a note on his tea tray in a scrawl he remembered of old, as well he might, for once upon a time a letter in that writing had broken his life in pieces.

He read:

DEAR JAMES,

I hear from Mr. Lucas that you are his guest for the next week or so. I am writing at the same time to ask him if you will both dine here with me on Wednesday next at seven-thirty.

I congratulate you with all my heart on your success. The fairy tales are exquisite, and your Spanish book is so vivid that it made me feel as though I were burnt by the sun.

I want so much to talk to you.

ORIANA CASTLETON.

P.S. Once, when I was very young, I laughed at you for wanting to write about the gypsies. If you should remember that, how you must be laughing at me now!

He read this letter over two or three times, his face expressionless. The formality of the first part in no way brought her back to his mind; it was only in the postscript that her impetuosity broke through, and then it was as though he could hear her speaking.

Jeffrey said to him casually at breakfast:

"It seems Lady Castleton wants us to dine with her on Wednesday. Will that suit you?"

"Perfectly." But he could not help adding: "I wonder how she knew that I was staying here?"

Jeffrey avoided his eye.

"I may have mentioned it when I saw her after church last Sunday. Have some more bacon?"

Wednesday was the last night that they would be alone together at Ardley, for Jeffrey had invited some other young men to join them on Thursday.

"I thought a bachelor party would be more agreeable."

"Do you know if Lady Castleton has many people staying with her?"

"I have no idea. Sometimes she entertains, and then again, for weeks at a time, she's here by herself."

When Wednesday arrived James discovered, to his amazement, that he felt numb, drained of all emotion. He simply could not believe that they were going to meet again. He kept on remembering, for some obscure reason, the day when he had first recollected her name, in Spain, the day when he had ordered Rosal to throw away her white hyacinths. As he dressed, he felt that strained feeling at the back of his head which sometimes presaged a bad headache, and did not even realise that this was due to the emotion he was so unconscious of feeling.

But he was very glad indeed that his new clothes had been made by a good English tailor.

They drove to Castleton Park in Jeffrey's gig.

"You don't mind, do you?" his host had asked. "It's a lovely night, and I thought you'd like the air."

"I do like it," James hastened to assure him, and indeed his headache had vanished by the time they drove through gilded iron gates down a drive arched over with beech trees and massed with rhododendrons. The park, he saw, was grander than the one at Ardley; he caught glimpses of a "ruined" bridge spanning a stream, of deer grazing on the hill beyond, and of a mock Gothic tower, ivy covered, frowning near the woods beside the lake.

The house itself was exquisitely proportioned according to the classical style of the period; here everything—fluted pillars, carved cornices, elaborate portico, and twin curves of shallow steps—was gracefully, almost frivolously expressed in the pearl-grey stone that caught the last light of the sun.

There was nothing sombre, as at Ardley, no richness of history; no sense of the past, nor of ancient things; here was something perfect, faultless, of its own time; delicate, lovely, stylized, and perhaps a little cold.

James, still unable to believe he was not dreaming, found himself in an Adam hall fragrant with masses of Candidum lilies. Here everything was light, airy, dominated by the beauty of the majestic staircase soaring upwards in a flight of loveliness.

Then they were shown into a drawing room of which, afterwards, he could have said nothing, save that it contained Oriana. Certain details, he supposed, must have etched themselves upon his mind—there were carnations blooming everywhere, which would, at any other time, have reminded him of Spain. Although the night was warm, there was a fire of glowing logs, but the french windows were open onto the lawn, and the impression of the room was one of fragrance and of spaciousness.

She was not alone; there was an elderly woman with her, and an indeterminate married couple, but their faces were clouded to him, for only hers was clear.

She was dressed in black lace that made her pale skin seem luminous. A fashionable wide skirt, herald of the future crinoline, emphasised what he knew—that she was tall, and slim, and straight of back. She wore her dark hair simply dressed, combed back from her cheekbones, but in it was set a diamond spray, and he noticed more diamonds glittering at her breast.

She was exactly as she had been five years ago. For her, time had stood still. Perhaps there were dark shadows about her eyes that had not been there before, but the eyes themselves, wide apart, wallflower brown, were the same. And her skin was what he had once called it—"pale as moonlight." The tip of her nose was delicately mocking, as it would be until the day of her death, and the vivid curve of her mouth perhaps was richer, for her beauty was, if anything, enhanced since he had last seen her, and there were no traces of immaturity in the assurance of Lady Castleton.

So he thought, looking at her, and saw, for a second, her clear glance waver, for he had quite forgotten that time had dealt less kindly with himself.

"James!" she said, in her warm voice, and then: "Your hair? When did you go grey?"

"I was ill long ago in Spain."

She turned, to introduce her friends, hoping that she had disguised her emotion at his changed appearance. Apart from the prematurely grey hair he looked thin, almost ravaged; he was dark, too, bronzed with years of sun and wind. It was then, as she talked conventionally, that she realised how grave must have been this illness to which he had just referred so lightly.

When a footman in yellow plush brought round a decanter of Bristol Cream, she said:

"I don't suppose this sherry will seem much to you after your Spanish wines?"

"On the contrary," he said, "it's better than most we had out there!"

He smiled at her for the first time, then looked quickly away.

She, who had always known him so well, knew then that, despite all his fame, which she had savored as her own, he was lonely, unhappy, ill at ease. He was no longer the wild boy who had walked so boldly into her bedroom one summer night long ago. He was now a man who looked ten years older than he was, and she divined immediately that, despite his success, he had endured some bitter experience or other, had suffered in some way that no one could guess, who had only read his book.

So she said gently:

"I've put you next to me at dinner. We've much to talk about, haven't we, James?"

"Quite a lot," he answered calmly, but she noticed that a muscle twitched in his cheek.

He had no idea of her other guests' identities; no conception as to whether they were only dining or staying in the house. He had not even noticed Jeffrey since first he walked into the drawing room.

There was nobody, nothing else in the world for him, but Oriana. He wondered whether she knew it, or whether, with her smiles and her serene gestures, she was still playing some mischievous game of her own, like the spoiled child she was.

"Not with me again," he thought; "not ever again with me. This time she must learn better."

The butler announced dinner, and then, since he was her guest of honour, he touched her again when she put her arm in his.

They walked across the Adam hall into the dining room, and he knew that he would never forget the scent of lilies that seemed to be everywhere in her house.

CHAPTER LIII

THEY SAT DOWN in a formal and classical dining room of cream, and he was placed on Oriana's right.

On *his* right was a hay-coloured lady, wife of the straw-coloured gentleman who sat on Oriana's left. As soup was served, this lady told him how much she had enjoyed his book.

"I'm so glad," he said, drinking a second glass of Bristol Cream.

"You must have met strange people—gypsies, smugglers, bull-fighters . . ."

"Indeed, yes, but so long ago it all seems like a dream, especially in such a house as this."

"You like the house, Mr. Darrell?"

"With all my heart! It's a jewel, perfect of its kind, isn't it? I've never been to Bath, but I've heard Bath is much the same style."

The lady confided as her soup was taken away:

"I would have liked to meet smugglers and bullfighters."

"Oh," he said, "they're rough and wild, and no fit company for women, except such as understand them. In fact, they're not at all romantic stripped of their gay clothes!"

"Then you must be a most untruthful person!"

"Why?"

"Because, Mr. Darrell, you've made every respectable female in this country long to visit Spain!"

"Well," he said, "they would scarcely enjoy themselves once they got there! Personally, I'd rather be dining in this lovely house!"

"So sad they no longer share it together, isn't it?"

"I know nothing of that."

"Surely, Mr. Darrell, you must have heard that Sir Francis is much of an invalid these days?"

"Is he?"

"To be sure he is! He's sick, you know, in London."

Then Oriana turned towards him, and the hay-coloured lady was most abruptly and disconcertingly left talking to herself.

Oriana

He said:

"That mocking nose of yours makes time stand still for me! I can never make up my mind whether it's more devastating in profile or in full face! Which do you yourself prefer?"

She hesitated for a moment, and then asked:

"Do you remember Oxfordshire, when I first drove over for saffron cake? Do you remember how muddy my red shoes got out there in the farmyard?"

"There's nothing," James said, "that I've forgotten about you all this time."

"Nothing?"

"I remember the coaching inn in Surrey one summer night, if that's what you mean. I think I remember everything!"

"Do you like this hock?"

"Oriana, I *must* speak to you!"

"I agree," she said coolly. "But not at the moment. I'm glad you like the hock, James. I've laid down a stock of wine these last three years I'm rather proud of!"

"You?"

"Yes. My husband's ill, and I—well, I've always been interested in wine, although I suppose you think that's a masculine taste?"

"Your only one?"

"James, we're not going to quarrel before I confess myself in the wrong. I never thought you'd become a famous writer, and I want to admit myself a fool."

"Ackland Wood!"

"Not only Ackland Wood! Do you know I'm very proud of you?"

"That pride," James said, "comes a little late. Forgive me for saying so, but it does."

"I *told* you I wanted to confess myself in the wrong! Do you think we should speak to our neighbours?"

"No! And after dinner I want to talk to you!"

"That can be arranged. But don't look so cruel!"

He said:

"You expect everything to be as it was when we parted, don't you? In that inn?"

"I don't! That's what you can't understand!"

She turned towards the straw-coloured gentleman on her left, so that all he saw was the ivory of her shoulder, the diamond spray in the darkness of her hair, and the tip of her averted nose. Mechanically, as he talked to the hay-colored lady, he thought suddenly of Spain—not of the Spain that he knew, but of the Spain they might have known together had she consented to marry him and journey with him to Madrid. There would have been no question of a robbery then, for they would have travelled together in a diligence. There would have been no Rosal——

She got up at last, in a cloud of black lace, and the ladies followed her out of the dining room.

Left alone with Jeffrey and the straw-coloured man, he fell into a reverie. He thought, had he been born Frank Castleton, that he would have continued to live happily forever with Oriana in this lovely house. He mused then on the bitterness of fate, and knew how gladly he would have sacrificed all his recent fame for the opportunities of the man he had always despised.

As they drank their port he joined mechanically in the conversation, wondering why anyone with Castleton's good fortune should have degenerated into an opium eater.

Jeffrey, noticing his abstraction, plunged gallantly into reckless conversation, by no means sure whether he had done the best thing by his friend in bringing him and Lady Castleton together once again. If they were lovers, or had been lovers, they were a stormy pair, he thought; although perhaps only because they were both remarkable to look at, and even with other people present it was impossible not to notice some gleam or flash of understanding that passed, sparkling, between them.

While he chattered, the straw-coloured man, bored with both of them, suggested a move to the drawing room, where James was fascinated by the skill with which Oriana immediately ordained that the other four should play whist.

He said:

"I expect you to entertain me."

"Would it amuse you to see something of the garden before dark?"

"I should like nothing better."

"Well," she said, "my cashmere shawl's on the couch over there. Give it to me, will you?"

Outside, dusk was flowing over the lawn, and on the terrace a peacock passed, trailing its plumes indifferently.

"Like your skirts," he said. "But I remember you never seemed to notice the dew."

"James, what has happened to make you so much older?"

"My life hasn't been an easy one until lately."

"I gathered that from your book. What was the matter when you were ill?"

"Oh, that's an old story. I'm quite recovered, except for an occasional headache."

"Oh, don't be so exasperating! I want to know what *happened!*"

They crossed the lawn towards an enclosed rose garden in the centre of which stood a sundial. The scent of roses was sweet and heavy in the dusk.

He told her briefly of his adventures with the diamond necklace; of the robbers, and of the Bear People, suppressing any mention of Rosal. He was not yet prepared to talk of her.

"And are you in love with anyone?" she enquired after a long silence.

"You know I am."

She said:

"It has always been the same with me too."

"You call that love? My dear, I should have thought one of your own stableboys would have served your purpose admirably!"

She said nothing.

"You never loved *me* that night! You never wanted me! Anyone else would have done as well!"

"That's not true, James. I loved you! I still love you, and always will! Try to understand a little!"

"What is there to understand?"

"A great deal. I was very young when I married Frank. It amused him to teach me many things I had no need to know. He's a queer, perverted creature, and I'd rather not discuss him, except to say never has anyone more bitterly regretted a marriage than I have mine. Well, I was younger then, James, and I wanted to possess you, having always loved you. And it amused me to send you away—I was so sure you'd come back. But you never did."

"Have you had many lovers since?"

She laughed, but not as though she was amused.

"One. I sent *him* away soon enough. Yes, I even sank to the banality of a lover, trying to get you out of my mind! It was a failure from the first. And you? Were there many women in Spain?"

"Only one."

Her head rose swiftly, and he saw that he had hurt her.

"All those years? You *must* have loved her!"

"She's dead."

CHAPTER LIV

HE TOLD her briefly then of Rosal.

As she said nothing, he concluded:

"I didn't even marry her properly, although I expect she would have liked that. I never thought—I was selfish beyond belief! You see, if I had never crossed their lives, they would have been happy enough together, she and Juan."

"Perhaps you are wrong. If she had had to choose, she might have chosen three years with you rather than ten—twenty years, with the bullfighter!"

"Why do you think that?" he asked curiously.

"I suppose because I chose wrongly myself."

"You got everything you wanted," James retorted.

"You think it's made me happy?"

"One can't have paradise on earth!"

"I suppose we had better go in," she said.

"Oh no!"

"We must."

He caught her hand. It was nearly dark, but as he kissed it he could still see how long and delicate it was; it seemed fragile beneath the weight of her rings.

"You don't think we are going to separate again?"

He took her in his arms, and it was as though they had never been parted. He drew her close, and her perfume, the warmth of

her body, consoled him then for much unhappiness, so that at last
he was at peace.

"You see?" he said, after a pause.

"When can you come back?"

"Tonight?"

"Of course not. I've got guests!"

"Tomorrow?"

"Let me go, James, while I think!"

"Let you go? I've waited years!"

"You must!"

He obeyed, his eyes never leaving her.

"Listen, James! Jeffrey Lucas has people coming to stay tomorrow, hasn't he?"

"I believe he has. Don't leave me—I might lose you again!"

"The Leightons go tomorrow. I shall have only old Mrs. Conway
here, and she goes to bed at eleven!"

"I'll come after dinner—across the fields! Before midnight!"

"I'll leave the drawing-room window open. You'll see the light
across the park."

"Come here," he whispered.

"Ah! no, James! That appalling game of whist!"

"We'll stroll back slowly."

As they left the rose garden for a walk arched over by rhododendrons, he confided:

"The night Rosal was killed, she saw your vision in her glass."

"Saw me?"

"Yes. Occasionally she was uncanny, as gypsies sometimes are.
That night I remember she described you minutely. She thought
it an omen."

Oriana shivered.

"I don't want to be the omen of a death!"

"You think it unlucky?"

"Very!"

"Well," he said, "you'll be pleased to hear I've finished forever
with gypsies, fortunetellers, witches, and wizards!"

"What was she like, Rosal?"

"Very young. Wild, charming, and gay. Primitive as a savage
—brave as a lioness."

"Beautiful?"

"Exceedingly pretty."

"How many other lives we've managed to spoil, between us!"

"You haven't told me anything about your husband."

"He's dying."

"Dying? Of drugs?"

"Yes. I suppose it's a sickness like any other. And he is consump-
tive, you see."

"Surely——"

"He began to drug even before we were married."

"But he was in love with you!"

"I know. He thought at first that I could save him. I thought so,
too, when I first found out what was the matter. But I couldn't,
of course. I was too young. And now . . ."

"Now?"

"He's incurable. It's hateful! I don't want to talk about it! Have
I not already admitted how hopelessly I've wrecked my life? Yours,
too, I suppose, and Rosal's, and the bullfighter's! It's not a pretty
thought."

"But it's not too late for us."

"I suppose not—for *us*. I can't help wondering whether we have
any right to be happy!"

"Oriana, if Castleton were not dying, I would have asked you
to come away with me!"

"I would have said yes," she answered candidly.

"Well, I've learned to be superstitious, so I won't, not yet."

Outside on the terrace they paused for a moment.

She said:

"Swear you've recovered from your illness?"

"I swear it!"

"Thanks to Rosal?"

"Thanks entirely to Rosal."

"O God!" she cried. "How I wish I'd gone with you to Spain!"

"We've got the future."

"I was so spoilt. I couldn't bear to be poor!"

"Let's agree to forget the past."

"It's not always so easy. When you got my letter, long ago, breaking everything off, what did you think?"

"I don't know that I thought at all. Everything stopped. I sold my fairy tales about that time, but I don't remember much about it. I only wanted to get away."

She said:

"I don't think I'd been married more than a week when I wrote, but already I was frightened."

"Frightened? You?"

"Yes—of Frank. I knew even then that he wasn't like other people."

They were close to the windows that blazed out into the deep blue of the night, and before they went inside he took her in his arms, behind a huge cedar tree, the black shadow of which sprawled across the wet silver lawn.

"Tomorrow?" he said, after a pause.

"If you don't come, I shan't want to live!"

"Why can't we still be young, now we're beginning to see clear?"

"We *are* young, James! You're only twenty-six!"

"Perhaps in years, but there's nothing young about me! I lost my youth when I lost my memory. Don't you understand?"

"My dear love . . ."

"Once, when I remembered you for the first time, I made Rosal throw away some white hyacinths she had in her hair—they reminded me of your skin!"

"We *must* go in!"

"Listen," he said, "we're going to be happy now: we've been through enough hell!"

"I agree. But we must be discreet. Come in before we wreck our lives a second time!"

"That was a damned boring game of whist," Jeffrey announced as they drove with the greatest rapidity towards Ardley Manor.

"Was it? I'm afraid I don't play."

"Lucky dog! James, do you think I'm a bit drunk?"

"Only a bit! Do you want me to drive?"

"You might as well. Yes, you're a lucky dog—wandering in the moonlight with Lady Castleton."

"The *twilight!* The moon's only just up!"

"Just as romantic!" Jeffrey protested, and then he sighed.

"James!"

"What?"

"This girl I'm going to marry—Georgiana—I wish I could want to wander with her in a garden at dusk!"

"Well, don't you?"

"Not particularly. I can't help wishing she looked a little more like Lady Castleton, if you know what I mean?"

"Lady Castleton," James said, "looked exactly the same when she was ten!"

"Come, James, you don't mean it! You're drunk too!"

"I am not drunk, and I do mean it!"

"I didn't know you were such old friends," Jeffrey commented.

"Why should you? Here we are. Shall I drive straight to the stables?"

CHAPTER LV

THE NEXT DAY Jeffrey's three friends arrived to stay at Ardley. They were charming young men, pink of cheek, exuberant of whisker, cheerful of disposition. They arrived with gigs, fishing tackle, and retriever puppies; they had known Jeffrey at Cambridge, and were at first inclined to regard James with nervous suspicion, as being a writer, and therefore some kind of singular animal it was not even permissible to shoot.

But by dinnertime they were all on excellent terms with one another. After dinner, in the middle of a game of billiards, James led Jeffrey aside to confide:

"Between ourselves, I'm off to bed. I've got one of those damnable headaches coming on."

"My dear fellow, what can we get you?"

"Nothing, I'm afraid. There's only one thing for me to do—lie in a dark room until tomorrow morning."

"Shall I look in on my way to bed?"

"No, on no account! If I try to sleep now, I shall be all right tomorrow."

It was easy then.

He ran upstairs, to close his bedroom door, and a few minutes later slipped out again through the hall. The night was dark and the stars overclouded, but he had been trained by the Bear People to possess a catlike vigilance of sight, and in a few moments his eyes became accustomed to the night. He walked across the park, where the wet grass brushed his legs, trees rustled, sighing, and owls called softly to one another from the firs of a covert near by. Once again he was entranced by the sounds and scents of an English summer night. Cows lowed in the distance, the stable clock chimed at Ardley, a wood pigeon clattered over his head, and the air was sweet with a mingled scent of mushrooms, dew, and clover.

Soon he found himself on the road, walking straight towards Oriana's house. He decided against disturbing the lodge-keeper and slid through a gap in the hedge near by. There were rabbits scampering about the avenue beneath the arched beech trees.

He was conscious not only of a fierce exaltation, but of a sweeter feeling, a feeling of peace, as though at last he approached his journey's end. He turned past the tumbling spray of the waterfall and cut across a grove of rhododendrons towards the great lawn. And then, as the graceful shape of the house etched itself darkly against the sky, he saw a light shining from one of the french windows on the terrace. This light, bright and unwavering, made his heart beat. He felt even more strongly that he was coming home, that he had been a wanderer for many years.

His feet fell softly on the terrace, and he saw that the french windows were wide open.

When she heard his step, she came out to meet him.

She wore, for some fantastic reason of her own, a Regency dress of chalk white, its folds falling so as to mould her long limbs. There was a gold jewel in the darkness of her hair, a knot of gold ribbons at her breast, and on her feet were gilded sandals. She was so much a figure from the past that for a moment he paused, uncertain.

"I'm not a ghost," she said, laughing. "Come in!"

There were fresh flowers in the drawing room, which was, he noticed for the first time, decorated in turquoise blue. Masses of lilies and carnations clustered everywhere, and, as on the night before, a fire of logs glowed in the hearth.

"You like hock, don't you, James?"

She went to where the slim bottle nestled in its pail of ice and began deftly to open it.

"Let me do it." As he filled their glasses: "Is that your grandmother's dress? It's exquisite!"

"It's a copy of one of my mother's. James, you look better today —rested—more tranquil."

He said:

"I had a strange feeling tonight, as I crossed the fields, that I was coming home."

"You haven't kissed me yet."

He said, taking her in his arms:

"I haven't felt that about anywhere for many years—not since Oxfordshire, in the old days."

"Never in Spain?"

"Never. You see, you were right—I wasn't meant to live with gypsy people."

"Drink your wine, James! I was cruel then."

"I used to think you had a genius for cruelty."

"But not any more?" she asked, speaking very seriously now.

"Not any more, Oriana."

"You were such a strange, wild boy! I was never sure of you."

"Sure? You *knew* I loved you!"

"I knew that. But I was never quite certain you wouldn't run away from me in search of adventure!"

"Well, my adventures are over now."

For some time he was content to sit beside her on the sofa, staring at her as though she were something conjured out of a dream. Indeed, he had dreamed of her for so long that he was by no means sure she was tangible; it seemed to him a miracle that after so many lonely and haunted years they had found each other again.

For some time they talked.

He told her more about Rosal and his life in Spain. She talked to him of her husband.

"The doctors don't think that he can live many more months. He was never strong; one of his lungs is diseased, and you can imagine that the life he's been leading has not done much to cure that."

"Do you hate him, Oriana?"

She considered for a moment, her head on her hand.

"No. I'm sorry for him. Indeed, I never had any particular reason for hating him—he gave me all that I wanted—this lovely house, jewels, money—all the luxuries I was determined not to live without and with which I was soon so intolerably bored."

"Try living without them!" he suggested ironically.

"I'm ready to do that."

"Is Castleton really so desperately ill?"

"Yes. But I'm not going to discuss any future plans with you. It's too unlucky."

"But we'll not be parted again?"

"Never, my dearest, except once in a while. And never partings as we've known them!"

Later that night, in her bedroom, the episode of the coaching inn was erased forever from his mind, and it seemed grotesque to him that he had ever thought of her as a sorcière, a voodoo woman.

There, in her lovely ivory room, where gold stars sprinkled the white wallpaper, where bright carnations were massed everywhere, he found, lying beside her in the great gilded bed, that the possessiveness of her youth had vanished, along with her passion for luxury, along with her highhanded ways.

Now, although tireless in loving, she revealed a tenderness, a glowing warmth, that he had not known before, and when he had possessed her, he discovered that her cheeks were wet with tears. She could not endure to let him go, and it was not until daylight that he left her, swearing to return again that night, however late.

As he walked across the bird-haunted park to Ardley in the sweet freshness of that early June morning, he thought that he would not mind very much if he were told that he must die.

For the first time in all his life he had known the delight of perfect happiness.

CHAPTER LVI

WHEN HE TOLD HER SO, the following evening, she laughed.

"I'm glad you were not taken at your word!"

"I'm worried," he said, "lest Jeffrey should know where I go at night."

"You needn't worry. I don't particularly mind who knows. Everyone will sooner or later."

She was perfectly indifferent, as had always been the case, to the opinion of others. The child who had ruled her governess, dismissed grownups as fools, and run wild in the woods, had grown into a woman to whom convention meant little or nothing, and this in an age unparalleled for its hypocrisy.

They continued to meet every night in her house, and in the mornings they rode together, as they had done many years ago. He decided that she had matured delightfully; her enjoyment of books and music and painting was no keener than was her interest in the estate, which she administered in what her more old-fashioned neighbours described as an "unladylike way." Which is to say that while she seldom visited cottages with broth and jellies, she bullied the agent, worked at her own desk in his office, and was acquainted with the names and family history of every one of her tenants. The village people worshipped her, swearing that she made a better squire than her father-in-law, old Sir John Castleton.

She drove herself about in her fast phaeton, daring as ever, and only laughed when he remonstrated with her on her reckless driving.

She was, as she had always been, quick-tempered, impulsive, and intolerant of criticism. She could be exceedingly disdainful to those who opposed her, and she was still overfond of having her own way.

With James, since she had found him again, she was all warmth and tenderness and sparkling enchantment. It was as though she were determined to compensate for what she called the "lean years."

She said:

"I made you unhappy once. Now you shall see how happy I can make you."

And indeed every night spent in the Palladian house seemed more entrancing than the last. The house itself, classical and yet frivolous, existed as an exquisite frame for their love, and she took pleasure in making it seem as beautiful as she could. Her favourite flowers, lilies and carnations, were massed everywhere; no matter how warm the nights, she lit a fire of cherry wood in the drawing room, because they loved the fragrance of the logs; in her white-and-gold bedroom there was always a bowl of gardenias from her conservatory; when she found that he loved wild strawberries, she went out herself to gather them in the woods; she saw that the wine was always perfectly iced, and she herself took pleasure in wearing her most fascinating dresses. She staged their love in the most luxurious setting she could devise, and sometimes, on these passionate June evenings in the Palladian house, it was as though the Spanish years had never really happened.

Then he remembered vaguely, as though in a daze, the camp of the Ursari, with flamenco music on guitars, and everyone drinking from wineskins. He remembered the bears to train, the colts to sell. Rosal, with her spells, and Juan down in the arena, bravely and valiantly killing his bull. Rosal dancing naked in a cloud of blue smoke. Crude wine in cafés, and violent brawls with knives. Blistering sun, and sweat, and the endless windings of a dusty road. Rosal again, with blood seeping through the bodice of her white dress.

"It can't really have been true," he said once to Oriana; "there can't be two lives so different!"

When he explained, she only laughed.

"There may be a hundred different lives for all of us. What do we know?"

"Not much," he admitted.

"You were growing old, although you were young, out there in Spain. In a few days you've become young again, here with me. You're not so old, now, as that arrogant boy who stormed my room one night at the coaching inn. Not so young, and far more charming."

"And you? You were so perverse that night—so sweet now. Oriana, when can we really be together?"

"Always—you know that! When you've finished your proofs!"

"I've got the Morocco book to write after that," he objected.

"I suppose you'll write it at Steeple Courtney?"

"I suppose so. To tell you the truth, I've thought more about you than about the book!"

She laughed, pressing her face against his.

"James, I've thought about it all. There's a caretaker at the Hall who is paid by me. I can always go down to my old home, you know, and stay there in two rooms."

"Would you really do that?"

"You see, I love you! What did you think I should do?"

The warm ivory of her throat was very near to his lips, and, when he had kissed her, he took a gardenia from the bowl beside him and held it near her cheek, laughing.

"What's the matter, James?"

"There's no difference between this gardenia and your skin."

Jeffrey Lucas showed an admirable tact during that enchanted week. To his friends, he explained that James was still an invalid, who must be in bed by eleven o'clock at the latest. To James himself he said:

"Listen, you're absolutely free here to do whatever you please and see whomever you please whenever you want. I don't exactly know what you do, and I have no intention of asking, but you look ten years younger since you came to stay here, and I only hope you'll stay as long as you want!"

James would indeed have stayed for another week had it not been for the proofs of *The English Journey*.

But he was in a lighthearted mood as he walked across the fields freckled with cowslips, to spend his last evening at the Palladian house. Never, never again would they be parted for more than a few days, or a few weeks at the most. They would be together in Oxfordshire and in London; they had a plan "one day" to go together to Russia for a year. He wanted to write a book about Russia.

She admitted him as usual.

She wore a rich dress of crimson, with a huge skirt, exactly the same colour as the dark carnation in her hair.

She said:

"Would you like to travel to London with me tomorrow?"

He kissed her.

"Since when have you changed your plans?"

"Since reading a letter I had today."

"A letter?"

"From the specialist who is attending Frank."

"What does he say?"

"Nothing—that's the damnable part of it! Only that he wants to see me as soon as possible."

"Do you think——"

"I don't know what to think, and we certainly aren't going to discuss it, my dearest! But I shall go by the ten-thirty train tomorrow. Will you come with me?"

"Yes," James said, "I'll even go on that infernal railroad to be with you!"

She asked thoughtfully:

"Can you arrange to stay in London until I know what all this means?"

"I'll stay, yes, of course. I can see Grant."

"Then," she said, "let us be happy here tonight. . . ."

He said, a long time afterwards:

"Oriana, why do you cry when I've made love to you?"

"I cry from joy," she told him.

"Will you ever fall in love with anyone else?"

"No! Never! And you?"

"Never, as you know. I think I loved you first when we were children, when you wore your red shoes."

"*I* thought even then you had an interesting face."

"And said so—being you! You were most imperious to our maid, Betty!"

"A spoilt brat, I suppose?"

"The worst I ever knew!"

"Do you remember how angry you were, when I stormed some inn, demanding to meet your gypsy friends?"

"I was angry before then! When you came back from the Queen's Coronation, wearing white pantalettes and a plaid silk dress!"

"Oh," she exclaimed in sudden melancholy, "that was when I met Frank for the first time!"

"I shall always hate tobacco flowers," James confessed.

"Tobacco flowers?"

"Yes. He came every summer to the Hall when they were out! I shall never forget."

"So he did! We fished, and gathered water lilies."

"You and he gathered water lilies! I had to row—he couldn't."

"He was never strong."

"And now, Oriana? What happens now?"

Caravan

"Will you come and see me tomorrow evening, in Cavendish Square, James? I shall know then."

"Yes. Meanwhile, there's tonight."

Soon she lay again in his arms, pale as the moonlight that, streaming through the open window, blanched her cheeks to crystal, while her warm lips enchanted his, and a tress of dark hair, falling across his mouth, was scented with the gardenias gleaming so close beside them.

Perhaps she was as much of a sorcière then as she had ever been.

CHAPTER LVII

He said:

"I don't understand what you mean."

It was the next day, or rather the evening of that same day, and they were in her drawing room at Cavendish Square.

A heavy, impersonal room, he thought; remote from the charm of Castleton Park; something, obviously, in which she took no interest.

She said, a note of weariness in her voice:

"I thought I'd made myself clear. Why pretend not to understand?"

"Clear! Castleton's dying—a wreck—eaten up with consumption and drug taking—aren't I right? And you come to me saying the doctors insist that he must go to Switzerland! My God, let him go, but don't stand there telling me it's your duty to go with him!"

She sat facing him, her lashes lowered. They were like tiny but exquisite black fans on the pallor of her cheeks.

"Well?" he continued. "Why don't you answer?"

"He wants me to go with him," she said. "He clung to me today. It was painful, horrible. The very sight and touch of him made me sick. But, you see, I've got to go."

"He's dying, isn't he?"

"That's why I must go."

"Why do these doctors want to send him abroad if he's dying?"

"He may live six—eight months longer if he goes, and he *wants* to live! It's their duty to keep him alive. James, he doesn't want to die."

"Why should *you* go with him? What possible good can *you* do?"

"None," she agreed, sighing; "but as he wants me, I must go."

Her resignation made him feel almost demented.

"Oriana, have I not had to do without you for years?"

"In a way. But in another way we've never really been separated, have we? James, be reasonable! I married Frank with my eyes open! I got money and jewels and luxury! He's always loved me, in a queer, perverted way. Do you really think I'm going to let him die alone?"

He said nothing.

"If it was Rosal, would you have let *her* die like that?"

"That's just what happened to her, Oriana. Only—I didn't know."

"You see?" she said. "Another good reason for not letting it happen again. We love each other, and we have years before us because we're young. You didn't know Rosal was going to die, or you would have been more patient with her. Well, I *do* know Frank is going to die, and I'm going to be patient with him! I'm going to see that he's as happy as he can be these last months."

He said, after a pause, "You're right. I can't argue with you. I don't want any more on my conscience."

"Is Rosal still on your conscience?"

"In a way, she always will be. I was so indifferent, so impatient, sometimes. I took no trouble about her. I couldn't be bothered. Sometimes I think about it, and then I can't sleep."

"Would you sleep any better if I stayed behind with you and let Frank go to Switzerland alone?"

"When do you expect to leave?"

"In about a week from now."

"Well," he said, "I think I'd better go down to Oxfordshire tomorrow and come up again to spend your last night with you. May I do that?"

"Yes, James, you may! I'll write to you at Steeple Courtney."

"It's a strange thing," he commented. "We can only be together for a short time, and then the fates contrive to separate us."

"Do you really think that anything could separate us after last week?"

"Death, Oriana?"

"Least of all, death. Isn't there something of the spirit about our feeling for each other that must survive even that?"

"I don't know. How can one tell?"

"James, I *know* one cannot tell! But don't you believe, for instance, that if I died before you, I would always be somewhere close to you?"

Gypsy superstition, long dormant in him, became alert once more.

"Oriana, I hate morbid discussions!"

"I don't mean as a ghost," she persisted, "because I'm not sure I believe in them. What I'm trying to say is that when people have been as close as we have, for so many years, surely death can't really mean that the candle's blown out? You and I—— Well, I'm prepared to swear that, whichever one of us dies first, we'll always, in some way we don't understand, be together."

"Stop talking about it!" he commanded. He got up, and she saw that he was pale. He took both her hands.

"Oriana, you're right to go to Switzerland. I was selfish tonight, because I can't bear losing you again just as I've found you. But I see he's got the right to have you with him. I see that now. I saw it a moment ago, when you reminded me of Rosal."

"You'll come up to London to say good-bye to me?" she urged.

A week later they dined together in the chophouse where, long ago, he had first seen Don Ignacio. Oriana behaved with her usual lack of convention in meeting him there. Ladies of fashion were never, in her time, seen in restaurants.

They drank some claret, and she asked:

"What did you have for dinner, the first time you ever came here?"

He considered.

"Far more than I could afford, but I was really hungry! I remember wondering whether I'd given the waiter a proper tip."

As they were leaving, she coaxed:

"Now show me the place where Don Ignacio was attacked!"

They paused for a moment in the dark slit of the alley, and then they wandered to the Strand, where they took a hackney, for she had dismissed her carriage.

She wore her black lace, and seemed surprised when he hinted that it was somewhat ostentatious for the chophouse.

She remonstrated:

"It's quiet, isn't it? And I'm not wearing jewels!"

When they returned to Cavendish Square, he gave her a present.

It was a tiny cage woven of gold and platinum, containing a minute bird fashioned from a blue jewel. The bird was no larger than a fly, but when James pressed a spring they both heard the nightingale sing, and this, he explained, was a mechanical marvel that had travelled all the way from China.

She was enchanted.

"Whenever he sings, I shall think of you! And he shall sing for me every night!"

It was then that she gave him the two seals that she had had made—a butterfly and a turquoise heart.

Later that night he asked her:

"Do you remember everything I love about you?"

"Oh, I remember the sweet things you've said to me. I shall never forget them."

"They're true. Your skin *is* like moonlight! Your nose *is* fascinating. Your eyes are more beautiful than a gypsy's, which is saying a great deal, and the word temptation was made to describe your mouth. But all that, in a funny way, is nothing! You're Oriana, with all her faults, and all her virtues, so dear to me that sometimes, in Spain, after my memory had returned, I would feel sick with longing for you—unable any longer to write, or talk; detached from everything in the world but memories of you!"

Early that morning, in the hall, when it was time for him to go, they agreed to write frequently to each other, and she said:

"Promise me that whatever you do, you won't, even secretly, pray for Frank to die? I have a feeling that to do so would only bring bad luck."

"You can be assured I won't. I'm too superstitious myself. Not that I'll be able to pretend the slightest grief!"

"I wouldn't ask you," she said, "to be such a hypocrite. Tell me what you'll do when you get back home tonight?"

He considered.

"Go out in the garden, I suppose. Dine alone; work after dinner. Sit up late, perhaps, thinking of you, and go to bed at last, to dream of you."

"When two people part," she reflected, "it's always worse for the one who has to stay behind."

"Tomorrow," he said, "I shall ride out towards the Hall, and come home by Ackland Wood."

"And then you'll write to me?"

He nodded, and, taking her in his arms, he kissed her mouth and her throat and her eyes and her hair. He said nothing; he was incapable of speech. Without another look at her he let himself out of the front door. As he walked down the street, he thought suddenly of the warm pulse beating in her throat. A moment ago he was touching it; now that their parting was over, it no longer seemed like a moment; it was as though a hundred years had passed since the door was shut between them and he was left alone, on the other side.

CHAPTER LVIII

THREE MONTHS LATER James sat working in the room that once had been his father's study. It was even more untidy now than it had been in the past, piled as it was with shelves of tumbling, dusty books. The old-fashioned desk was littered with papers, but the open windows overlooked a garden misty with the blue-grey of Michaelmas daisies.

Sometimes, as he sat working in what had always been his favourite room, it was as though people from the past still roamed the house, ready at any moment to wander into the study and interrupt him. His father, large, weatherbeaten, stiff from riding miles across the fields to a confinement; Betty, peony-cheeked, red-armed, whispering of potato cakes waiting in the kitchen; the remote figure of his mother, with her strong French accent, her petulant complaints, and the perfume she used to hide the smell of gin; his lovely little forgotten sister, who had so much enjoyed listening to his stories. Outside, tapping at the window, the dark, faunlike face of the gypsy boy, Sylvester, waiting to lure him away from all that was civilised; and, of course, more vivid than any of these, a little girl in a red hood, with a mischievous face and eyes like great black cherries.

All these shades belonged to his youth. There was, of course, no Rosal to prowl about the Queen Anne house in search of him.

James was as happy as he could be without Oriana. They wrote constantly, and her scrawled, passionate, and sometimes ironical letters made him see her as clearly as though she stood beside him.

He found that she had that rarest of all qualities—she was one of those to whom he could write of anything and everything. And so he wrote to her, not only of their love, their passion, and their friendship, but also of everyday matters—the neglect of the empty hall; gossip of the villagers she had known; the gorgeous autumn turning of the leaves in Ackland Wood; gypsy *patrin* on the cross-roads near the church; the progress of his book; and a hundred other little details that would have interested no one else in the world. She was furious to learn that her father's grave had been ill-tended; when James occupied himself with the matter she wrote back:

It makes me particularly angry, because when I die that is where I wish to be buried. Not only because of all the old Camperdenes in the church, but because your father is buried there, too, quite apart from so many village people that were part of our childhood. That little churchyard we know so well is the most peaceful place I ever saw. I love the way grass and nettles have grown about those old battered tombstones, so that in summer there is clover; there are harebells and butterflies; all sorts of sweet, familiar things that make death seem natural, devoid of terror. That, surely, is how it should be.

Now, on this September morning, he sat working on a chapter of *El Moro*, determined that he would finish it before he allowed himself the luxury of writing to her. It was difficult, sometimes, in England, to remember those secret, hidden cities he had only been able to visit disguised as a Moor.

As he rewrote carefully, he heard, with one part of his mind, a peal at the front-door bell. Another, more active part, was so busily occupied with the description of a mosque in Tangier that he dismissed the interruption almost with impatience.

A few minutes later Taieb, his Moorish servant, came timidly into the study.

"Sir, a gentleman—he desires to see you."

"Don't you realise I'm working? Who is it?"

"Sir, a Mr. Lucas."

"Oh, then I'll see him! I expect he'll stay to lunch. Ask him to come in!"

Now, what on earth, he wondered, pushing his papers on one side, what on earth is Jeffrey doing in this part of the world? Surely he could have written?

"Come in, Jeffrey!" he called, hearing footsteps outside, and then, as Jeffrey obeyed, one glance at his pale face and downcast eyes made him ask, gripping the edge of the desk:

"Something's wrong, isn't it? Oriana?"

"James . . . "

"What is it? Please tell me!"

"She—Lady Castleton—she asked me, if ever——"

"She's dead, isn't she?"

"Yes," Jeffrey said.

"What happened?"

The room swayed in a crazy way as he spoke, and he felt sick. He sat down.

"There was an accident," Jeffrey said, not looking at him.

A deathly chill made him shiver, as though an icy hand touched his heart, and he could not believe that it was still beating. He felt as though cold grey waves were breaking over his head, and his mouth was dry.

"An accident?"

"Yes. You know how she loved to drive her own horses. Well, those mountain passes in Switzerland—I suppose she was driving too fast, and, you see, the heavy diligence came round the corner— there was a collision, and her light phaeton hadn't a chance. She was killed instantly."

"She was?"

"Yes. James, you must believe that!"

"How do *you* know, Jeffrey?"

Lucas fidgeted.

"I'm not a fool," he said at last. "This summer I guessed what was happening between you. How could I not? She talked to me one day when you were fishing. She wanted me to know. She realised I was your friend. Perhaps she had a premonition that she wouldn't live. I don't know. Anyhow, she gave me a letter to give you. Here it is."

"Thank you," James said, in an absent tone of voice, taking it. "I am sorry to have caused you to travel so far. It was kind of you— you're always kind! Good-bye."

"I'm staying here tonight," Jeffrey said.

"Here? I'm sorry; nothing's prepared. You can't. Another time . . . "

"I'm staying here tonight," Jeffrey repeated. He added, like a schoolboy, "I'm sorry nothing's ready. But it doesn't matter. It doesn't matter in the least."

"I've got to finish a chapter," James said vaguely.

"Would you like me to leave you?"

"Yes, go now. I don't want anybody. All this—I can't—I'm behind with this chapter, you know. I can't think properly! I'd better go on writing."

Jeffrey went out of the room, but James did not go back to his desk.

Instead, he opened Oriana's letter. It was brief.

He read:

BELOVED,

I have left this for you in case I die first. You will probably never read it. But if you should, I want you to know that all my happiness in life has been derived from you. You are not only my dearest love —you are a part of me that always has been, always will be. I suppose our roots are somehow entwined, like those trees we used to see in Ackland Wood. Apart, we only seem to make other people suffer, but when we are together we are one flesh, as they say in the Prayer Book, although they have never said it about us, and never will, now, if you read this letter. I hate that, because my only sin against you was refusing to marry you.

Beloved, since knowing you all over again I have left instructions to be buried in our own churchyard, where I shall be close to you. Don't grieve too much, because I am quite sure that this is not our final parting. Don't ever come to me piously, with flowers; I should like the briars and long grass to grow above my headstone. Since it cannot say I am your wife, I would rather be forgotten. You will know where I am, and that is all I care about.

Good-bye, my dear and only love.

ORIANA.

He sat down heavily at his desk after reading her letter, and tried, like a drunken man, to scribble words across the pages of his manuscript.

But of course it was useless. He was far away. He was at the Hall, and at the Palladian house in Hampshire; he was in Ackland Wood; he was at Cavendish Square; he was at the chophouse near the Strand. He was everywhere, chasing her ghost that flashed across his vision. There she was, near to him, elusive, laughing in her crimson dress, or in her white Regency robe, or her black lace; her dark hair was sweet with the perfume of gardenias; her eyes mocked him; he chased her tempting mouth and tried to touch her pale cheek; once again he saw the warm pulse beat in her throat, but she was intangible, a wraith—she was dead.

Soon he found relief in his anguish, for his eyes were no longer like stones, and he was able to weep.

It must have been much later when Jeffrey came to him, for Taieb came, too, bringing candles, and he saw that it was dusk.

"Yes," he said, in answer to their arguments, "I'll eat anything you want. Anything! But afterwards I am going to the churchyard. I'm going alone. I want to find a place there. . . . A place for her. . . . Somewhere she'll like. . . . Somewhere peaceful. . . ."

EPILOGUE

"WANTS to see *me?*" Mr. Edward Scales repeated in a shrill tone of protest. "The *editor?* And my lunch hour too. Jiminy!"

Nevertheless, he removed, if with an ill grace, his boots from his desk, combed his hair, straightened his tie, and insinuated himself with an elegantly concealed timidity towards the inner sanctum.

"Sit down, Scales," said a grizzled, bearded, ferocious-looking man.

Mr. Scales complied.

"I've done nothing wrong," he told himself privately, to bolster up his courage.

"Listen, Scales, do you remember a story you did last winter, on James Darrell?"

"Yes sir, of course I do. He was seventy—it was his birthday, and he asked me to lunch!"

"Precisely. I liked your story. Well, he's dead."

"Dead? Darrell?"

"Yes. He died—somewhat dramatically—yesterday."

"Yesterday?"

"You wouldn't realise, I suppose, that yesterday was All Souls' Day?"

"Well, no sir. I didn't know."

"You know nothing! Even your racing tips are the bane of this office! However, we wish to do a particularly detailed obituary of Darrell, whom many critics consider the finest writer of our day,

273

and it so happens that, as he was such a recluse, you were the last person we know to have seen him alive."

Dead! That old cove!

"I'm sorry he's dead," Mr. Scales blurted out abruptly.

"While your feelings doubtless do you credit, Scales, I did not request your company to hear them! Cast your mind back—dig up your article, if you like, and try to remember any details about the man, his house, his life—anything you can think of! His servants, for instance—would it be worth while talking to them?"

"How did he die?" Mr. Scales asked impulsively.

"Oh, he was over seventy, and it appears he'd wandered out late at night. To the churchyard, of all places! Well, he was found in the morning lying across some old tombstone. His heart had given out, of course. Not to be wondered at—playing the fool at his age. Don't sit there dreaming! What can you remember about him?"

"He was lonely," Mr. Scales said, after a pause.

"How do you know he was lonely? What reason have you got for saying so?"

"Well, he lived alone, with an Arab manservant. The house looked neglected, not properly dusted—all that sort of thing! He gave me the impression of being rather a monkish sort of chap—I mean, I shouldn't think he'd ever taken much interest in women, if you know what I mean."

"Did he talk to you about the gypsies?"

"No. When I tried to, he turned the conversation. I don't think he was interested in them any more."

"Well, what *was* he interested in? I'm tired of negatives!"

"He didn't seem very interested in anything," Mr. Scales confessed, adding generously, for he had liked the old cove—"But of course he was very old, wasn't he? Seventy!"

"If that's all you've got to say, Scales, you can get back to your work!"

"I'm sorry, sir———"

"Get out!"

Mr. Scales returned lugubriously to the office, where, for at least ten minutes, he was exceedingly crestfallen. He even forgot about his lunch, thinking of Darrell. Poor old chap, wandering out like that at night into a churchyard! He should have had a wife to look after him, Mr. Scales decided, temporarily determined himself to get married. Neglected, that's what he'd been! All Souls' Day? Was that the same as Halloween, something ghostly, and ghastly? Ruminating, he looked out of the window, where a wintry sunshine, gay as daffodils, suddenly decided to brighten the November day.

"Lunch!" Mr. Scales leaped from his chair.

As he clattered down the stairs, he remembered how, not so long ago, he had read *The Spanish Journey* in a train, and how much he had enjoyed the vivid writing of the old man who had just died so strangely.

Outside in the street the sun still glowed, and costers were selling mop-headed chrysanthemums from barrows.

He heard a shrill tootling sound from the corner, and saw, as he dashed towards the nearest chophouse, a tiny red-curtained theatre from which Punch's raucous accents could be heard proceeding. Yes, there was Punch, Judy, the thin terrier, Toby, shivering in the cold, and a fat, florid man banging his drum outside.

For one moment Mr. Scales, who had never read *The English Journey,* was unaccountably and extraordinarily reminded of James Darrell.

"Poor old cove!" he thought again, but he could not understand why he had taken what he would have called a fancy to a rather unfriendly, aged writer, who was, in any case, nearly forgotten.

"Dead, as well," he reminded himself.

He pushed open the door of the chophouse, and there, in a rich atmosphere of food, he found his friends, who were talking noisily in a crowded box.

"Late again!" one of them taunted.

"Well, James Darrell's dead."

"Who's he? Try a better excuse!"

"I'm hungry," Mr. Scales declared. He sat down to study the bill of fare, forgetting Darrell in the familiar excitement of his own colourful, restless, and unstable life.

Outside, on the street corner, Punch played, as usual, to a crowded audience of children, nursemaids, errand boys, loafers, and muffin men.

James Darrell had once described Punch and Judy as containing the essential elements of all tragedy. Their drama, in any case, was destined to outlive the popularity of his own works, which would not in the least have surprised him.

The November day was drawing to a close. It would soon be dark.

The fat man stopped banging his drum and, shrewdly eying the sky, went forth ruthlessly among the spectators to collect pennies.

Soon it began to rain, and then all the city was veiled in a mist of leaden grey.

It was raining down in Oxfordshire, too, and the old crusading Camperdene dripped his usual tears of damp in the musty Norman church where he had lain for centuries, his pointed feet crossed like those of a ballet dancer.

Rain fell in the churchyard outside, pattering down upon the overgrown forgotten graves. Here, where briars and nettles grew, and long, wet grass, Oriana's tombstone was half concealed by so much wildness.

There was nobody living in the village to remember her family, and so she had been left undisturbed for many years, as had been her wish, and on her headstone the letters were already fading.

Now she would be alone no longer, for once more, after so much loneliness, he would be beside her again, in that quiet place they both had known so well.

Later, years later, credulous people would swear that at night they still walked together in the churchyard, and then there would be wild tales told of their love for each other and of their parting. Soon, before the end of Victoria's reign, they were to become a legend in their own country.

But the truth was that they rested tranquilly in the little churchyard with its yew-darkened lych gate. There were never any ghosts. The slumber of these two was as quiet as their lives had been stormy; so that in the end, their story finished, they lay in peace together beneath ivy turning above headstones on which were cut their names, but nothing more.